SEVEN KINDS OF HELL

DANA CAMERON

SEVEN KINDS
OF HELL

47NORTH

Text copyright © 2013 Dana Cameron
All rights reserved.
Printed in the United States of America.

Published by 47North
P.O. Box 400818
Las Vegas, NV 89140

Cover Illustration by Chris McGrath copyright © 2013

ISBN-13: 9781611097955
ISBN-10: 1611097959
Library of Congress Control Number: 2012948380

To James:

Here's to the next twenty-five years.
Usual terms.

Chapter 1

I was sorting a box of objects in the Museum of Salem's accession office when the call came. My mother was dying. I knew this day was coming, had known for months, but the news hit me like a freight train all the same. Numbly, I saved the work file, turned off the computer, pocketed my pen, phone, and the antique clay figurine I'd been working on. Locked the empty artifact box in the cabinet. Dug my keys from my bag.

The drive across town to the hospital seemed to take forever.

I stood there, frustrated that there was nothing I could do to help her, wishing I was back at the museum or, better yet, at the bottom of a nice, square hole in the ground, excavating and recording a thick Native American hearth with a scatter of stone flakes in it.

Ma had lost so much weight, and she had never had any to spare. Her hair had thinned, the once-vibrant red dulled against the pillow with dark roots showing an inch. Once she'd been tiny, but a dynamo. Now she barely had the energy to breathe. She turned and spoke what I knew were her last words to me.

"Your father, goddamn it," my mother said. "He was a good person. But you see any of his family, you turn, you run as fast as you can."

I nodded, not wanting to say anything. Running and distrust had always been our way of life. But I wished she'd talk about something else. I didn't want her to waste her breath on what I already knew.

"Ma—I love you—"

I knew she wouldn't say it back, but I needed her to hear it from me.

My mother's hand tightened on mine. For such a sick woman, her grip was incredibly strong.

I couldn't stand it. I knew she'd been hoarding the breath for this final set of instructions. It wasn't long now.

"Promise me. You see them, you'll run like hell."

"I promise, Ma." I kept swallowing so I wouldn't cry. I didn't want to worry her. We knew this was coming. "I talked to Ian at work and let him know…about you. That I might have to move. He put me on lab and office work, so I don't have any field projects outstanding for him." I brushed my eyes. "He even offered to call a couple of colleagues, to help me get another contract job. And the museum, the grant they hired me for is almost done, so…I can go."

"OK, good. You lose yourself now; you have a good, quiet, dull life. What we did was only to keep it together until you were grown and could look after yourself. And I'm sorry you had to worry about me the past coupla months. Now you can fade away, settle down. I kept you hidden; they don't know about you. When I'm gone, they won't look for you."

I knew that was a fairy tale, but nodded anyway. Ma was usually tight as a clam; this was volumes.

"You go visit your grandma. I left something there for you."

"Huh? Grandma—" It took me a minute to figure out what she meant. My eyes filled up and spilled over when I nodded again. "OK, I got it, Ma. I'll do everything you say." That much I could do, to make her happy.

"OK, good." Satisfied, she sank back into her pillow, all effort spent. "Good."

A few moments later, Ma moved her hand. I leaned in to hear.

"Ginger ale?" came the hoarse whisper.

I nodded and went down the hall, glad I could do something for her. When I returned two minutes later, my mother was gone. Her eyes were closed, her head tilted, but it was nothing like sleep. Her face was free of pain for the first time in months.

I set the ginger ale down on the table. "Ma, don't—"

Don't what, Zoe? I thought. *Don't go. Don't worry. Don't hurt anymore.*

She didn't even look like herself. Something had left her body, and there was no more Ma.

I felt my eyes start to burn. Sensors beeped and a nurse appeared.

"DNR," I said robotically, turning away and wiping my eyes. "She didn't want any extreme measures."

She didn't even want me to see her die. Didn't want me to have to say good-bye.

The attending nurse, a new one, was very nice. I filled out the paperwork I'd become so familiar with, all the while biting the inside of my cheek. I'd cry later.

I took the next few days to work out the funeral arrangements before following Ma's orders to take off. I wasn't a fool, but there were some things you had to do, no matter what. I let the folks who worked at the university dean's office with Ma know. I gave notice at the contract archaeology company I'd been working for and wrapped things up at the museum, grateful my skills as an archaeologist were transferable and I'd be able to find another job shovel-bumming wherever I ended up. I filled out yet more paperwork and answered interminable questions. I cleaned out the apartment we'd been renting, sold everything I could, and emptied out my mother's checking account.

I wanted to make three calls. I'd left a message for my cousin Danny, but wanted to talk to him. He would have been there in an instant, but, disastrously, was out of town with work. And Will and Sean didn't want to hear from me. Not after...

That was it. After the funeral, I'd run. I'd lose myself and figure out what to do with the rest of my life. I was almost twenty-five years old. The rest of my life seemed a very long time.

It was a good plan, but the day before the funeral, my last day temping at the museum, I could barely control my emotions. One minute, I thought I'd explode, feeling too much. The next, everything seemed distant, and I felt numb and detached.

I opened up the file of acquisitions I'd been working on the day Ma died. A quick look around; I was alone. I took out the figurine I'd stuck in my pocket on my way to the hospital and looked at it. It was dirty and ugly, not much longer than my middle finger. It looked a little like a doll of painted clay, its colors faded almost to a uniform beige, a woman with her hair piled on top of her head and dressed in what looked like Greek robes. It was so crudely done, so battered, it couldn't possibly be real; it was just a souvenir from some classical tourist trap, an imitation of a votive offering or a miniature of a famous statue. It had been rolling around loose in a box of objects from a donor's collection, probably swept up when they were clearing out her house. The box it came in could have been a museum piece itself, having originally held a Radio Shack TRS-80 Color Computer, with—dig it—four whole kilobytes of memory.

An honest mistake, picking it up that day. I'd found it that night and realized I could return it as soon as I got back to the museum. No harm done.

Looking at it now, something about the figurine spoke to me. Reminded me of something, maybe from a dream. Maybe it was the wall of sadness surrounding my better judgment, but impulsively

I deleted the description I'd just typed—*Greek, late 19th-century replica, clay*—and put the figurine back in my pocket.

I'd never stolen before, not really, and certainly not an artifact. I was as ethical in my archaeology as only the righteous new professional can be, as rigorous in my recording as in my analysis, never ignoring data that didn't support my theories. Never even touched an artifact out of context on the spoils heap without checking with the crew boss, and even then, I marked the object with the site location.

But the box was full of old junk the donor's heirs clearly didn't want to be bothered with, and that thing was just…calling to me. I couldn't look away from it, couldn't make myself enter it into the collection, where it would be ignored again for the next hundred years.

It wasn't gold or in any way precious; it was dirty and it was really hard to identify it until you looked hard, I told myself. It had no provenience other than the box it had come in.

I had just erased its official existence. No one would be able to tell anything was missing. I was good at leaving no trace of my passing in the world, and this was no different.

I didn't give it another thought the rest of the day.

That night, a few of the museum folks invited me out for farewell drinks. I went, surprised they'd noticed me at all, and even more surprised when they presented me with a glossy program from a past exhibit on daily life in ancient Greece. It was out of print, hard to come by, and expensive. It was an unexpected kindness, and it made me nervous. I liked thinking I'd been invisible.

On my way home, my skin began to crawl. I'd been mugged twice in my life, despite all my vigilance and despite what I'd learned from Ma. It had turned out very badly both times. Now I saw no one. This made me even more afraid.

Then I caught a passing glimpse of a man, but my eyes are sharp, and that glimpse, in the dark at fifty meters, was enough.

The jawline and nose looked too much like the faded picture I kept in the bottom of my backpack. While he didn't have my dark hair, cut above shoulder length in an attempt to mitigate split ends and the occasional Kool-Aid home coloring, I could see other resemblances to me in his big eyes, small nose, and pointed chin. Slight build, Harley-Davidson T-shirt...

I didn't need to see whether he had green eyes to know. He was my father's people.

My family, the people I was never supposed to meet.

The enemy we'd been fleeing all my life.

I turned and ran, even though I saw nothing obviously dangerous. I knew the neighborhoods well enough to avoid tight spaces and dead ends. But my apprehension only increased.

Small and stealthy, I made the most of the shadows when I could, but mostly I relied on speed.

The two other muggings—attacks, let's be honest and call them what they were—had been too horrible to remember, too terrible to repeat. I'd burst my heart before I let it happen again.

I vaulted a low chain-link fence and ducked between two houses. As I tried to catch my breath, I saw more of them, spread out and running as silently as I was. I felt the hairs on the back of my neck prickle, the world begin to swim before me, a familiar thrill of adrenaline.

Oh no. Not now, not when they're so close...

Maybe I could still outrace it. I tightened my backpack straps, almost to the point of pain. With any luck, I'd keep my meager possessions with me in the flight to come.

Things got worse, more intense, as they do when you're in a panic. Reality receded. Whoever they were, they hadn't found me. They had never *lost* me, I now understood, my legs going wobbly. They'd chased me to exactly where they wanted me. Herded me.

My blood boiled, my despair transmuting into something else, more powerful. An anger that was cleaner, nearly irresistible. I knew I was giving up and I knew what would follow as I did. As my rage grew, it wiped away the last of my resistance. They wanted me so bad, let them see the *real* me.

Let the Beast come.

Footsteps behind me. Ahead of me. Shadows from a street-light showed familiar profiles, features similar to those I saw in the mirror.

I gave in to the Beast.

I felt the shame of unleashing the Beast only until I was washed in a flood of righteousness. The guilt evaporated, sizzled, then vanished like water on a hot skillet as my body shifted. I always expected pain, and the few times this had happened before, I'd been surprised: nothing but goodness, like I'd had an injection that made me somehow better in my Beastliness. My spine arched and stretched, my legs and arms lengthened, my fingers shortened. My jaw grew long and narrow, my ears pointed. My backpack straps were now comfortable, conformed to my new body. As I stepped out of my cheap black China-doll shoes, I felt elegant, sleek, graceful. The wind ruffled my fur.

I could think, I could keep a plan in my head, I knew who I was, but didn't think I was up to complex math or philosophy. Maybe that was to make room to deal with all the information my heightened senses fed me. I felt like Zoe, but stronger, more elemental, and the Beast guided me.

Go ahead, guys, I thought. *You'd have to be nuts to stick around, having just seen that. And even if you are nuts, you probably aren't stupid enough to mess with the Beast.*

I growled, low but palpably audible. I ached for them to attack. I'd end this nonsense now. They owed me for haunting my mother and me. They owed me two lives.

A glimmer—but of what? My sharpened senses weren't easily fooled, but something was happening I couldn't explain. The air around me was charged with electricity. Another moment and we'd all spontaneously combust.

It was coming from the men at both ends of the alley. The air was full of Beastliness.

It wasn't just me. The others were…

I turned and bolted.

I ran as long and as hard as I could until I felt the Beast relax and no longer sensed those around me posed a threat. I trotted, catching my breath, but still kept to the shadows; people in Salem might expect to see a coyote these days, but I didn't want to draw attention as a wolf in a short cotton dress with a backpack.

I pulled up behind a huge rhododendron, shifted my pack, and…concentrated. Praying I'd be able to turn back, terrified I'd stay in the Beast's form, trapped in my own brand of insanity. The Beast had come upon me about a dozen times since I turned sixteen, and sometimes it took ages to turn back, and then I despaired of resuming human form. Those were the worst times.

I lucked out, and it happened quickly. Shifting back, I surveyed the situation. The hem of the dress I'd been wearing was shredded by my escape, but it'd do for the moment. I pulled a pair of flip-flops out of my pack and looked no more remarkable than anyone else out on the street that time of night.

As I found my way back to our triple-decker, over fences and cutting through backyards, I wondered about the men who'd just followed me. Ma'd always told me Dad's family were bloodthirsty killers who considered themselves above the law. She had implied they were "Family," with a capital *F* for "Felonious." She said they killed my father and were after her because of what she knew about them. That's why we moved around so much. I had no reason to disbelieve her. But I knew all along it probably wasn't the whole truth. I never dreamed maybe she meant this family shared my problem, one I'd worked hard to hide from her.

Was it possible she knew what I was? Had she been the same? Impossible. For all her paranoia, if she had known, Ma would have told me, given me some way of coping with the Beast. She had always been straight with me.

Once home, it didn't take long to pack the rest of my things. I slipped a note under the landlady's door and then went for the last box of stuff. I'd leave immediately after the funeral tomorrow. I'd wait till I had to decide between going west, on the Pike, or south, on Route 93, then call Ian to ask for that recommendation.

On my way from the car, parked down the street, I stiffened. I felt a tingling in my spine until I saw it was Hunk coming around the corner toward me. He was, as he put it, temporarily between permanent residences. On nice nights, he slept on the Common; I don't know where he found shelter on the nasty nights. He was far from his usual haunts. I almost sneaked past, but I heard him mumble my name.

There's always someone worse off than you. No matter how squirrelly our life, I knew there was always someone who could use what little I had to give.

I fished a tattered bill from my pocket. "How's it going, Hunk?"

He took it, nodding thanks. "Snakes are bad this time of year."

Not one of his better nights. "Snakes?"

"All over your house. I seen 'em."

"OK, Hunk. It's OK. They're...gone now."

"Did they find you?"

I went cold. "Did who find me?"

"Your cousins. Said they were looking for you."

I knew he wasn't talking about garter snakes now. "I...they weren't my cousins. They're bad men. I don't want them to know you saw me or that I left, OK? You see them, you duck out of sight."

"Hey, I'm an old guy who sees snakes. Who's gonna bother me?"

"You don't want to find out. You take care of yourself."

But Hunk had already wandered off.

I knew my plan, had been rehearsing it in my head when I couldn't bear to think about Ma's pain. Tomorrow I'd drive until I felt safe, then start a new life.

But the apartment was empty, and my footsteps reverberated strangely now that all our stuff was gone.

Now that Ma was gone.

I hadn't let myself feel her absence before, driving myself with the details of my flight. The place wasn't really ours anymore, not now that she was gone. The apartment was bereft, the way Ma's body had been when she passed.

I'd been fending off emotion for weeks. Tonight was just too much. I didn't even care anymore if my pursuers were hallucinations brought on by stress, sadness, mania, and fear, or if the world was actually full of monsters who were after me. Who were just like me.

I curled up on the stripped bed and let the tears come, my sobs echoing though the empty rooms.

Chapter 2

The first time the Beast had come, eight years ago, I was certain I'd lost my mind. It was shortly after I'd turned sixteen. Ma was at work when the landlord came up to badger us for the rent. We'd already told him he'd have it when Ma got paid that night, but he was being a prick, yelling and threatening eviction. When he opened the door—something he should not have done—I felt something come over me, and all I could do was think about ripping out his throat. The images played out in my mind, and I knew exactly how it would go down. Never had I felt rage as simple and clean and demanding as that before. The look on his face as he backed off rocked me. It was all I could do to shut the door and chain it behind me.

That kind of violent response shouldn't have felt as good as it did. That was my first clue that I was going nuts. The experience was like opening a door to a whole different suite of rooms I never knew existed inside me. I was as terrified as I was exhilarated. If I hadn't felt the alien, destructive feelings—and if I hadn't seen the flash of retracting fangs in the mirror as I splashed cold water on my face—I would have spent the whole day trying to get that feeling back. As it was, I was so convinced I was going crazy, I had my bag packed and was ready to leave when my mother came home. All I could tell her was that the landlord was hassling us—hitting on me—and I wanted to move on.

No, I didn't tell her the whole truth. If you had no family, and friends you only saw once in a blue moon because you're always moving, would you risk losing the only person you had in the world when you thought you might be mental?

We left. Ma was ready to jam anyway, and I did my best to convince myself it was a flash of hormones, or a bad burrito, or anything besides me going loopy. Until that point, I had never touched drugs and had sneaked a beer only once in a while, so I had no idea the Beast would return.

Until it did.

A year after the landlord visit was the first time the Beast caught me out in public. That time wasn't the worst, but it changed me forever and sealed the deal for me that Something Was Not Right With Zoe. I wasn't exercising good judgment that night, and I now wondered if this had been purely coincidence. Yes, it was a full moon, and some nutcases claim they can feel the moon directing them, strengthening them. I felt those urges myself, and rather than try to figure it out, I tried to blot them out. That night, I found myself at a party at a friend of a friend's. Being young and stupid, and thinking it would be all right *this time*, I drank too much. It didn't work, not the way I needed. No matter how much I drank, the more I *wanted* to get drunk, the less I could shut off my feelings. I craved a little oblivion, even at the cost of a raggedy, personally embarrassing night. But it wouldn't happen. No matter how hard I tried to get wrecked, I couldn't.

Eventually, very late, I said good-bye and took the long way home, hoping the cold air would somehow force the alcohol into my system.

Down the block, the last lights in the darkened cinema clicked off, the late show having let out twenty minutes earlier. A young man set an alarm and locked the door. The manager, maybe, or the last of the late-shift workers.

He looked around, put the keys in his pocket, and set off down the street ahead of me, another lonely soul.

Lonely, maybe, but not alone. Three men stepped out of the shadows in front of him.

"Faggot. We told you we'd be back."

He kept his head down, kept walking. It was a pretty stupid thing to do; if someone is threatening you, you don't turn your back on them. I knew from experience you can't wish away trouble like that. But he quickly lengthened the distance between himself and the others, so maybe he knew what he was doing.

"Hey, faggot! I'm talking to you." One of them raced up and, before he could move, grabbed his arm.

The kid *did* know what he was doing; he pulled out a can of pepper spray and soaked the guy with it.

The attacker grabbed his eyes and screamed. The kid stepped in and aimed the stream at him. He should have run. His attacker flailed and, with a lucky shot, managed to knock the canister out of his hand.

The kid ran, then. The guy he nailed was screaming curses and crying, rubbing his eyes, which only made things worse. Made it worse for the kid, too, because the other two decided it was time to join in. One rushed him, throwing hard punches at his head. The kid went down.

The other, having checked on his blinded friend, was now screaming himself. He kicked the prone kid several times.

It all happened in less than a minute. It took forever.

I was frozen, unable to scream for help. I stared as the scene unfolded, unable to think. The cheap, prepaid phone in my pocket never even occurred to me.

Everything slowed to glacial pace. Eternities passed between heartbeats, and even as the violence seemed to pause, it was as if a movie was running in my head, several minutes faster than the reality unfolding before me.

I knew exactly what was coming next—
I had no idea. How could I have known?

—They would drag the barely conscious man over to the sidewalk, blood streaming from his face, his hand bent back at an unnatural angle. They would place his head on the curbstone, open his mouth, and stomp his head, splitting his jaw on the anvil of asphalt.

I shuddered. An orgasmic surge tore through my body. I felt the confinement of flesh fall away, and a strong, sure connection with the universe seized me. It was coupled with an equally foreign feeling of strength, and suddenly the men before me, between punches two and three, sloooowed and stopped.

Two thoughts struggled to make themselves known in the tumultuous rush of emotions and sensations.

One: The energy drinks and vodka had definitely caught up with me. I was unhinged with power and, oddly, goodness.

Two: If I'd once been labeled a "troubled child," trouble was calling me, louder and more comprehensively than ever before.

I was going to stop this.

I could smell the sweat on each of the men, scents as individual as the men themselves. The dissipating odor of pepper spray tingled and burned. I could practically taste the blood as it streamed from the prone man; its molecules dancing, ruby-luminous and hypnotic. I could hear heavy breathing and heartbeats, crickets from an empty lot down the street, a radio from a car a mile away.

And the moon, oh, the moon. The cold silver light suffused my veins, animating me, making me magic.

Time snapped back into its groove, but the men did not continue the beating. The idea of the curb—so vivid in my mind, as if a direct link from them—faded. They turned away from their victim and froze.

They were staring at me. I was growling.

It was not the noise of a small woman frustrated with the unfairness of the universe. Not a personal, muffled noise of determination or resistance. It was animal violence, loud and warning. The louder it got, the more I felt it and the strength, *omigod*, the *power*...

I stepped forward, and found myself hindered, tangled in my clothing. Nightmarishly, I couldn't make my hands pull at my jeans.

I had paws.

A distant part of me wanted to stop, but I didn't. It felt too... right.

Instinct drove me now; if I had paws, I had claws. I had a mouthful of teeth. I snapped and tore at the fabric. My legs—and tail—were freed.

With the moon singing in my blood, power coursing through me, a lifetime of unfairness and fear falling away, I had one objective: *fix this*.

There was one other thought in a corner of my brain: *What the fuck was in that Red Bull cocktail anyway?*

I turned back to the men, who were still staring when they should have been running. Three long, leaping paces, and I was on them.

Although I felt entirely capable of tearing their throats out, something kept me from doing so. An impulse suggested they weren't worthy of that kind of punishment. My intervention would make them reconsider their role in the world and their all-too-willing use of violence.

How could I have known that?

I shook one by the scruff, then nipped at the other one, almost playfully, savoring their fear, enjoying my power. If it was a hallucination, it was a good one. I'd willingly pay six or seven hangovers for that sensation again.

The first two ran. The other remained, stunned.

I didn't feel the same urge to limit violence with him. I felt a compulsion, a need to *end* him. A natural urge, and unnatural.

I hurled myself at him, my soul blazing with its righteous mania. I clamped onto his shoulder with my teeth, reveling in his screams. His blood was ambrosial and...wrong. The taste of his wrongness told me I had been correct in my assessment. He needed to go.

Instincts ablaze, I should have anticipated he wouldn't run away. I should have anticipated the response, a yank on my clothing and the brick upside my head.

I fell, stunned, a cathedral landing on top of my skull. Yet the compulsion to attack remained.

I struggled up, shaking my head, and saw him heading around a corner. To a car, I knew, somehow. I tried to run, but tangled up in my clothing, I stumbled, landing hard, skidding on my chin.

I saw stars. I passed out, and awoke with my clothes knotted around me, twisted, torn, and dirty. The young man who'd been the victim of the attack was sitting up, gingerly dabbing at his nose, which was streaming blood. He stared at me, dragging himself away painfully, his wounded hand useless, cradled in his lap.

"What. The. Fuck."

"Sorry...I...they're gone?"

He shook his head. "You turned into a *wolf*."

Somehow I was less concerned that he and I were having the same hallucination than the fact that he seemed to believe it. That increased my panic. I shook my head, rearranged my clothes as best I could without seeming too nervous. Time to leave.

Terror filled his eyes. His back hit the wall; he couldn't get any farther from me. "What *are* you?"

"I'm..." *I'm really scared.* "I'm...I'm...late. Gotta go."

Then I got up and ran away, hard as I could.

I got home, sneaked past my mother, and stripped off my remaining clothes. I got into the shower, as hot as I could bear, and scrubbed off all the blood. Then I turned it all the way to cold until I knew I was neither drunk nor dreaming.

I stared at myself in the mirror. Nothing unusual there: bloodshot eyes, bad haircut, lips faintly blue from the cold shower. I was shivering, too, but that was nothing to do with temperature.

I stuffed the torn clothes into a bag and threw it into the back of my closet. I didn't want my mother to find bloody, torn clothing. I went to sleep.

At the time, it was easiest to ignore it all, write it off as a bad alcohol experience. After that I had three choices. I could either hide the Beast, stifling it with beer and dope, shutting the door that had opened unasked. Or I could tell someone I thought I turned into a wolf when threatened, then probably eat the leather strap while that someone jabbed my brain with a cattle prod. The third choice was even less palatable.

I could remove my dangerous self from the equation altogether.

For the next several years, until I graduated high school, I made it my mission to become the calmest teenager in history. It wasn't easy; my sudden interest in the occult and ancient history wasn't the most direct path to the Kingdom of Cool. Vodka and pot became my best friends; I was too scared to try anything stronger, afraid it would unleash the Beast forever. The reputation as a stoner was marginally preferable to that of a target. The bad days were when I had to pull up my hood and keep my head down to keep the fangs from showing.

Summoning up all my courage, I tried once, when Ma was cooking, to ask her about any...unusual behavior...in our family. She scowled, but asked like what.

"Uhhh, I dunno. Anger issues? Mood swings? Violence?"

She froze, her face went ashen. "What?"

"I was…just wondering. You know, about family traits. And stuff." Inspiration struck me. "It came up in biology."

She tried to replace the lid on the pot, but slipped, hitting the pot at an angle. Spaghetti sauce splashed onto the stove, vivid red against cracked white porcelain. "Why are you asking me this, Zoe?" Her hands were trembling; it took her three tries to turn off the heat.

"Uh…"

"Why is this coming up, all of a sudden?"

Her urgency scared me. I wasn't about to tell her about my problems, not with this kind of reaction. "Uh, class—?"

She let my lame answer hang there, too caught up in her own thoughts. She wiped up the spill, rinsed out the sponge, and gave me a questioning glance.

"You know we don't want to run into your father's family. They're bad people, nothing but trouble. But you listen to me. You and me, we're *nothing* like them, do you understand me? *Nothing*."

She grabbed my shoulders, her fingers still damp. "The only reason I left your father was that he was…in something over his head. He wasn't a bad person, just…lost. I couldn't risk you getting caught up in his family's antics. I work as hard as I can, don't I? Our life isn't the greatest, but we have nothing to be ashamed of, do we, Zo?"

No way would I ever say anything about her not working hard enough for us. "No, Ma. I…we don't. No way."

"And it's getting better, slowly but surely. Right?"

"Yeah, Ma." I let a little exasperation into my words, trying to diffuse the situation, trying to sound like a normal teenager. "I get it. I'm just asking, because of class, that's all."

"Yeah, well." She turned away from me, reached into the cupboard for the box of spaghetti. "Anyone ever says anything different, anyone says anything about your father, you tell me, right?"

"Yeah, Ma. 'Course. I know the drill."

"OK, then." She smiled weakly. "Dinner's in ten, so go ahead and set the table."

As I got out the plates, somehow I knew Ma wasn't evading me. She believed everything she was telling me, even if she wasn't telling me everything she knew. I could tell, in her mind, our life was about keeping on the straight and narrow, about family dysfunction and crime. Not about monsters.

That was the only time I'd tried asking her about the Beast. She'd never seen me when I was in the thrall of the Beast, and I never saw her sprout teeth, so I assumed it was my own exclusive problem.

If others fled, seeking refuge into comic books, fantasy, and arcane books on witchcraft, I devoured them wholesale, hoping I could learn something about myself and the Beast. I don't know whether I hoped I'd find more like me or find the cure to what I was. A simple, logical explanation would do. All those museums we loitered in—free on Wednesday nights, and warm and full of security guards—they had reproductions of cave-wall paintings and statues of people with animal heads. Or animal bodies with human faces. I thought there must be some connection. I told Ma I was interested in art history and the past because it took me away from the present. The past can't hurt you, I said. Archaeology did calm me. The focus it demanded kept the Beast away, and, later, the quiet of libraries and labs made me feel safe.

I tried to tackle the problem head-on, though. I read, but there's only so much useful information a teenager can glean from psychology texts. Worse, the more I learned, the more afraid I became: "psychotic" and "schizophrenic" are terrifying words, especially when you believe they may apply to you. So it was only when I was feeling exceptionally safe—and brave—that I took that direct approach.

I tried twice on my own to talk to a professional. Once, after narrowly avoiding a fight in school, I was sent to a counselor there, and I got the impression, after two or three mandatory meetings, that I could trust her.

One day I told her I had dreams about being a wolf. About attacking people.

She didn't laugh. She didn't mock me. She listened, and after I finished, she asked questions.

I think I eventually might have opened up to her even more, but Ma got one of her feelings, and we moved on the next week.

For a while I began to believe what little the counselor had told me, that the "dreams" were a way for me to feel some control in my unsettled, and sometimes scary, early life. And shortly after, during my first attempt at college, I sucked it up to try another session, but by then I realized: I could talk all I wanted about dreams and urges to violence, but I'd never be able to prove what I was. I had no control over the Beast. I couldn't *show* anyone.

I canceled the appointment and never tried again.

But it started to get better after that. As I delved into my all-consuming interest in the past, I developed skills, which led me to finding a place where I felt I belonged. I began to wonder if my own personal demon would be banished. It gave me hope then, but now I knew otherwise.

Ma had no reason to doubt me, seven years ago. I'd learned to be a good liar, and thanks to my "research," I always had a glib, deflective answer. In any case, now I had to obey her last instructions to me.

Up until now, I'd worked awfully hard not to use the word "werewolf" to describe the Beast.

Until my first encounter with my father's people, I had no idea there really might be others like me.

Chapter 3

The day of the funeral was bad. I'd wanted to avoid as much of the public side of mourning as I could, but Ma had friends, other assistants in the dean's office. So against my every antisocial desire and habit, I let them know about the burial. I hadn't put anything in the paper because it would only draw my father's people, which was the last thing I wanted; but if the obit was optional, the death notice was not. I just wanted it all to be over.

I put on my skirt and my one dressy jacket and thought longingly of the vodka bottle that was still one-third full in the box in the kitchen. Not today; fear or anger, not grief, brought the Beast, and I owed it to Ma to do her proud in front of the few people who might have cared about her besides me.

It was a cloudy day that refused to either cool down or actually rain, and I kept telling myself to take it in increments. I drove to the crematorium, no problem. Listening to the polite, nondenominational words of the minister I'd only met minutes before and who'd never even seen Ma was harder, but he didn't screw it up, so I held it together.

Greeting two of the other administrative assistants from her office was tougher than I expected. I didn't know them well, but they'd genuinely cared about Ma, which broke my heart. With one or two notable exceptions, most of our connections didn't survive our moves, but in the past few years we'd stayed put while

I finished college. In the last years of Ma's life, she'd put down tenuous roots.

My control was almost to the point of snapping, thinking of the normal lives we might have had, when it was shocked back into place by two surprises.

The first was the dean, who I'd always thought a little full of himself. "I'm so sorry, Zoe. Nancy was a good friend to us all, and I know she made my job a hundred times easier. If you decide that you want to stay and start a PhD, you let me know. We'll find a way to make it happen."

Of all the things I had been expecting from him, that was just about the last. An offer, totally unsolicited, to continue my studies? Past regrets fled in the face of future hope.

Stunned, I nodded. "Thank you, Dean. I don't know what I'll do next, but…thank you."

He put his hand on my shoulder, then joined the two women by a car. I looked up to see the second to last thing I had expected to see. Sean Flax was standing by the door. Used to the jeans, work shirts, and heavy boots he wore when working on archaeological field projects, he was supremely uncomfortable in a suit. I was uncomfortable for him; apart from my graduation, we had never seen each other dressed up. His sandy-reddish hair had been brushed into a semblance of order, his round face scrubbed, his Van Dyke trimmed, his nails clean.

Sean was trying hard.

I didn't know what to do. I had to talk to him, I wanted to talk to him, but it had been a long time. Where to start? I'd been in love with his best friend, Will; we'd all worked together and we'd all shared an apartment, so shaking hands was absurd. Between us, knuckle-bumps were more likely, but not here, now—

"Zoe, hey." He shook his head and opened his arms.

I walked into his embrace and cried for what seemed like a hundred years.

"I'm so, so sorry," he said into my hair. He had to lean over; there was nearly a foot difference between us, and probably a hundred pounds. It was good to hang onto him. If nothing else, Sean was solid. Sean was real.

"I'm glad you're here. I should have called, but...I didn't think you'd want to see me."

He cleared his throat and stepped back from me. "Come on now."

"Well? We haven't spoken in a while."

"No. But this is different, and that other stuff..." He shrugged. "It's over. Your mother, she trumps whatever other drama we might have had going on."

His face was blotchy and his eyes were red-rimmed; having lost his mother at an early age, something about Ma had apparently hit him hard. And she'd taken to him right away, too, for some reason, despite her usual caginess. When she visited our apartment, he just liked sitting near her. It took the fire from him, in a good way. Calmed him, I'd thought.

"I'm sorry. I should have called."

"Yeah, you should have. But I get it. I wasn't sure I should come, either."

We both shrugged and looked away, because we both remembered why I hadn't called, and why he hadn't been sure. I decided to point out the obvious.

"Does Will—?"

"I shot him an e-mail, but he's out of the country now, and his connectivity might not be all that great. So."

So. Having broached the topic of Will, and especially with Sean, it was now impossible to ignore the hundreds of mental snapshots of Will I'd tried to forget: the light-brown hair, cut short to thwart the cowlicks; his good jaw; the way one eyebrow was slightly raised in perennial skepticism. A shade below six feet, Will had a runner's build augmented by time in the gym he claimed was to clear his head after classes, but maybe was also habit from growing up in a neighborhood where using your fists wasn't uncommon. Then there was his smile, which first caught my eye when I was in his class section. A little crooked, but so, so sweet—

I swallowed. "Does Will—is he doing OK?"

"Yeah, he's fine." A little of the familiar, stubborn Sean resurfaced, and he frowned. "Zo, I'm not going to get into all that, OK? You guys want to talk, you should decide you're gonna talk to each other. I'm not getting in the middle of it."

I nodded quickly. Of course, no question. "But maybe you and me—we're OK?"

He sighed. "Will's been my best friend for years. You broke his heart with what I thought was a bullshit excuse. What am I supposed to do? I'm not as angry as I was. It's been two years. Maybe someday you can explain it to me, we'll be a hundred percent. But now?" He rocked his hand back and forth. "Maybe eighty-five."

I smiled. "Thanks, I'll take it." I had to take it; no way would I *ever* tell him why I broke up with Will so suddenly. "And I'm sorry I hurt you, too. If I could've avoided hurting anyone—"

"Yeah, OK, ancient history, done with it." He walked a few steps, coughed. "Any chance you could give me a ride back to the train? Call me a cab? My car is in the shop."

"Jeez, Sean, I'll give you a lift. Just give me a few minutes to change, OK?" A thought occurred to me. "Um, you don't still happen to have the bag, do you?"

He shook his head. "Not on me. I remembered it about halfway here. I felt like such an idiot. You can pick it up, once you drive me back."

I glanced at him; I didn't think he'd forgotten the bag. Maybe he'd said so, because just showing up here with it would have been weird, like he was saying, "OK, your mother's dead, and here's the last of her stuff."

Sean knew the story Ma had told him; that we were hiding from dangerous in-laws. That's why he'd agreed to hang onto a bag stuffed with insurance papers, the car slip, and other things she wanted to keep safe. He'd been established in his apartment for ages and had a steady job. Ma didn't trust our flimsy apartment door or want to rely on the schedules of a bank safe.

I drove us back to our apartment. The excuse of the funeral now gone, things got more awkward. We found ourselves trying to reconnect, the reason for us having to do so resting squarely on my shoulders.

He mentioned he'd decided to forge ahead and pursue his doctorate to start his own contract archaeology company. I told some lies about maybe looking into a museum studies program in New York. There was an uncomfortable silence for a few blocks.

"How's Danny?" Sean asked suddenly.

Danny was my cousin by affection, not blood, but he was all the family I had left now that Ma was gone. I pulled into the drive, switched off the ignition. "Good. He's working in Cambridge. I helped him move into a nice place there, couple months back."

"Tech job?"

I paused. "Computational linguistics."

"Get the fuck out. There is no such thing."

"There is. And not only is he good at it, there's money to be made."

"Well. That's one way for him to put all those languages to use." Sean followed me up the stairs. Archaeologists are expected to have a few languages under their belts; Danny put us all to shame. "I wouldn't have gotten through my Spanish proficiency if he hadn't helped. But…he wasn't here today?"

I nodded, sighed. "Business trip, three time zones away. Not much we could do about it."

Danny's mother, Louise, and Ma met working at a temp agency when I was young. When their paths crossed a year later, in another town, Ma decided to accept Louise Connor's friendship. Not until she asked Sean to hang onto her papers, years later, did I ever see Ma trust anyone like that. Louise and Danny were all Ma and I had for a long time. Junior-high frenemies had made comments about me "having two mommies"; I would have killed for that kind of stability. That's what friendship is, I guess: Ma and Louise were never huggy-huggy—Louise no more demonstrative than Ma—and we weren't living in each other's pockets all the time. But they were always there for each other, and for us, two underemployed single mothers struggling together.

I shrugged, unlocked the door, let us in. "Have a seat. The fridge is empty, but if you want a glass of water?"

"I'm good."

"Let me get changed, and we'll get going."

Sean's voice followed me to my room. "Zoe, where are you going to go? You got this place cleaned out."

The reason for my leaving so hastily—another tricky topic. "Um, dunno."

"Zoe."

"Yes?"

"What's up?"

I finished pulling my hoodie over my head and grabbed my backpack. "Um."

"What aren't you telling me?"

"I think my father's family has located me." The detail of their similarity to me wasn't important.

"Shit." A pause. "So no idea where you're going yet?"

I knew I had to visit my grandmother, but after that..."Nope."

"Oh." He flushed red. "Well, if you want, you can stay with me—"

I shook my head. No way was I going to lead those other Beasts to Sean. "Naw, thanks. I'm going to put some distance between me and them. Then I'll figure it out."

"Well, let me know if you change your mind."

I locked up and debated leaving the key. I didn't know if I'd be staying here tonight, but figured I should hang on to it because I still had to stop by my grandmother's.

Things got quiet between us again on the drive to Boston. Two-thirds of a team isn't quite the same when they're doing their best not to talk about the other third.

"Seeing anyone?" I asked as I negotiated the merge onto Route 128. Driving in Massachusetts was a little like playing *Grand Theft Auto* without the rewards.

"No. Too much going on with the survey. The hours are ridiculous. I come home beat-up, exhausted, and smelling like an animal. No woman wants that."

I nodded, remembering the laundry the three of us had generated when we were all in the field at once. At the end of one particularly noxious project, working near a Superfund site, we'd buried our work clothes. We didn't dare burn them and wouldn't risk leaving them in the trash for a homeless person to find. "All the glamour of working on a road crew with none of the union benefits."

"Maybe next winter, when we're out of the field and in the office." Sean hitched and squirmed. The suit fit fine but was wool, and it was warming up outside.

The closer we got to Boston University, the easier and harder it became for me. The traffic was even worse than I remembered, but I felt like I was fitting myself back into the flow of the area. The university might have been attended by smarter and more important people, but it belonged to me. The last year I was there, I'd been able to live on campus, which was new to me, despite my six-year undergraduate tour of public institutions in three states. Until Ma got the steady gig at BU, we'd moved so much, my transcript was a patchwork of classes from colleges up and down the East Coast. Living on campus was a revelation: in the cafeteria, you could eat all you wanted, and if you were quick about it, you could sneak food out. Other students might grumble about the food's quality and doing unfamiliar chores, but I shook my head in wonder. They'd never been as hungry as I'd been on occasion, or they would have concentrated on eating, not bitching. And you don't complain about doing laundry if you've ever had to wash your clothes with the same bar of soap you showered and shampooed with.

The archaeology department might not have had the biggest budget in the world, but if you can do 90 percent of your work with a few old shovels and buckets and handmade sifting screens, you don't need much else. Same for the lab: I learned I could do a passable job of conservation with distilled water, old cardboard beer flats, a toothbrush, rubber cement, masking tape, and some marking pens. Give me a gift card for the drugstore and I'll work miracles.

I'd never had much, and given just a little—a little instruction, a few materials—I learned how much I could accomplish. I learned how far I could go with just the smallest encouragement.

And the libraries—there were lots of them and they were open almost continuously. A major chosen and a degree nearly within reach, I dove into my studies, excelling for the first time. They let you take out all the books you wanted. For free. The world was at my fingertips.

The hours I'd spent there allowed me, for whole stretches at a time, to forget the Beast.

In those two years, I'd found friends and, eventually, a boyfriend. People smiled when they saw me, asked me to work with them on their weekend research projects. I made money, I got skills, and I felt normal for maybe the first time ever.

I, the rootless wonder, the girl blown about by the wind, *belonged*.

I missed the place terribly.

Luck smiled on me, and I found a parking space on Commonwealth Avenue. It was several blocks from Sean's street, but a parking space in Boston is a gift from the gods and I no longer had a valid parking sticker.

"Um." Sean looked really uncomfortable now. "You want to wait here? I can go and—"

"No, I'll come with you. I need to stretch my legs."

"If you're sure."

We got out, and habit caught me glancing down the street to the faculty and graduate student lounge, otherwise known as The Pub. I'd celebrated my twenty-second birthday there with Will and Sean.

That's when I began to worry. I'd felt better coming to Boston than I had in weeks, but I hadn't counted on the other memories that would come back with the scenery.

We played *Frogger* with the traffic and trolley tracks, and then I started to realize it wasn't such a hot idea going to the apartment with Sean. As we crossed St. Mary's Street, my heart pounded. I tried to stay calm, but memory is as powerful a drug as anything on the market today. The more I recognized, the more I remembered, and the worse it got.

I did some breathing exercises, trying to calm myself. The Boston University student ghetto was no place for the Beast. It was no place for me, either, and the faster I got out of there, the better it would be for everyone.

I could have found my way up the weathered granite steps to the foyer, the elevator, the third floor, blindfolded. If memory is a drug, smell is the trigger. Maybe it was just my senses playing tricks on me, but Sean's apartment was identifiable from down the hall.

Very little had changed since I'd last been there two years ago, when my life had gone to hell. The living room looked like a garage sale had exploded, but that was Sean all over. When Will had been here, there'd been a modicum of order, and when I had lived here, there'd even been acceptable levels of hygiene. Now there were only pathways from the doorway to the kitchenette, the couch, and the bedroom. The rest of the space was piles of clothing, tools, and books, all very orderly, but out of place in a living room. There was a desk somewhere under a mountain of paper and notebooks. I had to assume it was a desk, based on the topography, but it could as well have been a stack of snow tires. Sean was ready, at a moment's notice, to run a dig out of this apartment. On several occasions, the three of us *had* run a dig from this apartment.

I tried not to look toward the room Will and I had shared. I shoved the memories aside and tried to believe when I told myself I should be grateful for what I'd had, not crying over what I'd lost.

Somewhere, under all this crap, was my inheritance. And maybe, a clue to the Beast.

"It's still here?" I said.

"Yup."

In spite of everything, in spite of the catastrophic, investment-grade bust-up I'd had with his best friend, Sean still had the bag. He hadn't let his feelings about me keep him from keeping his promise to Ma. I don't know if I would have been that big a person.

He went into his bedroom for a minute, shutting the door behind him. I heard rustling, the sounds of clothing being shifted and books skidding on the floor; finally, silence.

As quietly as I could, I went over and touched the door to what had been Will's room. Our room. I didn't dare open the door, any more than I dared think about the one perfect summer I'd shared with him. Will had moved months ago, I was certain, but I could still sense his presence here.

I couldn't not remember the summer I'd moved in.

There is nothing quite like being young, working outside, and coming home with your boyfriend. Will and I worked in the field all day together and then spent summer evenings on the fire escape drinking beer with Sean. We argued about everything under the sun, swapping allegiances as fast as we changed topics. I had worried about bringing Danny over the first time, but he'd held his own against Sean's bluster until he gained his respect, helping him with his language exams and translating the occasional article.

Better, Danny really liked Will. Wary of Will's motives all the while he helped me move into the apartment, Danny was sold when, having realized I'd left my notebook computer in a "safe place" at Ma's, Will offered to make yet another forty-minute drive to go get it for me. Danny had gone with him and had come back approving of Will.

As the three of them came home one Friday night, I was reminded of the picture of the "ascent of man," the one that depicts the transition to modern man from apelike creatures. Sean crashed through the doorway, a transit case strapped to his back, a broken tripod over his shoulder, and a six-pack in his free hand. Will, looking tired as he juggled a stack of books for his own research and a backpack full of exams to be graded, was apparently soothing a hysterical student over the phone. Danny followed—his head down and unconsciously bobbing to the music of any one of several Bach family members playing on his ear buds—texting madly. It made me giggle to think of them as states of evolution—from a dense brute, to an athletic professorial type, to a soul better acclimated to computers than the physical world—even though I knew that was as an erroneous oversimplification.

We four had exactly the right chemistry: enough of the same taste in reading and movies to be passionate about it, enough overlap in our professional interests so that no one felt left out. We all came from the Northeast—Sean from central Maine, Will from western Massachusetts, Danny from upstate New York, and me from all over—so we had some things in common but could still argue over what to call a sub sandwich. Personalities just added flavor, and arguments never lasted long. During those four months, we shared the kind of long evening discussions where you believed if you had just a little more time, you could solve all the world's problems.

Then Will and I would go to our bedroom, and that was simply magic, too. I don't know if it was because Will was my first long-term, serious boyfriend, but all it took was one smile, one look, for my knees to turn to jelly and my usually cautious nature to be cast aside like I'd forgotten everything I was. Maybe the sex was cataclysmically good because it did allow me to forget for a while, or maybe it was the danger, the thrill of losing control, that made it so sweet. Maybe it was Will's body that made me crazy, and he seemed a little bit psychic about what would please me most, at any given moment. Whatever the reason I fabricated for breaking up with him, whatever problems in our relationship I might have invented, the physical side couldn't have been one of them.

I felt bad leaving Ma alone so much, but when she met Will and Sean, she understood. I knew she was happy for me.

Gone now. All of it. I tried to be happy I'd had it once when I'd never expected so much.

Sean emerged red-faced but clutching the duffel bag. It looked OK; there's only so much you can do to secure a cloth bag, but when I checked it, the only really important thing was still there—an envelope with a sheaf of papers I remembered Ma tucking in there. There were a few other things, including one that surprised me: a yellow plastic pencil box I'd used as a treasure chest when I was a kid.

I closed my eyes and let myself sag with relief. The papers were safe. I owned so little now, preparing to vanish after Ma's death, that what really mattered to me could just about fit into my backpack.

"Zoe, what now?"

"Um, I got some errands," I said. Not wanting to tell Sean what I had to do next, I glanced out the window, down to the street. Four men were entering the building.

"No, I meant about you and—"

I turned back to the window. I'd almost dismissed it, but something about one of them looked familiar. And they were too old and too well-dressed to have normal business in a student apartment building.

The one holding the door was no longer wearing a Harley T-shirt but a very expensive suit—was he the one last night, in Salem? The night I learned I wasn't alone with the Beast?

Didn't matter who it was. They'd followed me, I was certain of it.

I tried to shove past Sean. He was about as easy to move as a refrigerator, so I got only about halfway past because I surprised him.

"Zoe, what's wrong!"

"Can't now." I was starting to hyperventilate. "Thanks for—"

"No, tell me—"

I shoved at him, but he wouldn't budge. "My father's family! Here! I need to leave, now!"

The hallway was too dangerous. Rather than wait, I went to the window and the fire escape.

"Zoe, we can call the cops—"

I was trapped, and I didn't like being trapped. It was just the kind of thing to invite the Beast, which was the last thing I could afford in bright daylight.

The window had been painted shut. Before Sean could protest, I picked up a shovel and broke the glass, using the blade and shaft to clear a safe way through.

I was out and clambering down as fast as I could, but sickeningly felt my hands slip when my foot expected to find a rung that was missing. The whole apparatus shook, making my stomach lurch.

Shouts from inside the apartment. I paused and saw the men force their way in. Saw Sean grab one of them by the collar and swing him into the wall. He turned and shoved another away, then ran for the window.

I climbed down faster.

I hit the ground and ran like hell toward campus. Hoping to lose myself in the crowds of students, I ran out into Commonwealth Avenue without looking.

Bad idea.

With Boston's crazy-assed drivers, I barely made it across the street intact. I stumbled in front of an oncoming Green Line trolley. A horn blast sent yet another surge of adrenaline through me, and I got out of the way, stopping just short of another train bearing down from the opposite direction. More horns and middle fingers from the drivers. As soon as the last trolley car passed me, I caught a break and a crossing signal—not that it mattered around here—and bolted across the street, narrowly missing getting hit by a BMW. I cut down to Bay State Road and briefly considered calling on the Beast. That's how desperate I was, to risk the Beast in front of normal people, going into whatever brief span of lunacy my broken mind took me when I imagined I was a wolf. Although I might have gotten away with it—a big dog with a backpack wouldn't be so out of place on a college campus—I could not, *could not*, risk losing that duffel bag. There was no way for me to carry it as a wolf. I had to stay sane, calm, and human long enough to get it away safely.

Watching the faces of the students I ran past, I could tell there was no one following me. One girl, running with a backpack and gym bag, was late for her train. Four men running, in suits, was another situation.

I'd lost them. With any luck, I was leading them away from Sean. With any luck, he'd gotten away.

I slowed down, and a form stepped from the narrow alley just past Classics House.

It was Sean.

"Hola." He gave the traditional BSR greeting, took my arm, and kept us moving briskly toward Kenmore.

"They behind you?"

He shook his head. "I ditched them by the falafel truck."

"I'm so sorry, Sean. I never expected they'd actually—"

"Zoe, what's going on?"

"Like I said. I think they're my father's folks. They seem to be particularly interested in talking to me." I shivered. "I don't know what they want."

"Zoe, no way! This is the second time they came by my place."

"What?" I pulled at him, a tiny anchor barely slowing an aircraft carrier. "When? What did they say?"

"About a week ago. They were looking for you. I blew them off when they wouldn't tell me who they were."

My stomach lurched. "But they found *you*."

"They found Will."

I started walking again, not seeing where I was going. They'd found *Will*, and he hadn't been in my life for years. How much did these guys know about me? Who were they?

Above the law. Hopelessly well connected. Knew about me, and apparently were intimately acquainted with the Beast.

Shit.

"The best thing for you to do is go back, forget you ever saw me. Tell them I asked you for help, and you said no. They won't bother you again, it's not you—"

"I wouldn't be too sure about that."

"Sean, they won't care about you roughing them up. They broke in. They don't want the cops, they won't press charges."

"There's that, but…" He shrugged, a little angry, a little pleased with himself. "I don't like people thinking they can boss me around."

I stopped, closed my eyes. Sean had always reminded me of Porthos the musketeer, appetites and violence included. "It was worse than you slamming that one into a wall?"

"I didn't hurt any of them," he hastened to add. "Probably. Nothing permanent, anyway. But the thing is I don't think I want to go back there just yet."

I opened my eyes and started walking again.

"You gotta take me with you, Zoe."

"Best thing is for us to split up. They're not interested in you. They won't bother going back, too afraid you'll call the police."

"Um. Yeah. Thing is…they know I won't do that."

I kept walking, fearing the worst. He probably hadn't actually *killed* one of them…

"I might have found a wallet, in the scuffle. I might have taken it with me."

"There are a dozen ways to argue that, Sean. Tell the cops you took it so you could report the intruders, that it was self-defense."

"But you want to know who they are, don't you? Take me with you, Zoe. You owe me that much."

Like I said, Sean's always had a crappy poker face. He knew he had me, and his jack-o'-lantern smile showed it. He held up the wallet, tempting me. "Just a couple of days, till things cool off."

"Sean, you're not going to like where I have to go next. And I really don't want to get you into any more trouble than you're already in."

In the growing dark, the ambient light of the university around us, I could see his piratical grin.

"Too late."

⌣

The cemetery was already locked up for the night. We parked on a dark side street and walked back, aiming for a section of fence that was obscured from the road.

I rummaged in my backpack and pulled out my trowel and flashlight.

"Little unauthorized excavation?"

I shook my head. "It...it belongs to me."

"What does?" He followed me over to the fence.

"Something buried here."

Sean looked around the cemetery. "Uh, lots of things are buried here."

"One of the last things my mother said was I should visit my grandmother."

"Never heard you mention her."

"She's been dead a long time now, before I met you. I think Ma left me something at my grandmother's grave. Something even more important than the bag you kept for us."

"Wouldn't she have been buried next to your grandmother?" Sean asked. "You know, where we were earlier?"

"Um, no. Father's mother," I improvised. "Long, complicated story—you know that."

I motioned impatiently, eager to be off the subject. Sean nodded and gave me ten fingers, which got me to the top of the fence. It was a long jump down. I would have thought with his larger size, Sean would have had a harder time clearing the fence, but long years of mischief and fieldwork had made him an expert. He landed heavily next to me, and I led the way.

"The last time Ma came here, she didn't take me, but she did bring a taped-up package, a brand-new garden trowel, and a potted plant. Ma wasn't a gardener; she came from the supermarket carnations school. I'm pretty sure she buried something."

It had started to rain hard now. The only light came from my flashlight and the city-night glow of Cambridge.

Water plastered Sean's hair to his head. His clothes were soaked through. "Zoe, what the hell are you doing? This is...it's seriously messed up."

That hurt more than I imagined. I knew I had problems, but I didn't like Sean thinking I was anything but normal.

I shrugged. "Ma told me she left me something with Grandma, something that would tell me about my father's family. All those years we were on the move, she somehow kept us two steps ahead. But she only told me about this when she couldn't protect me anymore. I need to know, now."

We'd arrived at a modest headstone, just where I remembered it, at the intersection of two lanes, near the tree missing a branch that had come down in a blizzard.

He stared at me, wondering how crazy I'd gotten in the past two years, the rain running down his face. He rubbed his hand over his eyes, wiped his nose.

"OK. Give me the trowel. You don't have a shovel, a trenching tool or something? This is going to take all night."

"What?"

"You can't afford to get busted for grave robbing, not with those goons after you. Give me the trowel. I'll get us started."

I couldn't help it; I started to laugh. Call it giddiness, fatigue, nerves, or burnout, I lost it. Sean thought I was going to dig up my grandmother and was now offering to help.

I pulled my trowel from my belt loop. One look at the tiny thing, worn down from years of work, and Sean was ready to explode.

"No, Sean, I'm not going to open the coffin. Just dig under the roses."

It took him a minute to parse that information; it would have taken anyone a moment. Finally he said, "OK, you can start."

He settled down two headstones over and tried to look relaxed. Hard, with the rain plastering his hair down, dripping off his nose.

It was hard work, made no less easy by the weather, the dark, and the dead little roses. I didn't want to just dig them up, leaving my work for everyone to see, but it would have been easier to work without the thorns grabbing at my sodden sleeve and bare wrist.

"Just like old times, huh, Sean? Working on your grad school projects?"

"What?"

"Me working, you watching, pretending to take notes."

That brought a smile, but any retort he might have made was cut short by a small noise, something barely audible above the rain but to which we were both well attuned.

Metal on metal.

I scraped the trowel through the wet earth and heard it again. Something was there.

We both worked now, me defining the edges, Sean shoving the overburden aside. Different noises now; it wasn't just metal.

Once I felt it move, I stuck my trowel in the ground and felt. I moved my fingers across the surface, obscured by mud and pebbles. Round, with something wrapped around the edges.

I pulled, and it came away, grating against damp, sandy soil beneath. Sean held up the flashlight. I brushed off the surface, tried to wipe away the smears of dirt and rust.

A blur of blue and gold. The letters OY and NSK were visible.

It was a tin for Danish butter cookies.

It took me a minute to realize it probably wasn't cookies, not if my mother had buried them in a cemetery, having sealed the top with duct tape. Not even Ma was that crazy about cookies.

I shook it; it didn't rattle, just a slow *thunk...thunk* as something heavy—wrapped—shifted inside.

I tried to find an edge of the tape to remove it, but kept slipping. Age had caused the tape to melt into itself. The cold and wetness did nothing for my dexterity. My hands were shaking; I set down the tin and grabbed my fingers, trying to stop the trembling. Then I pulled out my knife.

"Zoe, wait."

I looked up.

"It's too wet out here. Whatever's in there might be fragile. Let's find someplace dry, get some light before we open this."

It took me a minute to realize he was right. I nodded and handed the tin to him so I could put my knife away.

I froze. Something was out there. Suddenly I felt as though we were surrounded, but I couldn't see a thing through the rain.

I felt the call of the Beast.

Five of them, I knew without knowing how. Closing a circle around us. "Sean, we need to get—"

A twig cracked.

"Zoe!" Sean grabbed my arm.

"Run!"

"The hell I will," he said. "I'm not leaving you!"

"Sean! You can't let them get this!" I shoved him in the direction away from whoever was out there, willing him away. "Get out of here, now!"

He shook his head but took off. That was a first; he must have heard something in my voice, because Sean almost never did what he was told.

Didn't matter. I needed to keep the tin from them. They'd leave Sean alone, surely, if they were after me?

I felt a rippling down my spine. Two of the men I sensed…weren't there anymore. There was something else out there now in the spaces they'd occupied. The air all around me felt just like last night.

The men were gone, but now I sensed *wolves*.

I knelt down, stowing my knife and my trowel. I stepped out of my shoes and rolled up my jeans. And then I tried to recall the feelings I'd had when the Beast came before. I *needed* the Beast.

I heard a shout. It was Sean.

Did I want them to get Ma's last bequest to me? The hell I did. I thought about them opening the tin, seeing what was in it before I did—

The Beast arrived. *Arrived* was too small a word: a roaring in my ears, a riot in my soul. I welcomed it, for the first time in my life.

Good. If anyone deserved the Beast, they did.

Two wolves were chasing Sean. I tore after them. I got close enough to bite one in the haunch, and he yelped, staggered, and plowed over into the other. Lucky for me, Sean never looked back, just booked out of there.

The two wolves untangled themselves, one reddish, one with a dark black pelt. I ran. In and out and around and among the gravestones and monuments, it was easy to dodge and duck.

Suddenly, on an intersection of two roads, I was surrounded: two wolves behind me, a wolf-man and a sort of horrible walking snake before me.

The snake-man's face was barely human: two enlarged nostrils instead of a nose, yellow-and-brown scales instead of skin and hair. He walked upright, wearing a tracksuit, but he was a monster, fangs gleaming in the rainy night. His large black eyes were the deadest things in that acre of burials.

But the half-wolf, half-man was even worse. His ears stood up on his head, his face and jaw elongated, full of sharp teeth. I'd seen wolf-headed gods in the museum, but never one wearing a Harley-Davidson T-shirt and jeans. He was the one I'd seen in Salem.

My growl turned to a whine. My tail wagged, involuntarily, and I paced a step or two, uncertain of what I was seeing, of what to do. They were just like me, and they couldn't be.

Maybe this is it, I thought. *Maybe this is where I finally unspool. This is where the world goes crazy and I wake up in the rubber room.*

"Zoe," the wolf-man said, and my ears pricked up.

He reeked of Beastliness and he could speak. Holy shit, he knew my *name*.

"Zoe, there's no need to worry. We just want to talk to you. You can trust us."

I shook my wolfy head.

"You need to know what you are." He nodded to another figure behind me. I turned to see the fifth, a human man, emerging from the tree line, removing a glove carefully as he negotiated his way around the headstones. "Download, if you'd be so kind?"

"This won't hurt a bit." Before I could move, the man put his hand on the back of my neck. That's when the movie started.

As I stared, frozen, images played out in front of me. No sound, no words, but impressions accompanied them.

A variety of artifacts from around the world with transformed humans, wolf, or snake imagery seemed to suggest the long history of these creatures among humans. Some of them I recognized, like the Egyptian god Anubis, the caduceus of Asklepios, Hindi nagas, ouroboros, the Norse image of Fenrir. Other images were totally unfamiliar to me. But the one common theme was images of monsters—wolves, giant snakes, and every shape in between—attacking humans.

No, not simply attacking. Making the world better. Tracking and killing murderers, rapists, evildoers. But the viciousness of it all—

It was too much. I shook off his hand, backed away. They were exactly what my mother had warned me about, but she'd never said anything about wolf-men.

"I know you're confused, Zoe. You must trust us. What Download showed you, that's just the merest surface."

Trust was not in my vocabulary, or the Beast's. I moved a few steps, then backed up, uncertain.

"Let us help you—"

The two behind me tensed, ready to fight.

I bunched, ready to leap over them. I was drenched, my clothes and fur were matted down. There was no way I'd get away. At least I'd given Sean a chance.

The snake-man went on point; the others followed him, sniffing at the air.

I sniffed, too. I recognized the smell without being able to identify it, until I remembered the night at the cinema. I felt ill.

Something *wicked* was out there and I had the insane urge to do something about it. Fix it, make it right.

One of the wolves howled, making me shiver. The two wolves and the wolf-man tore off away from me, but also away from Sean.

I had the worst urge to go with them. If it hadn't been for the cookie tin, and my need to guard it, I'm sure the Beast would have carried me off with them. I wanted to run, chase whatever they were after, and be there for the kill—

If the snake-man hadn't spat just then, breaking the thought, I would have gone.

He hissed. "You're becoming a problem, stray."

With that, he melted into the rain and mist, following the others, making no sound at all.

Goddamn.

I stood, confused, angry, and thwarted. I waited a few minutes to make sure they were really gone, then resumed my human form. It was one of the easy times; I was so tired, it just sort of happened.

I found my shoes, put them on, and headed for the car. I hoped Sean was still there.

Every kid dreams they have a secret family, I thought as I trudged across the wet gravel pathways. It was just my shitty luck that I actually had a secret family full of threatening, dickhead monsters.

Chapter 4

Sean was in the car. He had it turned on and was ready to tear out as soon as I appeared. I was glad for the heater; the spring rain was freezing and I was soaked.

"What about those guys? Who were they?"

I thought about the one with the Harley T-shirt, the one who'd shown up in Salem and then Boston. "I didn't get any names. But definitely my father's people." I shuddered. "I was mostly running. Not a lot of talking."

We drove until we found a coffee shop, but then sat in the parking lot. I wasn't going to open the tin in public.

Under the dim yellow light of the overhead, I pulled the tape off the lid, brushing bits of roots and dirt from it. My hands were clammy; the cold of the metal didn't help. With the last of the tape gone, I slid my fingernails under the lid and pulled: no luck.

Rustle of cloth, followed by a sharp click: Sean handed me the screwdriver on his knife.

Nodding, I turned the tin over and jammed the screwdriver under the lid. Two good whacks and it started to move. I chased the loose edge around until the top came off with a grating noise and a shower of disintegrating metal.

Inside a sealed baggie was a swaddled package. I unwrapped several meters of plastic wrap until I uncovered a plain mailing envelope with a clasp closure, yellowed paper faintly discolored by foxing around the edges.

I unfolded it, and in my mother's handwriting was my name and a date, from six months ago. The date of her diagnosis with brain cancer.

I ripped off the top. Inside was a smaller, sealed envelope, addressed to me, which I was not about to open in front of Sean; I stuck it into my pocket for later. The rest was a collection of photos that slipped out in a cascade across my lap. A sheaf of yellow legal pad paper was folded in half.

Somehow, I wasn't as concerned about Sean seeing these, even when I saw the images on the photos. If this had anything to do with the Beast, surely Ma would have told me before she died.

I had come to the conclusion she didn't know anything about my personal problem.

The photographs were hard to look at. There were a dozen, all told, from what looked like crime scenes. Murders—maybe two, maybe three different cases.

They weren't tidy deaths, like in an Agatha Christie book, where the body would be artistically sprawled on the library carpet, a glass of poisoned wine spilled alongside. *These* were bad deaths in dark places: a badly lit alley, a storeroom, a basement. The bodies were torn apart with a viciousness difficult to fathom.

I don't know what kept me studying them, but I did. My stomach was in a knot, but otherwise I was dispassionate. Sean had gone green and sweaty.

Shuffling the photos, I saw they all were blurry, dark, and taken in haste. Amateurish. They showed the bodies fully, emphasis on the wounds. There were numbers on all of them, one through ten, in the same hand.

The first sheet listed numbers I assumed corresponded with the photographs. There were dates and place names, none of which I recognized, all from before I was born.

"That," Sean said, looking at a nearly decapitated body, "is one *hundred* percent fucked up."

"Welcome to my world. I guess this is why she didn't want me near my father's family." I wondered privately: Had Ma somehow had a baby with a werewolf? That brand of mayhem looked all too familiar. Is *that* what I was destined for? I remembered the urge to run with the others from the cemetery, to do…what? It made me ill to think of it.

"What now? You're not going to go—?"

"Not to the police, no. I have no idea what this is, and I don't want to know." I realized after the last interlude, I wanted to put as much distance as possible between me and my father's family—which now had a whole new twisted meaning for me. "I'm leaving, Sean. Tonight."

"But what about—?" He pulled the wallet out of his pocket. "You can find out more about them, maybe even your father now."

I took the wallet, went through it: license, some cash, a couple of credit cards, all in a name I didn't recognize. I shoved it into my bag.

"The more I see of those guys, the less I like." I wasn't about to stick around and let them tell Sean—or anyone else—about what I was. "It's safer this way."

"At least let me try and talk you out of it over a cup of coffee. I'm still soaked."

I nodded. We hadn't eaten and I was ravenous.

We went in, and I plugged in my phone to charge. There was a text from Danny waiting for me.

I'm back home now. Call me!!!

I could tell from the number of exclamation points just how anxious Danny was, but I hesitated, not wanting to draw danger to him, too.

It was just a phone call, I told myself as I hit speed dial.

"It's me," I said when he picked up.

"Zoe, I'm so sorry. I tried to get back early, for the funeral, but I got delayed and missed the connection. I'm so sorry."

"Danny, it's OK." I had a lump in my throat. "Thank you for trying."

"What are you going to do now?"

Danny was worried about me, but I couldn't tell him about the tin and the photos, that Ma's warnings had been about something even worse than violent in-laws.

On the other hand, if someone looking for me knew enough to look for Sean—or Will—they might find their way to Danny. I'd be damned if I'd let that happen. Sean could take care of himself, I knew.

I was never so sure about Danny. Danny had started out college in history, then went to anthropology, then ended up with a degree in linguistics, which I thought was even less practical than art history. But he found himself a nice job doing computational linguistics for a software startup, and actually had a job with benefits, which was more than I could currently say for myself.

Now that I thought of it, Danny was doing OK. Maybe I worried about him to keep from worrying about myself.

"I think it's fair to say I discovered some of Ma's concerns have some basis in reality," I said finally. "In fact, you might want to keep an eye out. They've been…reaching out, looking for me."

"Zoe, where are you? Please. We need to talk."

"Look, I'll send you an e-mail when I get…wherever I'm going."

"Zoe."

I don't know how he did it, but he managed to freight the two syllables of my name with history, guilt, and obligation. He knew as much as anyone why we'd been on the run, or as much of the made-up story my mother told anyone about why we kept moving. Yes, there was the year we'd spent sleeping on the pull-out sofa in his mother's tiny apartment, and there was a summer where Ma and I would have missed any number of meals if his mother hadn't invited us over regularly. I kind of thought the month he spent with us while his mother looked for a new job made up for it, but I know it didn't, not really. Not when my father's people might be on his trail.

"I'm not far," I said. I'd realized there were no documents, like the lease at BU, to tie Danny and me together. Our lives had been in parallel for some time now. The risk was there, but it was low. And I missed him. "I could stop by. But I am leaving tonight."

Where would I go besides…*away*?

"Stay with me, for just a few days."

"I can't."

"Just come over to my place. Please? Just for a drink or something?"

I thought about it, trying to tell myself that I would tell him just enough to put him on guard. It was more likely the threat would evaporate as soon as I took off. "Sean's with me—"

"All the more reason," he said. "You need *Homo sapiens sapiens* advice, not Neanderthal advice. See you both soon." He hung up.

I turned to Sean. "I'm going to stop by Danny's before I leave. You don't have to come."

"Like hell I don't. Who knows who else is waiting for you out there?"

"Sean, it's Cambridge. A city dense with responsible do-gooders, as well as campus and local police. The best place to hide out from people is in a crowd."

He shook his head. "Maybe Danny can talk you into forming a reasonable plan before you take off."

I felt better as soon as I saw Danny framed in the doorway of his brick apartment building. I felt genuinely happy for the first time in ages. Not much taller than me, maybe five-eight, and lighter than me by ten pounds, Danny's is the picture you see in the dictionary under "geek," "dweeb," and "nerd." Or maybe it would have been ten years ago; despite the glasses, the pale skin of the habitually nocturnal, and the curly dark hair perennially in need of a cut, once Danny had found his niche, he'd grown a confidence that was rare in anyone.

The bond Danny and I had was strong enough to last when I fell in love with Will and moved in with him and Sean. It had outlasted Will.

I knew I had to keep my distance, though, so the Beast and its kin wouldn't jeopardize him.

But I settled into that hug, feeling a weight come off me for the first time in I don't know when.

"What do you need?" he said.

Rather than argue with him, I said, "Strong drink, something to eat. In exactly that order." I suddenly felt epically tired and wanted to crash. I could barely see straight and didn't want to drive. I had no idea where I was going, anyway. "Um, and if you'll still have me, a place to stay. Just for tonight."

Danny knew me too well. He raised an eyebrow. "And?"

"Can Sean stay, too?"

"Oh." He looked past me, into the night. "Where is he?"

"With my stuff. Just wanted to make sure you were fine with me bringing him along."

"Love me, love my dog?"

"Danny."

Danny sighed. "Fine, sure, whatever."

I whistled sharply; Sean came around the corner with my backpack.

The two eyed each other before they extended their hands. Lines had been drawn when I split with Will and they hadn't seen each other in some time.

"Sean."

"Danny."

"Can we get inside?" I said. I was still dripping wet. "I'm freezing."

We climbed to the second floor. Inside, Danny dug out a beer, which he handed wordlessly to Sean, and a bottle of vodka, which he kept on hand for me. We ordered Chinese, and while we waited for the delivery, I brought him up to speed, stopping just shy of discovering the Beast's new kin.

"So, yeah, they're real," I finished, trying not to think about the pictures in the tin. "I got a look at them a couple of times. At home, Boston, and the cemet—and more recently."

Sean nodded. "I beat the shit out of three of them after Zoe jumped out my window."

Danny thought about that, and nodded back. "Good. Zoe, what's next?"

"I'm not sure. I'm going to head out of here, try and lose them. I've got a choice between New York and Providence, thanks to Ian, so I can get a job someplace crowded." I shook my head. "I'll decide which tomorrow."

I had a plan in place as soon as Ma got really sick. But somehow making that last choice seemed like too much to ask before the funeral, and now I hated that I finally had to decide.

The food arrived; we ate and talked. Tension eased somewhat, and it was almost like the three of us were back to normal. Danny and Sean covered the familiar territory of *Star Trek: The Next Generation* versus the movie reboot of *Star Trek*, and I relaxed only when Danny offered to agree to disagree.

Sleep settled in on me as they argued. It had been a long day, and I still had something left to explore. Danny showed me to the guest room. That's how far Danny had come in life: he had a real guest room with a bed, not just a futon.

"We can talk more tomorrow, after you get some sleep," he said, handing me clean towels. "I'll work at home."

"You don't have to."

He shrugged. "'Course I do. Don't worry about it." He hugged me briefly. "G'night, Zoe. I'm glad you came."

"Me, too."

Revived and calmer, I closed the door, then pulled out the smaller envelope from the tin. I stared at Ma's handwriting for what seemed a long time. Then I sat on the bed, opened it, and began to read.

Dear Zoe,

I love you. That's probably not enough for what you're about to learn, but if you're reading this, I'm gone. That's my last wish, that you know that you were the most important thing in my life. You didn't have the childhood I would have chosen, but you grew into the adult I always wanted to know, so I can leave believing I did my best. That's a lot. The only other thing I have is the truth, as best I know it, about my early life and what I learned about your father.

I ran away from the home when I was fifteen. I was raised in an asylum that was probably for orphans, but seemed like it was at least half lunatics as well. Some kids raved and hollered, some just sat in the corner and stared, harmless enough, most of them. But no matter how bad they were, they were always worse—mute and a little dead behind the eyes—after they received the treatment. That was what decided me; when I found myself hearing whispers when there was no one there, I decided I could live with voices better than electroshock therapy, or drugs, or whatever they did to those other kids. I took off in the middle of the night, hitchhiked to the first bus station, and chose a destination based on the amount of money I stole from the petty cash behind the desk.

I'd asked the teachers about my parents a couple of times and got variations on "car crash" and "somewhere up north." New England or New York, maybe? Vague, but possibly true, so I don't know who my people really were. The lady I called your grandmother—I left this at her grave. She was a good friend to me, but no relation. I thought you could do with a grandmother, even if it was only for a few years. I'm sorry; I hope the slight lie of blood is outweighed by the kindness she showed you and me both.

So that's me.

Your father, I thought he was it. I thought we were _forever_. He seemed to understand me, didn't push me or rush me. We met when I was waitressing, and he kept coming back for coffee, which I later realized he hated. For a few years, we were a couple, and it was bliss for me.

You probably get that I might have had problems with trusting folks, but when he told me he worked as an insurance claims adjuster, I believed him. But I knew he wasn't telling me the whole truth: claims adjusters don't get calls in the middle of the night and come home covered in blood.

It's kind of like Bluebeard's wives. Maybe if I hadn't peeked, we would still be happy. But when I saw the clothes he washed, with bloodstains that wouldn't come out, I had to find out what he was doing.

I followed him one night. He joined up with some men, none of who I recognized, but he called them "brother" and "cousin." Somehow I was able to avoid them seeing me, and I'm glad. I lost them for a few hours, but when I saw them later, it was horrible.

The last couple of times, I followed him with a camera. The pictures I left you? That's their handiwork. Best I can figure, they were some kind of mob enforcers. My thought was I could use the photos as evidence against them if I had to, but all I wanted was to get away from this man I loved who seemed to have two lives and monstrous habits.

Why didn't I just go as soon as I knew? I was confused. I hate to admit it, but I got a kind of rush the first time I saw the mess that your father and his friends made. It took me a while to figure out it was just seeing the forbidden, or shock or something, but I knew I couldn't have a baby and let those feelings lead me to places I knew *were wrong. I might have occasionally heard voices, but I knew right from wrong. Murder wasn't right.*

So I chose you. And I left.

You need to know, he's gone now, but he was always good to me. Whatever else he was, he never raised a hand or even his voice to me. I trusted him as long as I did for good reasons. Doesn't mean I ever want you to run into his family.

That's why we were always on the run. I didn't want them to find out about you, and I didn't want them to find us. Hard, to keep dragging you around, but better than the alternative, I think.

Zoe, I hope you'll understand a little, as far as I've been able to tell you, why I did the things we did. You don't want to burden a child with too much, but you're grown, and maybe you can settle someplace and do a little better by your own kids. I don't think they'll be able to find you. I was careful, and you've probably guessed by now, Miller's not really your last name either. It's a nice name, though, one I took from good folks I met along my way. You should know that much, anyway; there's not much more I can tell you.

Remember what I said at the beginning of this? It's the same now, and always: I love you, Zoe.

Your Ma

I put the letter down carefully. It sounded like "Ma-at-home," not "Ma-at-the-university," when she'd finally been able to start taking college classes herself; it was comforting, and the professional analyst in me speculated that the intimacy of the language implied truth as well. The contents explained a lot, but opened up more mysteries. All I'd ever wanted was to have a normal life, in one place, for more than a year or two. Now I understood what drove Ma, and it helped, maybe just a little, to know she worried about being nuts, too.

She was wrong, though. My father's people had found me. I didn't share his last name—I guess now I didn't even know what his name was—and yet they'd found me.

I began to consider the facts of the letter, began to wonder about the asylum, and wondered whether it was still full of people who might be like me. Were the ones in charge of the asylum coming after me? How many of us were there, and who knew about us?

Maybe Ma had never turned into a Beast in front of me, but I began to suspect both of my parents must have had something crazy going on, genetically speaking. I didn't know much about biology, but it seemed to me you'd need both parents to contribute something to a Beastly child; otherwise, we'd all be monsters.

I pulled out the one picture I had of my dad and stared at it. It was the only way I knew him; the paper was blurry and creased, a candid taken in a lighthearted moment, with him backing away from my mother's camera, his hands up in mock protest, bad eighties hair with a flop of bangs. Green eyes, like mine. Maybe I was imagining it, but his head was tilted in a way I found familiar from the mirror. I wanted to think they'd been happy.

Didn't matter. I didn't even know if he was dead or alive now. Maybe I'd share this with Danny, and maybe we could do some Internet research, just to see if anything popped up.

I glanced at the little yellow pencil box Ma had kept at Sean's place, but was too tired for more ancient history. I wasn't ready to expose the meagerness of my early memories. I spared one thought, wondering whether Sean had let Will know I'd popped up again, before I fell asleep.

———

Next morning, I got up early. I wanted to sneak out and pick up a few things and be on the road after breakfast. I regretted staying the night, though I hadn't slept so well in ages. I just didn't want to draw the monsters to Danny. I'd had a lucky break last night in the cemetery. Had they abandoned me, acting on the impulse I'd also experienced?

I was dressed and found my way to the living room. Sean was awake and dressed, sitting on the couch flicking through the local news channels.

"Anything from yesterday?" I asked.

He shook his head. He noticed I was dressed and had my bag. "Where are you off to?"

"I need to get a few things."

Something in the way I said it must have tipped him off. Sean's face darkened, and he reached for his wallet. "I'll come with you."

"Honestly, Sean. I'm just going to find an ATM and a drugstore. I'm not going to take off without saying good-bye."

Though I had considered it.

"Well, I could use the walk, and you could use the protection."

"From what?"

"From guys like the ones we found in the cemetery last night. From the guys you jumped out a window to avoid."

I grinned. "You make it sound so bad."

But Sean wasn't buying my attempt at levity. "I'm coming with you."

"Keep it down, then. Danny's sleeping in and gonna work from home today."

"We'll bring him coffee."

I found a CVS and bought panties and a toothbrush—I realized my toothbrush was still in the bathroom in Salem and I hadn't had time to do laundry. I love pharmacies that are open twenty-four hours; you can get almost anything there. Ma always said you were ready for anything if you had a pair of clean knickers, a toothbrush, and your passport. I did have my passport, from two years ago, when we drove up to Nova Scotia in an attempt to distract me from Will.

Purchases made, I got Sean away from the motor sports magazines and we grabbed some coffee before heading back to Danny's apartment.

We were crossing a lot that was between teardown and rebuild when I stopped.

"Something's wrong," I said, a prickling growing at the base of my skull.

"Zoe, relax. It's a vacant lot." He was right; I couldn't see anyone. "And who's going to bother you with me around?"

He might have had a point if we'd been dealing with anyone but...them. Not that he didn't enjoy trouble, the getting-into and the getting-out-of, but most troublemakers would take one look at his size and I've-got-nothing-to-lose demeanor and decide it wasn't worth the effort.

My bad feeling persisted and grew, however, until finally I wasn't sure I could go any farther. Every part of me hummed with a warning so bad, I was reminded of the time outside the cinema. Then the really bad time.

I didn't want any repeat of that. Definitely not in front of Sean. "Let's get out of here. Now."

"Zoe, I don't think—"

Too late.

A sensation washed over me, telling me the Beast was near. Irretrievably, irrevocably, irresponsibly here, in an urban center, in broad daylight.

"Sean." My mouth could barely form human words as I found myself being sucked under the onrushing current of Beastliness. Never mind him not seeing me; I couldn't afford to bite Sean. He'd be a terrible werewolf.

A growl. "Run."

And then it was too late again.

Chapter 5

Four figures came from the shadows of the construction trailer, three men and a woman. At least, I thought it was three men; one of them had a snake head. Scales, fangs, pinpoint nostrils, wide eyes...Hugo Boss suit.

Sleestack? Silurian Lizard Man? He wasn't the one in the cemetery...he's new, he means business, something's changed...they're not asking me, cajoling me, anymore.

Then the Beast was on me in all its glory and violence. I let it wash over me for two splendid seconds.

Enough of these ambushes. I dropped the coffee with a wet splat. *Enough of these surprises. Let's end this now.*

I turned, snarled at Sean (*get going!*) and launched myself at the nearest figure. Snake-man dodged me, incredibly fast, held his hands up. *I don't want to fight.*

Tough luck, buddy. I do.

I leaped again, then zigged when they were expecting a zag. Pinned one down, and then—I wasn't exactly sure what to do.

He wasn't fighting back. He wasn't cowering. He didn't even flinch. I expected him to transform himself—the smell of the Beast was all over these guys, a heady perfume from deep within—but he didn't.

I knew these were dangerous people, but like the dog chasing the car, now that I'd finally caught one, I didn't know what to do with it.

If I were human, I could ask questions. With the Beast, I could intimidate most people. But if he refused to be scared, and I couldn't interrogate him, how could I get anywhere?

So I bit him. Hard. He was already a werewolf, or a weresnake, or whatever. It wasn't going to be like *I* did it to him.

That got a reaction. I felt a surge of Beastliness roll over him (*it felt good, it felt right*), and being on top of him, in contact with his bare skin, was like a chemical reaction, sizzling and popping. I yelped and dodged away.

Risking a quick glance, I saw no sign of Sean. Good, he got himself gone. I could explain, maybe, later. Burn that bridge when we came to it.

Snake-man was talking to me. Actually, now in place of the humans, there were *two* snake-men, a wolf-man, and a wolf-woman.

Holy Anubis, Batman.

I shook my head. I'd seen this in the cemetery, but with the rain, even with my good eyesight…I'd just been in denial. This was daylight and I was definitely awake.

He was a snake, with large eyes, scales instead of hair, and fangs. A snake, but lizardy, walking on two feet.

"…And I don't know what you've been told, or what you've learned about yourself, but we can help, Zoe. Family, understanding. A history. You don't need to be alone, if you trust me—"

I could have listened to his voice all day long. As a matter of fact, I had to shake myself. It was like I was about to fall asleep, but suddenly I found I was nearly five feet closer to him than I had been. That wasn't right; I didn't even remember doing it. I whined, shook my head, backed off.

Suddenly there was a snake-man missing.

An unearthly scream from somewhere down the path we'd come.

A man's scream.

Sean.

I was still backing off, getting ready to run toward the scream, when the others melted into the shadows. Not waiting to find out what they might be hatching, I turned and bolted.

Directly behind me, I saw two people, a young man and woman, walking toward us.

Damn it. It was still early, but none of us could afford to be seen by anyone.

I hit the shadows, ran like the devil. Maybe I *was* the devil, maybe I was the devil's daughter, but that didn't mean I'd abandon Sean.

Sean sat in the middle of the Cambridge side street, alone and dazed, as if he'd had too much sun or too much to drink. He looked OK…then I saw it.

Sean had two red marks on his neck. They were already fading, but I leaned in and sniffed hard: the smell of the fleeing snake-man was all over him. It was like…it took me a minute to decide, my Beastly brain familiar with an encyclopedia of smells, but not having the words to describe them. Definitely not like the reptile room at the zoo. More like…clean things. Grapefruit, lavender, rubbing alcohol…not those smells, exactly, but those… feelings.

I stumbled, bare feet under me now, staggering to keep balance as my hands/paws left the ground. The Beast was leaving me, and I was becoming human again, but in the wrong position in my clothes. I hoicked up my panties, wrangled my bra, and adjusted my shirt as soon as I had something like hands. I still had sharp claws and barely managed to escape tearing my clothes beyond repair.

It occurred to me how odd I must have looked: a small black wolf in a white shirt, black skirt, and denim jacket with rolled-up sleeves.

My shoes. My bag. Still back in the middle of the lot where the Beast had found me.

Shit.

Making sure Sean was OK, woozy but otherwise unharmed, I ran back, cursing the uneven asphalt and pebbles and glass beneath my naked, human feet.

Shit encore. The two strangers were still there. Right next to my bag. The guy stooped down to examine it.

I ran faster. "Hey, that's mine!"

He straightened; they both looked toward me. I felt foolish, barefoot and childish, as I approached them. He was broad, dark, and tall, probably had been a football player, with that easygoing, entitled corn-fed look. He was dressed in jeans and a polo shirt. He'd never had to work for anything. I just knew it.

Immediately, I didn't like him.

She reminded me of too many school principals who'd called me down. With her jeans and the little twinset, I knew for a fact that this was as casual as she ever got. This one never let her hair down, and as if to prove the figurative point, the knot of her chignon was one crank off "amateur face lift." I don't know why, but somehow I trusted her more. Women need to work for what they get in this world. If Ma hadn't caught that lucky break, with her friend recommending her for the senior administrative job, I never would have gone to BU.

"I was just checking to see if there was some ID in it," the guy said, holding his hands up.

"Yeah, sorry. Things got weird with some guys, and I ditched my shoes in case I had to fight—er, run," I said. "Which I did. Thanks. I guess you scared them off."

"I'll call the police," she said, reaching into her bag.

"We could," I said slowly, "but what would I tell them? Some guys hassled me, I dropped my bag and ran off, then they were gone? I doubt the cops would be able to do anything; I barely saw them." I slipped into my shoes, snagged my bag. "Thanks, though. I'm really glad you showed up when you did."

"No problem," the guy said. "I'm Gerry Steuben, by the way. This is my sister, Claudia Steuben."

"Zoe." We shook hands, and I tried not to look nervous. In my experience, siblings don't hang out together, wandering around abandoned construction sites, unless either they're actually not siblings but swingers looking for playmates. Or maybe Jehovah's Witnesses.

"I'd feel better, though," Claudia said, giving her brother a glance, "if you let us walk with you back to civilization."

"OK. My friend...is kind of winded. He's over—" I nodded my head in the right direction, and we set out. I brushed a few coarse hairs from my skirt. "So what were you all doing down here?"

"Real estate," she said promptly. "Friend of ours is looking to buy. We said we'd check out the state of things. You?"

She was lying. I knew it instantly. "I got lost."

"Zoe, I really think we should—"

"Claud, she already said she didn't want us to call the police." Gerry stepped all over whatever she was going to say and gave her a pointed look. "Let's respect that, shall we?"

Shall we? OMG, the guy really was some kind of banker or real estate agent. I would have been happier with swingers *or* Witnesses. My unlove of authority and status was showing.

We found Sean, who seemed clearer headed now, but still not too with it. He was smiling beatifically, and if I hadn't been worried about him being concussed, I would have assumed he was high. Of course, with Sean's good sense, he might well have sparked up while I was gone. I sniffed. No sign of smoke.

"And who are these, then?" Sean clapped his hands together and rubbed them expectantly. "I'm about ready for breakfast, Zoe. How about you?"

I stared at him. No questions about the attack, nothing about me turning into the Girl Who Bays at the Moon. Not a damned thing but that dopey smile and too-innocent eyes.

Which was reason enough to be suspicious, but I can usually read Sean pretty well—remember, no poker face? At the moment, there was nothing going on. No one at home.

I made some introductions, and was making excuses about getting Sean home when Claudia said, "Look, I'm a doctor. Let me have a quick look at him. That way, you can decide whether to stop at the emergency room."

I gave her a look. A doctor? Then what about the real estate?

"Look at me, check me out, examine me, my darling!" Sean did a passable two-step. He grabbed Claudia and whirled her around. I was surprised; she managed to stay upright, feet unscathed, even laughing before she gently disengaged herself from the maniac.

"All right, simmer down. Follow my finger." She held up an index finger, moved it left, right, up, down. "You know the date, right?"

"Wednesday. June eighth," he said. "Or maybe the ninth."

"That's as close as he ever gets," I said. I really wanted to ditch these two, but Gerry stepped in.

"I wouldn't mind an iced coffee or something," he said. "It's warm out here."

Claudia said, "C'mon."

I felt something—instinct?—nudging me. I resigned myself to another half hour with these guys. I hated the idea; Sean might snap out of it and start asking odd, unpleasant questions about me turning into a wolf at any minute.

"No, I don't see any worrying signs," Claudia said finally. "Perhaps a slight inclination to overindulge in stimulants?" She made it a question, giving me a chance to roll my eyes. Sure, Sean was high. Whatever; she wasn't much of a doctor if she didn't know the smell of dope, or the lack thereof. That story gave me a lot of cover, anyway, and as long as he didn't start talking, we'd be fine.

We walked to a breakfast joint that was open and inviting. As we sat, I was dreading the chitchat, the utter irrelevance of it all, and yet looked at the menu. My phone rang, a number I didn't recognize.

Even if it was the creeps with pointy teeth, anything was better than this awkward socializing and waiting for Sean to come to his senses. His movements were still a bit wobbly.

"Yeah?"

"Is this Zoe Miller?" The voice was almost familiar.

"Who wants to know?" I cringed; not only did my defensive answer sound juvenile, it caught the attention of my two new friends. "I'm sorry. Who's calling, please?"

"This is Mick, the manager of Danny Connor's building. He'd said you'd be visiting, right?"

That's where I recognized the voice, from moving Danny in. "What's this about?"

"There's been a break-in, your...cousin's?...place. It's pretty bad."

"Is Danny OK?"

"I don't know."

"What do you mean?" Panic rose in me.

"Well, he's not there. There are a few bloodstains, but he's nowhere to be found. I called the police. They're on their way. I figured I should call you, too."

Police? *Bloodstains?*

"I'm on my way." I hung up.

"What is it?"

I turned to Claudia. "An...emergency. My cousin's place was broken into. They don't know where he is."

"Should he be there?"

"Yes. He's not...there're...bloodstains." I felt dizzy.

"Gerry, trouble!" Claudia said. "Zoe, we have a car. Did you walk, take the train?"

"Walked." The world was still spinning. Sean just sat there, looking confused, and that worried me.

"Let us drive you. It will be faster."

I nodded dumbly, breathing regularly, trying to stay calm. This was not the time for the Beast, that was for sure, not in this coffee shop, not at Danny's, not with these strangers, and Sean, and oh my God, police…"Thanks. I…I'm going to try Danny's cell."

Nothing.

Gerry threw a couple of bills on the table, smacked Sean on the shoulder, and we were off.

Danny's apartment looked as though Sean had been living there a year. Worse—my heart sank as I saw just how bad it all was. Whoever had been here was not interested in subtlety or secrecy. The way the place was torn apart—cushions eviscerated, curtains slashed, the refrigerator emptied and left open—told me the perpetrators had been as interested in intimidation as in finding whatever it was they sought.

Hoping I was wrong, I pulled out my cell and dialed Danny's number again. Almost too faint to hear, a Sousa march played, the one I always associated with Monty Python. I eventually found his phone down in the sofa cushions.

"Your ears are better than mine," the super said when he arrived. "I tried that, but couldn't hear anything."

"I knew what to listen for," I said. "Where did you see—?"

But I'd found the answer myself, before I finished my question. Something drew me over to the office door, where a lurid splash of blood painted the wall.

I felt drawn to it, when any other day I would have been out of there like a shot. It glittered on the wall, shimmering like living rubies, calling to me. The closer I got, the more the blood drew me in.

I told myself that I didn't actually touch it, but I was so close, it was as though I could see the individual molecules dancing, still struggling to live.

"Zoe!"

The shout startled me from my reverie. A gentle hand was on my shoulder.

I looked up.

Claudia was there. "You don't want to contaminate any evidence the police could use."

I shook my head, a bit dizzy from the rich smell of the blood. "It's Danny's," I blurted.

"You don't know that, Zoe," Sean said.

"Of course I—" I caught myself and shut up. Sean wasn't disputing my assertion so much as trying to reassure me.

Normal girls can't identify who left a bloodstain by smelling it.

"No, you're right," I said weakly. "I'll try not to get ahead of myself." I looked at Claudia, whose eyes narrowed. "I don't want to anticipate the worst without knowing for sure," I said.

"No. But it doesn't look good, does it?" she said.

My eyes filled. "No." A wave of empathy washed over me, and I was sure she understood where I was coming from. The blood was Danny's; he'd been injured, and, if the streaks were any indication, he'd been taken from the apartment by violent force.

Alive, a small part of me said, *don't lose hope. Danny's still alive, I can tell.*

The cops came, and before I could ask myself how I knew he was alive, their questions overwhelmed me.

I gave the cops my story about going to the drugstore and for coffee. I wondered how they'd feel about me inviting two strangers back to my cousin's apartment—I was barely sure I understood myself. I didn't want to discuss the creatures in the lot, but they didn't seem to notice the Steubens were out of place here. They were the most chilled-out cops I'd ever run into, über eager to please, supportive, agreeing with me at every turn.

It had to be Claudia, I thought. For a plain Jane, the cops did seem rather attentive to her. I shrugged. It didn't matter. I'd take whatever help I could get.

They took down notes, and for some reason, they were willing to start an APB for Danny. I always thought you had to wait forty-eight hours to report a missing adult, but maybe it was the blood. In my experience as a troubled youth, civilians didn't get these kinds of helpful breaks.

I didn't care. *Just help me find Danny*, I thought.

They left, eventually. Too soon and too late for my taste; they shouldn't be talking to us, they should be looking for him. They shouldn't be running off, they should be calling in the CSI guys to come and look for clues.

I was glad Gerry seemed to be taking an interest in the apartment the cops hadn't. He stared at the bloodstains and examined the floor around them. He spent more time on the busted door than the cops had, too, but as quickly as my hopes were raised, he dashed them by looking at Claudia and shaking his head slightly.

What was she asking? What did he mean?

My phone buzzed in my pocket, a "private caller" number.

"Danny?"

"I have your cousin, Miss Miller," a heavily accented voice said. "You want him back, you do what we say."

"Who are you? What do you want?" I could barely get the questions out; I couldn't keep the panic from my voice. Who would take Danny? I didn't want to think my father's people had found him.

The Beast whispered from the back of my brain.

"First, listen. Do not call the police back. We know they've left, we'll know if you contact them again. If you contact anyone, it will be bad for you and your cousin."

"What—?"

"I said *listen*." The voice was stern, a rebuke. "I will not continue if you do not. Do you understand?"

Dizzy with misery, I said, "Yes."

"You have information about certain...objects we wish to acquire. Artifacts of some antiquity. You've taken what I want, so now you owe me. You help me procure these items, Danny goes free."

Chapter 6

I wanted to scream, "What do you mean? What do you want? You're mistaken, you took the wrong person!" But I didn't dare speak again, until the kidnapper had given me leave.

I hated myself for that cowardice.

"You have an object in your possession, one you stole."

I thought back, with a sudden flash of guilt and horror, to the figurine from the museum. How could he know about that? I'd forgotten about it myself.

"I was told the figurine had gone to the museum. When I made inquiries, both you and it were gone. That artifact is similar to one owned by a collector, Rupert Grayling, in London. His is in the shape of a woman with a shield and helm. I want both of them. You use yours as an introduction, or trip him on the way to the market, or break into his house—I don't care how you meet him. But you must find a way to get his figurine, and bring that one and yours both to me. Use money, sex, whatever you think will loosen his hand. You fail, Mr. Connor dies. It may be that you do, too. It will be slow. It will be ugly. You leave tonight, in four hours. A ticket will be waiting in your name at the airport."

I knew absolutely that the caller was telling the truth. As crazy as this was, he believed everything he was saying. And I believed his threats.

Then something about the caller...*spoke* to me. Not with his words, but something about his voice triggered something. I felt something akin to the Beast, and as he gave me directions—a credit card and a new cell phone were hidden in Danny's bedroom—I found myself cataloging what I observed.

The accent was Russian—he reminded me of a student I'd met from St. Petersburg a few years ago. The man sounded middle-aged, but he was younger than his voice suggested; a hard life, a vicious life, added gravel to his speech. He'd learned English in Europe. He was educated. He was a practiced thug.

I knew two more things, as surely as I could feel the sweat running down my back, as surely as I could see my shaky handwriting as I copied down his instructions.

I'd know him as soon as he was within one hundred meters of me. And...

I'd obliterate him if I could. I'd leave nothing more than could be swept up in a dustpan.

The violence of my response shocked me. Where there should have been fear was nothing but cold-blooded calculation.

"Why me? Why Danny?"

"You've proven yourself adept at stealing artifacts. Call it...a family gift. You have this talent, and now I've given you the motivation."

"How do I know you have Danny?" What did *he* know about *my* family?

"Check your phone messages. I'm sending you proof now."

My next question surprised me. "What do I call you?"

He laughed. (*He'd had a rich lunch. He sounded congested, but he wasn't out of shape*—how did I know these things?) "For now, you may call me Dmitri. Call me when you arrive in London."

The absurdity and horror of what he was proposing suddenly shook me out of my dispassionate focus. "Wait, wait, I don't underst—"

The line was dead.

Only then did I notice I was shaking.

"Zoe, what is it?" Claudia crossed the room.

I backed away from her. "I...someone...I can't say."

"Gerry specializes in finding missing people. I've studied a lot of violent crime and criminal types. I know we can help you. It's about Danny's disappearance, right?"

I nodded. "He said his name was Dmitri." The entire story, in perfect order and organization, came spilling out.

Under my relief at having someone to talk to came the question: Why on earth did I tell her? Why had I gone with them to the restaurant, then brought them back here? Claudia and her brother were exactly the kind of people Dmitri would not want involved in this. They would be all over this. They would cause trouble. They would involve the police.

"How did you do that?" I asked suddenly. "Why did I just tell you everything, when doing that could get Danny killed? I don't even know you, and somehow you...you get people to do things."

A light dawned. "Like the cops. When have they ever done anything close to what I wanted? When did I ever get treated so kindly, so efficiently? Something's not right. *You're* not right."

I looked over at Sean, who was sitting, a look of patient concern on his face.

Patient? *Sean?*

I recognized the feeling now. Why had it taken me so long? It was nearly identical to the one I'd felt in Salem and in the cemetery. This morning, in the empty lot.

The whisper of other Beasts.

Thing was, there wasn't a crowd of werewolves and snake-men threatening me here. It was just Claudia and Gerry.

But they were the same as the other guys, I realized. The same as me.

I bolted for the door. Gerry beat me to it, blocking my exit. Jeez, he was huge. Bigger than Sean even, like a minivan.

It didn't matter. I was going to leave, even if it meant going through him.

I wouldn't have bet I could move him at all. I did, but only a little, so I shoved at his face. "What are you? What do you want with me? Why can't you leave me alone?"

Sean wasn't sitting patiently anymore. He sprang up, lunged at Gerry.

"Claud! A little help here?" Gerry grabbed my arms, held them with difficulty. He turned us away so his back was to Sean, who was trying to pull him off me. A few of Sean's punches landed on Gerry's head.

I heard a growl from Gerry, sensed a frantic energy in the room.

"Zoe, calm down! Sean, back off!" Claudia commanded.

Sean sat again as if nothing had happened.

The frenzied urge to fight drained out of me like sugar from a ripped sack. I sagged against Gerry. In its place was a sense of calm...and I knew that couldn't be right.

I jerked away. Not very effectively—it was like I had no will to do it—but I tried. I wrenched one arm loose and swung, smacking Gerry in the face.

One eye was screwed up tight while Gerry tried to keep out of range of my flailing hand. "Shit! *Claudia!*" he bellowed.

Claudia pulled my freed arm back, and then, my God, the bitch *bit* me.

Rage filled me, only to dissipate almost immediately. I slumped down to the floor. Gerry let go reluctantly.

Limp as a rag, calm as a pebble, I felt safe and inclined to listen to them.

Didn't mean I was happy. Somewhere in the back of my brain, something still *me* was furious.

Must have been some kind of hypodermic, maybe some kind of contact poison, to make me think she'd bitten me. I didn't remember getting drugs this good when I had a root canal.

"You need to listen to us," Claudia said.

I saw fangs retracting.

Fangs. I'd seen them in the mirror, once or twice. And most recently across the empty lot and in the cemetery. Now Claudia had them.

More of my father's people. Why hadn't I felt the Beast in them before? Maybe the Steubens were better at disguising their nature. The others had wanted me to recognize them right away, and I'd been preoccupied with Sean there...

It was one thing to think I was a werewolf, quite another when others kept appearing out of the woodwork.

"You bit me," I said. I looked at my arm and saw tiny puncture marks growing increasingly smaller, as if they were evaporating. I rubbed at the spot; there was no pain at all.

"I couldn't calm you down any other way. It's important you hear what we have to say right now."

Then she...started to shimmer, blur. She *changed*.

As she did, I felt the call of the Beast. I didn't even try to resist; if the world was going crazy around me, being a wolf seemed like the best response.

The air around me was filled with weirdness. I was sure my hair was standing on end, with all the energy—more than electricity—in the room. Adrenaline pumping, like I'd done a mocha with six extra shots. I was so jazzed up, I wanted to launch myself into orbit, tear the guts out of a bad guy, right wrongs, run forever.

Emotions like I'd never felt rushed over me, and suddenly the Beast seemed like the best thing in the world. I felt like a force for *good*, me, who put the "difficult" into the "child" and the "troubled" into the "teen."

Not bad. Not dirty. Not crazy.

In my wolfy shape, I couldn't express this excruciating joy. I jumped, then rolled around on the floor, but then got hopelessly tangled in my clothing. I wuffed, trying to untangle myself.

Way to diminish the moment, Zoe.

Claudia, now a snake-lady, exchanged looks with Gerry, now a wolf-man.

She knelt down beside me. "Zoe, stay still. I'll help."

My wolfy brain didn't have room for the shame I usually felt at the Beast's victory. It didn't have room for the humiliation I might ordinarily feel having a stranger rearrange my human clothing over a lupine body. If I could just stay like this forever, I'd be happy. It was like chains had dropped away from my limbs.

But Danny needed me. I tried to dismiss the Beast.

No luck.

I whimpered and tried again. Still no dice.

A shimmer of light, a frisson of energy, and Claudia was human again. "Zoe, can you Change back to your skinself?"

Crazy lady. What else could I be trying to do?

"Gerry?"

He shook his head. "I don't know, Claud. She seems like she knows nothing at all."

He turned back into a human. And suddenly, so did I.

"Know about what?" I rearranged my shirt and shrugged my bra back into place. I should have been angry, but whatever Claudia had done to me was sticking.

"Anything about what you are, and how to control it."

"Um, no. Until a couple of days ago, I just thought I was out of my mind. I'm still not sure what's going on. Care to fill me in?" These two didn't remind me of what my mother had said about my father's people.

The Steubens exchanged another glance.

"We haven't got much time," Gerry said.

"I'll keep it short," Claudia replied. "Zoe, we're Fangborn. That's what it's called. Vampires, like me, who clean blood and heal. We can also use our venom to make humans forget, and we tend to be very perceptive. And persuasive. Werewolves, like Gerry, whose power and speed help them track and fight evil. And oracles who have all sorts of powers, from precognition to telepathy to…just plain luck. Since the beginning of time, we've worked, mostly in secret, to protect humanity and eradicate evil; all the myths, all the popular culture—whatever you think you know—is wrong or at least deliberately misleading. There are lots of theories about how we came to be, but some call us 'Pandora's Orphans,' the hope that was left in the bottom of the box when evil was let out. Whatever story you believe, we're the good guys."

The Steubens, the guys who'd cornered me—these were my father's "family"? They were all Fangborn?

"So that other guy," I said slowly. "The one who…showed me that history reel? He was telling the truth?"

"History reel?"

I shook my head. "He sort of put his hand on me, and I *saw*… lots of this. 'Download,' I think someone called him? It was freaky. I busted out of there in a hurry."

Claudia and Gerry had worried looks. "'Download?' You know him?" Claudia asked.

Gerry shook his head slowly. "This ain't good."

"Why?" I really didn't think we needed more badness. "What's going on?"

Gerry shifted his weight, rubbed his shoulder where I'd hit him. "We were looking for you, because we'd heard rumors of a female stray—"

"Unacculturated pack-sister," Claudia corrected. I was kinda glad they had words for these things, "Change" and "skinself" and "pack-sister." Made me feel better about myself, not so rudderless.

"—in our area, and we were sent to find you. The fact that this other group is looking for you is …irregular."

"What do you mean?" I nodded. "Who are these other guys? And..." I rummaged through my bag, found the wallet Sean stole. "What do you know about this one?"

"Where did you—?"

"Wallet fell out of his pocket when he attacked Sean," I said.

"Ah." Gerry flipped through the cards, and frowned. "Claud, it's like I said: someone is bringing in Family from out of state."

"There have been some political tensions among our people lately," Claudia said, almost apologetically.

Gerry snorted. "What it means is that some Fangborn, who want to reveal themselves to humans, are adding to their side by rounding up any stra—Fangborn who might not have been raised in a pack or nest. Some think a preordained date for announcing our presence is coming up. So they're listening for news, then pouncing before the local Families can find them."

"The Identification Issue has been heating up." Claudia gave Gerry a "you're not being helpful" look. "Identification, revealing the Fangborn to Normal humans, is incredibly dangerous, I think. If it happens at all, I think it should be taken very gradually, a slow reveal if you will, very carefully orchestrated and supported by the vast majority of all the Fangborn. Even then, many of us worry about how Normals will respond and what will happen to us all. Others believe the world would be a better place if Fangborn ruled. Some think we'd be able to organize searches for evil, streamline the justice systems of the world if we identified ourselves. Both sides have their points, and their radicals, but so far no one has taken it upon himself to reveal us for what we are."

"Look, I don't have time for this. I need to get to the airport. I need to get on that plane and try to find whatever this Dmitri wants."

"Who's Dmitri?"

"The asshole who's taken my cousin and is threatening to kill him! I don't know who he is!"

They shook their heads. "We don't know anything about him," Claudia said.

I ran a hand through my hair, ready to pull it out by the roots. As much as I wanted to know all this stuff, answer the questions that were my life, I needed to focus on one thing. "You're devoted to defeating evil and I'm not crazy: check. Let's use these powers to get my cousin back from that evil sonofabitch!"

"OK. We can do that, only—"

"No only! We go now! And…and what have you done to Sean?"

"We've done nothing to him. But by the way he responded to my suggestion, it looks like someone in the Family has given him a little forget-me juice."

Suddenly my hackles went up. "Wait, why should I believe you? If you can manipulate us—make him forget, make me stop resisting you—how do I know anything you're saying is true?"

"You can sense it, can't you?"

"I…I don't know." The question caught me by surprise. I dug in, tried to concentrate. I *could* sense good intent, if not truth. And at least the Steubens appeared to be trying to help me—the other…Fangborn?…had only seemed interested in getting me to go with them. I had to make a decision.

"Look, trust isn't my strong suit, but if you're willing to help me, I'll give you the benefit of the doubt. But please: my cousin's in danger and time's *wasting*."

I looked over. The whole time, Sean had done…nothing. Had said nothing, even when we'd all transformed. "Can't you…do anything about Sean?"

Gerry glanced over at him. "I like him docile."

Claudia frowned. "Gerry."

"What? I'm just saying. He's easier to deal with."

Gerry was determined to work my nerves. "Is it fair to let him just sit and drool?" I asked.

"Zoe, he's not drooling," Claudia said. "There's no indignity; I wouldn't allow it. He's just waiting for someone to give him direction, which I will do." She glanced at me. "Even if I weren't bound by oaths to keep my secret self...secret...would you want him to know about *you*?"

She had a point. "Uh, not yet. Not until I know more myself. Just...make him as normal as possible."

"Don't worry. I'm good at this." She knelt by the immobilized Sean, looked him in the eyes. He was already mesmerized by her.

"You got knocked about when you ran into those muggers on the construction site," she said. "Things have been a little crazy, with Danny's disappearance, but you feel fine, and you, my brother, and I are going to help Zoe however we can, right?"

"Absolutely. I like Danny, even if he can be a little smartass sometimes."

"That sound about normal, Zoe?" Gerry said. He tried, and failed, to keep a straight face.

I felt a flare of anger; he had no business making fun of Sean, being amused by our imperfect selves. *Deep breath, Zoe; you'd have made the same joke under other circumstances.* "Let's get going," I said.

Claudia held up a hand. "Wait. Your flight leaves in four hours. We'll come with you. That gives us time to think, to plan. This Dmitri needs you to make contact with someone, make an exchange?"

I nodded. "He wants me to find another object like the one...I already have."

"Why doesn't he do it? Why doesn't he just ask you to give him the object you have for Danny? Then he can get the other himself."

I thought about it. "Maybe he can't. Maybe he's known to this guy Grayling."

"How do you happen to have this object?"

"It's nothing, it's a small figurine. And it's a long story," I said, my face burning. "Save it for the ride. For now, I want to focus on Dmitri. We don't know much about him."

Even as I said it, I recalled what I'd been imagining about Dmitri while he spoke. Gerry noticed my hesitation.

"I bet you know more than you think. Even if you don't know what you are, you still have your Fangborn powers, however untrained. And we have resources most people don't." He pulled out a gadget and waved it over Danny's computer. He typed in a few commands and then nodded. "There was something there, but now I've zapped it. Your cousin has some very sophisticated software on here. As in, not 'off the shelf,' and close to 'hacks just brushing the law.' He spends a lot of time coding?"

I nodded. Memories of Danny working on a piece of code all hours, of Sean and Danny trying to whip each other at *Halo*, came flooding in. *No tears*, I told myself. *Not now.*

Gerry's fingers flew over the keyboard, hitting the keys so fast I couldn't follow what he was typing. "What did he sound like?"

I spilled all the details I'd gleaned—however I'd noticed them—from my conversation with Dmitri. He nodded and went through one database, entering all the key words. Then he typed some more and I saw an FBI database come up.

"Whoa! You're not supposed to be in there!"

"Nope. But a Cousin of ours is. And it's a great catalog of bad guys." Gerry kept typing, searching. Pictures began to flash across the screen, some of them mug shots. "It's also how we found you. Once we heard rumors of a…that you were in the area, we made a call to our Cousin in the Federal BI, and we were able to find your phone and track that by GPS. We only managed to home in on you a few days ago."

I thought about someone stalking me via my phone. It gave me the creeps. "Above the law," "vigilante," and "gang" were words my mother had used more than once to describe my father's people.

I wasn't sure what to think; the Steubens were definitely dangerous. Clearly I was like them. I still couldn't reconcile what I was
learning about them with what I'd been raised to believe. And they
didn't seem the same as the other Fangborn following me.

The computer had paused in its flickering. "What do you have
there?"

"List of possible 'Dmitris.' All have associations with antiquities theft or smuggling, all have the characteristics you described...
Uh-oh. I don't think this one is a coincidence. Dmitri Alexandrovich Parshin."

Claudia made a small noise in her throat. Her eyes narrowed.
"I thought he was in prison?"

"Not anymore." Gerry turned to me. "He's kind of obsessed
with the Fangborn, werewolves, especially. He's made a living—
after dealing in antiquities and illegal arms—of hunting us down
and torturing us. I know of at least three stories of him killing vampires, slowly, over days, depriving them of sunlight, injecting them
with vile things like a distillation of black hellebore, which really
weakens us Fangborn."

I swallowed. "And now he thinks I'm one? Why take Danny,
then?"

"I don't think he's hunting you because you're Fangborn. If we
only discovered you, chances are he doesn't know, and if you're
lucky, he'll never find out. I think it's really the artifacts, just as
he said."

"But why? Why does he hate you—us—Fangborn so much?"

"It's not that he hates us. He wants to *become* us. He still thinks
we can turn him, but we're born, not made." Gerry ran his hand
through his hair, frowning. "And I think he believes the artifacts
you have will make him a werewolf."

Chapter 7

"Wait, you just said we were born." So maybe I couldn't have turned Sean by biting him. "If we're born this way, how can these artifacts make him—?"

"They can't," Gerry said. "Reason's not Dmitri's strong point, if this is our guy. The files we have about him, his family history, tell us he's obsessed with the mistaken idea he's descended from werewolves—"

"We'll discuss it in the car." Claudia reappeared suddenly; I hadn't even seen her leave the room. "Zoe, do you need anything else besides what I found in the guest room? Do you need to go somewhere to get the figurine?"

I hadn't even had time to unpack since I'd arrived at Danny's. I'd made sure the figurine was in the bottom of my bag, made sure my passport was where I put it when I left Salem. "No. I'm good."

She threw a bag to Sean, who had dozed off. "We're heading to the airport, Sean. I'm glad we had a chance to meet you. Time for you to go home."

"I'm coming."

"You got your passport on you?" I piped up.

"Go out partying in Boston on Friday night, wake up Tuesday in Cabo, you learn to take precautions," he said.

"You can afford to leave your job?" I demanded. "I doubt it. And those guys who broke into your place in Boston, they won't bother you anymore." I didn't want to drag Sean into this. I didn't want him to find out that I was a monster. I didn't want to worry about him while I tried to save Danny's life.

But the selfish part of me didn't want to leave him behind. He was the last shred of normal I could call my own.

Besides, as long as Claudia was with me, she could keep rearranging Sean's world to a reality where I wasn't a werewolf. However imaginary or chemically induced that world was, I wanted to hang on to it.

In the car, however, nerves overtook me. I couldn't shake the feeling I'd be better off without the Steubens. They were exactly what Ma had warned me about. They were clearly adept at manipulation, and I'd known them, under adverse circumstances, for less than a day. A day during which I'd been threatened and my cousin had been kidnapped, his blood spilled.

But they were helping me so far, and they weren't telling me I was crazy.

Claudia drove her BMW like someone used to getting where she needed to go, fast and without getting caught. Gerry sat with a notebook computer, working on the files he'd acquired at Danny's place. Sean sat up front, asleep, at Claudia's suggestion. He'd always called shotgun for as long as I'd known him. Didn't matter that he was almost thirty.

"So, how could Dmitri kill Fangborn? Aren't you guys pretty much impervious?" It was only then it clicked for me: Claudia hadn't been affected by daylight. If anything, her color had improved since we left the apartment. And didn't she say Dmitri tortured vampires by keeping them in the dark? Not even what I knew from fiction was accurate.

"We're not immortal, just long lived. Hard to kill and quick to heal," Claudia said. "Forget what you know about a stake through the heart—it *would* kill me, but the same as any massive trauma. But holy water, crucifixes—" She touched the little gold cross at her throat. "Not a problem. Plus, it would make going to Mass awkward. But with the call to Change, we know there's trouble brewing and we are compelled to help prevent it, if we possibly can. We're strong in human form, but much more powerful half-Changed, or in fur- or scaleself."

"Yeah, but you kill people." I'd blurted it out before thinking, then decided it needed to be said. "I know you said, and the other guys said, you're trying to protect humans, fighting evil. But... there is such a thing as due process. How do you know it's justified? You guys are never wrong?"

"Never," Gerry said firmly. "We've never been mistaken in identifying predators. Fangborn aren't capable of true evil. And no Fangborn has ever killed another Fangborn."

Logic and suspicion made me wonder how that could possibly be true. His statement certainly told me a lot about Gerry, though. "How do you know?" I asked carefully.

"Our history."

"History isn't a perfect record," I said. "I can tell you that, as an almost-professional."

Claudia stepped in. "I had similar questions when I was younger. I finally decided the world was better because of us, because of our actions."

I felt as if I was treading in the dangerous territory of faith or religion; time to change the subject. "How was it Dmitri was able to kill so many Fangborn?"

"From the autopsies we performed, we learned he's aware of some of the chemicals that will weaken or disable us, like the black hellebore we mentioned. It worries me, because he seems to know so much about us. That's one of our most carefully guarded secrets." She clutched the wheel. "I hate to think how he got that information."

"When we get to the airport," Gerry said, shutting down his computer, "I'll send this to your phone, not the one Dmitri left for you."

"What are the numbers for your phones?" Claudia asked.

I recited my number, then read off the new one to Gerry, who entered them. "How about yours?" I wasn't about to let them off the hook for their contact information. "Quid pro quo, Dr. Steuben."

Gerry snorted a laugh—Claudia wasn't much like Hannibal Lecter—then rattled off the numbers for his phone and Claudia's. OK, so I didn't trust him, not entirely, but he seemed...OK. Hard not to start liking a guy who laughed at your lame jokes.

The next few moments were filled with plans for how we'd travel. Somehow there had been no question they would try to go with me, and I was steadily more impressed with the idea that there was more going on than just me and Danny. I already had my ticket and I was going to use it. I stopped by the ATM to get as much cash as I could, this last time; maybe, if Dmitri was capable of tracking me, having even a little currency might help if I needed to get off the radar for any reason.

Claudia and Gerry would buy their own tickets. Dmitri didn't know them, and as long as they were helping, I was resigned. Sean, determined to follow me, would buy one, too.

"It's probably OK for him to come with me," I said. "If they know so much about me, they know he's with me, that he'd come even if I asked him not to." I looked hopeful at that last comment, but Sean shook his head.

"I'm coming. You can't stop me."

But the ticket counter could.

The flight to London was sold out; even Claudia's persuasive inquiries couldn't get seats on a plane that was full. Not even first class, where, I was surprised to find, I was seated.

"Probably the better to observe you, if he has someone following you," Gerry said, handing his sister his passport. "I'll be over at the coffee shop over there, the table out front—next to the bar? Claudia will get the tickets. There's Wi-Fi, and I'll send the rest of the files to you."

Inquiries at the counter and we had a last minute plan: the flight for Berlin via Munich left shortly after mine. There were seats and they booked three tickets. We'd arrange to meet up in central London as soon as everyone landed, and pray it wasn't too late to find some kind of plan that would give us an edge over Dmitri.

I glanced at my watch. About a half hour before the flight boarded. We joined Gerry, sitting at one of the tables just outside the coffee shop. He held up a finger: he was almost done.

Sean glanced out toward the concourse. His face froze. I saw something go dead behind his eyes, then light up again, as if he'd been rebooted. "Zoe, the muggers! From the construction site!"

"Get to the gate," Claudia said as she rose. She looked for all the world like someone whose flight had been called, purposeful but unhurried. "We'll deal with this."

"The Wi-Fi cut out, damn it," Gerry said. "Don't wait; I'll e-mail you the rest of the files, what we have on Parshin. You'll have them by the time you land."

Nothing else mattered but getting on that plane and saving Danny.

The sight of the team of other Fangborn coming toward us decided it. I turned and legged it for the security line.

And stopped dead. A moment before, the line had been nonexistent. Now several groups converged on it. They were moving, but far too slowly for me to avoid the other Fangborn.

I didn't think the Fangborn wanted to draw attention to themselves—not with their secrets—but neither could I afford the attention, not with what was in the bottom of my bag. I didn't want them to get too close; I remembered the snake-man at the construction site uncomfortably. And now there were enough of them to "suggest" I get out of line and go with them.

I glanced around, as casually as I could, and saw Claudia approach them. Gerry was still in the coffee shop, trying to get the files sent to me.

The group of six Fangborn split up. Three stayed with Claudia and three came toward me.

I turned, trying not to think about what would happen when they caught up with me. If I stepped out of line, they'd catch me. If I didn't, and a ruckus ensued within sight of security, chances were almost nil I'd be allowed on the plane. I had to make that flight; Danny's life depended on it, it seemed.

I closed the minuscule gap between me and the family of six ahead, four little girls with their pink Hannah Montana backpacks. I checked my watch. Twenty minutes till the flight boarded.

The line stalled as the little girls struggled to get out of their backpacks. The other line was no better, a group of traveling seniors who weren't up to speed on their liquids allowance, every other one of whom had a pacemaker or a metal prosthetic. The third line was looking likely until a sizable flight crew, wearing uniforms identical to the woman who'd checked me in, cut ahead of the two business travelers. I realized with a start that they were probably staffing my flight, now just minutes from boarding.

A gasp behind me, followed by a shout.

Don't turn around, Zoe, I told myself. *It doesn't have anything to do with you.*

A shove, and I swung around, ready to demand to know what was going on.

The guy behind me held up his hands. "Sorry—there's some maniac back there."

Maniac sounded oddly familiar.

I nodded and glanced around with an awful feeling that I knew what I'd see.

The coffee shop had seating adjacent to the bar on the concourse floor, separated by only a railing. Sean had reached over the railing and grabbed a beer from someone sitting there; the owner objected. The Fangborn following me also objected as Sean careened right into them. The beer he was holding crashed to the floor, foam and glass splashing them all. He slammed into one of them and grabbed at the ones on either side of him.

The Fangborn tried to shove past Sean, the most inconvenient human speed bump ever. He staggered into them, clutching their clothing to hold himself up.

True to Claudia's suggestion, Sean was helping me make my flight.

TSA guards emerged, then the state police. I saw Gerry join the fray, acting as if he was trying to separate the struggling parties, but in actuality, he was slowing the other Fangborn down even more. At the sight of the cops, all but two of the Fangborn melted away as fast as they could.

No one was going to be bothered with me when they had angry cops asking questions. I turned; the Hannah Montanans finally collected their belongings, tied their shoes, and moved on. They left, a pink comet tail vanishing, the security gate suddenly duller.

I dumped my bag onto the conveyor belt, took off my shoes, and handed my ticket and passport to the TSA guy. "I'm tired just watching them," I said, gesturing to the pink posse as they headed for their gate.

"It's gonna be a long flight for Mom and Dad," he agreed. He nodded me through, and I waited on the other side of the body scan. My bag rode out of the scanner, then paused.

My heart stopped as the belt reversed. They were taking a second look at my carry-on.

My figurine was in there. And, oh hell, my trowel and my knife. I didn't need delays while they…

An inspector called a second one over. They conferred, pointing at the image on their screen.

I wondered if they'd believe my concocted story about teaching examples and replicas.

Don't worry about those things in my bag, I thought as hard as I could. *These aren't the droids you're looking for. I'm totally harmless. Don't notice, don't notice…*

Another moment passed. I vaguely wondered where I was getting my oxygen from, because I knew I was holding my breath.

I heard one mutter "cell phones," and realized they'd paused over the two I had in my bag.

The bag slid out again, and I grabbed it and my shoes and moved out of the way as fast as I could.

As I put my shoes on, I glanced through the security gate. Claudia had joined the TSA and was smoothing things over. She didn't look at me. Gerry did.

He gave me a thumbs-up, then turned back to the discussion with the police.

I breathed out and picked up my bag. My gate was to the left, and if I hurried—

"Hang on a minute, miss!"

The security guard was calling me. I wondered what would happen if I just ignored him, kept walking.

"Hey! You in the blue hoodie!"

Cursing, I turned.

He held up the plastic bowl containing my watch. "You forgot this."

I nearly told him to keep it, but I managed a sheepish smile and retrieved it. "Thanks."

"Gotta keep it together," he said.

"I'm doing my best, brother." I trotted down to my gate. They invited the first-class and business passengers to board almost as soon as I arrived. I found my seat.

First class was nicer than many of the places I've lived, and almost as private, with the seats that extended into beds in their little cocoons. But as solitary as much of my life had been, for the first time, I was truly alone.

I looked around to see if I could spot one of Dmitri's men. Everyone looked reassuringly boring, but then so had Claudia and Gerry. No one, including me, was what she seemed.

As I shut the overhead compartment, I saw my hand trembling. I sat, and immediately the cabin attendant offered me a glass of champagne.

This was new; clearly she didn't know who *I* was. I smiled as I accepted it, trying not to giggle insanely. In fact, I wasn't sure *I* knew who I was anymore. From an early morning ambush by my so-called family, to the revelation of what I was, to Danny's kidnapping, I couldn't say it had been an ordinary day. I *must* be someone special for all this to happen.

As I stared at the champagne glass, watching the bubbles rise up in steady lines to the surface of the pale gold liquid, I wondered what it must be like to expect treatment like this all the time. For some people, it was just life, just as my life was all about gypsy peregrinations. As far as anyone here knew, *this* was what I was used to. I flew to European capitals all the time, swilling champagne and having people worry that I was happy. Hell, I'd never even been to Europe. I didn't even know anyone there—

Wait.

My hand stopped shaking, but not because of the alcohol. A plan came to me, not just about getting what I needed to save Danny, but also to keep Dmitri from turning around and killing us both after he got the figurine. The more I thought about it, the more it made sense—*if* I could pull it off. Dmitri might know too much about me, but he didn't know everything, and he didn't know all my resources, scant as they might be. The idea grew and blossomed, and the more I tried to punch holes in it, the more I found answers. All through dinner, served on real porcelain with real glass, I thought about it, and by the time I was offered a brandy, I thought it might work.

That's when the trembling started up again, twice as bad as before.

Chapter 8

After dinner, I went through my bag, looking for my own phone, the one with my address book in it, the one I hoped still had Jenny Kelner's old address in London. That's when I came across the yellow pencil box. Curiosity overcame me, and I opened it, wondering what childish keepsakes I'd find.

There wasn't much. A small notepad with no cover and a crushed spiral binding; inside was a flip-page cartoon of a flower growing. A bundle of ancient playing cards, their corners bent and their surfaces rubbed blurry. Two SuperBalls, their brilliant colors now cloudy and the plastic disintegrating. An Optimus Prime action figure, whose joints still moved, albeit arthritically. A shiny mechanical pencil with no lead. A small doll...

Not a doll. It was clay.

I turned over the object, my fingers suddenly cold, my heart racing. I recognized it, but not from my childhood.

It was nearly a twin to the figurine I'd taken from the museum. Like the one Dmitri had described, in Rupert Grayling's collection. This was male, but with the same stylized robes and faded painted coloring. It had suffered more than mine through the years: an outstretched arm was missing, along with part of its face.

I shivered.

There was a string tied around the base, with a small tag. On the tag was my mother's handwriting:

This was your father's. It's the only thing of his, besides you, I took.

I didn't remember playing with it. And yet here it was, among what I valued most as an eight-year-old. Clearly Ma had put it in the box, but perhaps there was some vague recollection of this figurine that prompted me to take the other from the museum?

A thrill ran through me when I realized it didn't matter where the piece had come from. It might give me an edge in getting to Rupert Grayling, in somehow convincing him to give me the figurine in his possession.

Unless I could convince Dmitri this was the one he was looking for?

I banished the thought immediately. If he was willing to kidnap Danny, he was also quite clear about the object he wanted. He'd described it as female, with a helm—an image of Athena probably. This wasn't even close.

So maybe I could use this fragment of a third figurine as insurance, to get me and Danny out alive.

As I wrapped up the new figurine, it took me a moment to realize there was one last thing in the bottom of the pencil case. A creased postcard from Will, from before we broke up. It said:

"Dear Zoe, Rome is amazing—and dangerous!! There are masterpieces everywhere, and I've never seen driving like this, not even in Boston. I've eaten like a Sus scrofa *every night. Since you can't see Rome properly in a week (yes, yes, I am going to the conference, too!), I'll have to come back, and bring you with me next time. Love you, Will."*

On the reverse was a picture of the famous bronze, the she-wolf suckling Romulus and Remus.

I hadn't put the card in here, but I bet Ma had—and I realized that's probably when she put the figurine in here as well. She had never accepted my trumped-up reasons for leaving Will and had always pushed me back toward him. Maybe she'd put it in here hoping that if I saw it again someday, it would change my mind.

It wasn't my mind that needed changing about Will.

Will and me…a complicated situation made more complicated by my secret personality disorder.

We shouldn't have happened, according to him, because he'd been a TA teaching one of my sections.

We shouldn't have happened, according to me, because my mother and I were always on the move. Maybe I stayed with my mother longer than most kids would have, but we were all we had, and I was convinced she needed me as much as I needed her. Permanent boyfriends weren't an option in my teens, and even when we stayed in one place for more than two years, while I *finally* finished up my BA after six years of patching together credits from various programs, I still shied away. I mean, why get close to someone when you could turn into a werewolf and bite him, maybe turn him into a Beast? Or why get close to someone if you were afraid the Beast was a psychotic hallucination? Either way, dating didn't make sense to me.

When I found myself engaging in class only to hear him talk, when I realized I was hanging around in the hallways afterward, reading flyers for field schools abroad and teaching positions and fat fellowships for Mayanists, I firmly told myself to put Will out of my mind.

When he emerged from the office he shared with three other graduate students, I turned to leave.

"Anything I can help you with, Zoe?"

I shook my head. "Do you want to have a coffee with me, sometime?"

I wished I could have dropped through the floor. Was my mania worsening? What had I just finished telling myself?

About six different expressions crossed his face. My heart leaped when I thought I saw a flash of happiness, then crashed when he shook his head.

"Wouldn't be right. Not with you in my class."

"I get it," I said. But no sooner had I resigned myself to his answer than I found myself saying, "But you hang out with other undergraduates all the time."

"Yeah, in groups. Hanging out. This isn't that, is it?"

"No, I suppose not."

"Look, if you're still interested at the end of the semester, ask again."

"Any hint what answer I'll get then?" I said. I liked his forthrightness and strict sense of morals.

He just shrugged. "Gonna have to wait and find out." Had it been a hint of a smile I saw as he turned?

At the end of the semester, I lingered after he handed out our graded exams, making sure I was last in line so we'd be alone.

"So...coffee?" I said, my blue exam book crushed in my hand behind my back. Of course I'd gotten an A. I busted my hump to do it. No sense showing yourself to be an idiot in front of the guy you're interested in, right?

Will had made it easy to succeed, too. He was a good teacher and had a talent for explaining things so even the densest student understood. And he had a way of communicating his own excitement about the classical past and how we explore it. It would have been embarrassing for us both if I'd gotten anything less than an A.

His face went blank. "Um..."

"Look, if you're not interested, just say so," I said. "I can take it."

"Thing is, you've signed up for Springer's method and theory class, right?"

"Yeah. It's the last one I need to graduate." After six years of wandering, taking an extensive tour of community and state colleges, I had enough credits to graduate. A miracle.

"Well, Springer isn't teaching it, because he's going to Arizona. I'm taking over. So it wouldn't be right, now, to get invol... coffee...with you. I'm sorry."

I nodded and figured in another four or five months I'd be on my way somewhere else with Ma. So it was all OK.

Except I didn't believe that. And I don't think Will did either, because whenever groups of the students were heading out for a beer or to a lecture, he made sure I was with them. And while he didn't ever just break down and take me on a date, we did spend some serious time talking. Never alone, but always...intimate.

By the end of the semester, when I showed him the completed forms that said, yes, finally, I would graduate, we were friends.

Which made it kind of awkward when we went to get that coffee. Enforced chastity becomes a habit, and habits shared by two people are hard to overcome.

We both sucked at small talk and ran out of chitchat after catching up with where everyone would be working for the summer. Suddenly I found myself wishing I hadn't tried so hard to get a job at the same contract company Will and Sean were working for.

"Let's get out of here," he said. Then he spilled his drink in his eagerness to leave, and we spent a few awful, embarrassing minutes cleaning it up.

We strolled down Bay State Road. Found a bench with a view of the flowering cherry trees and the freshly resodded verges, made pretty for returning alum and parents coming for graduation. Spring in Boston can't be overrated.

I turned back to Will as he leaned in to kiss me.

What we couldn't sort out with casual talk, we worked out with kissing. Within a week, we'd slept together. Inside of two weeks, I had a drawer at his place and was kicking in for the grocery bill with him and Sean.

During those four perfect months, I was nearly able to forget all about why Ma and I had been so peripatetic. I was nearly able to forget about the Beast. I broke my cardinal rule, the one that had guided me since I was sixteen.

I let myself think about the future.

I let Will talk about how we'd do contract work until it was time for me to decide about doing an MA, about how he'd finish his PhD, and then we'd take a summer and hit the Mediterranean sites. I let him use words like "when" and "if," because, on his lips, they were intoxicating.

Served me right, what followed.

Didn't matter now, I told myself as I flagged down the cabin attendant. I asked if I could have another brandy. I didn't really like brandy, but the burning in my throat distracted me from thinking about Will.

Problem was, I'd already let myself think about Will. I fell asleep remembering why I'd broken up with him, which led to a dream.

I'd been in a bar, celebrating something with someone, but couldn't get into the mood. Will was visiting family, Ma and I had had a fight, and there was something about the frustration and tediousness of writing boilerplate field reports that brought the Beast very close to the surface. Liquor and drugs helped only if I was alone, it seemed, and there was nothing in the party to make me happy. Some of the guys were arguing sports, which seemed about the stupidest thing in the world to me; the ladies' room had long ago exceeded acceptable levels of filth. It was crowded and hot.

I thought I was showing good judgment when I left. Turns out I was only looking for trouble.

I heard him behind me, before he made his move. For a moment, part of my brain, practiced in hope and denial, assumed it was a roughhousing friend following me from the bar, but another part, deep down, knew better. Even when he grabbed me by the arm and started dragging, I knew I should fight back, but I didn't. I knew I should go in the direction he was pulling me, just quick enough to let him go off balance before I yanked myself away. But I didn't.

Even when I saw the other man, and the knife, I didn't do anything. Didn't scream, didn't pull, didn't put up any kind of struggle. I wasn't stunned or shocked or drunk. I knew my life was almost certainly in peril.

And yet, I went with them.

My bad mood had vaporized. I felt completely calm, as if I'd been waiting for this to happen. Despite the reek that filled my nose, worse than the sewer leak last spring, the Beast was whispering to me, telling me to bide my time, wait until we were in the abandoned building, out of sight.

The darkness was almost absolute, but I didn't need a light to sense the knife just below my chin.

Neither man spoke until we were deep in the shadows.

"We won't be needing this," one of them said. I felt my shirt tear.

Now, the Beast whispered.

The oblivion I'd been seeking all night came as the Beast rushed in: I was suddenly a wolf. If I hadn't been resisting the rapists, it was because I hadn't been resisting the Beast.

I snapped my head around, seizing the wrist of the man with the knife. I bit through flesh, snapping fragile bones, feeling blood—dark, coppery, and filthy—rush out as I severed an artery. As his blood hit the floor of that dank basement, I felt a glorious satisfaction: his blood was better outside his veins. The more he bled, the better I felt.

His screams brought me back to myself. No time to waste: I ripped at his throat as he was bent over his mangled hand. I tore it out, feeling the foamy blood wash over my muzzle.

A joy came with the kill that was nearly inexpressible in human terms. It was every note of Beethoven's symphonies and every word in Shakespeare's sonnets and more.

Footsteps. The other attacker was backing away, ready to run.

I couldn't let that happen. He was as wrong as the first, as badly in need of removal as the first. The glory that washed over me only made me stronger and quicker.

He pulled a pistol out from behind his back. I knew (*how did I know?*) that I had just a moment before he pulled the trigger.

Just a moment was enough. Ignoring the gun, I ran forward, and once I was inside his range, I lunged.

He fell back, and I followed him down. I missed grabbing his throat—the quickest and quietest kill—but felt my teeth sink into his eyes and the soft flesh of his face. I tore, and before he could draw breath, I found his neck.

His blood spilling dwarfed even the experience of the first kill. I was rooted to the ground, the Beast exultant within me.

For the first time, I howled my joy.

That alien noise summoned the human in me.

I chased the Beast away and found myself sitting, half-naked, in a dark basement with two mangled corpses. Their blood pooled around us.

I'd killed two men.

I started to shake. I gathered my scattered clothing around me as quickly as I could. I grabbed my shoes and ran like hell.

I'd killed, viciously, happily, willingly. And I knew, without a shadow of a doubt, I'd do it again.

I ran back to the apartment, showered for an hour. I climbed into bed, next to Will. When he rolled over and put his arms around me, I put my hand over his mouth. The Beast came; I nuzzled his cheek, then quickly, efficiently, tore his throat out—

I woke with a start, the cabin attendant offering me a hot facecloth before breakfast. I scrubbed the tears from my face as I finished the rest of the real memory: hiding more bloody, torn clothing. The trumped-up excuses I fed Will the day after about "going too fast"—anything was better than telling him the truth of what I was, the danger he was in. His anger and disbelief, my own heartache. Telling myself, over and over, that I'd saved Will's life by leaving him didn't make the months that followed any easier. Before that, I had always believed that dying of a broken heart was mere poetry; after, I learned it was entirely possible, because something in me died.

But I had been right, then. I couldn't expose the man I loved to a side of me that lured men, no matter how evil, to their deaths. And reveled in it.

The Beast had saved me from being raped, and taken my soul in exchange. What does that tell you about God? If it hadn't been for the material proof of what had happened—more bloody, shredded clothing I couldn't afford to lose, and the newspaper reports filled with speculation of a rabid pit bull on the loose—I would have been able to pass off the earlier incidents as one of the freaks of psyche.

I still don't like to think about that night. The blood, the screams...

...the satisfaction.

The Beast had saved me, but a gift that comes with a price isn't a gift, is it?

When the plane landed, I used Dmitri's card to get some cash and found a train that would take me into the center of London. When the train lurched into Paddington Station, I put the past behind me.

Didn't matter what I'd learned from Claudia and Gerry. I was right to leave Will back then, and now I had more pressing matters, no matter what my subconscious wanted. With a sigh, I hoisted my backpack up.

It was time to see if I could get Danny back. I had a plan now, and if it worked, I'd have made up for so much I'd ruined in my life.

If it didn't, it wouldn't just be Danny who was dead.

Chapter 9

Navigating the maze of the London Tube, I found it a Habitrail of white tile tunnels, odd place names, and echoing orders to "mind the gap." When I reached the Russell Square stop in Bloomsbury, I emerged, a little dazed by the new sights, the smell of diesel, accents I only recognized from PBS, and traffic that was doing the opposite of what I thought it should be doing. Having very carefully crossed the street to a quieter corner, looking left and right several times before I dared move, I left a message for Dmitri, stating I'd arrived in London and that I would contact Rupert Grayling this evening. I called the University of London Institute of Archaeology and asked the department administrator about Jenny Kelner's class schedule, which was keeping her busy until the afternoon.

I was left with nothing to do for several hours, my first time out of North America. I oriented myself; Ma and I had moved so often that learning the layout of a new city seemed like second nature to me, and when you added all the time I'd spent reading and drawing maps, it was that much easier. Looking at the tourist map I'd snagged at the airport, I realized I was in the middle of archaeological heaven. I was within a mile of the British Museum.

Walking up the steep white marble steps and stepping between the massive columns of the facade, I was swarmed by tourists and busloads of children. It took a while to get oriented, but I knew exactly what I wanted to see first. In the Egyptian Sculpture gallery, I approached the Rosetta Stone with something like religious awe. A byword for discovery and communication, the artifact had appeared in almost every class I took my first year of college. The same decree carved into stone three times—in hieroglyphics, the demotic or everyday script, and Greek—allowed the first translation of Egyptian hieroglyphs by Jean-Francois Champollion, unlocking that world to scholars in the nineteenth century.

My meditation was interrupted when a band of French school kids went tearing through the room. One made a game of slapping the flanks of the stone sphinxes, one after the other, as if he was running bases.

So much for that moment of reverence. I hightailed it away from the throng and spent the rest of my time wallowing in the delight of seeing the artifacts that had filled my textbooks: the gorgeous gold and enamel objects from the Anglo-Saxon ship burial at Sutton Hoo; the detailed carvings of religious feasts on the Parthenon Marbles; the giant bronze gates and winged lion sculptures in the Assyrian rooms. In each case, I was struck by the long history of research behind all these objects, and felt a little proud that I was a part of that tradition, sharing this knowledge with the world.

I ate lunch in the café, and then stared at the Greek pottery, painted with scenes from the Trojan War. It made me wonder: were these vessels more like the early American pottery with pictures of George Washington, or more like today's fast-food giveaways decorated with cartoon characters? Commemorative, commercial, some of both?

The French kids came in for lunch, and I began to think about the sphinxes near the Rosetta Stone again as I made an escape. Human faces, animal bodies—it reminded me of the images "Download" had shown me before I'd broken the connection. It reminded me of my Fangborn cousins. If he was to be believed, there was evidence of the Fangborn throughout human history. Maybe not a one-to-one correspondence, but perhaps, in a few places, at a few times, the Fangborn had made their mark on humanity felt.

It called into question every piece of art, every artifact, every scrap of literature that combined the human and the animal. It all bore study, I realized, a little dazed.

Finally it was time for me to leave. I found my way to the University of London Institute of Archaeology, past the graying stone buildings darkened by the soot of centuries and tiny, dark pubs with curious names. Every step seemed filled with history.

It was just a few blocks' walk from the museum, and I nearly got run over once by traffic going the wrong way. A burly man with an Australian flag on his jacket grabbed me by the collar and hauled me out of the way of an oncoming car with a "Careful, love!"

I reached the right address and considered going in to meet Jenny. It didn't seem right to me, to discuss what I needed in such a place. In an enclosed garden across the street, I found a bench with a view of the front door and waited.

It was a quirk, Jenny and me becoming friends. Our interests overlapped somewhat, but visiting postdocs on research grants don't usually hang with undergraduates. I, of course, was a year or two older than most in my class, and with much more life and work experience, and in the convivial atmosphere of The Pub, we got to be close before she figured out I wasn't actually the graduate student she believed me to be.

Soon a woman, reed thin with short blonde hair, emerged, walking quickly toward Tavistock Square. I placed my pinkies in my mouth and let out a piercing whistle. The other people in the garden—mostly students—looked up at me, startled. I ignored them and focused on her.

C'mon, Jenny. Turn around.

I got up. She tilted her head—it couldn't be Zoe, could it?

Jenny looked both ways, then crossed the street to the garden. "Zoe! Is it you?"

I shrugged, smiling, and held out my hand. "Hi, Jenny."

She laughed and shook her head. "None of that now." She hugged me. "When did you get here? Why didn't you tell me you were going to be in London?"

"I didn't know I was coming," I said. Truthful and surprising—who suddenly runs to Europe anymore?

She stepped back, frowning. "Why? Is something the matter? Why didn't you come up?"

When I told Jenny what I wanted, I was pretty sure she wouldn't want to be seen by anyone she knew. And she certainly didn't want an electronic trail to her phone or computer.

"I'll tell you everything," I said. "But let's get away from here first. Somewhere quiet. I'll buy you a beer."

Jenny picked up her briefcase, studying me. "Zoe. You're in London, when you've never had a brass farthing. You're here, and you didn't call or text or e-mail me."

I nodded.

"OK," she said after a moment's hesitation. "Follow me."

We walked away from the quieter university streets to the bustle and business around Euston Square Station, waited for a Circle Line train, then changed at Moorgate. About twenty minutes later, we emerged at London Bridge, walked down the street crowded with businessmen and tourists in packs. Tiny, almost comical, cars vied with huge black taxis and honest-to-goodness red double-decker buses. We dove across the pedestrian traffic into the crowded, cobbled courtyard of the George and Dragon Inn. I tried to keep myself from gaping; it was like something from a Shakespearian set. In London, I realized, half-timbering in the architecture meant sixteenth or seventeenth century, not 1920s; here "gothic" meant, well, "gothic," and not some nineteenth-century revival. Jenny didn't even seem to notice the age of the place. It just was a good pub to her.

A couple left one of the picnic tables outside the pub building. Jenny snagged it. "I'll hold the fort against Pictish invaders if you're buying. I'll have a bitter," she said.

I went inside—my eyes took a moment to adjust to the dark—bought two pints, and wound my way back over to the table. My friend was resisting the advances of two young men in expensive suits.

"No, you may not join me and my friend. No, we are not interested in going to dinner with you. No, we are not lesbians. Thank you very much. Good afternoon."

The men turned away reluctantly—they, too, had started their weekend early—and saw me standing there in my jeans, hoodie, and hiking shoes—the only things I had that weren't packed—holding the two pints. They gave me a frank look, but left.

"What was that?"

"Boys from the City. You were no help."

"But I brought beer." I set the glasses down and sat.

"And for that, many things may be excused." Jenny grabbed a glass, clinked briefly. "Cheers."

"Cheers."

Jenny swallowed nearly half of her pint before she set it down. "Christ, that's good." She settled back against the wall and closed her eyes, enjoying the warmth and the sunshine. "Just give me two minutes. This will be my summer holiday. Sun and beer. No students, no husband, no babies. No papers, no looming deadlines. Just two minutes, then we can talk." She swallowed two more large gulps of her beer, her eyes still closed.

I owed her a moment to collect herself—brace herself—for what I was about to ask.

I went in and fetched two more pints, even though I'd barely touched my own. When I returned, Jenny's eyes were open, she was leaning on her elbow, her hand in her hair, a new frown of annoyance knotting her mouth. She was on the phone.

"And how did he get the bean? Never mind. You can still see it? Use a flashlight. Good. Just sit him up, put one finger on his other nostril, and have him blow. Yes, he may figure out how to do that when there is no bean up there, but—it did? Good. What? Yes, he's done it before. No, I didn't call you, because if I rang you every time beans went up noses or filled diapers were hidden or fistfuls of curry powder were eaten, you'd never get any work done. No, that was not a pointed remark about your parenting skills, it was a pointed remark about your demeanor. You lack confidence, Lawrence, and it will only get worse when they grow up and sense this. Ruthlessness is what is required. No, I'm not coming home now. Nope, never; I'm never coming home...OK, two hours. I promise. Yes. Yes. I love you, too. Kisses. Bye."

She slid the phone shut, looked up, and saw the other beer. "Thank you. I will." She drew the glass over.

"Well, it was really almost three minutes you got there," I said, shrugging.

"And we are grateful for it." Another sip of beer, and Jenny was back to the real world. "So. You don't often hang out in the park waiting for me. In fact, if I recall correctly, you've never really been out of the States. What's wrong, Zoe?"

I decided to come right to it; I still had a schedule to keep. I was desperate. "I need your connections. I may need some kind of letter of introduction."

"But why? Why are you actually *here*? Why not call or e-mail?"

I explained about Dmitri and Danny. I left out the part about Ma and my newfound family tree. Danny was bad enough.

Jenny's face grew more disbelieving, then horrified.

"Heavens, Zoe." She set down her beer. "You're...you seem rather calm about this. Cold-blooded, even."

I shrugged. I'd been pummeled with so much in the last week. "It must be the jet lag."

"Still, you're worrying me. And...how is it you think I can help?"

"It's not your professional connections I want." I took a deep breath and wondered if two beers would loosen my friend up as quickly as it used to. We still e-mailed and Facebooked, but it was four years ago that we'd hung out in Boston; BW, Before Will.

I said in a rush, "It's your father's connections. I wouldn't ask if—"

"No. Absolutely not." Jenny stared. "My God, I can't believe you would ask me such a thing, Zoe. I told you that in *strictest* confidence. Honestly!"

I held up a hand. "I wouldn't ask unless it was the only thing I could think of that would help Danny," I said quickly, hoping no one had heard Jenny's outburst. "I would *never*. This isn't morbid curiosity. You know that. You know I'm not like that."

Jenny's body was rigid. "I'm not exactly sure what you're like anymore. You want me to give you the names and addresses of a load of thieves." She exhaled. "I'm not even sure why I ever told you about my father. I don't do that easily, Zoe. You just had this way about you. You drew things out of me, things I never told anyone about my...family."

I began to wonder if that wasn't attributable to two things: perhaps some element of persuasion, thanks to my newly identified Fangborn powers, and the fact that we'd both had early lives influenced by criminals and criminal behavior. It had just made sense at the time. Jenny was thawing, if not warming, to the idea. "I'm just asking so I can do this quietly, maybe save Danny's life. Maybe mine."

"These...people...they're dangerous, Zoe. It's not like my... the old days, which were bad enough. It's a high-tech livelihood now, and they're no slouches. They do their homework. And they're the same people who deal in weapons and drugs. Same routes, same buyers oftentimes. So, to recap: heavily armed, greedy, and amoral."

It sounded like a fair description of Dmitri. "You don't need to tell me. I'm only asking for Danny." I took a sip of my beer to hide my fear she'd say no.

Jenny put down her empty glass and fidgeted. "Officially I have never wanted a cigarette as much as I do this moment. Thank you for that, Zoe."

Jenny had spent her life making up for her father's trade as a dealer in stolen art and antiquities, a life that he intended she continue after he was gone. She had gone in exactly the opposite direction, making her subspecialty the study of archaeological law and ethics, working to protect antiquities around the world. It was only to be expected that her exacting standards of professional behavior might not make exceptions for me and our friendship.

I shoved my own second, untouched beer across the table.

Jenny frowned. "You can't bribe me with alcohol, Zoe. It's a long time since my postdoc in Boston."

"I'm not trying to bribe you. I'm trying to make up for making you want a smoke." There was no lightening the moment. "Jenny. You know what Danny means to me. This situation requires whatever I can do to fix it."

Jenny sighed, then reached for the pint. "Are you absolutely certain?"

"I'm here in London. Yesterday I was going to drive to New York City maybe."

"I don't like it. I hate it, as a matter of fact. But I can't think of anything else that might work. If I do this, you may be able to save your cousin." She took a deep breath. "So I will help you."

"Thank you."

"Only because I know these people. If you go to the police…" Jenny drained her beer. "Which one is it you think can help you?"

"Someone named Rupert Grayling."

The glass paused on its way back to the table; she clearly recognized the name. She set the glass down very carefully and took a deep breath.

"You're in luck, only in that I know him, and I believe he knows me. You're out of luck, because the only person I know less obsessed, less dangerous than Grayling is this Dmitri character, if you've described him correctly. Zoe, are you sure?"

"No. But I have to do it."

"Come along, then. The offices will have cleared out. No one will see us while I mortgage our souls."

Jenny's office was lined with bookshelves that were stacked to the top and overflowing. There were mugs and an electric kettle in the corner. The place smelled of floor wax, paper, and stewed tea.

I showed her the figurine from the museum.

"I think it's some kind of souvenir, right?" I said as she examined it under a lighted magnifying glass. "The sort of thing they sold back in the day when rich people were going on grand tours and seeing the world?"

"You're right, it looks mold-made, so there could have been a lot of them, but I don't see any seams." Jenny shook her head, turning the figurine around. "No, it's definitely much older than that."

"Well then, a votive figure, maybe? An offering to the gods?"

"No, I suspect not. If it's not just a toy—and I wonder how many 'ritual objects' in the world are nothing more than toys a potter made for his kids—I'm betting it was a decoration, possibly for a ceramic vessel. See how the figure's body is somewhat curved? A series of them might have adorned the neck or waist of a pot." She thought for a moment, then turned to her computer, typed briefly, until an image appeared. "This is one like it, from the Metropolitan Museum. An unusual form, but not unheard of."

I glanced at it and nodded. Eighteen inches high, with a flared, angled mouth, almost no neck, and a bulbous body, the pot was different from anything I'd ever seen before. It was made of terracotta, pale whitish over red, and there was a flange around the waist with dozens of holes. Although the decorations on this museum piece had pegs beneath their feet to fit into the band around the pot, I could see some similarity to my figurines.

"Not identical, of course, but I just have one of those feelings." She made a face. "I hate that. I know there should be a good reason why I'm thinking of this piece, but sometimes you just end up saying 'I just know that's what it is.'"

I nodded. She was the expert, and I trusted her gut instincts. Besides, I was starting to get the idea—for another reason—that my figurines weren't mass-produced, the same way she "just knew."

"And—wait! There is an article, just came out, with a reference to one." She dug around, tossed me a copy. "Take it. I have an offprint. Some reference to a decorated pot in one of those letters from the Roman fort of Vindolanda; Professor Carl Schulz in Berlin ran it past me. He might be able to help with identification. He's the one who taught me—but of course, identification's not your problem, is it?"

I shook my head. Mine was not the usual academic puzzle.

"This plan of yours," Jenny said while flipping through her Rolodex—she wouldn't trust this address to her computer. "Contacting Grayling and hoping for some sort of cooperation? It's full of assumption and hopefulness, Zoe."

I shrugged. "I'm open to other suggestions."

Jenny seemed to struggle with something. She took a deep breath. "I'm going to call Grayling. I'm going to arrange a meeting for you."

I froze. I almost said, "I can't let you do that," but the truth was I needed whatever help I could get. I'd been on thin ice hoping Jenny might know Grayling or how I could appeal to him. I never really considered my friend might actually lend me the credibility of her father's dishonorable name.

I nodded and bit my lip. "Thank you. Jenny, I mean it."

Jenny scowled. "I won't have your death on my conscience. But there are conditions."

I nodded, not quite crossing my fingers under the desk.

"This is a one-time deal, and I'm telling Grayling so. It's for your own good."

"OK."

"He will get *nasty* if he thinks his goodwill is being abused. Never for a minute underestimate the viciousness of these people."

I tried not to let my dismay show. This was a side of Jenny I'd never seen before. To be fair, she'd devoted her life to concealing it, and I had asked, but now...I was getting scared.

Then I remembered: Grayling had better not underestimate my hidden viciousness.

"Next: Anyone besides Grayling asks you anything about me, my family, anything, you lie your head off. The story is you'd never be so self-involved as to ask this favor of me, and even if you were, I'm too much of a stickler to admit such a thing was possible. I'm just thinking of my kids and Lawrence, here. You understand."

I nodded. Who was being cold-blooded now?

"Lastly: You mustn't get hurt."

"I won't." I shrugged.

"I'm serious. I'm reluctant to give you this introduction because it is so dangerous. And I'm afraid if I do, it will only get you in out of your depth. But if I don't, you may be in worse trouble. If you get hurt or killed or sold or something else dreadful, I'd have to work very hard to remember the blame is on you."

"I'll do my best."

"No," she said with the same tone she'd used on Lawrence. "Promise me you'll do more than your best."

I nodded. "I promise. Now may I have Grayling's number?"

"Oh no. This has to come from me. And that means a walk to King's Cross."

"Why on earth—oh." Jenny didn't want the call being traced back to either her mobile or her office line.

Jenny arched her brow. "Exactly."

Chapter 10

The meeting was set for late that night. I had assumed that it would either be in a really ratty part of the city or the most expensive. Instead, Jenny told me to take the Tube to Islington, an upscale but unremarkable borough of streets lined with row houses. I would meet Grayling at a nearby restaurant.

"He lives somewhere on the South Bank," Jenny explained. "But he can't afford to be seen doing business there."

Grayling didn't look like anything at all. If I hadn't known what to look for, I'd have thought he was an old-age pensioner, sitting alone in the back room as on a thousand other, identical nights. Portly, with wisps of curly graying hair, jowls sagging to dewlaps, and owlish eyebrows. He had soup and a glass of wine in front of him, making a racket when he slurped either of them. There was a stain on his tie that looked like the same tomato soup, only from a month ago.

"Mr. Grayling?"

"Miss Miller?"

I nodded, and he gestured to the chair opposite. "Please sit down." He didn't offer a hand, so I didn't either.

"Forgive me if I eat while we talk," he said. "If I don't eat when I remember to…"

I wasn't sure I bought his frail old man act. The waiter came over; I ordered a glass of wine.

I waited until Grayling pushed his plate of soup away, not half-finished. He nodded at the waiter. "Would you heat this up, please?" The waiter took the plate and disappeared into the kitchen.

"So I'm told that you're interested in...archaeology," he said. "Yes." "Don't say much, do you?" he grunted. "That's fine, that's fine. I was very surprised to get a call from...our friend. About this sort of thing."

I shrugged.

He wiped his mouth, returned the napkin to his lap. "I am very interested in seeing this piece you claim to have."

"But not here."

"Not here." He wasn't done vetting me, not by a long shot, I knew. "You know our friend...how?"

I wasn't going to say more about Jenny than necessary. "We have mutual interests."

Just then he held up a hand. "A moment." He turned, gestured, and placed his napkin on the table.

A short, thin man, nearly as old as Grayling, had shuffled to our table. Dressed in a soiled jacket and a threadbare shirt, he waited at Grayling's side until Grayling nodded. "Marco."

"Evening, Grayling." The old guy didn't exactly tug his forelock, but his respect was close to obsequiousness. He reached into his jacket and pulled out an envelope, nearly as dirty as his fingernails, and slid it under the napkin.

Grayling cocked his head. "I hope that's everything."

"Absolutely..." Marco tried a game smile. "...very nearly. Only, I need an extra day or two—"

The waiter returned with the soup. "Careful with that. Shall I get another setting?"

"He's not staying," Grayling answered, never taking his eyes off Marco.

When the waiter left, Marco said, "It's been a bad week, that's all. I can have the rest in two days, three tops."

Grayling nodded. "Absolutely. As long as you can add on the extra interest."

Marco crumpled then. "I…I can't. I can't keep going on like this. I'm an old man, and I don't earn like I used to. And…with this hand…" He held up his right hand, recently bandaged, the only thing on him that wasn't greasy or worn. "Grayling. It's been ten years, after all. Can't you this once—?"

"I'll be dead soon, and then you'll be done, just as we said. Two days, with a point."

"I can't—"

Before Marco could finish, Grayling stood up and patted his shoulder. Then he slid his hand over Marco's mouth, took his bandaged hand, and jammed it into the plate of steaming soup. Marco's scream was muffled, barely.

"Hey!" I tried to get up, but my chair was so close to the wall, I was trapped. The Beast paced in its cage, but I couldn't give in, not now…I needed this bastard. I tried to focus.

"Zoe, Marco stole from me and is paying me back. He's been short twice, if memory serves." He held up Marco's hand; the man gasped, tears running down his cheeks. I could see stumps where there had been two fingers. "He pays me back, I don't go to the police. We had an agreement. Gentlemen honor their agreements, don't they, Marco?"

"Ye-es." He swallowed. "Two days, a point."

The violence past, the Beast was somewhat quieted. But it hurt not to be able to stop what had happened.

"Good." Grayling sat back down, frowning at the stain on the tablecloth. "Otherwise I have as many kitchen knives as you have digits. Please, Marco, don't make me. We used to be friends."

Marco shook his head, backing away and clutching his hand. "I won't, Grayling. Thank you." He left with a rapid, unsteady gait that was painful to watch.

Grayling picked up his wine. "Why do you want...this particular piece?"

As if nothing had happened. As if I hadn't just heard his threats—

Danny's life is on the line, Zoe, I thought. *Be cool.*

I swallowed my protests. Jenny had warned me that the more I lied, the more it would show. I went with the truth.

"I need the piece to save my cousin. I've been sent by a man calling himself Dmitri."

"'Need' and 'save' are interesting words. Can you tell me why I should help, when I'm sure Dmitri told you I would have nothing to do with him?"

The truth was all I had; why hadn't Dmitri told me this would be an issue? "Dmitri kidnapped my cousin," I whispered. "Is... threatening him, unless I can get that piece from you. Maybe he thought I could find a way to...persuade you." I tried to look like I was open to anything, but the truth was I knew I was sunk.

"And yet he knows I would rather die than see him get something of mine." He blotted his lips with a crumpled napkin. "I have neither the time nor the interest to help you."

"I have money," I said, desperate, thinking of Dmitri's credit card. "I can pay, whatever you want."

He frowned, looked ashamed for me. "Money's not the point. As with Marco, there's a principle at stake. The doctors give me six months. I can no longer travel, nor work to the level I wish. I am spending what time I have amongst my treasures, as quietly as possible."

I couldn't let the conversation end there. I was desperate to keep Grayling engaged until I could figure another angle.

"Show me them." Maybe, if he was as crazy as Jenny said, it would get my foot in the door.

I knew my instinct was correct as soon as I said it. He hesitated, so I pushed a little more. "I want to see your collection.

If you haven't much time, I may never get another chance to see material like this, all in one place, ever again. *If* it's as good as I've heard. You know if Jenny made this introduction, I do know the field, I do know what I'll be seeing."

Pride and suspicion tore at Grayling. I made myself finish my wine and used every remaining bit of self-control to seem calm. Even if he wouldn't sell me his figurine, I might learn something else I could use to force him to give me what I needed. I wished there had been more time to learn about my curse and powers, but I had to keep them under control. For now.

The opportunity to show his collection to someone who could properly appreciate it—the rarity, the perfection, the antiquity of it—was too much. Grayling carefully counted out the banknotes for his dinner and pushed his chair back. "Come along."

I slapped a note on the table and followed him into a cab. We traveled back to King's Cross station, which looked incredibly seedy at night after rush hour. We took another cab, doubling back somewhat before we crossed the river.

"My habits are too well known these days," he said, taking my arm. "I like to be careful."

He's crazy, I thought. *The urge to show off his collection borders on lunacy. Why else take the risk of showing me, a stranger?*

We climbed the stairs to a row house on a short block. I turned away discreetly when he entered his alarm code. That I have excellent peripheral vision and make a habit of picking up and remembering information like other people's alarm codes by their tones, he didn't need to know. A click, and we were in. Air—cool and dry like a museum's—washed over me, and I realized he had environmental controls in his house to store his collection safely.

It wasn't until after he locked the door behind us that I began to worry whether I'd gotten myself into even more trouble than I'd expected. Than I could manage. Even before the restaurant and

Marco, I'd known through Jenny that Grayling was a borderline personality. I knew he was more than half a criminal, given his "profession." What other plans might he consider to amuse himself at the end of his life? When had I ever gone alone to a stranger's house like this?

It was for Danny, so I was prepared to risk everything. But Jenny's reference, and her knowledge that I was with Grayling, suddenly seemed like a very thin sort of protection. The very unreliable powers of the Beast didn't reassure me, much.

The house held a collector's dream. I forgot almost everything else at the sight of it all. It was a hodgepodge: Some rooms had been designed to show off one spectacular piece. In others, artifacts were piled up on every flat surface, stacked without regard for their age or provenience.

One room was nearly a shrine—a mosaic floor with a three-dimensional pattern, plaster walls painted with the muses, an apparently genuine Roman table, and in a case, three perfect, beautiful clay bowls with molded patterns. It reminded me of the villas from Pompeii. With a jolt, I realized it was because an entire room had been removed and reconstructed here, if not from Pompeii, then some other site, ravaged for its finds.

In a moment, within arm's reach of these amazing antiques, no Plexiglas barrier or velvet rope between me and them, I understood exactly what drove Grayling. I understood his impulse to want to touch and to own such things and have them all to himself. I understood what it was to crave something, to remove it from the shared view of the rest of the world.

The stolen figurine in my backpack was testament to that— and why, oh dear God, hadn't I left *that* someplace safer?

But in that house, I saw no space for Grayling, no place that was where *he* lived. For him, it was ownership, or with regards to Dmitri, the denial of that pleasure to someone else. For me, my only instance of unethical archaeological behavior—actually stealing something—had gotten me into *serious* trouble. I wasn't built for crime.

And then I saw *it*.

It was a marble statuette, a Venus, modestly posed as if caught emerging from the bath, maybe twenty inches high, but perfect in every way. Intact sculptures of this sort were rare, and when they were found, much was made of them. This one had been displayed at the Hermitage with huge fanfare. I remembered because it made all the news and was the sort of find people asked you about, no matter what part of the discipline you specialized in. Three months later, a curator and a security guard were murdered late one night and the statuette taken. Nothing else—including gold and religious objects—had been touched. It had been a brutal, and very specific, robbery.

I now couldn't imagine Venus's marble without bloodstains.

Rupert Grayling wasn't an aging crank with a fetish for classical history. He wasn't someone who skimmed the rough edge of unethical behavior, buying goods with a provenience no more detailed than "the private collection of a recently deceased gentleman from Geneva."

He was someone who dealt in violence to feed his obsessions.

What would happen if he figured out I had the clay figurines with me now? I thought of the dead museum employees. Marco's maimed hand.

He caught me staring at the statuette a little too long. He knew that I knew its recent history and he was waiting for my reaction.

Would he prefer my horror, fear, or disgust? Quick, Zoe! What would set him off, what would placate him? What would get me what I needed to save Danny?

Something nudged me, and I took another risk.

I went closer and examined the marble carefully. Never touching it, yet giving every indication I wanted to.

Finally I looked up. "It's superb. Extraordinary."

He beamed.

"It's almost perfect."

A dangerous light kindled in Grayling's eyes. "Almost?"

"There's a certain heaviness about the legs that I think diminishes it. But that slight flaw, that element of human imperfection, of course adds to its…charm."

Grayling's mouth twitched, then went still. Under his stare, I felt exactly like one of his artifacts. His was a weighty and penetrating gaze.

I'd called an astonishing artifact "charming," as if it was Grandma's quilt or a Victorian silhouette. He'd either kill me, stroke out, or…

"Almost perfect, indeed. Quite right."

There was an invitation in his words. I prayed I wasn't mistaken. "What do you have that *is* perfect? That's truly peerless?"

I could tell by the way he fussed over a speck of dust on the base of the marble. He wanted to show me something else, and yet he still hesitated.

"You wish to see that which is peerless. You come with a startling reference, one I certainly never expected to see. It is almost enough to recommend you to me. You come with a story, one guaranteed not to please me, but which has the ring of truth. That interests me. But you claim to know Dmitri. Knowing him, in whatever capacity, works against you."

I held my breath. The longer I kept him engaged, the better chance I had of getting near that figurine.

"Follow me," he said finally. "Touch nothing."

I'd passed some kind of test.

We went into the kitchen; even those hoarders on TV would have drawn back in disgust. No wonder he ate out. There was no room to eat here among the filthy plates and piles of reeking trash bags, so different from the other rooms. A door that led, presumably, to the basement or a mud room, or whatever it was called in

England, had another door behind a shelf. He moved a dusty jar and hit a switch or a lever I couldn't see. The shelf unlatched from the floor, and he was able to swing it out on hidden hinges. The door behind it was nearly invisible, certainly not recognizable as a door, until he pressed a release, and that swung away, too, to reveal a panel. He looked at me pointedly, until I turned my back. I heard him press in a code.

Like I said, I'd always had pretty good hearing, though, and a memory for sounds. Just recently, I'd found out why those skills came to me so easily.

An almost inaudible *click*, and another door opened. Layers and layers, but all to protect his pride and joy, I hoped.

I was only slightly surprised, then, to see a small room, nearly empty, save for a chair, a pedestal, and a carefully adjusted light that flickered on as the door opened. Triggered, no doubt, by the correct alarm code signaling the owner's entrance.

On the pedestal was the crowning glory of Grayling's collection. His prized "perfect" object.

It might have been perfect, but it wasn't peerless.

I had two of them in my backpack.

This figurine was the same size as mine, about four inches long. It too had a human body, but this one had the obvious helm and shield of Athena. Amazingly, the spear and arms were intact— such slender clay fragments should have broken off long ago—and the painting was less faded than on the figurines I had. With her arms outstretched, I could now see how the figurine would fit the curve of the pot it decorated.

It wasn't the archaeologist in me that was riveted; it was the Beast. Oddly, it wasn't snarling for release, but quiet, patient.

Wait was the surprising impulse I had from it. *Restraint.*

Circling the pedestal, taking it in from every angle, I realized it was the closest to pure reverence I'd ever felt. I reached for it, then caught myself, glancing at Grayling, who nodded once. His own eyes were riveted by the object, and to judge by the wear on the chair and the floor, he'd owned this for decades. Stared at it for hours at a time.

It was cold to the touch; I'd expected it to be warm, the way it glowed, blue-white. Then I realized it might not be glowing; it was some trick of my Beastly eyes.

I could barely tear my gaze away from it. I felt certain that if I turned, I would miss something terribly important. For all its humble appearance, it was, quite literally, enchanting.

"So?" I said, finally turning my back on the thing, working to make my voice casual, even dismissive. "Maybe it's not tourist junk from the nineteenth century like I thought when I first saw one; but it's not even a votive offering. It's some kind of pottery decoration. Old, but not that valuable."

"So wrong, so wrong. You see, it's the key to Pandora's Box."

"Pandora's Box—?"

"Of course you've heard of it. Pandora, the first woman, created by Hephaestus, and given all the gifts of the gods: talents and curiosity. When Prometheus gave fire to mankind, as part of his punishment, Zeus gave Pandora to his brother Epimetheus. He also gave her a vessel, which he warned her never to open. With her gods-given curiosity, she couldn't resist, and on opening it, unleashed all evil onto humankind. Which was the plan of Zeus all along, if you believe the traditional stories."

I waved my hand. "Yeah, yeah, I know the story. It's just… stupid. Pandora's Box is a myth, a metaphor. No real Pandora, no real Box."

"No more a myth than you or I." Grayling blotted his face with his handkerchief. "There are objects in the world with untold powers to confer on their possessor, scattered and hidden. That idiot Parshin wants these because he wants the unspeakable power that he believes comes with them. I have seen documents, carefully guarded, by those who don't want the Box found. But my colleagues and I are very close to locating it, so close. Do you have any idea the value of such a thing? Of what secrets it would unlock?"

He gestured to the figurine. "And this is the key. Rather, one key of four."

Hadn't Claudia said something about the Fangborn being "Pandora's Orphans"? But it had to be a metaphor, nothing more. Right? And, oh God, who were Grayling's "colleagues"?

I couldn't help looking back at the figurine. The Beast certainly thought it was real; it might be nerves, but I could almost feel the two figurines vibrating inside my backpack.

A prickle up my spine forced me to turn away from Athena.

Grayling held a large pistol, pointed at me. He wasn't enchanted any longer, but he was very pleased with himself.

"Give the figurine to me," he said. "I know you have it with you."

"I don't—"

"You wouldn't dare leave it anywhere else. Open your bag, now."

"I can't! Dmitri—!"

"I have no desire for Dmitri to get near this. You can leave that over there and then remove yourself before I call the police. I'm sure they'd be very surprised to hear you broke into my house in order to add to your collection of ill-gotten antiquities."

"Your word against mine," I said. "People saw us in the restaurant."

"Yes, but I'd have shot you first. *You'd* have no words at all."

I stared. The Beast was strangely absent when I could have used it most. I reached into my bag and pulled out a figurine.

Disaster. It was the wrong one, the broken figurine I'd identified from my treasure box just that morning. Why on earth—?

Too late. I'd never felt so human, so vulnerable. The Beast should be raging, that pistol so close to me, but there was nothing. A calm hollow in the back of my head that I couldn't extend to the rest of me.

Grayling glanced at the figurine in my hand. His face paled, then flushed.

After a moment he said, "My dear. You are full of surprises. This is not what you acquired from the museum. The source that tracked that key to the museum had a description of it; many people are looking for it. And in this room, *we* have three of the four keys to the Box, from the oracular temples of Didyma, Delos, and Delphi. That puts us close, oh so very close. We only need that from Claros." He snapped his fingers. "Place it on the pedestal. And the other. Quickly. *Now.*"

Cursing the lack of the Beast, instead of placing my figurine on the pedestal, I grabbed at Grayling's. It was fastened to the base and didn't move.

The pedestal was rigged. An alarm went off. Grayling did not look concerned. "You have thirty seconds before the police come. You can leave the other figurines here now and live, or you can stay and die."

He was telling the truth. I couldn't even attack him in my human form and hope to escape in time. The police wouldn't help me rescue Danny, and he knew it. I dumped out the third figurine, took my bag, and fled through the secret door and out into the garden, tears burning my eyes.

I didn't go far. Hugging the wall, I watched and waited from the shadows of the next house over. This wasn't over, I promised myself. There had to be another way; crazy as he was, dangerous as he was, Grayling wasn't invulnerable.

I had to get back in there, get my figurines and the one Dmitri wanted.

Seconds later, a police car pulled up. Grayling met them at the gate, an apologetic look on his face. My hearing was so acute, I could follow it all: He traded pleasantries with the two cops, an accidental trigger of the alarm. There was no mention of me. They returned to the car and left shortly thereafter.

I waited a few more moments, giving Grayling time to reassure himself he was safe. I was about to go in there and try again, but just as I was summoning myself, another car pulled up to the house.

This was driven by a man I hadn't seen before, but for some reason, when he got out of the car, I was paralyzed by the sight of him. I've learned if you pay attention to the little things about people, you can read them pretty well, and this guy was the worst kind of trouble. Didn't need the Beast to tell me that. His menace was subtle. It wasn't a swagger, but a kind of assurance that said he knew how to get what he wanted. It was like a billboard, too: clean-headed with three parallel scars along the back of his skull; clothing that was expensive but too tight because his muscles were jacked; nose busted and rearranged a few times; eyes that saw everything.

He went to the door, knocked. When Grayling answered, he invited himself inside and shut the door behind them.

I looked at the passenger seat of the car; it was one of the cops who'd been by earlier.

The television went on then, too loud. A police drama, by the sounds of it; a repeat of an American show I'd seen a dozen times. Then I realized that some of the noises didn't make sense.

My skin went cold, the hairs on the back of my neck stood up. I was listening to the sounds of violence between Grayling and his guest. I tried desperately to summon the Beast—now was exactly the time for it! I closed my eyes, tried to remember what it felt like, tried to play on my fears, the bad taste in my mouth when I saw the clean-shaven guy—

But the Beast was strangely absent. I knew it wasn't only a threat to me that brought the Beast, not after the episode with the guy at the theater years ago. I cursed my ineffectiveness.

Any impulse I might have had to do something—rescue Grayling, call the police—was quashed when I looked toward the unmarked police car. The officer was smoking, his head turned away. No way he couldn't hear it. He was in on it.

I waited, praying it would end soon.

It ended too soon. The stranger left hurriedly, tucking something into his pocket, a frown on his face. He hadn't gotten what he'd gone in there for, I could tell. The cop stubbed out his cigarette on the heel of his shoe, placed the butt in his pocket. Without a word, they drove away.

I hated what I was about to do, but I was desperate to save Danny. I was about to take advantage of what I knew was a crime scene—possibly a murder—in order to get my figurines back.

To my shame, the thought that I might save Grayling's life hadn't occurred to me.

The smell bludgeoned me before I reached the front steps. It was like a butcher shop, meat and blood heavy on the air. Holding my breath, I went in—the front door had been left unlocked—and was astonished at the amount of blood. Although the walls and the artifacts were dripping with scarlet spatters, a massive puddle had been spilled in the center of the room, soaking into the mosaic floor. Although one side of the puddle retained its perfect edge, the rest had been smeared, by Grayling being dragged or crawling away. A small amount of rough twine was soaking scarlet, a visceral image. His pistol was on the floor, its bullets scattered and useless. He'd never had a chance to use it, had been overpowered too quickly. The bloody smear led out to the room with the reconstructed painted walls.

The Beast was back, making up for its brief, calamitous absence with its response to Grayling's blood. The effect was the same as in Danny's apartment: Grayling's blood smelled like *him*. I would recognize it again, even just by the sight of it, I was convinced. The molecules danced, eager to share their story with me...

I felt the Beast pacing in the back of my skull, but couldn't afford to be a wolf now. Why hadn't it showed up before, when I could have used it? I tamped down the wolfy urges, even though I had the distinct impression that if I let the Beast out, I would be able to read Grayling's blood like it was the contents of his wallet. But there was no time for that now and no place for a wolf now.

Grayling had, quite remarkably, pulled himself up against the nearest wall. A hundred little cuts covered his body, leaving a bloody patchwork. A piece of duct tape covered his mouth, abrasions on his wrists where he'd been tied. Panic filled his eyes when he realized someone was in the room with him, but he relaxed, only a little, when he recognized me.

I stooped, motioning to the duct tape. He nodded. I made a face—*this is gonna hurt*—and he nodded again. I pulled it off, taking a bit of skin with the tape. But now he could breathe more easily; his nose had been smashed in. I could see a splinter of cartilage gleaming through the tear in the skin. This wasn't good.

"Who was it?" I asked.

He shook his head. "I don't—" He coughed. More blood. "Don't know. Not Dmitri. Someone...I've never seen before. He smelled of the law, of governments, to me."

No time for a dying old crook to wax poetic. "What did they want?"

"The figurines. I could not...would not...let him have them."

I swore.

"He also asked about *you*," he said. He gasped as he tried to sit up. "There wasn't much I could tell him."

A cold, lead weight settled in my stomach. "I'm going to call 911," I said.

"No—"

"I'm sorry. I'm not going to stick around. I'm going to take my figurines and leave. I'll call before I leave. Fewer questions for everyone."

"No, I mean—" He coughed again. "The emergency response number is 999."

"They're in the secret room?"

He nodded.

I went to the kitchen. The door was shut, but the shelves were askew. No one looking, however, would have noticed anything else.

Careful not to touch anything, using the sleeve of my hoodie to cover my hand, I pushed the keypad, entering the code Grayling had used. I opened the door.

My two figurines were there. But this time, so was the other figurine, the one Dmitri wanted, loosed from the pedestal. Grayling had been comparing them when his unwanted callers arrived.

Now I felt the Beast grow urgent: *Go now, quickly.* Was it some kind of Beastly magic, or just common sense and panic?

I didn't think about it. I snatched them up and returned to the main part of the house, shutting the doors behind me.

I held up the three artifacts. "I'm taking yours, too. I would have paid before, but now I'm thinking I'm owed something for having a gun pointed at me." Maybe I could use the third to bargain for Danny.

Grayling was gray now. I stashed the three figurines in my bag, found his phone, and using a pencil, tapped on the buttons. When the operator answered, I gave him the address. "An ambulance. Hurry."

I hung up and turned back to Grayling. He held something in his hand, and for a moment I was afraid he had another pistol.

It was an address book.

"Take it. There are two keys tucked into the back. At the Paris address—Rue Mouffetard—in the cupboard opened with the smaller key, there is something that may help you. Someone else is now interested in the figurines. Take it, but whatever you do, keep all these things out of Dmitri's hands."

He made a noise that might have been a laugh. "Of Dmitri Parshin, and all my visitors tonight, you are the least bad choice.

Save these things from the others, but don't let them fall into the abyss of history..."

I didn't have time for the truth or his ramblings. I couldn't tell him the *first* thing I'd do with the figurines was trade them to Dmitri for Danny. "I'll do my best. I have to leave now. Tell them a stranger walking by called the ambulance, then left. It's close enough to the truth."

He nodded, his eyes half-lidded, his gaze only for the paintings of the muses in the room. I might as well have already gone.

The two-tone wail of an ambulance grew louder as I fled down the street.

Chapter 11

I found my way back to the Tube station. There were a flock of messages for me on both my phones, and I flicked through them nervously. The one Dmitri had given me rang, and I jumped a mile.

It was Dmitri. "Did you get it?"

My next sentence counted. I'd only get one chance to keep Danny alive. "Grayling is dead."

"You killed—?"

"No. He pulled a gun on me and tried to take my figurine. I barely escaped with it. Shortly after, someone broke into his house and tortured and killed him." If it wasn't true yet, it would be in a matter of minutes. "I'm afraid he told whoever it was about me. It wasn't your people, was it?"

I could practically hear the sneer over the phone. "You do not warrant that kind of redundancy."

"Convince me Danny is still alive."

"A photo, within ten minutes. Let us say, I will send two a day until we make our exchange. Danny may not look as pretty as he does now, the longer you wait."

I bit my tongue, willing myself not to respond to his threats. "I'm hiding. If they find me, they'll get the figurine." A flash of inspiration hit me. "As it is, I have a lead on how I might get the other figurine. A contact of Grayling's is supposed to have it, for conservation," I improvised. "I'm going to get it from him. You'll hear from me in twenty-four hours, one way or the other."

"Do nothing until you hear from me. Danny's life depends on it."

Like he had to remind me. "I'm not staying put. You can reach me with this phone, but I'm not waiting for whoever killed Grayling to find me. You...you didn't see the body. You know what a creep Grayling was; the guy who killed him is *worse*."

A reluctant grunt was all the permission I got. Dmitri hung up.

A vibration alerted me; a message with the picture arrived. It was Danny. He looked OK, not beat up, but worried. He had one middle finger showing, a subtlety perhaps lost on this Russian captor; Danny knew enough international slang to be able to insult almost anyone he wanted. At least he was well enough to secretly express his discontent.

I checked into a crowded hotel in central London, then collapsed with fear, jet lag, and worry.

The next morning, I threw down the newspaper and tried to clear my head. Reading about Grayling's murder seemed to make the incident even more violent than I'd experienced nearly firsthand. I'd never expected anything like this. So quick, so bloody, so... utterly lacking in discretion. Whoever had done it hadn't cared who knew about it. It might as well have been a billboard: *We find you, you'll get the same.*

And how did they know about me? What did they want with the figurines? What was this mass hysteria about Pandora's Box, when not even the Fangborn believed it actually existed?

I read through the files Gerry had finally managed to send me on Dmitri, which confirmed many of my observations on the phone: his parents had been academics and he had gone to a good university, but shortly after leaving, he went down a different path. Something had driven him into a criminal life, and he'd taken to it with an alarming affinity. Unafraid of violence, he dabbled in moving drugs, weapons, and stolen art, but not always for profit. Many of his crimes, according to the Fangborn analysts, were attempts to learn more about the Fangborn, especially werewolves. He had a kink for the occult.

There was a comprehensive list of Dmitri's crimes and a few interviews with the Fangborn who'd been briefly in his hands, but escaped. They all came to the conclusion that he'd learned something about the existence of vampires and werewolves, but was ignorant as to the specifics of their culture. His obsession, they confirmed, was to become a werewolf, and he refused to believe it was a matter of birth.

I glanced at the pictures; the wounds sustained by the quick-healing Fangborn were shocking. My own experiences so far paled in comparison. I was glad, half-surprised, that I didn't recognize anyone familiar in the photos.

Was he really innocent of the attack on Grayling? It seemed to fit. But there was no reason for it to be Dmitri or his people, unless they knew I'd failed initially. And why deny it, when they could follow my movements? Why bother when he held all the cards? Why not simply kill Grayling to begin with and collect the figurine?

It had to be other Fangborn. That had all the hallmarks of what my mother had told me about my father's people. But I hadn't gotten the same feeling I did when I was near the Steubens, and the gruesome murder didn't seem to line up with what Claudia and Gerry told me. I certainly didn't want to get in the middle of political strife. That bald guy I saw going into the house... I shuddered at the memory of the raking scars on his head.

But why were *they* looking for the figurines? Claudia and Gerry hadn't asked me about the figurine when Dmitri had called, so I assumed they didn't know anything about them or about their supposed connection to Pandora's Box.

What had Grayling told his attackers? He had no reason to protect me, apart from his hatred for Dmitri and obsessive love for his artifacts. It might have spared him some pain to tell what little he did know.

I had to assume he had talked. There was no real reason for me to trust him, after all, including the details he'd given about the apartment in Paris. Who knew what was waiting for me there?

But I was going, that was absolutely certain. Even the slightest chance of getting an edge over Dmitri, while I had this breathing space, would help.

———

I had never been so aware of the crowds of a city pressing around as I made my way to the train station. Every person seemed to be staring at me, and rush-hour traffic was as hostile as it was confusing. When I inadvertently bumped someone with my pack, I got a muttered "bloody American tourist" for my trouble. I felt a wave of anger wash over me and tamped it down.

I'd decided not to fly to Paris. Trains weren't cheaper, but it would save me finding a room for the night. Frankly, I trusted them more. A fracas on a train, you can jump out halfway to your destination and still survive. OK, barring tunnels, bridges, and high-speed rail. Still, I was betting *I* could survive a leap from a TGV, even though it would hurt like hell. There was absolutely no getting out of a plane—neither Claudia nor Gerry had said anything about Fangborn being able to fly. I wasn't going to learn by myself at thirty thousand feet, that was for sure.

Plus, I'd already seen what could happen at airport security, and I didn't want to draw that kind of attention to myself. Didn't want to take the figurines through, either, and risk losing them.

When I got to St. Pancras and bought a ticket, I felt safe enough to call Jenny from a pay phone.

"It's me," I said when she answered. I felt foolish about my precautions, but at the sound of Jenny's voice and the kids fighting in the background over the blaring television, a massive weight rolled off my shoulders. "You OK?"

"Yes. You saw the news?"

"Yes." She couldn't know I'd been at the scene. "That's why I figured I'd better check in before I left, make sure you were… safe."

I could tell Jenny had turned away from her children; their racket was suddenly muffled. "I am. Not happy, but safe. Hence the precautions. I hope this will underscore what I've been trying to tell you."

"I got what I needed, in any case," I said. "I met with him before it happened. There was some unpleasantness at the restaurant. This might have been retribution." Several truths, and not necessarily in chronological order. "I'm leaving."

"Keep in touch," Jenny said after a long pause. "Let me know you're all right, if you can."

"Bye, Jen. I can't tell you… Just, thanks again."

I left messages for the Steubens and Sean, found a seat on the train, stowed my bag, and ate some breakfast, marveling at how mediocre the stuff from the dining car really was.

Once my ticket had been taken, I surveyed the car. It was full, but seeing no one who looked like a werewolf, an archaeologist, or a vicious international antiquities thief, I fell asleep.

I got into Gare du Nord in Paris a little after noon and bought a map of Paris. Then I realized I should also get a highway map of Europe since I was covering more ground than expected.

Like London, Paris was a blur of pale buff buildings, but these had gray-blue slate roofs to distinguish them—very nineteenth-century—with shutters and wonderfully colored window boxes filled with geraniums. More tiny cars tearing around as if in combat, or at least a contest. I craned, but didn't even catch a glimpse of the Eiffel Tower.

Grayling had given me the key to a small apartment over a flower shop. Knowing the idea of lockers in public places was as outdated as his antiques, he'd rented space on a larger scale. You still ran the risk of finding yourself surveyed, stung, or mugged, but a private home was as safe as anything.

The Rue Mouffetard was in a neighborhood of the Quartier Latin, an area crowded with students coming and going across cobbled streets. I rented the table at the café across the street from the apartment with a glass of juice and a sandwich far better than the one I'd had on the train. I watched over the next hour, but didn't see anything amiss. To be sure, I wasn't certain what "amiss" would look like, but it seemed prudent to wait all the same.

I looked at the patrons around me; I saw no berets, but a number of perfectly affected scarves. I was aware I lacked a personal style of my own. I listened with little comprehension to the discussions around me. Each speaker was very passionate about his argument, and everyone spoke with such a certainty and precision, I had no doubt they were all correct, at least in their own minds. Attitude must come by the gallon with the wine around here, I decided.

Finally I realized I was starting to doze in the warm sun, so I threw a few euros on the bill and crossed the street.

The flat was on the top floor. It was two rooms and a tiny kitchen: empty, dusty, and cobwebby. There were a few pieces of furniture—a couch, a table with one chair, and a futon frame with no mattress—and it looked as though it had just been emptied for the end of term.

I realized my senses were telling me I was in the right place. I could detect a faint scent of Grayling here, along with others, more transient, but still identifiable.

He'd said something about the cupboard.

The kitchen was full of cabinets, all of which, oddly, had locks on them. This was some kind of clearing house—who knew what was in the other cabinets? The second cupboard opened to my key, but it took some jiggling of the old lock to get it. The shelves were anciently lined and on the orange-and-yellow swirled paper, there were marks of rust where cheap cooking pots had sat. It smelled of dust and dead herbs, mold and rat turds.

Sometimes having a supersensitive sense of smell was a liability.

I examined the paper, but it was exactly what it appeared to be. When I pulled it up, however, to look beneath, I heard a rattling noise and a bump.

Something had rolled to the back of the cupboard.

Crinkling my nose and pulling my sleeve back, I reached back into the darkness. My fingers brushed something light; it slid over the gritty surface. I stretched and managed to grab a small container.

It was a small, empty spice bottle. It was the generic brand of oregano from Sainsbury's, an English supermarket I'd noticed yesterday.

I was on the right track. It *thunked* when I shook it; oregano doesn't thunk.

The top was sealed with tape. I started to peel it off.

The front door rattled.

It might have been nothing, it might have been students looking for a squat or a place to carry on an affair, but somehow I didn't think so. This place was a clearinghouse for criminal commerce. I glanced out the window: There was a car that hadn't been there earlier, illegally parked. I knew instantly it was trouble. It reeked of anonymous officialdom. Some of the neighborhoods I'd lived in had taught me such things.

No time for hope. The front door wasn't going to stand up to applied force. I pocketed the container, moved to the bedroom, and shut the door. I pushed the futon frame against the door, hoping to buy enough time to scream for help. I thought of my cell phone— but who could I call? I was consorting with criminals. Yelling might create enough distraction to slip away.

The back window overlooked a maze of steep roofs a story below me, a tangle of alleys. One flat terrace, covered with plants, offered me hope. No one was there.

I heard the front door clatter in its frame. I twisted the latch on the side of the window; it turned, barely. I pulled with all my strength, straining against the swollen wood and generations of over-painting.

I pried it open, with a creak of hinges, just as the front door gave. I could hear two sets of footsteps, one heavy, one light. Neither was speaking—they knew what they were looking for and it wasn't a rendezvous. The Beast opted for running rather than further cataloging my pursuers.

I thought about throwing my pack down first, but couldn't risk it being found by a passerby and taken, leaving me stranded and without the figurines. Better to keep it on my back.

It was harder than I thought, trying to wedge myself out the window while trying to aim for the open space of the terrace. I battled vertigo and the urge to scream.

I was stuck.

A strap of the pack had snagged on the window latch behind me. I tried hauling myself up with both arms to relieve the weight on the pack, hoping it would come off of its own accord. No luck. I tried reaching up with one hand to work the strap off, and that unbalanced me further. I scrabbled to keep from falling out while caught and tangled.

There was a tremendous crash. The bedroom door burst open, slamming the splintered futon frame against the wall.

One of the men saw me, pointed, and shouted in French. The other...

The other was the scarred clean-head who'd tortured and killed Rupert Grayling.

We stared at each other for a fascinated moment. His eyes were the gray of the sky seen from under a foot of icy water.

He cocked his head. "But you're the stray. *You* have the keys?"

Grayling's keys? My stomach fell away when I realized he meant the figurines, what Grayling believed were the keys to Pandora's Box. I struggled to pull myself free.

Three steps and he'd grabbed the back of my jeans. Yanked me out of the window, into the room. I landed on my butt, hard. He kicked me in the side, once, twice. The blows took my breath away.

The Beast roared. It flushed the pain away, gave me enough energy to vault up and turn on Clean-head. I snarled at him.

He pulled out a knife.

I slashed at him so quickly, I startled both of us. My fingernails left bloody trails on his hand and he dropped the knife. I turned and dove through the open window.

I had just enough time to hope I didn't turn into a wolf as I plummeted.

I crashed onto the terrace. I landed better than I had a right to expect. I destroyed a few potted plants in my fall, but I was OK.

I pulled myself out of the greenery and saw the men intended to follow me. I ran to the roof door, which was open, and let myself in, locking it behind me.

The easiest thing for them to do is follow me on the ground, I thought as I skidded down the stairs.

Maybe I could move a few buildings over before I took to the street. I'd managed the last jump OK.

I found a window and a fire escape on the second floor. I climbed to the top of the railing, and it wasn't far over to the next fire escape, but it was high above my head. I doubted even another werewolf could jump that high. I had to go down another flight before I found a window I could crawl inside.

I was surprised at how far I was able to travel this way, sometimes up a few flights to a close-by roof, sometimes down a bit to an open window.

It was *fun*.

If I'd only see Paris for a few hours, at least it was with terrific views of the narrow streets, the tiny shops with perfect produce, and the occasional stone church. And every time I looked around, I was able to see my attackers, moving farther away, looking for me in the wrong direction. I smothered a laugh, but it felt wonderful to use some of my abilities to my own benefit.

I still didn't feel safe enough to trust the sidewalk. I put another few blocks between me and my pursuers. My agility, even without the Beast, was a treat, and I moved faster than I ever dreamed possible.

I was moving toward the Seine when suddenly the adrenaline left me and I petered out. I hated how exposed I now felt, but pushed on. I found a wine bar down an alley near the Pont Neuf that was half-full. I took a corner seat inside where I could see who came in and out and who was on the streets through the long windows. I ordered a glass of wine and began to relax.

The door opened. It was Clean-head and his friend.

They were moving toward me, brushing aside the polite welcome of the hostess.

I began to cast about for an escape route. There, a back room.

I pressed back there, then stopped. The room was full of rough-looking men drinking steadily. They went silent as I entered.

Only one of the several dozen French words I knew seemed appropriate: "*Merde!*"

The resentful silence was replaced by a loud guffaw.

I turned back; Clean-head had stopped and suddenly taken a seat at a table nearby.

"Little girl, I think you want the other room," one of the men said, in English. "We have serious business to discuss here."

"And serious drinking and eating to do, too!" said another.

"*Mais non!* Come, sit with us! Stay a while!" one shouted, to the approval of his friends.

"*Pardon*," I said, backing out of there. I now was caught between that room of toughs and the seated killers.

The hostess came over to me. "The WC is downstairs," she said in English. "That back there is most of the police detectives in this *arrondissement*."

"Ah, I'm sorry to have bothered them." A flash of inspiration. "Perhaps I should apologize again."

"I do not think—" she began. I dashed back into the room.

"Ah, our little friend is back! Have a drink with us!"

"Or, two, or three," I said. "Madame? Three bottles of—" I glanced at the chalkboard and pointed at a wine I'd never heard of, in the middle of the price range.

This met with a roar of approbation. I sneaked a look past Madame as she went for the wine; Clean-head was still out there.

Drinking with the rowdy detectives won.

An hour later, I was starting to get nervous. The three bottles of wine had only lasted so long, and others were ordered. My days of swilling vodka to tame the Beast had helped me keep up with them, but I was starting to feel the travel, the wine, and my flight across the rooftops and alleys of Paris.

As if responding to my worries, the detectives began to stand and sort themselves out. A few new ones joined us, and I realized it was shift change. Some of these guys were going to work, some were going home.

I stood up and started to shake the hand of the detective next to me.

"*Non, mais non*, not like that!" He grabbed my shoulders and kissed me roughly on each cheek.

And since I couldn't kiss one and not the others, I went around in a circle. At the last cheek kiss, made scratchy by five o'clock shadow, I pretended to stumble.

"*Alors!* Be careful there!" Scratchy said as he steadied me. "You were drinking with professionals!"

"Veterans!" said another. "Of many campaigns!" More guffaws.

"A taxi, perhaps?" I said, seeing Clean-head glaring at me from the main room. "I need to get to the train station. I'll ask Madame—" I wobbled again, my fingers crossed.

"*Mais non!* We will find you a taxi!"

"Come, come, our little friend!"

In a scrum, the entire shift of police detectives escorted me from the back room, right past Clean-head and out to the sidewalk. In a few more moments, a cab had been flagged down and an argument had about the best route the driver should take. Then another argument ensued just for form's sake.

The cab took off. I was safe.

Once inside the station at Gare du Nord, I went to the ladies' room. I closed myself up in one of the stalls and took out the spice container. Inside was a piece of crumpled plastic, and when I unfolded it, I saw that it was an ordinary artifact bag, about two inches by three inches, with a ziplock. Inside was something wrapped in cotton.

I pulled the bag open and carefully eased the cotton out of the plastic. I unrolled it, wondering what could have cost Grayling his life. Some vital clue, perhaps even valuable in its own right. Gold or silver? Diamonds? Perhaps a rare—

It was a piece of thin red pottery. Samian ware, I thought, terra sigilata. It wasn't any bigger than a quarter, reddish-brown. It was just about the most ordinary sort of artifact one could find on any Roman site, apart from fragments of roof tile or brick. Like its cousin redware on American sites, it was ubiquitous, common as muck. Even if it wasn't gold or silver, a coin or brooch, I reasoned, maybe it was valuable as all artifacts were, for the information they contained, unlocked to the right questions.

It was nearly flat. There weren't any even molded patterns, which might have helped identify its origins. It wasn't a rim sherd, a handle, a lip, or a spout; there was nothing to tell specifically what kind of vessel it came from, though there was a blotch of extra glaze on top of the glossy red surface.

It was, outside of its context, useless. Worse than useless, because at least if it had been left in whatever location it had been deposited, it might have told *somebody* something.

Of all the things that Grayling could have risked his life for, this piece of pottery was about the last thing on earth to be worth it.

Chapter 12

I stared at the sherd, willing it to be other than it was. Perhaps its very ordinariness meant that it *had* to be meaningful. I mean, people who aren't archaeologists don't just happen to have small pieces of Roman pottery in their kitchen cupboards.

I pulled the sherd up to my face and stared at the blob of glaze. It was so similar in color to the body that it nearly blended in. When I examined it more closely, I saw there was a series of numbers and letters.

Not glaze. Clear nail polish. Applied by some archaeologist to protect the numbers, which detailed where on the site the sherd had come from. I'd done tens of thousands of them myself.

This was more like it—this, I understood. A provenience mark...but how to tell which site it was from?

The combination of letters and numbers could have been for anywhere, on any site.

I stared at the sherd, my fatigue and fear crashing on me all of a sudden. To have gone so far, risked so much, for *this*? Some teaching specimen culled from the sifting pile of a long-abandoned site? This was worth lives?

I must have misunderstood what Grayling wanted me to do. I must have gotten something wrong. He was dying, he was delirious.

Maybe he was trying to get back at me, setting me up so the others could find me. Certainly Clean-head and company might be evidence of that.

But at one point, the sherd had meant something. No one makes marks like this for no reason. They have meaning. If it's provenience, I could track it down, maybe in fifty years. If it's something else, a code or coordinates, I'll figure that out, too.

Another puzzle, and I still needed to negotiate what I'd found for Danny.

I left the stall and found a bench inside the station. I had some calls to make, but I didn't want to use either my phone or the one Dmitri had given me. I still had some cash from the ATM at Logan, so I changed it and bought myself a phone with an international SIM card. Dmitri might have connections, but he couldn't control all the kiosks in all the train stations.

I looked at my watch and risked a call to the Steubens. If I was very lucky, they were in England, having connected from Germany. After I struggled with the combination of country codes and area codes, someone picked up on the first try.

"Yes?" A female voice, strong but cautious.

"Claudia, it's me."

"Are you OK?" Either she was hoping to hear from me or her vampiric senses identified me.

"Yes."

"And Danny?"

"Still alive, as of last night."

"And did you find...what Dmitri wanted?"

"I think so." I told her what had happened at Grayling's house. I left out the bit about the other clues he'd given me, for the moment. Her talk of political divisiveness bothered me; I still didn't know much about her, so until dangerous men stopped chasing me, I was only going to tell her as much as she was familiar with.

I did mention the clean-headed guy, though; he scared me. "I thought humans weren't supposed to know about the, uh, Fang-born?"

"They're not, but we're not perfect. Dmitri, for example. There are others who've slipped through our safeguards, and believe me, we're trying to catch them and make them forget. What next?" she said.

"I...I honestly don't know." My eyes started to burn, and it took a second to figure out it had nothing to do with the diesel fumes. My throat was tight; I was on the edge of tears. I wasn't ready to share that with anyone. I shook myself and settled for an admission I rarely made: "I don't know what to do next."

"We need to meet. Where are you?"

"Paris."

"Good. We're in London."

I thought about the other Fangborn at Logan security, and that led to the wallet that Sean had—Sean. I hadn't even had time to think about what kind of trouble he might be in. "Is Sean OK?"

"I talked the police into letting him go, yes. Good thing he showed up when he did; we would have had a much harder time getting you through. He's here with us."

Sweet of Sean to be so worried. Silly of him to have come so far. "You couldn't just...you know. Make him forget?"

Claudia sighed. "I could have. But we couldn't leave him for the others to find, and they'd be digging into his head with a whole lot less restraint—or skill—than I."

"Wait, I thought you said Fangborn were good guys?"

"We are. It's just...we all want the common good to prevail, we want to protect humanity. We just differ on what that looks like and how best to do it." She paused, and I could practically hear a shrug. "We're only human."

It was going to take me a while to digest that.

"Where and when do we meet?" she said.

"Not here. Berlin," I said all of a sudden. I needed more information about my figurine, supposedly a key. "There's...there's someone I should talk to there."

"Can you trust him or her?"

That is what I liked about Claudia, I realized. She didn't tell me to wait, she didn't tell me to stop. She seemed to trust me to make good decisions. "I think so. There's no reason for anyone to suspect I'm there, and I hope it will answer a few questions."

"Good. Can we meet before you do? We need to talk."

"Sure." All I knew about Berlin came from a call for papers for a conference in Germany and what I'd read in *National Geographic*. "There's a place, loud, busy, touristy—the Sony Center. Meet me there—when?" I figured there'd be lots of ways in, lots of ways out, and lots of crowds to melt into.

"When can you get there?"

I looked at the schedule; there was a train leaving this evening. "Tomorrow morning. You can find me?"

"No problem. We'll call you when we get in. Take care, Zoe."

"You, too."

I hung up. Luck was on my side, and I booked the last seat for Berlin.

A little after eight, I settled in for the long train ride. Other, smarter passengers had booked a cabin and were making a party of the trip; I had to make due with a reclining seat for twelve hours. I could make the best of the discomfort with rest and research. I stowed my bag, took out my phone, and Googled Dmitri, but didn't find anything extra that told me more than the files that Gerry had sent. There was nothing new about Grayling's death, or Cleanhead. I found a couple of references to Jenny's colleague, Professor Schulz, who'd written on everything about Greek pottery, from decoration and style to regulations about standardized volume measures.

Academic research usually chills me out, but the prickling in my spine wasn't going away. If anything, it was getting worse.

It might have been exhaustion, seasoned with a lifetime's worth of paranoia and a week of monster stories and worry about Danny. On the other hand, maybe my paranoia was part of the Beast, part of being Fangborn.

Or at least half-Fangborn. It suddenly occurred to me: Ma sure wasn't a werewolf and probably not a vampire, either. Maybe she was some kind of oracle—was that what Claudia had called them? But though she'd complained of hearing voices in her letter, I'd never seen her do anything...Fangborn-y. I'd have to ask the Steubens.

I walked to the bathroom and back and didn't see anyone suspicious. I strolled down to the café car and bought some dinner—with something to take in my pack—for later. No one sprouting fangs or wielding machine guns there. Drunken students, uncomfortable families, late-traveling businessmen, lovers necking like it was the only thing that mattered. I remembered how it felt; now it just made me sad.

I went back to my seat and convinced myself it was nerves. Sleep came eventually, but no sooner did I nod off than it seemed that we arrived in Köln for the transfer.

Blearily I shouldered my bag, found the correct track, and found another seat. As I settled in for what I hoped would be several hours of uninterrupted sleep, I glanced out the window.

A beloved form, familiar features, a crooked smile.

There was Will MacFarlane, staring at me from the opposite platform.

What the hell was he doing here?

I ducked down. It was too much of a coincidence—wasn't it? I mean, he might be abroad for fieldwork. He might be here for any number of reasons.

I knew it wasn't any of these things. Somehow I knew he was looking for me.

Too many people were looking for me.

Nonsense. It couldn't possibly be Will. I peeked up; Will gestured to himself. *Zoe, it's me*, I could see him mouth. And of course it was: short light-brown hair, strong jaw, the skeptically raised eyebrow...

The train started moving.

He'd seen me. Will held up his hand—in greeting? Recognition? To stop me?

He started running.

I panicked and ducked back down.

My train picked up speed. If I could have gotten out and pushed, I would have. I leaned out the window to make sure it was really him. Disastrously, the train slowed.

Will ran faster, head back, arms pumping, legs a blur.

Of all the times I could have seen Will again, this was the worst. Even if it was coincidence, I didn't want him to see me up to my neck in this nightmare. If it wasn't, then I wasn't sure I wanted to know why he was looking for me just now.

As if awaiting my admission of desperation, the train sped up again, this time beyond even Will's capacity for speed.

He ran five times a week. Rain or shine, promise of Christmas presents or promise of sex, he ran seven miles. But not even Will was faster than a speeding locomotive.

The city gave way to countryside, and when I was sure I was safe, I had to put Will out of my mind. I simply didn't have the bandwidth for him at the moment. I slept a while, out of sheer physical and emotional exhaustion.

When I awoke, early, I checked my phone; there was the scheduled picture of Danny with today's *Herald Tribune*. Danny looked bad; pale, tired, thin, as if he'd been deprived of sleep or food. Dmitri texted me; we would meet shortly. He was delayed, investigating Grayling's sudden and bloody death. I replied I had lost my pursuers in London and would soon be in Berlin. I would meet him there late tomorrow, with the figurines.

I put my phone away. I tried to convince myself it was a good thing I'd bought myself another few hours to explore what the figurines—keys?—might mean. Maybe there was still a chance I could get some leverage out of them before trading them for Danny.

It was hard, though. Danny looked like hell, and I was taking chances with his life.

It's Dmitri, I told myself fiercely. *Dmitri was the one who kidnapped him, not me!*

Dmitri took him because of you, a little voice said. *Because you took the first figurine from the museum.*

Hours later, I stretched painfully, listening to my joints crack like wine-glass stems and feeling my muscles protest. I got out in Berlin HBF and found some breakfast in the station, a plate of cold cuts, bread, and cheese. I've always been hungrier than most girls—or at least more willing to admit it—and now I knew why. It was more than just low blood sugar or the habit of intermittent poverty. I needed to feed the Beast. I needed to keep my focus and get my cousin back.

I decided to walk the mile or so to the Sony Center to stretch my legs and orient myself. I was struck by how modern Berlin was compared to London and Paris, no surprise because so much of the city had been destroyed by war. Glass was used in all the buildings, in swoops and curved lines as well as in stark, uncluttered rectangles. Steel and brick, clearly the geometry of the late twentieth century; I was so used to the idea of Europe as "older" than the United States, and it took me a minute to miss buildings that might have been built in earlier centuries. This was a city that radiated youth and energy emerging from the past.

I was early, with plenty of time for another cup of coffee and a croissant. As I ate, I studied a tourist map of Berlin I'd snagged at the train station, located the museum where Professor Schulz worked, and tried to figure out some of the complexities of the U-bahn and S-bahn transit systems.

I put down my cup; I felt...something. Not a scent, but my sense of smell sort of...opened? Widened? Like another sense was just behind it, working overtime. It's hard to explain, but just as I was starting to realize my senses were in overdrive for a reason, Claudia and Gerry arrived, harried and relieved to see me.

Sean was with them, to my relief. He looked like hammered shit.

Gerry ordered breakfast in reasonable German; when I looked surprised, he said, "Our grandfather came over from Germany. He taught me some."

I nodded. Their food came—eggs and sausage and more lunch meat—and I waited while they put it away. No point in talking with their heads down like that. Claudia was very polite, but she ate even more than I had.

Sean was probably hungover and jet-lagged. He barely touched his coffee, barely spoke after a muttered greeting. Claudia's suggestion was probably still at work; he didn't ask any unanswerable questions.

When they came up for air, I told them what had transpired at Grayling's and at the Paris apartment. At first I omitted the piece of pottery I'd found, but both Steubens frowned so obviously that I found myself back-pedaling fast, but playing it down. I wondered about the extent of the Fangborn psychic ability, or their ability to detect truth. Useful skills, if I could develop them, too.

"The numbers and letters could refer to its location on a site," I finished. "Provenience marks generally indicate a position on a site and its depth below surface. But we have no way of knowing where the site itself is. And this kind of pottery, well, there's nothing special about it."

"Did you Google it?"

I nodded. "The number was blurry, but I managed to figure it out. And I got nothing but a part number for a plumbing company."

"What if it's not archaeological markings? Could it be longitude and latitude?" Claudia said, finally pushing a plate back. At least she'd left the glaze on it. Even the parsley garnish was gone.

"Not enough numbers," I said, and Gerry nodded. "And there are letters that don't fit."

"What if it's not in English? Or...what if it's a telephone number? The old-fashioned kind, with the letters in front?"

I looked at Sean, surprised. It was the last thing I'd expect him to think of. We tried it out, and I got out my telephone to check, but unless it was for a number on Mars, it wasn't a telephone code.

The telephone reminded me of Danny, and I checked, but there was no new message. But then a thought came to me. "Maybe it's Leet."

"What?"

I explained about the use of text, numbers, and UNIX codes on the Internet. "Danny's license plate is 1337," I said, "which is 'leet' or 'elite.'"

Claudia tilted back her head and closed her eyes. "They don't match anything I can think of in European languages, but the printing and numerals look like they were made by an American or European. Not much help."

Sean said, "I think you're right, Zoe. It's a provenience mark."

"But why would Grayling send me after this?" I said. "Unless we know what site it belongs to, we can't do much with it. These things aren't standardized internationally. Some countries have regulations and protocols about archaeological site marks, so I can start to check that out, but for now..." I shook my head. "I gotta think Grayling was trying to set me up in Paris."

"What time is your meeting with Professor Schulz?" Claudia asked.

"About two. He has classes all morning."

Claudia turned to Sean, who really did look green now. She took his hand, as if measuring his pulse, and peered into his eyes. "You're exhausted. We booked a room at the Westin." She handed him a map, pointed out the hotel. "Why don't you go crash for a few hours? We'll find you in time for lunch."

He nodded and got up unsteadily. "Thanks. I'm sorry. I just... I'm just wiped out."

I suddenly realized: Sean was the only one among us who wasn't Fangborn, who'd be feeling the travel and lack of sleep even more than us. "No problem, Sean."

"Zoe, a quick word?" he said.

"Sure." I got up and we stepped off to the side.

"I'm worried about you," he whispered. "I mean, I thought you'd just go to London, and we'd be back inside the week."

"I know. I appreciate your help—I never would have made my flight if you hadn't stepped in and caused that ruckus in Boston." I put my hand on his shoulder. "You should go home. You don't need to keep on."

He exhaled, frustrated. "No, that's not what I meant. Can't you leave this up to the Steubens? Or go to the police?"

"Sean, I can't. Dmitri warned me against it. Honestly, you should—"

"I'm not leaving, Zoe. Just...I'll catch you later, OK?"

I watched Sean leave. Gerry stood, having paid the bill. "Let's walk."

Clearly something was up; they wanted to talk without possibility of being overheard, even by Sean. After a few minutes, we found ourselves on the edge of a large green space in the center of the city, ringed by wooded areas. I had the impression it went on for miles.

Gerry looked around, then ducked down a secluded pathway, surrounded by trees. I followed suit and began to get very worried. It was as much a feeling as a sensation. I was keenly aware of where people were around us, as if all my senses were kicking into hyperdrive to reassure me I was safe.

I also realized it was a little like the feeling I had in Salem, right before the other Fangborn appeared at the cemetery, and again in Cambridge. Now that I was paying attention, that feeling of awareness seemed to get stronger. More accessible.

We came to a clearing, and Claudia nodded to Gerry. "I've got the perimeter." She took off.

OK, now this was just plain odd. I wasn't sure how I liked being left alone with Gerry, in the middle of nowhere.

"Calm down," he said. "Danny's safe, as far as we know, and we have a few hours until the meeting. It's the only chance we have to give you a crash course in being Fangborn. Teach you some of what you should have learned as a kid."

"Here? Out in the open?"

He nodded. "It's risky, and it's public. But it's quiet here. The park won't fill up until lunchtime. And some folks say being out in the open, near nature, helps them focus on the Change."

"What is this, some kind of induction ceremony? Solemn oaths and burnt sacrifices?" Sure, I was nervous. This was only *one* aspect of my life right now that terrified me.

Gerry shook his head. "We can fill you in on the cultural aspects later. I'll even buy you a cake that says, '*Mazel tov!* Today you are a werewolf!' That is, if we all survive this. But for now, we just need to get you to Change at will."

I shook my head. "I can't. I've never been able to control keeping it away or summoning the Bea—it when I needed it."

"When you've been a stray…not raised within a pack, you don't get the training. So I'm not surprised you think this, but yes, you can Change at will. You must unlearn, young Skywalker."

I backed off a step or two, mostly from the idea. A fern curled up from the leaf duff; I decided to be fascinated by it for a while.

I shook my head again. "I can't…no, I don't want to. I've worked very hard to keep the Beast contained. For a while I thought I was just insane. Then I worried that I was worse, some kind of serial killer. It's too much to take, on top of everything else."

"*Beast* is a nice word for *monster*." Gerry very gently put his hands on my shoulders, touched his forehead to mine. "You're not a monster. It's only your other self, as much a part of you as dark hair or green eyes. You don't have to be afraid of it—*it's* you. And the Change…don't tell Claudia I said this, because it's not dogma—"

I was nervous and creeped out, so I giggled. "You said 'dogma.'"

Gerry shook his head, not taking his hands from my shoulders. "Nothing funny here. Like I said, it's my own personal opinion that the Change makes us like angels. With it, we fight evil, we protect humanity. This is a good thing."

He was serious. He seemed incredibly naive to me, and what he was saying was a little too much like what my mother had told me about my father's people, all these years: above the law, vigilantes, a gang. I still didn't like the idea.

I thought Claudia was the psychic one, but Gerry maybe had a touch of that, too. "This will increase our chances of getting Danny back," he said.

OK. Sold. I nodded.

"You trust me?"

I shrugged.

He cocked his head, then kicked off his shoes. "Fair enough. Without the cultural background, without even the most basic exercises in focus and control, it's like getting someone…ah, to dance *Swan Lake* by telling them the steps, and without any music."

"*Swan Lake?*"

"I'd usually go with a mixed-martial-arts reference, but you're a girl."

"Fuck you."

He gave me a big smile. "For now, just...watch and be aware of what your senses tell you when I go."

Then he Changed.

It was like the feeling while I waited in the café this morning, times twenty. Somewhere wrapped up in the astonishment was the urge to laugh. A wolf can only look so fierce with an Oxford cloth shirt and jeans hanging off him.

He Changed back. Gerry was so good at shifting around in his clothes quickly you'd never have noticed anything was amiss.

I chewed on my bottom lip. "What about...those half-wolfmen? Can you do that? Could I do that?" Maybe being only half a Beast was a good start for me.

"Sure, but we're going to focus on this for now. Get the basics down first, then the flashier stuff. Remember how it felt when I Changed. Give it a shot."

I tried, but no luck. "Uh, what do you tell the kids you're training? The ones who have problems?"

Gerry opened his mouth, then closed it. "Uhhh, they're younger than you are by, like, ten years or more. By the time most Fangborn kids can Change, at puberty, it's all they want to do. And I never came across any who were kept in the dark about how to Change and what they really were, like you were." He thought about it. "With the kids I've taught, they have the ability; I need to get them to trust me, then we do a lot of exercises, learn to meditate a little, focus on my voice, that sort of thing."

"Well, what do parents tell their kids when they're little? Where's the first place you start when you're training them to get control of the powers they'll eventually have?"

He shrugged and started in a voice made for nursery rhymes, "*First* the wolf in you runs around and makes sure it's safe. *Then* the vampire in you chases away all the bad thoughts. *Then* the oracle in you tells you to get ready for an adventure. *Then* you *go!*"

I looked at him. "Yeah, that's not going to work."

"Told you. There are little gestures to help them remember each of the steps"—he mimed making wolf ears, vampire claws, and someone looking far away—"and help them not be afraid. I didn't think you'd get much out of those either."

"Maybe I'm really different. I keep telling you, it's danger, a threat to my life that does it. Or the moon. Most of the time, anyway."

Claudia stepped back into the clearing, nodding to Gerry.

"It's not the moon. We haven't got time to start grounding you in meditation, the first part of the whole training program, but relax, try to summon the feelings you have when you've Changed before—sensations, emotions, whatever."

"Um, usually anger."

"Go with that."

I tried it again, and this time, I felt the slightest tickle, but it was so far away, it vanished as soon as I identified it.

Gerry shook his head. "You're trying too hard. Bugging your eyes out, clenching your stomach, holding your breath. You look like you're trying to hold back a fart."

I had been holding my breath; I exhaled with a nervous laugh. "Look, usually this just comes rushing over me. Overwhelming me. Nothing active on my part."

"Stop thinking of your furself as separate from you. That way you're not using up all your focus and energy to prevent it. This is what they start us off with at the academy."

He began to recite: "*Breathe. You can't do anything if you can't breathe.*

"*Wiggle your toes. If you can't wiggle your toes, the rest of you is probably too tense.*

"Smell. What is nearby? Danger? Even if you can't smell it, are you afraid?

"Move. If you don't see or smell anything, start to cast over the rest of the area."

He shrugged. "Then you focus on the wolf."

I relaxed as he said, with no luck. I thought a moment. "You do it again." I recalled I'd felt the Beast come on me easily at home, in the presence of other Fangborn.

He did, almost as soon as I asked. It was beyond weird, watching it, but it wasn't as scary as it felt when the Beast took over me. Gerry was probably right, it was just training and getting used to it. He looked good as a wolf. He looked...not tame. *Benevolent*, that was the word. Even after seeing him do something I thought of as my own personal sin, I wasn't afraid.

Yet I was always afraid when I felt the Beast come upon me.

I tried again, using that little frisson of his Change to sort of pull me along. It was a bit like riding a bike in the draft of someone else who acted as a windbreak. I tried to put aside resistance, tried not to think the rush was bad or evil. I just let go—

It worked. I'd turned into a wolf, nearly on my own. No moon in sight, no danger—

Something was wrong.

During the moment of disorientation as I Changed, a familiar smell, a long-lost smell, wafted into a wolf's nose, then registered in a much slower human brain.

Danger...

My ears back, I turned around.

He's here, he's here...

There was Will, not twenty feet away from me, his mouth agape.

I had Changed into a wolf in front of the one man I swore would never see this side of me.

Habit and emotion won out.

I tore out of there like my tail was on fire.

Chapter 13

He'd seen me. He'd seen me. He'd seen me—
That phrase drove me on, running in a blind panic.
The man I loved, who I hated for getting so close to me, who I swore to protect, just saw me Change into a monster. How did he get here? How did he find me? Why is he here?
The Tiergarten takes up nearly a square mile in the center of Berlin. There are acres of woods around wide, grassy lawns, but a city is no place for a dog without a leash. I imagined it wouldn't be long until law-abiding citizens took notice and did something about it. Then they'd discover I was a wolf, not a dog, and then, perhaps, a girl, not a wolf.
I needed a plan. Something besides running.
I galloped into another wooded area and hid for a moment, catching my breath. I surveyed the fields, now full of mothers and children playing in the sun. A few sunbathers lounged as business folk packed up their lunches and returned to work.
I didn't have long; no doubt Gerry could track me if he wanted, and God knew what Claudia could do. Fly, maybe—isn't that what vampires did?
Remembering the city map I'd read earlier, I watched the picnickers. Even though I'd attacked humans before, that had been to protect myself or someone else. I'd never felt as predatory as I did now, spying and calculating. It was all a matter of one strike, pure physics, acceleration, direction, and mass. And...conscience.

One young woman in a bathing suit finished applying sunblock and then settled herself gingerly on her blanket. In a moment, she'd be asleep.

I tried not to think too much about it as I ran toward her.

My timing was a little off and my luck a little bad. As I snatched up her tote bag and booked it, she shifted, readjusting herself on the blanket. I stepped on her hand, and she startled, screaming incoherently.

What's German for "Holy shit, a big dog in a T-shirt and panties just stole my bag!"? If I kept this up, I might have to learn.

I booked it for the woods, then doubled back in the opposite direction under cover, angling toward a U-bahn station.

I tried to Change back; it took a minute because adrenaline and embarrassment were strong inducements to stay wolfy. I tried to remember what Gerry said, tried to remember that I had to Change back if I were going to figure out this whole mess and save Danny. Wiggling my claws? No problem. With something like a cross between soda bubbles up my nose and a burp, I Changed back.

I rifled through the girl's bag, pulled on her wrap skirt and sandals, and straightened out my hair. While trying not to think about what had just happened.

I'd turned without a threat to my life. Without the moon. Without a criminal nearby.

Will had found me. Had seen me as a wolf. Why was he here?

I'd just ripped off some poor woman.

I'm not really a thief. I'd stolen before, in minor sorts of ways when things were tight. Paper from a copying machine, a couple of pens from a bank. Once or twice, when things were very bad, I would find a hotel catering to families, and when the kiddies were put to bed, I'd go through the hallways like a ghost, checking the trays put out in the hall after room service. Maybe it wasn't nice, but as a teenager I was always hungry, and I didn't want to put any more on my mother's shoulders, especially after she'd given me the bigger of two scanty portions for dinner.

Taking the figurine from the museum didn't count, because I was paying for that momentary lapse with my cousin's life.

When I was dressed, I pulled out the wallet. There wasn't much money in it, a few euros. So while I was no newcomer to a few shortcuts here and there, abuses of hospitality at most, I was always aware of people who didn't have much. And the woman's clothes and wallet did not say "wealthy" to me.

I stared at the wallet for a long time, not looking at the license or other cards. Finally I threw it as far from me as I could. I wasn't going to take advantage of someone who might be as bad off as I was. Then I scattered the rest of the things around to make it look like a dog had stolen the bag and gone tearing through it.

The last thing to go flying was the cell phone, and that brought my other troubles into focus. The phone Dmitri had given me, my one link with Danny, was in my jeans pocket.

Back in the clearing. Where Will was.

Sweating with fear, I thought hard. OK, I'd have to find Claudia and Gerry soon, if only to snatch my things back—oh dear God, the figurines. In my backpack, along with everything I needed to save Danny, including my passport. Imperative, then, to find them, or rather, let them find me. I had no doubt they would.

Then it occurred to me—they had no idea who Will was. He hadn't said a word, had he? Not my name, nothing that I could remember. Perhaps he hadn't even seen me, and if he had...well, that's what Claudia was there for, to make him forget.

I sighed with relief. Maybe I'd be OK.

They'd find me. And maybe Will would be out of my hair even before they knew he was a problem.

But as I heard a clock toll, I realized I was now running late to my meeting with Professor Schulz. I scooped up about four euros of loose change and ran for the station.

I found my way to the Oranienburger Strasse stop and walked from there, across the "Museumsinsel," or Museum Island, where several of the most important collections in a city stuffed with fantastic museums were situated on a small island in a river.

For me, if you couldn't find "Cupcake Island"—and I hadn't stopped my search—"Museum Island" was the next best thing.

Down along the canal, past the Pergamon Museum, I found the place. I wasn't really sure what to expect, but the exterior of the Altes Museum was impressive. The museum formed one edge of a wide, square green space, with the Berlin cathedral on the next side and a line of trees along the canal. It was busy, a well-used space, even at midafternoon. The museum facade was lined with columns, and dramatic bronze sculptures of mounted hunters flanked the staircase leading to the central entrance. I was suddenly reminded that so many of the finest classical antiquities were now to be found in repositories outside their native lands. The nineteenth century had brought a gold rush for the best sites, and Germany, France, and England had gotten busy.

As I introduced myself at the desk, I was given a badge and directed to the main gallery. Row upon row of cases of the most exquisite ancient pottery were showcased by category: sacrifices, everyday life, women, warfare.

Clearly being a colonial power had its benefits.

"Miss Miller?"

He was every caricature of an aging professor. Untidy tweed jacket, tufts of gray hair poking out in a tonsure, smudged glasses. Folded papers stuffed in one pocket and, surprisingly, an Asterix comics mug nestled in the soft fabric of a basket from which he'd just taken a vessel that looked like a sort of vase with handles. He put the brake on the trolley he was using and held out his hand.

"I had an e-mail from Dr. Jenny Kelner, who told me you might be in touch. I'm so pleased you were able to stop by."

"Thank you for taking the time to see me." I shook hands, a little apologetically. "I'm afraid my bag was snatched, so I don't have my notebook. But I do remember my questions."

He tutted over my fictitious loss and nodded. "I was just replacing this kalyx krater. Mid-third century BCE from the Greek colonies in southeastern Italy. It depicts the release of Prometheus from his torture by Hercules, who killed the eagle feasting on his liver. It's such a painful story, Prometheus sacrificing himself for having gifted humanity with fire. I look at this and feel happy and relieved for him; it's a hopeful story about the end of pain and suffering."

He smiled at his silliness. "But to the matter at hand. You have an interest in pottery decorated with three-dimensional figurines? I think I can help. Have you seen my recent paper on the subject? I happen to have an offprint, if you would like."

He made one appear as if by magic. I took it and glanced over it. "Thank you. Mine...was in my bag."

"My specialty is Greek pottery, which seems very dull, until you realize it tells you of the movements of people, trade, and whole civilizations. The rise of nations and democracy. And," he nodded to the vessel he'd just replaced, "some of them tell wonderful stories, not only of myth, but of daily life."

"I'm not sure if you can help me," I said. "The object I'm interested in is clay, but not a pot. Though Jenny said it might be a pottery decoration, not a votive figurine as I first thought."

"May I see it?" Then he shook his head. "Of course. Your bag was stolen. Perhaps you can describe it for me?"

I turned the offprint over and sketched out the object I'd taken from the museum back at home, but without enough detail to indicate specifics.

"I think Dr. Kelner is correct. You see the little roughness at the bottom? A peg might have been there once. It would fit in a hole in a ridge around the vessel. There would be a half dozen or a dozen of them, and all together, it would make a very decorative piece. Unusual. I've just seen a reference to such a thing in, of all places, northern Britain."

"Oh? Where?"

"I found mention of a former Roman soldier to his brother, who was stationed at Vindolanda, on Hadrian's Wall, in the north of England. You're familiar with the wax tablets found there, the way that they were inscribed? How the marks were scratched onto the wooden holders so that when the wax disappeared, it left a more permanent record, capable of surviving in the archaeological record? Good. Well, we don't know who this ex-soldier Secundus was, but he wrote to his brother claiming to have found a pot decorated in this fashion in what is modern-day Turkey."

"Oh," I said. I'd heard of the tablets, but didn't really know how they could help me. I didn't need to know the whole history of these things, just the specific importance of the ones in my possession.

Schulz was on an academic tear, though, and hadn't noticed my lack of interest. "But most peculiarly, he described this vessel as an 'unbreakable,' perhaps of metal, at what is now the site of Notion. Clearly that wasn't where it was supposed to be, as something as different and important as that should have been in the temple of Apollo in nearby Claros or at the temple of Artemis near Ephesus. A pithos of metal. From the temple of Apollo."

He looked at me as if I should get the importance of that.

I didn't. I cleared my throat. "Um, how old was it?"

"The letter dates to the end of the first century CE. The Apollonian temple at Claros probably dates to the second half of the seventh century BCE, but there was almost certainly a much earlier presence of the worship of Cybele there, two centuries before that. No one knows how old the jar is, because it was never found."

I was missing the point. He kept looking at me so hopefully, wanting me to get it.

"The temple of Apollo. I mean, that makes sense to find a metal jar there, doesn't it? As a special offering to the god or something?"

He nodded, giving me a chance to work it out.

"Metal jars...not all that common, right? I mean, they're mostly always clay, right? Maybe some of carved stone?"

"Hesiod describes the 'box,' really a jar, given to Pandora as unbreakable," he said, unable to keep it to himself any longer. "Therefore, a metal jar. Though the description of this one is unusual, ornate and small, not your usual storage vessel."

It took me a minute to work it out. "You think a Roman in first-century Asia Minor found Pandora's Box?"

"Well..." Academic habit made him cautious. "No, no, of course not. But this description stood out as unusual in the letters, and, naturally, I couldn't ignore the Hesiod translation. Whatever Secundus found was rare enough, and certainly he was excited enough about it to write to his brother and give him a description of it. I am going through the letters exchanged between the brothers."

I thought of the figurines in my possession. In his last breath, Grayling had said something about Pandora, but I thought it was only a way of saying how untrustworthy Dmitri was. But Clean-head had also mentioned the Box in Paris..."Is there a description of the Box? Jar?"

"Metal, I suspect. Decorated, Secundus mentions, but he is circumspect. He did mention that there were four spaces, perhaps slots for adornments, along a flange around the belly of the jar. I think he believed he'd found something very, very important. Very precious. I suspect it also originated from the same region as this kalyx krater, for instance, in Apulia."

"Do you know where either of the soldiers ended up?" I asked. Four spaces jibed with what Grayling had told me, that there were four figurines or keys, each from a different temple.

"I believe Tertius died in the army, not long after this letter was received. This is no surprise; there was a great deal of disease at the time. A shame, because another letter from Secundus might have brought more information. I think he was trying to leave his brother a clue. Because Secundus became a merchant after his stint in the army, I suspect he would have lived in one of the major cities in the area, Ephesus, perhaps. But it's also possible he could have moved on."

And be anywhere in the Roman Empire, which at that time spread from Britain to Syria. "Do you have their letters?"

"Oh my, no. They're all at the British Museum."

"Oh." Just my luck.

"I have spent a long time studying them, though, and have included several very clear, very detailed photographs of the fragments in my forthcoming article. I have a copy, if you'd like to see an early draft."

"Oh yes! Thank you very much!"

"I would, of course, appreciate you not citing it until after the publication date this fall."

I stared at him, then finally remembered: I wasn't a student, researching a paper. I was working for a deranged thief who'd kidnapped my cousin. Intellectual primacy was not even on my radar. "No, I promise, I won't."

He pulled out the thick sheaf of papers from his pocket.

I took it.

"Interestingly, another party, an amateur from the States, has just contacted me with a similar question about decorated Greek pottery." He noticed his glasses were smudged and began to polish them.

I had never heard of this stuff before Dmitri, and suddenly it seemed as though Pandora—and interest in my figurines—was everywhere. This couldn't be a coincidence. "Oh yes?"

"I've never spoken to a real senator before," he said in an excited, reverent whisper. "It was rather exciting."

Given the context, it took me a minute to realize he wasn't talking about Julius Caesar and Mark Antony. "Senator? As in a US senator?"

"Oh yes. Your Mr. Edward Knight, from New York. Apparently he's an enthusiast, helping to organize a museum show to visit his state."

A woman in a severe skirt and blouse approached, caught his eye, and handed him a note, which he read. "Oh dear. A phone call I absolutely must take. If you'll excuse me? I won't be long."

I nodded, and he left, trailing in the wake of the woman. I gazed at the pot, remembering what I knew of Prometheus: His brother was Epimetheus, and they were responsible for doling out attributes to the animals. Epimetheus, or "hindsight," believed he had nothing left for humans. This prompted Prometheus to steal fire from the gods in order to let humanity develop culture.

Prometheus, who, in return for this sin, was tortured and given Pandora for a sister-in-law.

I didn't like to think how often Pandora, and her Box, and all the trouble it contained, kept popping up in my investigation. If chaos had followed the last time the Box was opened, I truly didn't want to see it happen again.

A susurrus behind me. I turned, expecting Professor Schulz, and was startled to see Gerry and Claudia, with my backpack over her shoulder. At least there was no sign of Will. I sighed with relief.

"Have you met Professor Schulz?" Claudia said.

I nodded. "He's taking a phone call. Should be right back."

"We have to leave soon," she said.

Gerry strayed over to one of the other cases. He peered at the pottery vessels and straightened, shaking his head. "Um, no problems about nudity in ancient Greece, huh?"

Claudia looked over his shoulder. "Whoa! Any excuse to wave your dick around. Penis here, penis there, get it out, lads, wave it in the air."

I clapped my hand over my mouth. She had *not* just said that…

"*Claudia!*" Gerry was aghast. I suddenly realized Gerry the Werewolf was prudish. And his sister, under the layers of buttoned-down shrink, had an actual sense of humor.

"I'm serious, it's nothing but penises over here. Zoe, how did they keep from getting sunburned?"

"Claudia! *Jesus!*"

"They probably used oil or fat or something, right?" She was genuinely curious now.

"Uh, probably," I said. "Never really thought about it."

Gerry shook his head. "I sure wouldn't be so proud if my junk looked like a bunch of small, hairy radishes." He caught my glance. "Which it doesn't."

Claudia had composed herself, as if the moment had never been. "What is that one, Zoe?"

I stepped back to show her the jug with the Prometheus painting.

She nodded, started to turn, then something caught her glance. "Gerry."

This time it was a command rather than a joke. He stopped counting genitals and came over.

"What?"

"Hercules."

He glanced at it, glanced at her. "Huh. Interesting."

I realized why they were looking at Hercules; I understood now his lion skin suggested a possible Fangborn connection. I resolved to add "animal skins" to my list of Fangborn attributes to be studied. But Hercules, another Fangborn, associated with Pandora and Prometheus? It all bore consideration now.

He turned to me. "But we need to get out of here. As in, yesterday."

"Yes. Zoe, come on."

"But Professor Schulz—"

"You can leave word at the desk," Gerry said.

I stopped by the front, and after a tentative *"Guten Tag,"* explained in English that I would miss Professor Schulz. "The police found my bag and I must identify it."

"I will tell him, thank you," the administrator said in unaccented English.

We hustled out, heading into the crowded tourist area full of shops and restaurants.

"Can we stop?" I said. "I missed lunch."

I didn't really want to stop, not with the discussions we had to have, but I was ravenous.

"Not quite yet. Let's get a little farther," Claudia said. "I know a place."

"What are you worried about? My next meeting with Dmitri isn't for hours, and I'm not even sure he's in the country yet."

We went a few blocks more, and the crowds thinned as we passed through a tony shopping district. It became mixed residential buildings and businesses, all very high-end.

I realized there were very few people I had to work hard to keep pace with, but the Steubens were among them. They weren't actually running but eating up the distance quickly.

We went into an alley. Four tall apartment buildings formed a bricked courtyard filled with outdoor seating for a café. Suddenly my mouth watered. Not only could I smell the strong oils of newly roasted coffee, but there was a trace of truly diabolical chocolate baking nearby.

We were seated quickly. Claudia ordered, then turned to me. I said, thinking quickly, *"Für zwei,"* which meant I'd be having whatever she was having. But at least I wouldn't feel like an ignoramus while I fished out my phrase book. My two years of flirting with German had been a long time ago, and while I might be a developmentally challenged werewolf, I still had some pride.

Gerry glanced at the menu and ordered something that took a lot longer to say. I wondered whether he'd gotten more food and whether he'd share, or if it was just more long compound nouns.

When the waiter cleared away, I was suddenly the focus of attention I'd not wanted.

"Nice skirt," Gerry said. "You mug someone for it?"

"I needed to get out of there fast. That guy in the woods? He's nothing but seven kinds of trouble."

"Thanks for the promotion, Zoe. I think I used to be only six."

I turned. That voice.

Will MacFarlane emerged from the basement of the cafe.

Chapter 14

What was Will doing here? After all the pain I'd gone through to protect him from the Beast, from me—

Habit drove me. I stood up, kicking my chair back, ready to run.

"Sit down, Zoe," Claudia said.

I sat.

I realized what she was doing and tried to stand up again. My legs wouldn't work.

"God*damn* it, Claudia!"

"Sit. The quicker you settle down, the quicker we get through this. And," she added, "the sooner you get a handle on your powers, the sooner you can resist me." She shrugged. "You'll have a better chance, that is."

As soon as she said "powers," my stomach lurched away and my face went aflame. "Not in front of—"

"It's OK, Zoe," Will said. "I know all about it."

"What *exactly* do you think you know?" I said. I didn't want to look at him. I was so mad he'd insinuated himself back into my life, but I forced myself. "*I* don't even know what's going on with me. How did you find me? What do *you* know?"

"More than you, but that's no surprise." He smiled for a second, but it vanished a heartbeat later. "I know all about the Fangborn, Zoe, because it's my job."

Impossible. After I'd sacrificed so much, it just got worse and worse. He'd known the very worst of me as a human, and now, somehow, he knew that I was a freak. Once again Will knew more about everything, more about *me*, than I did.

My breath came harder and harder, and I realized I was hyperventilating. The waitress came out with a loaded tray, and that gave me a moment to collect myself.

Will sat down at the table, right next to me, and ordered a coffee in idiomatic, ass-achingly perfect German. He'd aced his required language exams, of course; as a classicist, he'd come across Italian, German, French, Latin, and Greek, trying to keep up with archaeological reports.

I was trapped. If I thought I could have managed it, I would have Changed, right then and there, and taken off.

Instead, I took a sip of the hot chocolate and burned the shit out of my mouth. "Damn it!"

Zoe, chill out. If he knows… Taking a deep breath, I groped for words.

He reached for my hand, then caught himself and pulled back. "I can help you get Danny back."

"What do you know about Danny?" I turned on the Steubens before he could answer. "What are you people trying to do? Telling him could *kill* Danny! You want me to trust you, then you ambush me with *this?*"

"Zoe, *listen!*"

I wanted to say, "Claudia, cut that shit out!" but suddenly I couldn't say anything.

Damned vampire tricks. She wasn't wrong, though, so while I fumed, I listened.

"I think I can help you with Danny," Will said, "because I know who Dmitri Parshin is. You're going to get a call from him, right? In about two hours?"

I nodded. He did know everything.

"I want to listen in on that call, and when you go to hand him the figurine, I want to be there. At the very least, I want you wired."

"Are. You. Out. Of. Your. Mind?" I realized Claudia's suggestion was only so strong; the more I concentrated on speaking my mind, the easier I found the trick of resisting her. Maybe I was getting better at it, too.

"He's immensely dangerous," Will said. "We can't let him get the things he's looking for."

"If he finds out I'm working with you, he'll—"

"I know: Danny." He shook his head slowly. "We won't let that happen. I won't let it happen."

"How can you—?"

"I work for the government, Zoe."

"What, the Bureau of Fangborn Affairs?" Either Claudia was easing up on me or I *was* getting better at this.

"It's a long story."

"That's OK. I've got two hours."

He sighed, looked around, and leaned over the table, to close our ranks. "The formal name, for the bean counters, is the Biological and Historical Intelligence branch of the FBI's Technical Laboratory. We mostly call ourselves TRG, from the Theodore Roundtree Group, after the guy who established it back in the 1940s."

I saw Gerry nudge Claudia, none too subtly, in the ribs. She nodded, frowning, and shushed him.

"Yeah?"

"He was the first, as far as we know, to officially acknowledge the presence of Fangborn in the United States. We work with the Fangborn in roles of legal and diplomatic efforts. It's kind of a cross between law enforcement, civil rights, and public relations."

"You're the guys who help hide the existence of the Fangborn." I looked at Gerry and Claudia, then back at Will. "My...people."

"Yes. And we'll be the ones helping to orchestrate the introduction of the Fangborn on I-Day. There are even a very few elected officials at the national level who are Fangborn."

"Like Senator Knight?" I blurted.

"How could you possibly know that?" Claudia said. "That's… that's very uncommon knowledge."

"I…don't know." I was as surprised as everyone else around the table—where had that come from? Perhaps Professor Schulz's comments had put the idea in my head. "The guy at the museum said a senator was asking questions along the same lines as mine. It just…came to me."

"Well, keep it under your hat," Will said. "He's one of the oldest Fangborn around, born at the beginning of the nineteenth century; he'll step down at the end of his term in two years. But for the moment, we're looking for Dmitri Parshin, who's as big a threat to humankind as he is to the Fangborn."

I couldn't stand not knowing any longer. "So did your interest in the Fangborn start before or after we dated?"

"After. But not by much."

"To get back at me."

Will looked at me. "Yes. As soon as we broke up, I immediately went searching for a government organization specializing in the history and culture of an otherwise unknown group of superhuman, hypernatural beings, on the astronomically remote chance you were one. That way, I could spend the next years of my life finding a way to hurt you as much as you hurt me."

I couldn't help it; I grinned. "OK, that was dumb. But how…?"

"Zoe, you knew I was looking into government work back when we were dating. Park Service, Army Corps of Engineers, my résumé was circulating. And the TRG discovered your existence about the time you left me. Questions and long, long discussions ensued, followed by a job offer. For a while, I admit, I thought I might use it to get back *to* you, once I learned about your history."

He looked away, then back at me. "Now I'm just worried about getting Danny home safely."

"How did they find out about me?"

"Recently, a document about a certain…facility…came to light. There was a list of names with photos. I almost flipped out when I recognized your mother's picture among them. And that she'd somehow managed to leave and keep from being discovered for so many years."

"What?" I recalled the note my mother had left me. "What else do you know?"

"Nothing. All I saw was the list of names." He cocked his head. "But there must be more information to be had. It wasn't my brief."

"What about you guys?" I asked Claudia. "Are you part of this TRG?"

"Um, no," she said. "But I think we're connected by blood."

"What?" This time Will was the surprised one.

Gerry leaned forward. "I'm pretty sure our grandfather, Jacob Steuben, was one of the first Fangborn to become involved with them. I found some family papers, sealed up and buried beneath the back shed when I was replacing it last year. They were written by Grandpa Jake, and they told of some weird stuff he and his Cousins got up to, on the home front and abroad, during the Second World War. The papers mentioned an FBI agent, who Grandpa said introduced him to Mr. Roundtree." He turned to Claudia. "What was his name? Harry Green?"

"Gray," Will said quietly. "And you're not supposed to know any of that. It's dangerous for you, for us."

"Well, we do know about it," Claudia said. "And we're in this now. So consider us legacies."

I didn't care about institutional memory. "You're after Dmitri?" I asked Will.

His expression didn't belong in that sunny courtyard. It belonged among gravestones, on a battlefield, in a morgue, not within sight of laughing, chatting Berliners. "Yes. And I want you to go after him. I want you to wear a wire and lure Dmitri out into the open so we can get him."

I didn't know how angry I was at him, and Claudia and Gerry, at that very moment until I actually stood up. Growling, I felt the pull of Claudia's suggestion and ignored it. Will was back in my life, but was endangering Danny by being here. They'd told him everything; everyone knew more than me. I was nothing but a pawn to any of them.

"We told you back in Boston," Gerry said. "Dmitri is not just a threat to Normals interfering with his illegal activities. He wants to *become* Fangborn. He doesn't understand. It's birth, not biting, not a spell, not a curse. He's not only a danger to the human world, he also threatens us. Anything that draws attention to our existence is a threat. Right now, we're very vulnerable."

"It is possible, too," Claudia said cautiously, "that the objects he's seeking do have some power. We don't know what, but it's imperative we find them first."

I didn't care what Dmitri was, not really, beyond his present role in my life. It didn't matter how awful he was. I hated how casually they were willing to risk my life and Danny's to get what they wanted.

So far from hiding, I was now out in plain sight, with people I needed to trust using my existence to further their own ends. So far from avoiding authorities and other Fangborn, I was at the center of multiple conspiracies I knew nothing about. The security and anonymity I'd worked so hard for were only illusions, shattered by friends.

A last tug, like fingers losing their grip, and all sensation of Claudia's restraint left me with an almost physical *snap*. I fled downstairs and into the toilets, which were unisex stalls with a common sink area. I closed a door behind me and tried to get it together.

A moment later, a creak of the door, and a pair of women's shoes were visible beneath the stall.

"Go away, Claudia. I...just give me a minute." No response, but a folded piece of paper slid between the door and the stall partition.

I took it, realizing that the feet I saw didn't match Claudia's. She wouldn't wear green suede sneakers.

I took the paper and unfolded it.

It read: *The phone on the sink is now yours.*

As I stepped out, the phone rang. I slipped the earpiece on and pressed the button.

"Yes?"

"You are speaking to an agent of the United States government."

It was Dmitri. How the hell—?

"Yes, but I didn't know he—he found me! How did *you* find—?"

"You must leave him. Immediately. Very much depends on it."

"How am I supposed to do that?" I wasn't about to offer up that I was with two Fangborn. Shedding them wouldn't be easy.

I heard a scream. My blood stopped in my veins and froze to ice.

It was Danny.

Dmitri came back on the line. "Tell him you are going to meet me at the Natural History Museum, near the Berlin Central Station. One hour. This is what he expects, no? When the time comes, I will give you your true destination."

"What *time?* What are you talking about?"

"There will be trouble; I have unearthed one traitor. Do your best not to be killed or captured."

Captured? "Killed? By *who?* And you'd better let me see Danny, or I swear to God—"

The discussion ended with a click.

"You stupid, goddamned—"

The door opened, the same creak as before alerting me. I had just enough time to shove the new phone into my pocket.

It was Will.

"—showing up with all these demands on me!" I turned, glared at him as if he was the one I'd been cussing.

He reached into his pocket and pulled out a wire and a small battery pack. A roll of surgical tape. While he was distracted, I grabbed the earpiece and shoved that into my pocket, acting like I was ready to pull my hair out.

It wasn't hard.

He held up the wire, waiting.

I lifted my hands in resignation. Between Will and Dmitri, what choice did I have? "I need to know one thing first."

"What?"

"Tell me you weren't dating me because I…of what I am."

Will closed his eyes, tilted his head, and pursed his lips. It was the face he made when he was trying not to smile. I'd seen him employ it a hundred times with freshmen. "You asked me out, remember?"

"Yeah, but—"

"But what? But I made you want me? I made you wait for nearly a whole year? Yeah." He nodded, letting a faint smile appear. "I'm that good."

I shrugged. I was too confused and upset for humor.

"Zoe, I dated you, I lived with you, I loved you for no other reason than *you*. Right up to the point where you broke my heart." He thought about it for a moment. "However unselfishly, you broke my heart."

His words were simple, but they felt real, honest to the core. It wasn't the Beast but knowing Will that told me that.

Will cleared his throat. "The wire is just a precaution," he said, back to business. "We have plenty of circumstantial evidence on Dmitri, but if we can add Danny's kidnapping, so much the better. Much less likely he'll wiggle out of extradition if the Normal authorities get hold of him first."

He paused, looking uncomfortable. Not knowing where to start.

There was no time to process my misery. Dmitri was waiting. I lifted my shirt. "Go ahead. It's not like you haven't seen them before."

I tried not to jump when I felt his hands on my skin. I noticed he tried to touch me as little as possible.

The flood of happier memories—so out of place at the moment, so badly missed—made me turn away from the mirror. I couldn't look myself in the eye. I sure as hell couldn't look at him, not when I was about to spoil his plans for capturing Dmitri.

"You know," Will said as he worked, "I wouldn't be doing this if I thought there was any real danger to you. I would never do anything to hurt you."

He let his hand rest on my side. I let him. It felt warm, the skin of his hand a little rough. I wanted to embrace him; it felt right, but I didn't have time for right. Neither of us did.

He nodded, then turned away, gathering up his materials. "But what am I saying? You were almost always brave. Maybe not trusting, but brave."

He said it kindly enough, factually, trying to be nice, trying to reassure me. Maybe trying to mend what was between us, and just for that, I wanted to kiss him. I owed him something, at least for what I was going to do, which would probably ruin his career and cause havoc with the international antiquities and Fangborn communities, but never mind.

He hadn't heard Danny's scream.

I couldn't bring myself to kiss Will, though I knew the signs: he wanted to kiss me. A little human, hell, even superhuman contact wouldn't have been amiss, as I might be dead within the next few hours. Almost, I leaned in—I could smell his hair, remembered how his lips felt—but I just couldn't do it. If I did, I'd give in to my emotions, and I needed to stay sharp.

"Look. I'm…sorry." I took his hand, not trusting myself to move closer. "I'm sorry for leaving you. My God, I'm sorry I didn't find a way to figure out what was going on with me sooner. I didn't know whether I was a mental case, a murderer, or a werewolf, or some of each."

I shuddered, remembering the recurring nightmare where I savagely turned on Will and killed him. "All I could think was that I needed to protect you. There was nothing permanent in my life then, not even my human shape. But now I know: I'm a monster, not just a ghost who passes through other people's lives. At least a monster can apologize."

"Zoe, you're not a monster. I understand. I *know* all about the Fangborn."

"Yeah, but I don't." Damn it, now I was starting to cry. I snuffled and wiped my eyes with the back of my hand. If I started now, I wouldn't stop. "That's the problem. I have no time to learn what I am, what you and I…"

"Zoe—" He leaned toward me.

What the hell, I thought. I tilted my head up—

The door opened. It was Claudia this time. She was holding the cell phone I'd originally been given by Dmitri. It was ringing.

"I think it's time, guys." She handed it to me, along with the bag I'd ditched when I'd fled Will.

I hit the button and juggled the phone as I confirmed the figurines were still safe. "Yes?"

A voice, gruff, accented, but not Dmitri's. "Don't forget what you were told before."

"Yes."

"One hour."

The connection was broken. I turned to them and shrugged. "I have to be at the Natural History Museum in an hour."

"OK," Will said. "We know what we're doing."

I most certainly do not. But with any luck, I'll figure out how to keep Dmitri from killing Danny.

Will hadn't noticed I'd checked out. "I'll get my people into place; they're already making sure we're not being tracked ourselves. Claudia, if you and Gerry are still willing…?"

She nodded. "We're on it."

"Then let's get going."

Their plan was this: I'd do just as I was told. Will's people from the TRG would be surrounding the area, ready to snag Dmitri and his men, or, barring that, follow me if I got further instructions. Gerry and Claudia would wait in reserve, ready to follow me if a change of tail—as it were—turned out to be necessary.

Doing as I was told, by anyone, was not my strong suit. I began to sweat. Will might have loved me, but now the only thing he wanted was to catch Dmitri. I couldn't risk him jeopardizing Danny. I had no intention of obeying Will, and would shortly dodge out to my real rendezvous with Dmitri. And since I was going to use every bit of guile I had to thwart Dmitri once I got there, I wasn't feeling very sanguine. The minimum I could hope for was to rescue my cousin, giving up the figurines in return.

And if all else fails, maybe Dmitri'll take a broken werewolf in exchange for Danny.

Chapter 15

I wasn't thinking clearly about my plan, but at one point, when I stopped to retie my shoe, I grabbed a loose half of a cobble and stuck it in my hoodie pocket. I also inserted the earpiece to the new phone.

It wasn't a long walk back to the Oranienburger Strasse S-bahn stop, but it took longer than it should because everyone following me was trying to stay at a distance from everyone else. Even though I was nearly jumping out of my skin with impatience and fear, Fangborn instinct told me it must be obvious to anyone we were all moving in a big block, heading to the same destination. Every once in a while, I would see Will mumbling something to no one in particular, and I knew he was talking to unseen others. Thing was, I could start to *sense* these others, fit them into the grid they'd learned in whatever training they'd had. Once or twice I tried to sniff the air, but I couldn't smell anything over the city smells. Even when I couldn't see them directly, the idea of Will's team surrounding me was very strong.

I purchased my fare and got on the next train. I had barely settled into my seat when my phone vibrated. I turned it on, as nonchalantly as I could, as if I was looking at a map route. There was a hiss in my earpiece.

"Get out at Friedrichstrasse. Lose them there. Then go to Brandenburger Tor."

The plan had been for me to change lines for the train at Fried-richstrasse to the Natural History Museum. I hoped to be able to lose Will there, then continue underground. "Got it," I mumbled, moving my lips as little as possible.

Late afternoon crowds started to fill the platforms. I stood up and paced, as if I was anxious. Not a stretch. I could see Will watching me, and sensed there was at least one other of his people nearby. I smiled briefly, nervously, and tried to focus on the map of the subway line. I couldn't keep anything in my head for more than two seconds.

The stop came, the platform teeming. I was pushed aside by a group of schoolchildren, and trying to find a clear spot, I slipped out.

It was just a moment, then I could feel panic radiate around me as Will and his team realized I was no longer on the train. I pushed through the crowd, losing myself, and before he could get out, Will was trapped on the departing train.

I wasn't alone yet. I sensed others nearby, so I dashed across the street, entering the main part of the station. I hoped I wouldn't lose my own way in the snarl of U-bahn, S-bahn, and tram lines, a maze of concrete and yellowish tile on several lev-els. To make matters worse, there was an underground mall so commuters didn't have to go above ground to shop on their way home. Eventually I felt Will's teammates fade from my aware-ness and, with a few false starts, wound my way back to the correct line.

Shortly after, I got out at Brandenburger Tor. It was a relief to get above ground again. It didn't take long to see my destination, a large, open space several blocks straight down the shop-lined Unter den Linden.

I hurried, not knowing how much time I would have before they found me again. I wasn't so sure I wanted Dmitri to find me either, but I had to see him.

I hoped to hell I had the heart to do what I was about to do.

The phone buzzed again as I walked down the historic street, past the restaurants and coffee shops, trying not to look like someone for whom the world was about to end. I answered.

"Look up. The Hotel Adlon is on your left. Three floors up."

I pulled off to the side of the sidewalk, out of the flow of tourists. I was looking in the right direction a moment before I saw it: a hand was waving out an open window above the ground floor canopies.

I held up my own hand.

Suddenly Danny appeared.

"I see him."

He looked dazed, his eyes not focusing on mine; he'd been drugged. There was a bandage on his hand, and I could see a bruise on his face, but apart from that, he was alive and intact. The facade of the hotel was far too elegant a setting for a prisoner exchange, I thought. He was pulled back, the curtain falling back into place.

"Now go straight into the Pariser Platz," Dmitri whispered into my ear. "It's the open pedestrian square directly ahead of you. I'll walk to the far side with you, by the Brandenburg Gate, to make sure you weren't followed. When I see you've given me what I've asked you for, I'll let your cousin go."

I glanced down to the square, a wide space surrounded by low, modern buildings, the famous neoclassical eighteenth-century gates topped by a chariot driver and horses. I walked in.

I stopped just inside the square, found one of the concrete stanchions meant to stop vehicular traffic, and pulled out the figurine. And the cobble I'd stashed in my pocket. I set the figurine on the top of the stanchion and rested my hand on the cobble.

"Your cousin's life—"

"Is about to improve, big time. You bring him down here, let him go, and I don't smash what you've been making me work so hard for."

"But—"

"And you'd better do it quick because Will MacFarlane and his people will find me any minute." I hoped to hell Gerry and Claudia, with their superior tracking abilities, wouldn't find me too soon and spoil my plan.

A large man appeared out of nowhere. How he'd been concealed, I couldn't have said, because there was no place to hide. And he was enormous, like something out of the circus, dark-haired with muscles that looked like the result of chemical enhancement. Though he was clean-shaven, Dmitri filled me with the same kind of dread I felt as a child seeing Stromboli in *Pinocchio*. He was dressed like a tourist from anywhere, but I knew he wasn't as soon as he moved. Everything about him said predator, and there was an attitude that seemed to create a force field around him. People, not even aware of doing it, were giving him a wide berth.

My Fangborn instincts roused. My fingernails and teeth *ached*, as if the only thing that would ease the pain would be to tear his throat out. There was a thin, disagreeable smell filling my head, like mustard gas in my brain. I forced myself to be calm. I couldn't afford to Change, not here.

And yet…something was wrong. Dmitri was…worried. His type never worried about anything.

It wasn't my pitiful attempt to ensure our escape that worried Dmitri. It was bigger than that. But whatever it was might work for me. That gave me courage, and courage gave me control.

I had about twenty steps before he reached me. He nodded and gestured at the window, and I knew, even as he growled intimately into my ear, that he was only pretending to let Danny go.

As he approached, I tried the trick of locating people around me. Will was nearby, and though I couldn't see him, I could just about smell him. He was moving in fast. There were more vague sensory blurs of his team closing in around me from the busy street beyond the gate itself and behind me, on Unter den Linden. This wasn't what bothered Dmitri, though. He spared two glances, one at the window and one across the plaza.

Dmitri was confused. Someone was coming, someone he feared.

He was within speaking distance of me when he held out his hand. "Give it to me now, and I will ensure your cousin's release."

My knees shook, but I straightened my back. "Not until I see him out here."

"We don't have any time, you little fool!"

I made myself shrug. "I got all the time in the world, now that we're here together."

"We're both in danger! I've been be—"

Before he could finish "betrayed," he was tackled from the side. "Tackled" was too strong a word for how it *looked* as a man nearly the same size as Dmitri slammed into him. It looked accidental, but I could tell it was a carefully choreographed move. The blond American—he could be nothing else with that huge build and Red Sox cap—might have been apologizing loudly, but he was also pinning Dmitri's left hand.

Dmitri shoved him with such violence that the second man collided with two other men. Still the American held onto him. These men all looked less like tourists and more like they were here for the same reason the rest of us were.

Only I was unfamiliar with these new players.

Dmitri tried to twist away from the big American. Two more men landed on top of the struggling men. My Fangborn senses flared and went wild. Claudia and Gerry were on the other side of the plaza, also scuffling with men I didn't recognize.

I froze, not certain what to do.

Suddenly my eyes fixed on Dmitri's neck. It wasn't the killing urge I'd had before; there was something there, claiming my attention.

Something on a thin gold chain. Something I *needed*.

Two of the men pulled Dmitri back. I could see the chain and the small object on it clearly now. Without thinking, I darted in and grabbed it.

Dmitri roared.

The big American suddenly noticed me. Our eyes locked, even as I backed away, and he stepped forward. There was an intensity and single-mindedness in him that scared me.

He believes he's on the side of right, something told me. *He'll never stop until he gets what he's after.*

I felt a growl, deep in the back of my throat, and stepped forward.

Our staring contest had distracted the blond too long. One of Dmitri's men grabbed him and punched him, hard. One of the other men yelled, "Nichols! Adam, look out!"

The spell was broken.

Something drew my attention away from the melee.

Danny was being bundled into a waiting car.

I stepped forward to give chase. Someone slammed into me.

"*Entschuldigen Sie!*" Police officers had arrived. One grabbed me, set me aside. "Best get out of the way."

I nodded, but when I turned back, the car with Danny was gone.

Dmitri was screaming.

He was screaming to *me*.

He wasn't speaking English. He repeated the words, followed by something else. "*Quadriduum, ad Delos, iuxta cavalli!*"

This time I did understand, barely. He must have seen the light of recognition in my eyes.

"Go!" He turned his head and bit the hand of the man nearest him. He might not be a werewolf, but I saw blood run from the wound as I turned.

I couldn't see Will, but heard a familiar yell. Even then, I could only sense him in the thick of the fray.

"Damn it, Zoe!"

The confusion now was massive and getting worse. Civilians were screaming, and I could hear sirens closing in.

There was nothing I could do here.

Danny was gone.

I took Dmitri's advice and ran.

As though by magic, a narrow path opened to me through the confusion, and I took it, pelting as hard as I could. All around me I could feel familiar presences, was nearly overwhelmed with the raw emotion spilling out.

I put all that aside and concentrated on running as fast as I could across the wide plaza.

The famous Brandenburg Gate was a white blur as I raced through. I seemed to know where pedestrians would be before they arrived. Maybe it was scent? Maybe my newfound proximity sense?

Traffic was another situation. Maybe it was the lack of human scents. A lack of common sense.

I dove out onto the busy street, felt the whoosh of a bus go past as I stopped just in time. Three stutter steps and I made it to the other side and the Tiergarten. I went north, using what cover there was, and ran past massive modern architecture. My memory nearly failed me, but I slowed down and saw the massive train station on the other side of the river.

If I was breathing hard, it was only because of fear. I felt as if I could have run all day.

The more I embraced the Beast, the closer to the surface it seemed to be. If I was terrified of it, at least it was *fast*, even when I wasn't fully Changed. And at the moment, I was more afraid of the men at the Pariser Platz than I was of the Beast.

I slowed to a normal pace. I couldn't see anyone following me, couldn't feel anyone looking for me nearby. Just in case, I got into a cab.

"Tegel Airport, *bitte*," I said to the driver.

He grunted, "*Ja*, Tegel," and we were off.

I slunk down in my seat, ripped off the wire and the tape. The pain was sharp, and the tape left an angry red mark. Another wrench, away from Will. I stuffed it in the seat cushion, pulled a map from my backpack, and tried to organize my thoughts.

Some of the men had been Dmitri's—now I knew what they looked like. Some of the men I could have sworn I recognized from the airport in Boston.

The ones who'd caused the most confusion were led by the giant blond guy. "Adam Nichols" someone had called him. The fact that he went straight for Dmitri, then me, made me wonder.

For all the secret creatures and societies, I seemed to be the only one on the entire planet who didn't know what was going on. Or what to do next.

The traffic started to clear, and we made good speed. I exhaled hugely. I hadn't realized I'd been holding my breath.

I hadn't understood what Dmitri had said at first because he had been speaking Latin. I didn't understand all of it, like when he'd said something that I thought was a noun, *cavalli*? Something about horses? Or like the designer's name? But I had understood "Delos" and "in the space of four days." Four days would be Monday.

For some reason, Dmitri needed me to find out what "cavalli" was, and then be on the Greek island of Delos by Monday.

Chapter 16

Why did "cavalli" sound so familiar? And why was Dmitri, a vicious criminal, appearing to help me? If he really wanted to help, where was Danny? And why was he busting out the dead languages?

He didn't want the guy attacking him—Adam Nichols?—to know what he was saying, or he didn't want to make it easy for him. It sure wasn't easy for me; I got through my two years of Latin mostly by the skin of my teeth, picking out the cognates, using rote memory, and peeking at the back of the book.

And yet the word "cavalli" seemed familiar. It was a new memory, but try as I might, I couldn't place it in any of the conversations I'd had recently. Maybe I hadn't heard him right or maybe I hadn't translated it properly. I didn't understand and it would have to wait. I had a destination.

When we arrived at the airport, I paid the driver, then looked around for potential pursuers. Inside the long, curved stretch of terminal, I was suddenly lost. I was hungry, hunted, and had no idea where Danny was.

Delos it was. It made a kind of sense: Delos was one of the sites Grayling had mentioned to me back in London.

Thing is, a little web search revealed an ancient Greek truth: you can't get to any of the Mediterranean islands quickly. Delos, in particular, seemed unusually awkward: I'd have to travel to Athens, then to Naxos or Mykonos, then take a taxi or a tour boat to

Delos. Part of the problem was that Delos wasn't actually an inhabited island—it was a holy site, an ancient sanctuary and temple to Apollo. No hotels, no airstrips, no nothing, besides the ruins and a little museum. Apart from the archaeologists living there during work season, no one else was supposed to be there.

It looked wonderful. The more I saw of the tiny pictures on my phone's screen, the more I longed to be there. I wondered if they were hiring.

"Zoe!"

Spell broken, I whipped my head around.

It was Sean.

"Zoe, wait up!" He pushed his way past a woman wrangling two trolleys, a toddler, and a mountain of luggage. She shouted something angry at him in German. He nodded and waved without turning around.

"How did you get here?" I glanced past him. She was still shouting.

"What do you mean? I was out for a walk, I saw you go running past. I yelled. You didn't even hear me." He shrugged. "I had a hard time keeping up with you, but I saw you get into the cab, I followed you in another."

"What about Will?" His story was a little too pat for my taste. "Claudia, Gerry?"

"What about them—wait! Will's here? Will *MacFarlane*?"

"Yeah." Maybe Sean didn't know Will's real job and why he might be on the wrong side of the world with me. "Uh, you didn't see the fracas in the Pariser Platz?"

"I saw a crowd there, but it's always crowded. Then I saw you. You sure it was Will?"

"Um, long story." I turned back to my search. This time I tried searching for "Cavalli," capitalized and paired with "archaeology."

"Well, wherever you're going, I'm coming."

His insistence surprised me. "OK." I looked up from my phone. "Just give me a minute." I glanced down: I got a more reasonable result and realized I'd seen the name of a scholar named Antonio Cavalli in Professor Schulz's article. I struggled to dig out the article and not get crushed by the growing crowd. I flipped through the pages.

I found the footnote. Antonio Cavalli had written an article on Hesiod and the myth of Pandora's Box, which had been cited by Professor Schulz. Dr. Cavalli was based at the archaeological museum in Venice.

I did some quick calculations and figured I could make it to Venice and Dr. Cavalli before I left for Delos. I could still make it to Delos by Monday, if I timed it all perfectly, if there were no flight problems, none of the famous Italian strikes, no bad weather...

What were the chances of that, with my luck?

On the other hand, if I found something to help me, it would be worth it. And Dmitri could call me anytime he wanted if I was late.

"Come on, Sean. Let's find a flight to Venice."

I have to admit, I thought about ditching Sean a couple of times. He seemed out of it, a little dazed. Fine, I was exhausted, too, but there was too much to explain, and I wasn't certain he'd believe me if I did tell him. If he could extricate himself now, at least he'd be safe.

He never gave me a chance to slip away. The long line of ticket counters was confusing enough, but the crowds didn't allow a quick exit.

But as I paid for our two tickets with Dmitri's credit card, I admitted I still wanted Sean around. He kept me from feeling so incredibly alone.

The flight was short but late in the evening. In Venice, we found a tourist hotel by the Grand Canal on the far edge of San Marco and got two rooms. Hey, if Dmitri could order me all over the world, he could spring for a little privacy. I was starving and we managed to find a restaurant still open. We ate in a leisurely fashion, not out of manners, but because the waitstaff were moving on a schedule that had no regard for a young werewolf's appetite.

"You gonna tell me what happened back there?" Sean gestured with his glass of limoncello. "It's not like there's anyone to overhear us now. I really want to know."

"It's simple. I went to meet Dmitri. Some kind of fight broke out, and before I knew it, Danny was whisked away." I shrugged, chasing a last bite of gelato around my plate. "I'll go to Delos because Dmitri told me to, but I think I might find more information about...the figurine I have from Dr. Cavalli."

"Oh."

I was glad it made sense to Sean. I could barely keep up with the number of lies I was being forced to tell.

A shadow crossed Sean's face. "But you said that other guy was beating on Dmitri. How do you know he'll even be able to get to Delos by Monday? He might be arrested, or dead even. I think you should stay here until you learn more. Safer that way."

I shrugged. "You may be right, but until I hear otherwise, I'm going to keep the appointment."

Back in my room, my hunger temporarily assuaged, I studied the map. I located the Museo Archeologico on San Marco plaza and figured I'd try tomorrow, early enough that I could leave for Athens and get to Delos without delay.

But what was I supposed to do once I found Dr. Cavalli? Dmitri was too busy getting his head pounded in to elaborate. I guess Dr. Cavalli might tell me something more about Pandora or what my figurine might have to do with the myth.

Thinking of my figurines, I pulled them out to make sure they were intact. All was well, but when I cleaned out the rest of my backpack looking for my toothbrush, I found the gold chain I'd snatched from Dmitri's neck.

What had drawn me wasn't the gold chain, but the object hanging off it. Three slender bands of gold held a fragment of pottery, like a porcelain doll's arm. I worked the bands off with a pair of tweezers and examined the fragment more closely. It was an outstretched arm, holding some sort of wand or staff.

I removed the figurines from their box and unwrapped the one my mother had taken from my father. The one with the arm missing. Dmitri's fragment matched perfectly; I could have repaired it if I had any glue. I held the two pieces together; the wand now suggested the male figure was a priest of some sort. Maybe a general? That wand was definitely a symbol of some kind of authority.

I still didn't know who or what the figure represented, but it raised more questions.

Rupert Grayling had mentioned colleagues, other collectors in search of what I believed were Fangborn artifacts, possibly including Pandora's Box. Berlin had revealed the presence of government authorities who knew and sought control over the Fangborn. Clearly, many more people knew about the Fangborn than was good for me. They might be connected, but there was also animosity among them, given Grayling's murder and the American who assaulted Dmitri. Could I use that strife to my advantage? Might there be allies for me there?

Dmitri had a fragment of an artifact that had belonged to my father. He looked nothing like the picture I had, so I knew Dmitri couldn't be my father. But what was their connection? What could he tell me about Dad?

An obstacle in the shape of a vaporetto strike greeted us in the morning. It was challenging, navigating the walk to Piazza San Marco through the curving canals and labyrinthine streets; the waterbuses would have made it easier, and it would have been fun to see Venice by water. The houses were tall and narrow, pale shades of yellow, pink, green, and white, humped in against each other on the tiny blocks surrounded by water. Occasionally we'd encounter an open space, a *campo* or little plaza, each with the neighborhood church situated on one side, with a fountain in the center of the square. The traffic on the canals was busy so early in the morning. There were boats for everything we might have trucks for at home: vegetable deliveries, post, police, construction.

There were twists, there were turns, and we had to backtrack a couple of times, but strolling along the confusing, narrow streets and canals was the most relaxing thing I'd done in I didn't know how long. The smell of stale water and the sight of stray cats nibbling on the fish bones left for them was a relief after the bustle of Berlin and so many airports. Even Sean seemed a little more like his old self after a good night's sleep.

By the time we got to the Museo Archeologico, St. Mark's Square was filling up with tourists and those who would make money from them. Though I couldn't for the life of me understand why visitors would pay to feed the pigeons and, worse, to have someone photograph them with pigeons on their heads, I shrugged. It paid someone's rent.

The museum was still closed, so we strolled back into the square. It was odd, being someplace I'd only ever seen through movies—you don't expect it to be real. But the brick campanile tower, the pink-and-white lacy marble confection of the Doge's palace, and the imposing dome of the basilica of San Marco were real enough, as were the ranks of motorboats bobbing at the bank of the Grand Canal. It was almost impossible to imagine that real people lived and worked here.

Winged lions guarded the city from the tops of pillars and on towers, and made me wonder if the symbol of the city had roots in an antique Fangborn past. The more I looked, the more I thought I saw evidence of the Fangborn in every piece of art and sculpture.

I wondered how effective the Fangborn veil of secrecy was; I felt I was seeing them everywhere.

But Sean didn't seem to be enjoying Venice the same way and was by turns out of it or uneasy. Which was fair enough; jet lag and an unexpected trip would have been enough, but the reasons for both were pretty screwed up. He had no real reason to be here; for me, the sights provided an opportunity to forget Dmitri for a moment. By rights Sean should have been back in Boston, no part of this.

Inside San Marco, the basilica was dark and cool. The glittering mosaics that covered the ceiling kept us staring up until our necks hurt. I felt as if I was at the crossroads of the East and West, with the influence of Asia and Europe blending, and Sean and I whispered furiously, comparing what we saw with what we knew from classes. We both were agog; having been convinced that we knew the cultures, we knew the art, surely the real thing would disappoint? It did not. In the Doge's palace, which had housed courts and prisons as well as the Doge, we saw ornate reception halls, walls and ceilings covered in masterpieces of art and gilding. Even with all that splendor and history, I couldn't quite stop giggling at the ornate silliness of the Doge's hat, with a knob standing up in back. It was funny to see Sean, who usually put such a premium on maintaining an unimpressed attitude, with his mouth hanging wide open. For a little while, sharing that enthusiasm was like old times.

The museum was just opening as we arrived. Nervously I asked at the desk to speak to Dr. Cavalli. The guard eyeballed me, made a hushed call, and gestured to a bench.

"I didn't know you speak Italian," Sean said as we sat.

Wait till you hear me howl, I felt like saying. "Mama Luongo. She taught me when she babysat."

A woman approached, looking harried. In fact, I'd noticed most of the Venetians I'd seen seemed perpetually harried, but maybe it was just a cultural perception.

I greeted her in Italian.

She conducted her half of the conversation in reasonable English.

"I am so sorry to say to you. Dr. Cavalli is dead, several weeks ago."

My heart sank. I'd wasted valuable time when I could have been hightailing it to Delos. "Dead? Was it...an accident?"

Her face softened. "No, no, he was very old. A little sick, then at home, in bed. I would wish the same for myself." The harried look returned. "Is there something I can help you with?"

"I wanted to ask him about a pottery figurine. Greek."

"Ah, well, Greek writers, Greek religion, that was his specialty. Myself, I know nothing, nothing about them. Etruscans for me. I am sorry I give you bad news."

She seemed so adamant, I couldn't press the issue. "Thank you for your time."

"*Prego. Ciao.*"

I left, nodding to Sean, who'd been studying the map I'd left with him.

"No luck. *Il professore* died. Couple weeks ago." The bright sun greeted us outside and I admitted to myself that I was lost. "Maybe Dmitri meant to send me to where Dr. Cavalli excavated, on Delos?"

"Seems kind of an obscure thing to say to someone while you're getting your ass handed to you," Sean said. "'Ouch!' or 'Get your ass to Delos!' would have been more efficient. Instead, he yells in Latin? Screwy. Are you sure you got the Latin right?"

"I think so. And I think he was just trying to keep what he wanted me to do secret," I said. "Keep it from the other folks there?"

"It was a little too cryptic if you didn't get it either," Sean pointed out. "Maybe you're overcomplicating it. Maybe you misunderstood and you're meant to stay in Venice."

"How am I overcomplicating? I'm on an international trek to rescue my cousin, being chased and beat up by bad guys from many nations. How could I possibly make it *more* overcomplicated?"

"Well, maybe what he meant was this." He pointed at the map. There was the Via Cavalli, very close by. "Maybe it wasn't a person. Maybe that's, like, a common name or something, and there's something you should see *here*."

I shook my head. "Yeah, right, but remember, Dmitri didn't tell me to go to Venice. Let me see." I stared at it, then handed the map back to him. A tickle at the base of my skull prompted me to agree—the Beast, or Fangborn instinct, was urging me on. *Holy shit.* It couldn't really be what I was looking for? "OK, whatever. Might as well check it out, since it's so close."

I would have apologized for snapping at Sean if he hadn't been so obnoxiously pleased with himself, pointing out his excellent eye, his awareness of detail, and how he'd probably saved the day all the way to the Via Cavalli. In fact, he took it so far, I was starting not to enjoy the few more blocks of Venice I was going to be allowed before catching the flight to Athens.

"Yes, yes, you rule and I drool. I *get* it already, Sean. Enough, OK?"

"I'm just saying." He shut up, but still radiated insufferable self-justification all the way there.

When we reached Via Cavalli, however, I could see nothing obviously helpful.

"What are we looking for?"

That was a good question. Antiquities? Werewolves? Pandora's Box? Venice was pretty, ancient, and a cultural nexus, but it wasn't offering me any answers. "Dmitri is interested in antiquities relating to…Greek religious artifacts," I said, carefully vague. "He seems obsessed with acquiring them." Because he mistakenly believes they will help him become a werewolf, if Will and the Steubens were to be believed.

"Antiquities have a habit of moving around the world and Venice was always an important market." I glanced at the row of houses, the edge of the canal one last time. Nothing.

"Zoe, even if you find this thing…Dmitri may just kill you once you give it to him, right?"

With everything that had occurred in the last few days, I'd become inured to the idea. I didn't want to bring up that I was trying to keep Sean out of danger, too. "That's why you're here, right, boy-o? To protect my delicate pink self?"

"Oh." Pondering that, Sean was quiet. "We could wait for reinforcements. The Steubens?"

"They might be in jail, too, for all I know."

We looked as closely as we could without actually climbing inside someone's house. We took a break, found a place for espresso and drank without talking. Something of the Beast pushed me, so we returned just before dusk for one last look, not very hopeful.

I combed the street side again, trying to think of what Dmitri might have wanted me to see here. There was nothing. This was a meaningless detour, confusion on my part, a delusion to make sense of what I'd been told about the Fangborn. I sat down on the stone bench in the sun, checking the flights to Athens on my phone. There were a couple, none of them nonstop, but I was still on schedule to get to Delos in time.

I wasn't ready to give up yet. The Beast was telling me to wait, and I was learning to listen.

I sagged a little, let the sun soak in. Felt the grooves in the warm, rough stone beneath my fingers.

Grooves?

I stood up so quickly, I caught Sean—who'd been leaning over me—under the chin with the top of my head. Mutual "ows" and glares ensued, and when my eyes stopped watering, I pointed.

The stone bench was carved with ancient images. I held my hand up to shade my eyes and strained to make sense of the lines.

What I'd at first thought were grooves were the serpent swirls of a caduceus, the staff of Hermes. Snakes.

"Looks Greek to me," Sean said. I felt no urge to explain about the possible Fangborn meaning of snake symbolism.

Antiquities move around. They get reused, reincorporated, reinstated, recycled. What had once been a stone marker for some ancient city was now a bench in a quiet Venetian neighborhood.

A bench fixed to a house. The buzzing in my ears and prickling at the base of my neck got louder, then died away altogether. My hearing sharpened, as did my sight, but it was neither of them that made me look up. It was more as if someone had taken hold of the back of my head and suddenly jerked it, so I couldn't possibly miss what was now in front of me.

Terra-cotta tiles covered the rooftops, some of which were so close they were practically touching. But the tiles weren't the only objects up there. While two of the roofs from separate buildings touched or overlapped, there was one corner where the roofs actually commingled in a design. It surely was no standard form of architecture, but a kind of whimsy, perhaps incorporated when one owner held both houses. Instead of the usual half cylinders, alternating to provide drainage, or the chimney covers, these were unusually ornate corner pieces. They looked ancient; any glaze that had been on them had been worn away over centuries, and as I stared, I realized they had been shaped at one time.

If I squinted really hard, they looked like the heads of snakes. Almost the same configuration as the top of the caduceus, staring at each other. With a significant difference.

There was some kind of clay pot suspended between them.

Anyone else looking up might have only seen a flourish with a knob, a finial, a decoration. Suddenly, to me, it was fraught with meaning.

I knew I needed to get at whatever was in that pot.

"Sean!"

I jerked my head toward the pot, and he understood right away. He sighed but looked around for observers. Seeing none, he laced his fingers together.

I stepped into the cradle of his hands, and we nodded together in time: one, two—

On *three*, Sean heaved me up, and I stretched as far as I could to reach the window ledge on the second floor. I couldn't quite reach it, until Sean pushed me up farther. After some precarious scrabbling, I grabbed the sill. I found a toehold between aging brick and somehow pulled myself up.

"Nice going! Now get it and get down!" Sean hissed from below.

Easier said than done. I squatted in the window, hanging on to the inside of the frame with my left hand while I carefully reached with my right hand.

Three inches too short.

I tried to stand, half-hunched, and reached out.

My fingers brushed the pot. It swung back and forth, and now I could tell it was only attached to the terra-cotta decoration by a thin and rusted wire.

Another inch and I could unhook it.

I stretched with everything I had. Maybe a little more; I felt the Beast growing restless inside me.

Another stretch, and I felt my hand...lengthen. Fingers grew clawlike, bones shifted. I panicked and made another desperate grab at the vessel.

I snagged one of the little handles. The wire snapped and I had the pot. I'd also managed to pull off the corner of one of the terra-cotta decorations.

I lost my balance, nearly toppled over. I held onto the window frame with all my might and righted myself.

The terra-cotta embellishment continued to fall as I watched helplessly.

Craa-aack. Sharp and final, it hit the pavement. The noise echoed through the fading sunlight.

No time to see if anyone heard. I jumped down from the window.

Sean had the sense to not try and catch me.

I landed hard, but rolled, the pot tucked under my arm like a football.

No one else was on the street. No one else had heard.

My epically shitty luck was changing.

I dusted myself off, let Sean help me up. We began walking quickly down the street, back toward Piazza San Marco.

That's when the shout came up.

Two figures from the opposite end of the street were standing under the roofline. They gestured, shouted again, then began to run toward us.

We took off.

Chapter 17

When twilight falls in Venice, the whole city seems to fall into a mystical slumber. The crowds disappear, the fog rolls in over the canals, muffling sounds, and the lack of motor traffic is ever more noticeable. It's eerie, it's evocative, and I hoped it would help Sean and me escape.

The thing was, the prickling at the base of my skull made me more and more certain our pursuers were also Fangborn.

I didn't know—or care—what their politics were. I didn't want more new friends and family. I had stolen something they wanted back, and I couldn't let them have it. Maybe it was something Dmitri had sent me for, maybe it was just dumb luck I saw someone's antique bird feeder on their roof and thought it was an important artifact. Didn't matter. I didn't have time for the luxury of curiosity.

We hid in an alleyway near a shop closed up for the night. I realized it was a shop where they made the straw wrappings for Chianti bottles.

"The guy. On the backpacking-in-Europe show." Sean was wheezing from exertion, and even I was out of breath. "He never hung out. In alleys as nasty as this. The guy on the survival show might have, though."

"This is off the beaten path. A true Venetian experience." I started giggling, until a noise in the middle-distance caught my ear. "We've got to get going, if you can."

He nodded, and we were off again.

An hour or two later, I felt an...absence, as if our pursuers were no longer there. It occurred to me that they had been distracted from us by...what had Gerry called it? The call to Change. Perhaps they'd left off chasing us because something worse, something evil, had come along.

I wasn't sure I liked the idea of some evil in the world actually helping me. First in the cemetery in Cambridge, and now.

I was determined not to think about it. "I think we've lost them. Let's head back to the hotel."

Sean nodded, winded, and we trudged back. He must have been tired because he didn't even ask about the clay vessel. It was unlike him, but it saved me thinking up another story when he just went to his room. I heard a soft thud behind the closed door; I knew he'd just collapsed onto his bed.

As soon as I got to my room, however, I knew I had to examine the pot. It might be nothing, but maybe it would be my ace in the hole in getting out of this alive.

Besides that, I sensed the pot and its contents were hugely... Fangborn. My automatic recognition of it, the way it warmed as I touched it—this was powerful stuff.

My heart fell as I looked inside my bag.

The vessel was ancient, all right. No magic here. It had crumbled to dust.

I upended my bag in hopes of finding a larger piece.

A puff of reddish smoke came down from my backpack. Despairing, I pulled apart my clothes and carefully shook out each bit. Not only was everything I owned coated in fine red dust, but the pot was completely destroyed. I was at a loss to say how it had survived up there long enough for me to pull it down but then had disintegrated in our dash from the house.

I frowned. It had seemed sturdy enough during my fall and chase...

Then I saw the disk lying under a notebook, almost blending with the yellow bedspread. I picked it up; it was surprisingly heavy.

A sharp pain in my finger made me cry out, and I saw a drop of blood on the gold surface. There must be a burr on the metal, I thought, but as I gingerly pulled the disk closer to look for it, a light so bright filled my mind I could no longer see my hand or the disk.

Images followed the light, so many and so fast I couldn't pick any single one out.

I began to recognize the images in a moment, because they were my memories.

I dropped the disk and threw my arm over my face to block it all out.

My head ached as if I'd been clipped with a brick. I tasted copper and bile. When my breathing slowed, I poked the disk, very carefully.

Nothing.

I brushed at the surface with my blood on it, but there was nothing there, no telltale burr, no rough edge I could have cut myself on.

I took a deep breath, then another, and went to the bathroom to wash my hands. I examined my finger carefully, but could see no cut. Nothing to clean out. I rubbed antibiotic ointment into the fingertip anyway before I went out to examine the disk again.

Very, very cautiously I picked it up.

Nothing special happened.

It had to be pure gold. It was so heavy.

It was a very short cylinder, about three and a half inches across and three-quarters of an inch thick. The edges were ornately decorated in a continuous band. The side facing me was blank.

I flipped it over, carefully, carefully. Maybe I had a head-rush, maybe fatigue and my heavy conscience was catching up with me—

I paused.

There were marks. Man-made.

I wasn't breathing as I tried to find the sense in the lines that were fine, but deeply engraved into the surface. Some were curved, some were straight, and—

—and that one was a letter.

It wasn't English or any modern language. It looked like Greek, but while I could recognize the alphabet, I don't read Greek. Some of the letters were…well…archaic looking.

It was the circular form that gave me my first clue. There was a kind of squiggly circle, not entirely closed, that fit inside the edges of the circle. The letters formed four words, distributed unevenly across the surface.

It was a map. The ancient Greeks believed the world was round, the top of a column suspended in space.

Δελφοι.

OK, the first one was delta, and the next, epsilon and lambda… DEL…

Delpoi?

A thought struck me. I got out my phone and Googled it.

Delphi.

I grabbed my recently acquired and well-worn map of Europe, and compared modern Greece with the shape on the gold disk. It was hopelessly crude by modern standards, but even I could make out the stiletto heel of modern Italy, the mainland of Greece, and coastal Turkey. The names were scattered across what today is the Aegean. It didn't take me long to figure out what the words were, but a little longer to determine what they represented.

Delphi. Delos. Didyma. Claros.

There was a kind of mark I couldn't quite read, under Claros, like a compass rose. I assumed it represented the importance of Claros, because, as far as I could remember, compass roses were a later convention.

I knew they were all the sites of temples. More specifically, temples with oracles, all dedicated to Apollo. Importantly, they were places that Grayling had mentioned with relation to the figurines. But what connection might they have to Pandora's Box?

What I'd originally thought was just touristic trash seemed to be connected to some very heavy-duty temple sites. Sites associated with Apollo, sites associated with oracles. Claudia had said there were oracles among the Fangborn. It got me thinking about the snake aspect of the Fangborn; there were many serpents associated with Apollo. Perhaps this was yet another connection.

I had no idea what the disk might mean. Maybe it was nothing at all to do with my problems, a coincidence, but it was probably worth a fortune in gold alone.

As soon as I had the thought, I knew it was incorrect. The disk *had* to be related to my troubles. The reaction I'd had when Sean had pointed out the Via Cavalli, the way the thing had—*tasted* me was what came to mind—when I picked it up the first time; it was finding out who I was. It wanted to be found. It wanted *me* to find it. Somehow the disk was acting on my Fangborn nature.

That scared the shit out of me.

With shaking hands, I photographed all the objects from several angles with my phone. Just to be on the safe side.

Then I crashed. It was morning, just a few hours before we were supposed to leave. I fell asleep, the disk still in my pocket.

When I woke, I pulled apart all my things and set them on the bed, trying to reorganize and take stock. Underwear was becoming a priority and a problem; I was still OK for toothpaste and had one shirt that wasn't covered in red dust.

I pulled out the figurines to make sure they were still carefully wrapped. Realizing the cardboard box I'd kept them in was crushed, I cast about for an alternative.

I picked up my plastic pencil box, removed the freezer bag I had closed around it. Its vibrant yellow had faded over the past twenty years. I emptied out the playing cards and the SuperBalls, and sadly said farewell to Optimus Prime, setting him on the bed-side table. Nice for him to end his days peacefully in Venice.

I carefully tucked the figurines into the box and nodded, sat-isfied. A snug fit, but better protection. I slipped the freezer bag around it, another layer of waterproofing.

The door opened. Sean or the maid. Cursing, I jammed the pencil case into my bag.

"I'll be three more minutes. *Tre minuti, per favore, signora.*"

It wasn't Sean or the maid.

It was Dmitri's attacker from Berlin.

He seemed twice as large as he had in Berlin, close up and personal. Still with the Red Sox cap, blond, and sunburned now. He'd been out in the Italian sun, it seemed. His nose wasn't quite straight, as if it had been broken and badly set. Scary, intense light-blue eyes. "Adam Nichols. I'm a government official."

Government officials were more than eager to tell you which part they represented; this guy was a total phony. "Prove it. Better yet, get out of my room."

He held out a badge for an agency I'd never heard of, signed by Senator Edward Knight. The senator who'd been so very interested in Greek pottery, according to Professor Schulz. The one who was also Fangborn. He seemed to be awfully close to the trail I was on.

I nodded. "I got one of those, too. Came with furry handcuffs and a policewoman's uniform with the breakaway snaps."

"I assure you, my title, my badge, and my power are all quite genuine. I don't want to hurt you—"

"And I don't want to be hurt."

"But I want those figurines you have."

"Can't do it. I need to save my cousin. Dmitri, that guy you were pounding into Silly Putty in Berlin? He's got Danny. I need to meet him with the figurines, or he'll kill Danny." A thought occurred to me, and hope kindled in me. "Or is he out of the picture? Please tell me you locked him up someplace horrible, that he's no longer a threat to me or Danny!"

"Dmitri Parshin got away," Adam Nichols said, his face grim. "You can imagine he's not pleased with you."

I couldn't help it. I swallowed.

"And he doesn't need the figurines anyway, not for what he really wants. Nothing can give him that—not even you, Zoe, with all your powers."

The blood rushed from my face. "What? What do you mean?"

"I mean, Dmitri thinks he can become like you, Fangborn, a werewolf, with the right artifacts, the right spells. Only it's nonsense. You can't be bitten, you can't be made. You can only be born to the fang. You know that, or should." He shook his head. "It's gonna kill him if he ever figures it out."

He had the door blocked. I backed away. "Wait, how do you know this? How do you know about—?"

Adam reached for the backpack in my hands.

I took another step back until I could feel the cool of the wall behind my back, felt the rough stucco through my shirt.

"It will all be easier if you give it to me. Then all of this goes away. It would be a great relief, wouldn't it?" He closed the space between us with two steps, and I was trapped. "I'll get it back where it belongs, I'll capture Dmitri, and your cousin will be safe. All this will be behind you. No more running, Zoe."

His presence was more than menacing: he was very large, very strong, very determined, and at least a little crazy. I'd seen him beat Dmitri like a bongo, and the fact he'd followed me to Italy and broken into my room scared the hell out of me. But I didn't know what he wanted with the figurines, only that his interest in them seemed to make no sense. If they wouldn't turn you into a Fangborn, who cared?

There was no reason for me to believe him. Why did he know about the Fangborn? How did he know about me? There was no time to concentrate for the Beast; there were too many questions.

He reached for my backpack, managed to unclip the flap. He gave me a suggestive leer.

Angered, I jerked it away. "What do you want with Dmitri?"

"Don't be like our friend Grayling in London. The man just didn't know when to let go—"

My eyes widened. Adam snatched the bag away.

The door slammed open, knocking Adam over.

Sean shoved himself through the doorway. "Zoe, trouble! Some guys asking about you downstairs! We gotta go!"

Adam still held onto my now-open backpack, but I refused to let go. He reached inside, grabbed the carefully wrapped yellow pencil box. The slick plastic bag made it slide right out, as if it was jumping into his hand.

"No!" I cried.

"Yeah, now!" Sean said. He grabbed me by the back of my shirt and pulled me from the room. I managed to keep hold of my backpack, because as Adam tried to follow me, Sean stepped in and slammed his fist into Adam's jaw. As Adam crumpled, Sean shoved him inside, slammed the door.

"Sean, he has the—!"

"Doesn't matter what he's got." Sean grabbed my arm, practically dragged me down the stairs. "What you said about those guys in Berlin? We don't get out of here in about five minutes, we're gonna die here."

There was something powerful about the figurines, but I knew they wouldn't make Dmitri a werewolf. But that fact didn't matter much if I wanted Danny back. I still needed them because Dmitri wanted them.

I turned to go back upstairs; the door to my room opened. A gun appeared. Held by a very pissed-off-looking Adam Nichols.

Fuck this. If there was ever a time to unleash the Beast…

I yanked my arm away from Sean, tried to imagine I was squeezing my anger into a box too small for it.

I felt the stirring of the Beast. A prickle at the back of my neck.

"Out the back," Sean hissed.

I squeezed my eyes harder and held up a hand. "Shut up!"

Heavy footsteps coming down the stairs. Doors opening. I opened my eyes and found a little tourist girl staring at me before her mother took one look around and grabbed her back into their room.

There were too many people. Too little time. The Beast was nowhere to be found.

Amateur. Squib. Muggle.

With a curse, I turned back, fled down the stairs.

I ran through the kitchen, glad Sean had gone first. The cook was still screaming and waving her knife around. I didn't need to speak Italian to know how dangerous this shortcut was.

Sean was running blind, no plan in mind. I nearly overtook him when he dove down another alley. Maybe he was trying to lose our pursuers by going off the main tourist track, but we needed to be where we'd blend in.

And where there was bound to be a lot of cops.

I stopped, put my fingers to my lips, and whistled.

It's a piercing noise, one Sean has always hated. He stopped, whirled around, scowling.

I jerked my head and ran. He could follow if he wanted. If he was smart.

What were the chances?

A plan came to me as I ran and made the last corner. Through the archway and into the Piazza San Marco.

A final burst of speed that almost left Sean behind, and I realized I'd just caught a massive break. There, near the Museo. A young *carabiniere*, looking quite sharp in his uniform.

"*Signore*," I began. I spoke rapid Italian, gesturing to the men following us. I could see Adam Nichols and his three men entering the piazza now.

The *carabiniere* had smiled at first, no doubt pleased to see such a prettily flustered foreigner speaking such idiomatic Italian. Then his smile faded, his face grew concerned, and then finally angry. He compressed his lips; another piercing whistle echoed through the piazza.

A squad of young and muscular men, dressed in navy or black uniforms and bristling with automatic weapons emerged from the administrative building behind us.

The *carabiniere* motioned for me and Sean to stay where we were.

Sean looked questioningly at me; I shook my head almost imperceptibly, held up one finger. We had to wait another minute before—

When Adam Nichols and his men reached the piazza, he was surrounded by a grim-faced mob of soldiers all pointing their weapons at him.

When he began to protest—and he did, loudly with gestured Italian and flashing his badge—the soldiers reacted strongly.

I thoroughly approved of their roughness.

Sean was about to step forward and reclaim my possessions when I stopped him.

"You want them to find out all those things are really mine? You want *them* to ask you how I happen to have them? How do you think that will go?"

"I just thought I would help. Sorry."

Since when did Sean voluntarily talk to the authorities? I cast a last desperate look at Adam and realized, even if I had the figurines, Dmitri wouldn't believe me when I told him nothing could make him a werewolf if he wasn't born one.

I thought about the gold disk hidden in my shirt. Maybe I could trade on that if he was into Fangborn weirdness, which this seemed to be in buckets. Or for its monetary and antiquary worth, maybe. That much gold, at today's prices…it was a fortune.

After three eternal seconds, I nodded. "Let's get out of here."

We hurried away, all eyes on the exciting scrum in the center of one of the most popular tourist destinations in the world, and went around the corner and out to the water taxi stand on the Grand Canal. At last, luck was with me and the strike was over, so we jumped on the first vaporetto we found.

The last thing I saw as we passed the lion-guarded columns of San Marco was the team of soldiers piling onto Nichols and his men, now almost invisible beneath them. They handcuffed them as their fellows tore through the contents of their pockets and briefcases.

I thought I saw a flash of yellow plastic, and I turned away in distress. They had my pencil box. They had *everything*.

"What the hell did you tell that guard?" His breath recovered, his ego at full bloom, Sean had admiration enough even for me. "Whatever it was, it worked!"

"I told the guard that there was a man following us who'd been boasting about being able to slip past the border to deal with antiquities. That I'd heard him in the hotel today and that he was showing artifacts around, trying to sell them. I was afraid that he was after us because I told him off."

"And who were those guys? What were they about?"

"The *Tutela Patrimonio Culturale*, the TPC. It's the arm of the *caribinieri* dedicated to the protection of Italian antiquities." I settled back in my seat. I was shaking and sweating now that the moment of action was passed. "You do not want to mess with them. Imagine a group with the obsessiveness of archaeologists and the training and tactics of a SWAT team. With a government mandate to hunt down antiquities thieves."

Sean whistled and suddenly looked nervous. "It's a good thing I didn't run into them when I was at the field school in Ravenna."

I looked up. "What happened in Ravenna?"

"Another time." He ducked down, made sure his pack was secure. "I'm only sorry we couldn't stay to see what happened to that bastard! Who is he? What was he doing in your room?"

"Well, that guy—I think his name is Adam Nichols?—was try-ing to take some…things from me, which he did. Things I needed for Dmitri to save Danny. Things I risked my life for and broke the law for. So we're pretty well screwed."

I shook my head. "I say 'we,' but this isn't your problem. Sean, you should leave."

"Why? Haven't I helped? At the apartment, in the cemetery, at the airport?"

"You have. I'm just worried for you. This situation is getting worse and more complicated and more dangerous every minute."

"Yeah." He glanced out over the canal. He took a deep breath. "But it would be worse for me if you got hurt."

I waved my hand tiredly. "I'm fine, he just scared me."

"No, Zoe. I wouldn't…I couldn't take it if anything happened to you." He turned red and refused to look at me. "It's been like that forever, but you wanted Will."

I felt the blood rush from my face. I would have given anything to stop him speaking. *You'll ruin everything, just don't say it—*

"…And you don't say anything to your best friend's girl. Not unless you're a real shitheel."

I opened my mouth, closed it again. "Sean, I—"

"Don't. Don't say it, I know. And it's fine."

I didn't know what to do. His admission was as unexpected as it was badly timed. Best stick with the simple truth. "You're my friend, Sean. I wouldn't want anything to happen to you. It was bad enough, those, uh, muggers in Boston—"

At the word "Boston," Sean blinked hard and seemed to shiver. "I don't think you should go to Delos. I think you should wait for everyone to catch up to you here."

"But Dmitri said Delos…" Why had he so suddenly switched subjects? "Why do you keep saying that I should stay here?"

"I just have this feeling it will be better to stay put. Stay here, Zoe. Tell Dmitri you'll meet him here."

"I can't. You know that." Sean's sudden change confused me. Why was he so hung up on me staying in Venice? He'd been like that since Berlin. "Danny."

"Danny will be fine. He's got a good head on his shoulders."

Sean said it so mechanically, I stared at him. He didn't look like Sean. He looked...blank. The way he had when Claudia had drugged him.

Except Claudia had no idea where we were.

I summoned up every bit of concentration I had and suggested, as strongly as I could: "Sean, tell me what's happened to you. Tell me who's been talking to you."

"What the hell is your problem, Zoe?" He looked away, confused and angry. "What are you going on about? Why don't you just stay here, let someone else do the worrying?"

Something was wrong. And this wasn't the very public place to try and sort it out.

Someone had got to Sean. Hard, and probably vampirically. I remember wondering why he'd slept so long in Berlin, and now I knew, with an absolute certainty.

A vampire had tampered with Sean. Maybe it was someone working with Adam Nichols and Senator Knight, maybe it was my Fangborn cousins from Boston, but whoever it was wanted Sean to hamper me now, to get the figurines.

I reached down and tightened the straps on my backpack, tucked in my shirt, straightened myself. I took a deep breath. "Never mind, Sean. I'm beat and my brain's scrambled."

I leaned over and gave him a kiss on the cheek. He blushed, raised his hand to the spot, and stared at me.

I felt my eyes fill up and saw the heart of Venice blur behind my tears.

I jumped to the railing of the vaporetto. Screams and curses followed me as I leaped from the boat.

Chapter 18

I landed on the delivery boat at the edge of the canal, stepping over the carefully piled crates of fruit and onto the sidewalk. I ran back the way we'd come until I reached the piazza, where I made for a Blue Line boat to take me to the airport.

When I settled in, I said to myself, *Don't even think about crying.*

I had no figurines and no way to ransom Danny. Even if I did get them to Dmitri, if Adam was right, they wouldn't get him what he wanted.

I knew from what Gerry had told me about the Fangborn who'd escaped Dmitri that no one, least of all me or Danny, wanted him disappointed.

Once at Marco Polo airport, I bought a ticket to Athens and got in line. A slow, bunching caterpillar of tourists shuffled before me.

It was possible Dmitri wouldn't even make it to Delos. In fact, I had to assume Adam Nichols or those Italian vamps or who knows who else would be waiting for me there, despite his precautions.

Sean was bugged—vampirically tampered with, spooked, call it what you will. His insistence on following me so persistently was just odd. Now I knew: he wasn't traveling under his own steam, and I didn't know who had sent him.

I had nothing, not even company now.

And then I realized I had a new disaster.

I had to find a way to get an ancient gold tablet the size of a stack of York Peppermint Patties through customs.

I racked my brain. Despite what I'd seen in the piazza, Italian customs had a reputation for being lax and susceptible to a pretty face. I suspected I was red and sweating and far from my prettiest, but I unbuttoned another button of my shirt and worked on my posture.

Then again, remembering the TCP in San Marco...they could also be fierce. Italians guarded their antiquities jealously.

Was it actually illegal to bring gold out of Italy? Would they even think it was as ancient as I did? It wasn't as if I'd robbed a site—and yes, I was rationalizing—as the building was not more than eighteenth century, maybe, at the most. I tried to tell myself that was nothing really in European terms, but I felt guilty all the same.

Hell, I didn't even know what it was. They might sell them in the souvenir shop for the Festa Santa Fangbornia.

By the time it was my turn, I'd stashed it down the bottom of my bag and was mentally flipping a coin. Heads, it was a story about transporting something for a relative. Tails, it was something I found in a flea market.

I am so totally screwed.

When it was my turn, I smiled briefly, handed over my ticket and passport, and went through the metal detector. So far, so good. The inspectors looked bored as they glanced at the screen, and with some relief, I saw my bag coming toward me.

The belt stopped. Went into reverse.

They were pointing at something on their screen, speaking so low I couldn't hear them.

I began to concentrate. Maybe werewolves had a little suggestive push in their words. Maybe I could just brazen it out. I practiced saying in my head, "What? I'm sure this isn't illegal. You don't want to make me late for my plane."

One of them clicked on his keyboard, frowning.

The phone rang behind them.

"*Si?*" One inspector answered. "*Si. Si. No. Si. Ciao.*"

The belt began to roll again, and I made myself wait until my bag actually pulled up to me before I grabbed it. Made myself walk, not too quickly—I didn't have anything to act guilty about. But not too slowly, either—I had a plane to catch.

It's a lot of work, being a criminal.

I wasn't happy until I was at my gate, and I didn't really breathe again until I was on board and in my seat, the plane taking off.

I fell asleep about two minutes later and didn't wake up until we landed in Frankfurt. I had to dash to make my connection, but with two more connections in about eight hours, I was in Mykonos.

At my last layover, I had done some research, and after orienting myself, I trudged toward a hotel I'd picked at random. I checked in and collapsed.

I woke up, ravenously hungry. I had no idea what time it was, only that I was in Mykonos, the easiest way to get to Delos. I'd remembered eating something at the Venice airport and a cup of coffee and a package of cookies somewhere else, but I think I'd slept through whatever meals had been served.

I went downstairs and had breakfast. OK, maybe three breakfasts; I wasn't worried about dieting and was determined to make the most of Dmitri's credit card until it got refused. Besides that card, I had a bag full of dirty clothes, a little cash, and a couple of cell phones. I had no idea where Claudia and Gerry were, or if they'd survived the fight in Berlin, and I didn't dare call them for fear of leading the wrong people to me.

I didn't dare think about Will and how I'd betrayed him, leaving him in the lurch in Berlin. I didn't dare think about Sean and what he'd confessed in Venice.

So I did what I could. I went upstairs, because it was still early, and rinsed out my other shirt and underwear. My room looked as if it was bedecked for a parade, but smelled a whole lot better. Out my window, it looked like a postcard: white-washed houses and shops along a seawall, bashed by a ridiculously blue sea.

I went out to the harbor, where the water was calmer, to ask about launches to the tiny island of Delos. There were only three a day, all leaving in the morning, all returning in the early afternoon.

Problem was there were none on Monday. Tomorrow, the day when I was supposed to meet Dmitri, was Monday.

I arranged to go on the tour of Delos at noon. I hoped, by going early, I would discover a way to get back on my own later.

But what if Dmitri hadn't escaped Adam during the fight in Berlin? What did I do about Danny then? I hadn't seen a picture of him in some time...

I put that aside and got on the boat.

The trip took longer than the promised thirty minutes. Any thoughts I might have had about whether wolves could swim to the island were banished. The chop was huge, and several of the other tourists looked positively green. Located at the southwestern tip of Mykonos, Delos was a tiny island, long north to south and narrow east to west.

We motored all the way around the northern coast of Delos to the landing on the western side of the island. Most of the major excavations and monuments were clustered on this side, which I knew from the tourist map I'd been given.

Several other groups got out about the same time, but no one I recognized, and no one who might have been a contact from Dmitri.

I only paid half my attention to the guide, who explained that the island was sacred to Apollo and Artemis as the holy twins' birthplace. We tramped over the uneven paths on the rocky island, the astonishing quality of light suitable to the birthplace of a sun god. I was entranced by the ruins of an island city that had been the religious, trading, and political center of the Greek world. The "Lion Terrace," with its guardian beasts, was particularly evocative, and I was not surprised to find out that one of the original lions was now in Venice. The other ruins—the theater, the gymnasium, the opulent houses, the shops, the sacred ways—gave a sense of how big, how important the place must have been.

I had to watch where I was going. Walking around, gape-mouthed and wide-eyed, I'd end up with a broken leg in a drainage ditch. There were ancient pitfalls here.

I spent my time observing, seeing whether there was any way I could sneak away from the group. The guide, however, kept a strict count of her charges, and I had no doubt if she came up short, someone would come looking for me.

You don't mess with a site as holy, as revered as this and expect to get away with it easily.

I'd have to come back on my own, somehow. At least now I had a sense of where to look and what to expect.

I tried once again to slip away from the tour when we were taking a break at the museum and gift shop. Nothing makes a tourist scatter and swarm and lose his mind faster than the idea that someone will get the better souvenir.

The guide was on me as I tried to sneak around the back of the museum.

She smiled the whole time I explained I was looking for the bathroom and pointed out the door, clearly marked with the universally recognizable signage. She also waited for me, chatting the whole time I was in the stall, not giving me a chance to check out the window. There was no way to sneak off from the tour and camp out for the night.

I was practically jumping out of my skin. I couldn't settle down, but I had to accept the fact: unless I heard from Dmitri soon, I was going to have to steal a boat and get over here on my own steam. I didn't know how to sail; I could barely swim.

On the way back, I watched the other tourists cling to the sides of the motor. The seas were rough, even on a nice day, and the waves seemed huge to me.

That got me thinking about Dmitri and how he was likely to react when he discovered I no longer had the figurines. I thought about the pictures of the tortured Fangborn from Gerry's files and didn't like the probable outcome.

But I knew Danny was alive as of yesterday, and where there's life, there's hope. I thought all the way back to the harbor of Mykonos, then spent a few hours shopping. It took me a while to find what I was looking for, in the configuration I needed. Then I crossed my fingers and hoped Dmitri wouldn't see this large cash advance until it was too late.

I sat in my room, staring at my recent acquisitions, thinking how pathetic they were, until I received a text from Dmitri with instructions. I was to meet Nikolas at the marina at three tomorrow morning. He would take me to Delos. It was a relief that problem had been solved for me.

My relief vanished when I saw the latest picture of Danny. I gritted my teeth as I surveyed it. He looked dopey, out of it, and had a bruise and scrape up one cheek. It seemed that Dmitri had taken out his own mistreatment on my cousin. I shut the file and looked at the time: eight o'clock. Only seven hours, then Dmitri would pay for all of this. I don't know how he escaped from Adam, but he wouldn't get away from me.

The phone rang again, this time with a different ringtone. The screen said, "Accept video call?"

I pressed the button.

It was Dmitri, sitting in the shadows. "You got the last photo?"

"Yes."

"Good. Then you will have a baseline."

The phone's camera swiveled away. I saw Danny, tied to a chair, a dirty rag stuffed in his mouth. Another man was looking toward where Dmitri was. He nodded to something off camera, then punched Danny in the face. Blood spurted from his nose and he strained at the ropes around him, his screams muffled by the rag.

Stunned, I screamed into the phone, "Stop it! Why are you doing this? I have what you want, and I'm going to meet you!"

At my voice, Danny lifted his head up. The man punched him again, and I saw a cut open up over his eye. Danny's head sagged.

"Stop it!" I screamed. "Stop it!"

The camera moved, an image of a room blurred, and it was back on Dmitri. "When I find the man who sold me out to Senator Knight, I'll kill him. But I do not forget that you could have given me the figurines in Berlin. Instead, you threatened to smash them. You lost me time, so I take something from Danny."

"I…I—"

"One more time, so you do not forget." He didn't bother to turn the camera back on Danny, just watched my face as I listened to his screams.

He broke the connection.

I put the phone down, then rushed to the bathroom. I made it to the toilet just before I threw up.

There was a knock at the door, someone asking if I was all right.

"The television…I'm sorry. I…I hit the wrong button."

I didn't understand the reply, but whoever it was went away. I sat on the cool, gritty tiles of the bathroom floor, shaking.

Much later, I couldn't stand the confines of my room any longer. The night air helped, a little. I went to the first restaurant I found and sat with a glass of wine—a couple, actually—until just after two in the morning. Anything beat sitting in my room and worrying, waiting for the appointed hour when I would have to successfully break into a holy landmark to rescue Danny.

I was just thinking I should pay my bill and let the staff go home when I saw the couple walking along the rock-bounded promenade.

She was stumbling, and he was laughing as he held her up. She didn't look too good and the salt spray made her appear even more bedraggled.

Honeymooners who'd overdone the partying, I thought as I signed the check. One last meal on Dmitri—

My stomach lurched.

Maybe wine hadn't been such a good idea. I stood up, grabbed my bag, and stumbled away. I'm sure I looked drunk myself, but not on two glasses of white wine—it took a lot more than that. I turned to go back to my room and doubled over. Cramps like I'd never felt before, which seemed to get worse as I moved away. Another three steps, and I could barely move.

I hadn't felt this bad since—

—since the night outside the movie theater.

Oh no. Not now. I couldn't, I didn't have time, I had to go to the marina. Danny—

As soon as I had the thought, I felt better. Even just looking at the couple as they vanished into the distance, I felt better—and worse. A smell filled my nose so bad that I looked around for the dumpster that must be nearby.

No. I didn't have time—Danny's life depended on me being at the harbor in an hour.

The effort it took me to keep going was immense. The pain intensified, and I fell to my knees.

Something bad was going to happen, and I had to try to stop it. Maybe I could stop it and still get back in time to put my plan—

Plans didn't matter. The Beast simply wasn't going to let me turn away from this.

I turned, hitched up my bag, and ran after the retreating couple.

I felt better almost instantly. I felt better than I had since Germany. Stronger. Righter.

It wasn't as hard as I thought it would be to find them. The streets were a maze, narrow, curving. With so many whitewashed shops selling the same scarves, jewelry, and pottery, they all looked the same.

It was the smell that led me to him.

The closer I got, the stronger it became. And the worse it became; if I thought it was an open dumpster by the restaurant, it seemed more like a toxic waste site by the time I found the trail down the darker alleys off the main shopping district. It was as if the stench was hanging in the air, leaving a trail for me to follow. It was so distinct it may as well have been painted on the ground in luminescent green paint.

I was running now, so fast the shops and apartments were a blur of blue-white in the night.

I barreled into an alley that seemed to almost glow with the smell.

The Beast came. I gave in to it, and Changed.

There were none of the tentative prickles I'd felt in the Tiergarten. This was a rush of...everything. Furious glee, joyful rage. Boots gone; no problem. Clothes shredded and tangled; whatever. Killing this monster was worth it. An overwhelming, orgasmic flood only sharpened perception. I barely gave a thought to my backpack and its golden contents as I slid out of it.

The woman was unconscious. The drugs had kicked in—I could smell them now. Awareness grew, but the surroundings faded as I homed in on what was important.

Ending the monster.

He looked up, didn't drop the knife. The woman's blood was a narrow border on its edge. The sight of the blood dripping from the blade dazzled and focused me.

I growled. He smiled.

"Brother wolf, welcome!" he said. "I am happy to share my prey with you."

Psychotic, stupid, *and* an asshole. Couldn't even tell I was a girl-wolf.

I leaped at him, landed heavily. Heard his discomfort with satisfaction.

We bit at nearly the same time. His knife nicked my left paw. I grabbed his shoulder, felt the vise of my teeth crunch through skin, down to bone.

He dropped the knife then. Screeched, twisted, shoved.

Physics is physics. He was huge, I was the same mass I'd always been. I lost my grip, but tore off a large piece of flesh as I rolled away.

Another tingle and sizzle. Oh no, I can't Change back *now*, please, God...

He was scrambling up. I hunched up, launched myself, no thought of my wound, no thought but keeping him here, away from the Normals, the innocents. No thought but killing him.

The sizzle came again, but I didn't turn human. It was familiar, but it only intensified my Beastliness. I slammed into him, my heart joyful—

—as something—a freight train?—nailed me from the other side.

Cobblestones and gravel, over and over, as I tumbled away from the would-be killer. I rolled to my feet, shook my head, and got ready to—

There was another wolf tearing the throat out of the killer.

I shook my head again. A rush of emotion, confusion first and foremost. Then, fear and delight.

The wolf—bulkier and darker than me—worried the corpse a little, then stepped back, turned, and, with his hind legs, kicked disdainful dust over the body.

He raised his head to howl, and I felt drawn to do the same.

Before he could give voice to his victory, a silky voice said, "Thorben—control yourself!"

He froze. If a wolf can look annoyed, he did.

I turned from him and glanced into the shadows, where the woman was still unconscious. A form emerged. Not human—my quick eyes discerned scales and fangs, as well as a general lack of nose, and eyes that were too large and dark to be human.

I stiffened, recognizing their presence, their signature. They were the Fangborn from Venice. They'd come for what I'd stolen from them.

Chapter 19

I backed away from them as fast as I could and stood over my backpack, baring my fangs.

The other wolf responded by turning immediately back into a human. A completely naked male human, and I was eye to eye with his...I looked up.

"We've been looking for you," he said in heavily accented English. "We need to talk."

I stopped growling, but that was it.

The vampire coughed delicately. "It would be easier if you Changed back."

I believed her. Besides, there was something else...

I closed my eyes and concentrated, tried to recall what Gerry had said in the Tiergarten. Nothing happened. I whimpered and tried again.

I didn't want to be stuck this way, not when I still had—

Danny!

Maybe the panic forced it or maybe now that the killer—and I knew he had planned to kill the woman—was gone, I could focus on what mattered to me. I was suddenly human again, and scrambling to find my clothes.

"She'll be OK." The vampire looked up from the unconscious woman, who moaned and seemed to settle into sleep. "Don't worry. You're among Family."

"Yeah, well, if you don't mind, I can't stay. I have to be down at the harbor. Like…" No watch, where was my phone? My panties? "Like, yesterday. What time is it?"

"It is nearly three thirty," the vampire said with a glance at her watch.

"No, it can't—I can't stay here, I have to check, the boat might not have left—"

"There's no boat at the wharf. No one should be going out this time of night in any case," said the werewolf—had she called him Thorben? "We just did a sweep, looking for you, when we got the scent of…*that.*" He jerked his head at the bloody mess next to him.

I'd gathered my things, gotten dressed, and was tying my boots. I wished the naked guy would get dressed as well. "You don't understand—I have to get to Delos."

"No one is allowed there after three p.m., and not on Monday," he said. "And technically, it's Monday morning now."

"Don't be didactic, Ben," the vampire said. She'd fanged down, and instead of black-and-green scales, she was a stunning blonde. "And yes, we do understand. You are Zoe Miller and you need to get to Delos to save your cousin."

I wasn't surprised; everyone seemed to know my name, but "Delos" had only come up in Berlin, during the fracas. I had to assume Claudia and Gerry had heard Dmitri, too. "You can't stop me," I said, picking up my backpack and shrugging it on.

"We want nothing more than to help you. We are *bound* to help you."

"Yeah, right."

"Look—that thing you took? The disk? It's called the Beacon. We've never seen it, but we know it's ancient and it's important to the Fangborn. Both of us, Thorben and me, have sworn to guard it, but when it was claimed, and we knew someday it would be, we also swore to help that person."

"Uh-huh."

I clutched my bag nervously. It was too much talk of "swearing" and "claiming" and it sounded like something out of *Le Morte d'Arthur* to me. Worse, it sounded exactly like what the disk had done in the Venice hotel room: claimed me. That made me even more nervous, and I already wasn't sure I could trust them—

A cold shock settled in the pit of my stomach, and I looked at my watch. Their statement about the time had settled in. I'd missed the rendezvous. I'd missed my chance to save Danny.

Unless these guys weren't lying... "You can get me to Delos? Immediately?"

"We can leave now. We need to talk first," Thorben said.

"You need to put some trousers on first," she snapped. "You have no shame."

"Yes, please do," I said.

"I understand the American being backward about nudity, but not you, Ariana. It's warm out. It's Greece." He spread his hands, as if that explained everything.

"You don't go shopping naked, do you, you great idiot?" She threw a pair of cargo shorts to him, which he pulled on, then a shirt. "You don't go out in town naked, either! Any excuse, any excuse at all." She turned to me. "Yes, an hour. We can get you there, but we need to talk first. About what you took in Venice. The Beacon."

"I...I'm sorry. I can't, I won't give it to you. My cousin's life is at stake."

"I don't want it, and I wish you'd never found it. It's yours by... birthright is not the word. It's yours, though. I'm just sorry for you."

"What do you mean, sorry?"

"The Orleans Tapestry tells of...a curse? A prophecy. I can tell you while Thorben readies the boat." She shook her head sadly. "You seem nice enough, and you did a good job tracking this evil one down. But I've read the Tapestry and I wouldn't wish the Beacon and what it means on a dog."

She meant what she was saying. I felt a pit open up where my stomach should be. "What do you mean?"

Ariana—that was her name—said, "My Cousin Steuben called us because we were closest to Delos. To think we missed you by a block!" She shook her head. "I understand you don't know much about being Fangborn, but I'm going to tell you things most Fangborn don't know. There are some of us who are chosen for duties beyond what we Fangborn take upon ourselves—"

"You mean like the TRG?" I said. "I know about that."

"The TRG—?" She cocked her head.

It made a nice change to know something someone else didn't. "Never mind. It's an American thing. Government, possibly top secret. Forget I said anything."

Ariana shrugged and pursed her lips, a European gesture of dismissal. "There are some artifacts of Fangborn history, very rare, very precious, and very…odd. Most of which we don't know the meaning of. Ben and I were charged with guarding the clay pot suspended between the roofs, which contained the Beacon. Some of us are chosen to defend certain objects, certain places that are mentioned in the fragments of our histories. In those histories, we have the stories of our people the Fangborn from—well, from the time writing was invented. There are also records of predictions, of things to come. From our oracles."

"And the oracles mentioned *me*?"

"No. But the Orleans Tapestry mentioned that someone would come for the Beacon, and that whoever that was would need our assistance. So for hundreds of years, someone has been living in Venice, waiting for someone to come. Most recently, Ben and me. Ben, he always treated our position as an honor post—he doesn't believe in the more mystical elements mentioned in the histories."

"Tell me about the Tapestry."

"The Orleans Tapestry is five hundred years old," Ariana said. "Sewn into the back is an even older piece of fabric, and on this, in gold thread, is stitched a prophecy in Latin. The text itself is even older, probably from about 1000 AD, so I assume the Beacon has been hidden in Venice at least that long. Someone was working to preserve this prophecy through time—you can see the errors made by later translators and needlewomen, but they worked very hard to save the words, though the Tapestry itself was largely destroyed in a fire."

"But some part of it was saved?"

"Yes. The fragment remaining refers to someone stealing the Beacon, unchaining the Fangborn, and revealing too much to the world."

"What does that mean? Oracles were supposed to talk in riddles, weren't they?"

"We don't know what it means. Some say it will mean the time of Identification, when we reveal ourselves to humans. Some say it will be when humans are ruled by us. Some say it will be the release of the Fangborn from their obligation to humanity."

"Um, doesn't sound good, whatever it is."

Another Italian shrug. "I've never met an oracle yet who was either specific or optimistic, but you can't be sure. As you said, oracles speak in riddles. We can only assume it indicates some change, a massive upheaval."

I wasn't sure how that was better.

"When they say 'unchaining the Fangborn and revealing too much to the world,' that's always reminded me of the Prometheus myth, or perhaps Pandora."

"*What* did you just say?"

"Pandora—you know, the one who opened the box and brought ruin to the world?" Ariana frowned and reached into her pocket; her phone was vibrating.

"Yeah, I know—" And I wished I didn't.

"Ah, Thorben—Ben is ready. We should make our way to the boat." She nodded and replaced her phone. "We do know one thing now."

"What's that?" Certainty, in any form, was welcome.

"You're the one who'll bring this change."

———

I was still digesting the notion of me bringing ruin to the world when I received a text from Dmitri.

"I generously assume you are on your way. Remember the video. You have until noon."

I shut off my phone. No point in giving myself away now. I was eager not to think of Dmitri's threats, Danny's face.

"How did your English get so good?" I asked Ariana as we hurried to the wharf.

"I attended university in California. Business school."

"B-school?" I bit my tongue before I could exclaim, *But you're a vampire!* "Um, why not...law or, I don't know...medicine?"

"Vampires need marketing, too." She shrugged. "At some point we Fangborn are going to reveal ourselves to the world. It might happen sooner, it might happen later, but when the Identification Day comes, I'm going to be ready. I'm working on a game."

"Game?"

"I happen to think the easiest way for an outsider group to emerge and be accepted into the mainstream is through popular culture. Zeitgeist. I'm working on an RPG to soften the ground for us identifying ourselves to Normals. There's a sociologist and a psychologist I'm working with, too."

I thought about it; my skills might not be so useless to the Fangborn after all. "Any other Fangborn who are archaeologists?"

"Two, now. One is in Asia and the other is in New York, but he's close to three hundred. That's very old, even for us."

"Two in the whole world?"

"There were more, in the nineteenth century, when science of the past was, well, more respectable, and a good cover for us to travel and research. Frankly, the slowness of communication made it easier for us to hide in plain sight, and our numbers were finally increasing after the Great Reaping in the eighteenth century."

Oh, of course. The Great Reaping. *What?*

She continued. "Then, the world wars took a toll. Always the case with wars." Ariana shook her head. "Unfortunately, humans are just getting more and more efficient at them."

"Oh."

After we boarded and cast off, it was too loud to talk, and if Ariana had answers to my questions, neither of us wanted to shout them. I could see the first glimmers of dawn in the east.

Once we were on the northern tip of the island, Ben had to cut speed. We pulled up on a small beach. The sea was as rough as it had been yesterday, but not as bad as I was expecting.

"Here's the plan," Ben said. "I'm going to let you off here. They'll be looking for you to come to the main harbor. You'll have to go south and west, across the island, to your meeting. The most obvious place is the museum plaza. I'll see if the western landing is clear. If so, we'll come around and see if we can't thin Dmitri's herd a little."

"And what do I do?" I hadn't told them everything; that I didn't have what Dmitri wanted. And I might have skipped over the part where I'd be willing to trade him the golden disk they'd been guarding for Danny.

"Try not to get killed," Ben suggested.

Ariana glared at him. "Just try and get Danny back. If it looks like things are…going to go badly, get feral on Parshin's ass."

I couldn't help myself. I laughed. It helped.

"Seriously, you can do it. You did on Mykonos. You've done it at home. Take him out, save your cousin, and we'll go back to our place. Ben will cook—he's quite good—and after the falafel mishap, he almost always wears clothing when he's in the kitchen."

She made it seem easy. She made it seem…finite. I was finally coming to the end of this. It was a relief, thinking that.

Ariana continued, "Keep your eyes open, and get ready to take advantage, if you can."

They took off, and I began to trot down across the island. Not too fast; I needed to give Ariana and Ben time to make their landing.

It was dark still, but sunrise was in about an hour. I was surprised at how well I could see in the dark, even skinself. The more I thought about it, the more I could recognize times when I thought I'd been unusually lucky, or maybe physically gifted. Now I knew it wasn't because I was special.

It's because I am a werewolf.

Although it was really the first time I'd said it as a matter of fact, it didn't quite make sense. But I was tired and scared and drained, and it made me giggle. I thought of Danny and picked up my speed.

Over the next rise, and I slipped; gravel and cobbles rolled out of the way, and if I'd fallen, I would have pitched into the excavations of a house and eaten colored mosaic, busted a tooth, busted a bone.

But I didn't, because I caught myself. Actually, I saw the peril before I had to catch myself, and averted it. I had talents, I had abilities…

…because I am a werewolf.

That gave me an idea. I didn't want to give Dmitri the golden disk without making sure Danny was still alive; I had no idea how long Danny's beating might have continued. I came up to the edge of the largest complex, the gymnasium complex, if I remembered yesterday's lecture correctly. I found a piece of uncovered ground by the base of a pillar and pulled out my trowel. I buried the disk and covered over the area with loose gravel and weeds. Then I pulled out my notebook, checked my watch, and made the roughest of sketches. An uneven rectangle, about fifteen minutes' walk from where I'd been set down on the coast, within sight of two intact doorways. They weren't going anywhere soon.

This was the most familiar thing I'd done in a while. I stuck my trowel into the back of my belt, dusted myself off, and continued.

The museum was in the middle of the top third of the island. I was approaching from the northeast; the landing where Ben and Ariana were going to land was to the west. It didn't take me long to get there, and as I did, the sun was just starting to peek over the horizon. The last hundred meters seemed to take the longest; I was desperate to get there on time but reluctant to face Dmitri without the figurines. I actually stopped, but by this time I was so close I could see three men outside the museum. They saw me, spoke into radios, and gestured to me.

Dmitri was close.

I trudged up the path, almost paved with fragments of marble and rock, sherds among the poppies. There were wildflowers everywhere, and they were vivid red, yellow, purple, and blue against the radiant marble and dun stone as the sun rose.

Not a bad place for a confrontation.

With the sun rising, the place glowed almost white off the water; the reflections and refractions must have added to the liquid quality of the light. And even though I didn't have full control over my powers, I knew, somehow, in this place I could summon the Beast easily.

If anything had happened to Danny, I *would* go feral on Dmitri's ass. I could do that.

Because I am a werewolf.

As I approached, the men closed in. One pointed to the coffee shop I'd checked out yesterday. I went in.

There was no one else; the goons stayed outside.

I might be able to get Danny out, I reasoned, but could I outrun bullets, even in wolf form?

Probably not.

I'd just have to run interference and make sure Danny got to Ariana and Ben.

All but one of the tables were set up for the night's mopping, with the chairs on top. I'd done enough mopping myself to know the process. One was not, and there were chairs around it.

I sat down, facing the doorway.

Dmitri was here.

Chapter 20

Dmitri Alexandrovich Parshin was here and he looked like hell, even worse in the light of day than in the video call yesterday. Adam Nichols and his gang had hurt him back in Berlin. One eye was blackened and nearly closed; what I could see of the white was actually red with burst blood vessels. There was a serious case of road rash down that side of his face, and one arm was bandaged.

Good. Adam Nichols had taken a chunk off him.

"You are late."

"I was delayed—I had to steal a boat. I'm here now."

"I saw no boat in the harbor." He snapped his fingers and one of his men approached. Dmitri said something to him in another language—Russian, it sounded like—and he left.

"I'm not real good at navigating. Actually, I've never driven a boat before. I just aimed for Delos and tried not to hit any rocks."

"You would have passed Antonio Cavalli's excavations from the main landing, a man of great learning. No matter, you are here."

Excavations? Not the Via Cavalli in Venice? Maybe the Beacon really did want me, had been leading me to it in Venice. "Hey, I'm just glad I figured out what you were saying." I was in a bad mood and let it show. "Things were a little hectic back there in Berlin."

At the mention of Berlin, Dmitri scowled. "I trust you have the figurines."

"No. They were taken from me by that guy I saw in Berlin. Adam Nichols."

"How? *When?*" He strode over to my table, slammed a pistol on it. "How could you, when so much relies on it? One of my men betrayed me, and Nichols has been dogging my steps ever since."

"Trust me, it wasn't my idea." I eyed the pistol, and before Dmitri could pop an artery or do anything crazy, I said, "But I have something else, something that might be even better. A gold disk."

"Do not waste my time." He paced back and forth, then called one of his men in. He barked at him in Russian, and the only words I recognized were "Adam" and "Nichols." Didn't sound good for Nichols, whatever it was. Then I heard him say, "Connor," and my heart almost stopped.

He strode back to me. "It was only those things I needed. Only those things I can use to become *oboroten.*"

"Does that word mean wealthy? Because I have access to an artifact that will certainly help."

"That word means 'werewolf.' Here, today, I was going to become *oboroten.*"

I swallowed. "You can't. It doesn't work like that."

He leaned into me. "What do you know about it?"

"You don't get familiar with that kind of artifact without learning some weird shit," I said. I was lying so hard about my familiarity with the figurines and the Fangborn I could have made the Olympic team. "And the reason I knew about them was because one of them has been in my possession for years. I met the people who've studied those things. I've listened, and I've read—it's been my life's work. And the only way you can become a werewolf is to be born one. You don't get bitten, you don't use broken fragments of two-thousand-year-old rubbish."

"Nonsense."

"You've been watching the wrong movies. You have to be born *oboroten.* Trust me."

"Liar! I know I have the potential within me—it runs in my family! I have seen!"

That gave me pause—was it possible he was some kind of demented oracle Fangborn but not a shape-shifter? If so, he was almost as ignorant as I was, a stray, and I wasn't going to give away any of my hard-won information about the Fangborn. It wasn't up to me to solve his riddles.

"You know who has the figurines now; if you still want them back, you'll find Adam Nichols. I bet a tough guy like you would be up for a rematch."

No response from Dmitri, whose eyes had darkened and whose hands were clenched. I spoke in a hurry to keep his attention.

"I can buy Danny's freedom, though, with an object at least as old as those taken from me. It won't turn you into a werewolf either, but it's worth a bomb, the price of gold these days. But before I hand over that to you, before I leave here safely with my cousin, we're gonna have a little talk about what you knew about my father. See, I discovered the fragment around your neck mended with a fragment Ma'd had for years. A piece that belonged to my father. How did you know him?"

"Enough of this." He snapped his fingers. Another man stepped forward.

Was that a noise back there? In the courtyard, a kind of scuffling? Was it possible Ariana and Ben had been able to circle around, undetected? My hopes soared, even as Dmitri shoved my chair over next to the wall.

"Check her bag."

I had to buy some time and wanted to hold the Beast in reserve, so I made a show of hanging on to it. I tried not to let any of them see how the noise in the courtyard, real or imagined, had stripped away my fatigue.

Bad Guy One tore the bag out of my hands, unzipped it, upended it on the table. A half-drunk bottle of water: *thud, slosh.*

Pens clattered; random notes, a thousand itineraries and ticket stubs fluttered out. Toilet paper. A plastic bag with Band-Aids, antiseptic cream, aspirin, and the spice container along with a couple of tampons topped the pile, as did my ratty, perennially empty wallet. Almost as an afterthought, the pile of cell phones I'd accumulated fell out and off the table.

Dmitri pawed through it, faint amusement his only expression. "This is the detritus of a very sad life, is it not, Zoe? I myself… frankly, I would be ashamed of this kind of poverty, not of material wealth but a…a sheer lack of character. There is nothing to distinguish you here. And I do not see the disk you promise."

"Where's Danny?"

"Danny is fine, fine." Dmitri absently shoved the things back into the bag. He looked up and whistled sharply. "You can see him now."

Bad Guy Two dwarfed the doors to the entrance. He dragged Danny in behind him.

Danny was a long way from "fine." His face was purpled with bruises, both eyes nearly shut. His nose was bloody and twisted at an angle, and when he breathed through his mouth, bubbles appeared. He made a noise when he saw me, and got a fist in his stomach that doubled him over.

I cried out, stood. Dmitri pushed me back down.

"The figurines."

"Stolen! Adam Nichols has them!" I couldn't take my eyes off my cousin. Was this what I'd heard, just now, Danny being beaten up? "I can get you the gold disk! Give me ten minutes, I can get it! Take the gold, forget I ever had the figurines! They won't turn you into a werewolf!"

"How do you know?"

"Because *I* am a werewolf!"

I felt stupid as soon as I said it out loud.

He stared at me, and I knew what he saw: a small woman, dirty and disheveled, the opposite of the power he sought. He knew about the Fangborn, but he didn't know all about them, else he wouldn't be so obsessed with the figurines.

And it seemed he didn't know about me.

He laughed hugely, then gestured.

Bad Guy Two took out a knife. The sight of it made Danny sink, all strength gone from his knees.

The knife should have terrified me. It should have triggered images in my mind that would haunt me all the years of my life to come. It should have immobilized me.

Danny was the last thing I had on earth, the last indication that I mattered as a person, all on my own, no hinky family troubles, no bizarre shifts in reality.

Somewhere beyond the now-familiar buzzing that seemed to fill my head as I saw my cousin begin to weep, as Bad Guy Two licked the blade with a kind of lust, I had only one thought:

Never mind the Beast. I'll kill Dmitri with my own two human hands.

I began to catalog the vulnerable spots of the human body. Years of studying skeletons had provided a list.

Neck: Too narrow. I'd never hit it square enough.

Chest: Too many ribs.

Eyes: Too small a target…

Thought stopped. My head dropped. My hands fell to my sides. The buzzing grew, filled—charged—my entire body. The Beast was different, somehow, this time.

No time to figure out why. No matter. It was here and I embraced it.

I reached behind me, pulled the trowel from my belt, and stabbed it into Dmitri's thigh with all the force I had.

Dmitri howled. Blood drenched his trousers, began to spill onto the floor in a torrent.

I tried to wrench the trowel back, hoping to get another blow in or make the tear in his leg worse. Even with Dmitri's meaty hand crushing mine as he tried to remove it, the trowel was stuck. Sickeningly, immovably.

I'd struck deep, deep into bone.

Dmitri roared, hauled off, and backhanded me. My head snapped back; I hit the wall. My vision blurred for half a second then sharpened beyond human capacity. I grabbed his arm in both hands, bit as hard as I could. With horrifying ease, I felt my fangs slice through his flesh; I braced myself and, with both feet, kicked, shoving him from his chair.

There, I've bitten you. Maybe that will show you once and for all.

I grabbed my bag and scrambled away; the table went over on him. A rickety affair, but it landed smack on the trowel handle, jarring the blade that was stuck deep in his femur. Dmitri screamed again.

Bad Guy One was stunned by the noise his boss made, but grabbed me in a bear hug. I felt my ribs being crushed inward. I shoved my elbow into his groin and raised one knee as high as I could. Then, with all my might, I stomped on his foot.

Low-tech boots win over high-tech sandals.

I felt the crunch of bones, but better than that, felt the air rush into my lungs as Bad Guy One released me. I took a deep breath, put him from my mind. I had to somehow grab Danny and run.

I looked up and was stopped in my tracks by what I saw.

Danny was biting the wrist of the man who held him, and doing a good job with his laughably small, human teeth. The reason he was not being stabbed with that wicked blade was that Adam Nichols was holding onto Bad Guy Two's wrist and using all his strength to do it.

No time for questions, I thought. *Danny. Door. Run.*

I strode up, hauled off, and planted my boot in Bad Guy Two's crotch. Fueled by adrenaline, the man noticed but didn't let go. Determined to put an end to this, I leaned back and kicked again; I could feel the impact throughout my body.

Not hurt. Just surprised at how good I felt.

Bad Guy Two went down. Danny had the presence of mind to let go and get out of the way. Adam still held on, but freed one hand to reach into his pocket. He pulled out a wicked-looking sap and brought it down on the man's head. Bad Guy Two wouldn't get up again soon.

I grabbed Danny and followed Adam out the door. I paused; there was a jeep. The rest of the piazza was empty, but I was afraid we'd be visible forever. It was a small island; we'd be easy to track down.

"Zoe! Get in!" Adam had started the car.

Still I hesitated. Danny could barely support himself, but the enemy of my enemy wasn't necessarily my friend.

"You better get in, because I'm leaving!" Adam shouted. "Right now, *they're* madder at you than you are at me!"

Unable to help his boss, Bad Guy One was limping toward us.

An unearthly scream froze us all, and I understood:

Somewhere inside, Dmitri had wrenched my trowel from his thigh bone.

The scream decided me. I hauled Danny over to the jeep and shoved him in the front seat.

"Feet, Danny!" I yelled. "Get your feet all the way inside." My voice sounded strange to me.

My cousin moved, but not fast enough. Bad Guy One had nearly reached the jeep.

"No time!" Adam put the jeep into drive. He pulled away, heading north.

I ran, matching speed with the jeep.

I dove for the backseat and landed ass over teakettle.

I pulled myself in. I looked up, triumphant, but Bad Guy One had grabbed the door handle and was hanging on.

I righted myself and lunged for Bad Guy One, raking my nails across his hands. His eyes opened wide, his mouth worked. Then he let go of the door, fell hard to the stony ground.

Adam turned briefly, a small smile on his lips.

"What's wrong?" I yelled. It was as if my mouth was full of cotton.

"It seems you've mastered the half-Change."

I looked down and saw I had furred arms and clawed hands; I bet under my jeans my legs were similarly covered in fur. I reached up and touched my face; a muzzle and teeth, mine and yet unfamiliar.

The Change with two feet. The Change, when I got to keep my clothes, mostly, and keep upright. Mastered nothing; I hadn't meant to, but it was a gift at the moment. And how the hell did Adam know about Changing?

I tried to Change back, leave this partial-Beast behind. No luck.

For the moment, I didn't care. "Where we going?" My words were still somewhat unintelligible. Delos is a very small island, with not much in the way of roads. A bump almost jarred my pointy teeth out of my head. Danny moaned.

"We gotta get out of here, pronto!" Adam said. "There are people arriving at the main dock soon, and I want to get you away from them."

"Wait!" I said, suddenly remembering. "We need to stop!"

"Exactly what we don't need—"

"No, just a moment, up by that pillar over there!" Desperation aided my pronunciation.

"What pillar? There must be dozens—"

"Over there! Between the two doorways! Look where I'm pointing!"

He got close enough, and impatiently I vaulted out. Three long, loping strides, and I was at my pillar. I reached back for my trowel—it wasn't there. Out of habit, I tried the other hand, tried to turn around, before I realized I'd left my trowel back in Dmitri's leg.

At least I had claws.

But when I looked down, I didn't. A feeling of carbonated blood, then claws transformed into human hands, bruised from when I'd buried the disk, but no more furry than usual.

"Zoe! There's no time!"

Didn't matter. I grabbed a rock, scraped down, and dislodged the disk. I stuck it inside my bra, gritty and uncomfortable but secure, and ran back to the jeep.

Again Adam didn't wait for me to get in properly before he roared off.

"Where are we going?" I yelled. We were nearly at the beach where Ben and Ariana had landed me. There was still no sign of them; I began to worry. "I have a boat—people came with me! I need to—"

"We need to get you out of here." He glanced at Danny, who wasn't moving, then back at me. "Need to get him out of here."

I didn't have much alternative. Unless my new friends showed up soon, I had to find my own way out of here, and so far Adam was it.

I nodded, and he roared past the small yellow buildings I'd learned had housed the French archaeological teams who worked here. Up a hill, then—

"Oh shit."

I looked where Adam was looking and saw a large boat waiting in the official harbor to the west. It certainly hadn't been there when I arrived, and it didn't look like something Dmitri would have had, not with all those official-looking policemen and flags and...guns.

"You do not want to let these people find you," Adam said, frowning. "If we're very lucky, they'll still think I'm working for them."

"They must have seen us," I said. "Keep going!"

"They expect me to be here. They think I'm coming to get you and Dmitri. They don't know I've changed the game."

"This isn't a game! Get me out of here!"

"I have to go to them," he said, almost to himself. "I'll tell them there was nothing but blood and overturned tables in the museum center. They won't have seen you, probably, and Danny, well, his posture isn't too good right now."

The sun was very hot. Sweat began to roll down my neck and back.

"When we get past that next hill, I'm going to slow down and you get out. Try and reach your friends. When you see them, tell the Steubens: Knight believes he's the heir to the Beacon. He believes his time is coming, and now that he has three of the four figurines, he's not going to retire from his Senate seat. He'll begin the Identification *soon*."

"Huh?"

He looked back over his shoulder. "As for these guys, with any luck, everyone will think you've already left. You'd better get gone."

Was this some kind of trick? Some kind of joke? I stared at Adam's face, trying to read what was going on. I tried to sense whether he was telling me the truth and got nothing but determination and, beneath that, a little unfamiliar fear.

In any case, I still had to fly under the radar, and those flags meant official business. There was no sign of Ariana and Ben, so I nodded and tried to remember what I could of the layout of the ruins. If I kept moving north and east, I'd end up at the little beach I'd come in on.

I got out and helped Danny. Adam did a tight turn and headed back to the west.

Danny was conscious again, and he could walk, but not well and not far. He was skinny and pale, even for him, and I was getting more and more worried by the second.

"Hey." His voice was hoarse and faint.

"Hey."

"You got any water?"

"Just a little—don't drink too much, OK?" I dug the half-full bottle of water out of my bag and handed it to him. Stupid! If I'd been thinking I would have had a full bottle of water, a first-aid kit, a commando team...

I was sweating like fury now that the sun was coming up. More than that, I needed an antacid.

Wait.

Suddenly I had heartburn? Since when did the Girl with the Cast-Iron Gullet get heartburn?

It took me a moment, but I realized the burning wasn't inside me. I reached down into my bra and pulled my hand back sharply.

The disk was hot, hotter than body heat. I grabbed it out of my shirt before it burned parts of me I really didn't want burned.

I looked at the disk. Nothing had changed; still round, still the same crude/elegant map.

"OK, either I'm hallucinating or you're trying to get my attention," I said to the disk. "Whaddya want?"

I didn't really expect anything to happen, so when the damned thing started beating like a living heart in my hand, I dropped it. Clamped my hand over my mouth. Glanced at Danny, whose eyes were closed now that the water was gone.

I stared at the thing, then picked it up. "You didn't start doing this until we saw the other boat, the one that scared Adam. You want me to check them out."

Why I was thinking of the disk as a living thing and why I was talking to it was the least of my worries. When I thought *check them out*, I felt such an upwelling of enthusiasm I knew I had to do something.

My phone vibrated madly in my pocket. It was Ben. I was faintly surprised there was cell phone reception here.

"Zoe, what are you doing? We can see you. Why are you waiting?"

"Ben, my cousin Danny—he needs help."

Ben muttered something I was glad not to understand. "Stay there. We will come to you. Three minutes."

"Three minutes."

Three minutes wasn't long; it would give me sixty seconds to get out toward the official landing beach, sixty seconds to watch Adam with the other men, sixty seconds back. "Danny, stay put. A friend, Ben, is coming to help us. I'll be right back."

"Where are you...?"

"I don't even want to think about it."

I began counting as I ran, heading south. *One, two...*

I kept low, running between hillocks and ruins, feeling stupid hiding behind a pillar or fallen base. I just needed to get a little bit closer to the landing.

Thirty-nine, forty...

I located the best observation point and ran, crouching, as fast as I could, clutching that beating heart of gold.

Fifty-eight, fifty-nine...

I was getting faster and faster in human form, I noticed as I skidded on the pebbly pathway and hid myself behind a broken column base. As long as they didn't see me, I was fine.

I could see one man, an American, on the western landing. Tall, lean, unhurried, and impeccable in a blue sports jacket and open-necked white shirt. His hair was receding and distinguished gray about the temples. His nose gave his face a hawkish look. It was the nose that cinched it: I was looking at the senior senator from New York State, Edward Knight. Just by his bearing you could tell he was used to wielding power and receiving obedience from others. You could also tell from the way the Greek officials were behaving that the guy in the jacket, the one Adam was talking to, was important. Must have been; visits to Delos don't happen on Mondays, I reminded myself.

Then another American stepped from the boat, and I knew him almost before I saw him. He was Clean-head, the man who'd tortured and killed Rupert Grayling in London, who'd come so close to grabbing me in Paris.

He was working with a US senator. Working with Adam Nichols.

Fifty-nine, fifty-nine, fifty-nine… C'mon, Zoe!

My hackles rose, but I didn't dare get closer. More than that, I found my attention drifting away from Adam, his boss—Senator Knight—and Clean-head. My attention was drawn to the boat. I wanted to be on the boat, I wanted to go to the forward cabin—

I could almost *see* the *inside* of the cabin. How was that even poss—?

I knew that instant the figurines were on the boat.

Fifty-nine, fifty-nine, fifty-nine, sixty. Waaay past time to go, Zoe.

I couldn't drag myself away. I was desperate to get the figurines back, but there was no way I could sneak on board, no way I could get past that phalanx on the dock…

My phone buzzed in my pocket; it was Ben's number. I glanced back at where I'd left Danny and could see two dark figures picking their way to him.

I was late.

With one last glance at the boat—

They were also looking in my direction. I saw a sailor with binoculars scanning the ruins, looking for me, I was certain. But they couldn't see me, could they? Maybe they had satellite imagining—

Maybe Adam had ratted me out—

The disk seemed cooler now and almost…content. As if it had accomplished something. I pulled it out to look at it. Perhaps I'd been mistaken, hallucinating… Nerves, lack of water, heat, adrenaline—I was seeing things. I had to be.

The disk burst into a blazing white light. So bright I was blinded for a moment. Even brighter than in my room in Venice.

I wasn't seeing things. Even I couldn't ignore that light. With a wrench, I shook myself and stuck it back into my pocket.

Didn't matter. I ran back to where I'd left Danny; two men were carrying him at a fast, low trot back to the beach.

There was Ben, but Ariana was nowhere to be seen.

The other man was Will.

Chapter 21

I caught up with Will, Ben, and Danny. I tried not to stare at Will. I didn't know what he was doing here, but as long as he was helping Danny get away…

The two men had Danny securely and were moving quickly. There was nothing I could do to help, so after a glance at Will, who nodded, I ran ahead, looking for their boat. I tried to pick out the safest path for them to follow.

There was no sign of the small motor Ben and Ariana had used to get me to Delos. There was a fishing boat close to shore. I almost turned around until I saw Gerry Steuben was piloting it. He looked comfortable at the helm, and when he saw me, he nodded and revved up the engine, moving in toward the shore. A little rubber Zodiac outboard was on the beach; I headed for it. I didn't know much about boats, but I did know it wouldn't go anywhere with the line tied to a log on the beach, so I untied that and moved the rope to a safe place.

"Get in!" Will's face was red and he was breathing heavily.

"Into the bow," Ben said. "I'm driving."

I scrambled into the front, and they splashed into the water, heaving Danny in with me. I helped him pull forward best I could.

"Zoe, am I dying?" Danny was even worse now, if that was possible.

"No," I said firmly, swallowing. "No way. You're safe."

"But I saw Will MacFarlane—your Will—he's not—"

"Yeah, it's me, Danny." Will said as he and Ben shoved us off the pebbly strand and into the water. "It's me, and you're going to be just fine."

Once the outboard had cleared the bottom, Ben jumped in. We were off.

Another time, I would have loved being in the Zodiac as it skipped across the waves toward Gerry and the fishing boat. But each soaring leap meant an equally hard *thump* as we hit the water again and again, spray soaking us. Every bounce saw Danny go a little grayer.

Worse than that, I could see one of the official-looking boats coming around the northern tip of the coast. Heading for us.

Gerry met us halfway, stopping at a safe distance. He hauled Danny up by himself, and then gave me a hand. Will and Ben secured the Zodiac, then the fishing boat wheeled around and away.

The fishing boat had something special for an engine, or else it wasn't really a fishing boat, because we *flew* ahead of the official motor. I suppose we were lucky it was so large as it was more cumbersome, but it was slowly gaining on us.

There was no way we'd escape by the time we reached Mykonos.

We weren't going to Mykonos, I realized. Gerry took us farther south, where there were several smaller boats ahead of us. He was heading straight for them.

Ben leaned over. "We're going to get you on that boat over there," he yelled into my ear, nodding at a small speedboat. "We'll split up, different boats, then regroup off Naxos. If we're lucky, they won't try to follow all four of us."

"Who are they? Adam works for them, right?"

Ben shouted something I missed, but we'd arrived at the little knot of boats, and there was no time to clarify.

"I should have gone with you. He looks awful," Claudia said as she pulled Danny aboard. I clambered onto the deck and collapsed, as much from nerves as from fatigue.

"We had no time to spare, and Will couldn't manage the fishing boat. You can work on him now," Ben said. He looked over his shoulder at the pursuing boats. "Hurry."

"We got him! Go!" Claudia hustled back to the wheel.

"I'll be two seconds." Ben maneuvered the Zodiac closer to the third boat, and Will got out. He immediately went below and his boat roared off—I assumed Ariana was behind the wheel.

I found myself furious that Will hadn't even spared me a word. Barely a glance. OK, maybe I had disobeyed him back in Berlin and caused a lot of trouble, but that didn't mean he had to be—

It didn't matter, I told myself furiously. I'd done what I'd done, every time, for good reason. I hated hurting Will, but I had no problem taking responsibility for my actions. Why did I care? I'd dumped him. For his own good. It wasn't like he owed me anything.

When Ben returned, he pulled the Zodiac on board with astonishing ease. "Go now, quickly!"

Claudia peeled out of there, and now our three boats were heading in three different directions.

I struggled to get up and landed heavily. We were bouncing again, almost as hard as in the rubber dinghy.

"Stay down!" Ben yelled. "We don't want them to see you, most of all."

He crawled over to where Claudia was standing, trying to eke out a little more power from the engine. I saw them yelling to each other, but couldn't hear. Both cast worried glances behind us.

The official boat was still following us and had closed the distance since our short stop.

I picked up Danny's hand, closed my eyes, and began to pray.

His hand jerked; I opened my eyes.

Claudia let Ben take over, and now she was next to me and turning…purple. Violet skin and hair, nails almost midnight black.

Her mouth was latched onto Danny's other wrist, and while I could see no blood, her skin was…pulsing. Changing.

I felt the Beast respond, but I shoved it away, worried for Danny. Even though I'd seen Claudia Changed before, this was different. "What the hell are you doing?"

She looked up, closed her eyes, and shook her head gently, as much as she could with my cousin's arm in her mouth.

"That's how she works," Ben shouted. "She's among our best healers! Look at him, he's already better."

I couldn't deny the grayish pallor was gone, and his eyes were open, clearer, less bruised. The horrible swelling had gone down.

Claudia, on the other hand, looked less and less human every minute.

All I could think of was ticks, leeches, mosquitoes.

I turned away. If I hadn't, I would have said something offensive, and that was the last thing I wanted to do. I knew, deep down, Claudia was one of the good guys. I knew she couldn't turn Danny into a vampire. But I still didn't like it. Seeing her biting him, drawing his blood, freaked me out.

A laughing shout, one I could hear over the roar of the engine. "They've turned around! We're safe!"

Claudia rolled away from Danny, gasping. Danny had a dazed, happy, almost goofy look on his face. I had to admit, it was far preferable to the semi-conscious mess he'd been before.

He squeezed my hand lightly, then fell into what looked like a comfortable slumber.

Claudia had lifted herself up and was staggering toward the bow, using the rail for support.

I let go of Danny's hand and followed her. When I caught up, I put my arm around her waist and helped her forward. "Thank you. For what you did for Danny."

She sank to an empty spot on the minuscule deck, eyes closed. "I'm fine. I just had to do a lot of work on him. More than I expected." "Expected" sounded a little like "espected" around a mouth full of fangs.

I cast an eye to the sun; it was getting warmer and warmer by the minute. "Would you be more comfortable in the shade?"

"No! No, sssun is the besssst thing." She laughed; it was a strange, inhuman sound. Lots of hisses, lots of…vampire. And sure enough, her skin was rippling again; she was processing the chemicals she'd just injected and removed. "I won't get sssunburned."

I nodded, then found my way back to the helm. Ben had taken off his shirt and was singing as he steered.

At first I thought it was opera, from the deepness of his voice and the dramatic quality of his phrasing. Then I caught the words and realized he was belting out Gladys Knight.

I blinked. Well, it was no more outrageous than anything else that had happened today.

I fell asleep to a German werewolf in a Speedo joyfully singing "Midnight Train to Georgia" as he steered us over the choppy waves of the Aegean.

It was late afternoon when I woke up. The sun was dipping into the horizon, and I was hungry. We'd stopped and dropped anchor. There was a cluster of small islands ahead of us, no sign of pursuit behind us, and, better, the smell of food cooking nearby.

I hoped it was someone I knew. I didn't really want to jump onto someone else's boat and snatch the gyros out of their hands, but I would.

I was saved from causing an international incident because it was Ben, on the boat moored across from ours, carrying food to a long table under a canopy. No sign of Danny or Claudia on board, so I got into the dinghy that was tied between the two boats, cast off, and hauled myself across.

This boat was larger—a yacht—and made for cruising. Ben put a plate of food on the table. "Danny's asleep below," he called over his shoulder as he returned to the galley.

Nearly everyone else was seated, and I bolted to the last chair. The food was gorgeous: small fish, tomato salad with basil, eggplant stewed in a fortune's worth of olive oil, tiny meatballs, and bread. But no one was eating.

Ben set the last plate down and sat. He looked at everyone gravely, solemnly, and said,

"Eat and enjoy."

Then it was like someone had fired a pistol, and Fangborn and Normal alike were eating as if for a time trial. There was no talk for the first ten minutes, just solid chewing and the occasional "pass the tomatoes" and "cheese?" and "is there any more of that lamb kofta?"

The worst of hunger at bay, wine was served and the plates were passed around again. Now we looked like any other collection of tourists enjoying a civilized meal. We even said "please" and "thank you," but conversation was still limited to the food and praising Ben for his cooking until he went to get coffee and dessert, fruit and baklava.

When it was clear that no one was going to go hungry and we could talk without choking on our food, Gerry looked around. "We have a lot to talk about."

"Danny will be OK?" I asked.

"Yep." Gerry grabbed another piece of baklava, popped it into his mouth, and wiped his fingers.

Ariana said, "I've been wondering about something. You were supposed to meet Dmitri's man at the harbor but missed the rendezvous when we tracked that would-be killer on Mykonos. If we hadn't been there, how would you have made it over?"

"I hadn't heard from Dmitri for a long while, after Berlin," I said. "So I didn't even know if he'd be on Delos, much less offer to ferry me over. So I took a cash advance and bought a small raft with an outboard motor."

"You were going to motor over there in, what, some inflatable thing?" Ariana murmured something in Italian I felt sure Mama Luongo wouldn't have ever taught me. "Crazy girl!"

I didn't like to think of having to navigate my way over those rough waves. "Where's Claudia?" I asked.

"Forward, still sleeping in the last of the sun. She already raided the galley," Ben said. "You know, there really is an order to this kind of discussion, where so much is involved and there is so little time. You should follow the protocol."

Casual enough about being naked, Ben seemed to care a great deal about the rules. "Sorry, I didn't know."

"You should have known, or you should have asked," he said.

I set my cup down, trying not to swear at him—after all I'd been through, parliamentary procedure was the furthest thing from my mind. "I'm *sorry*. I didn't *know*."

"And you should mind your temper."

Before I could respond, Ariana said, "Perhaps you should remember she's been unacculturated?"

"And how else will she learn," Ben said, "if no one tells her?"

"We have more important things," Will said before I could respond. "What was that light we saw from the beach, Zoe?"

"What light?" I went suddenly shy. "And what are *you* doing here?"

Ever been stared at by two intimidating uncles, an equally formidable aunt, and an ex-boyfriend? I can't recommend it, especially not when three of them were built to detect the truth and the other knew you better than almost anyone alive.

"OK, there was a light," I said. "I'm not sure what—"

"Zoe, I saw it," Will said. "It came from *you*."

"Not really me," I said. Reluctantly I reached into my shirt and pulled out the disk. "I found this in Venice, when I met Ariana and Ben here."

"You mean when you broke into our house. Ha!"

Several hostile glances at Ben.

"What? It's funny," he said. "All the time we were meant to be guarding the Beacon, and when, after generations, someone finally showed an interest in it, we thought she was a house thief."

"House thief?"

"Well, at first. She doesn't look like the one foretold in the Orleans Tapestry, does she? The one who will 'unchain' the Fang-born?"

Everyone seemed to go on point. I felt like slinking under the table.

No one actually moved down the table away from me, but I could tell they were considering the ramifications of what Ben had said.

"Wait, how did you know to go there?" Gerry asked me. "Why did you go looking for the Beacon?"

"I didn't." I told them about Dmitri's instructions to me in Berlin. "When he said 'Cavalli,' I thought he was talking about the professor, but he meant where Cavalli had excavated on Delos. It was Sean who suggested the street name was Cavalli, in Venice. I found the bench with the caduceus there."

"Ariana?" Ben asked.

She shook her head. "That bench is just a signal to other Fang-born, to let them know it's our place. There's no way Dmitri or this Sean person could have known about the location of the Beacon. I can only assume your instincts took you there. Maybe a little nudge from the hand of fate."

I didn't like the sound of "fate" at all. "I wasn't going after the pot thing for any reason but to get Danny back," I said quickly. "It started...I don't know. Throbbing? Pulsing? Beating. It started beating when I was near the ship." Just saying it flooded my mind with memories: the way the Beast had reacted, making me bide my time at Rupert Grayling's house until I could recover the figurines safely; the way the disk had "bitten" me, drawing blood and memory; the strong interaction and blinding light when it was close to the stolen figurines on Delos.

"Is it possible…I don't want to sound conceited or anything, but is it possible that the figurines have been acting on my Fangborn powers and sort of, I don't know, guiding me to bring them all together? I shouldn't have gone to Venice, but maybe they… prompted me, somehow. I felt the Beast urge me to take Sean's advice about looking down the Via Cavalli. And then the disk kind of…well, *tasted* me, in Venice—there were all these memories, and now I'm wondering if it wasn't finding out who I am."

There was stunned silence around the table.

"I guess," I finished, "it would kind of explain my powers coming in and out of control, even when I should have been trying to stop Grayling's murder, right? I don't like to think I'm being driven by something magical, but it's starting to be the only thing that explains all this."

"Ariana?" Ben said. "You're the one who's been so diligent about combing the histories? Is it possible these things have that kind of power?"

She shrugged. "There are no dates, no places, no names. But since Zoe's the only person in a thousand years to claim the Beacon and it seems to be communicating somehow with other artifacts of Fangborn origin, I'd say the chances are, yes, they are having an effect on her. And therefore, the Unchaining is at hand."

I tried not to gulp and kept my eyes on my plate. I did not want to believe, as Grayling had said, that I held three of the four keys to Pandora's Box. I didn't want to think that I was the one who would unchain and reveal too much. Chaos and upheaval. Ariana was right; I wouldn't wish that on a dog.

That reminded me of something, and I looked at Gerry, eager to change the subject. "Adam Nichols, the one who beat up Dmitri but took away my figurines, then helped me get away from Knight? Who is he?"

The Fangborn exchanged looks, shook heads.

"I know the name," Will said slowly. "He's attached to Senator Knight's office. I've always just thought of him as an aide, but he seems to be inserting himself into the Fangborn side of the senator's business now. Why?"

"Well, he told me to tell Gerry and Claudia that Senator Knight has decided not to retire, because he believes the time is coming soon. He has three of the four keys and believes he's heir to the Beacon, too, so he'll begin the Identification soon."

Questions erupted from all over the table. I glanced around helplessly until I met Ben's glance.

"This is why we have rules," he said loudly. "What's supposed to happen, Zoe, is that in any group of more than three, when there is serious business, we pick a moderator, usually someone senior, to help organize who speaks and keep things organized when there are so many strong personalities involved. Formality is a good thing here. Order is good." He frowned, nodded once. "There. Now you know. Maybe others will follow suit."

The others stopped. Ariana rolled her eyes, but Gerry nodded. "Allow me, Thorben. Zoe, why don't you start from the beginning?"

I started from Berlin. I told them how I'd taken the necklace with the figurine fragment from Dmitri, and how he'd told me to meet him at Delos. About the clue he gave me, the disappointing trip to the museum, and my discovery of the caduceus and the golden disk. How Adam broke into my room and stole all three figurines while Sean almost broke my arm trying to drag me away from him. Ditching Adam and the tussle with the TPC as we tried to escape Ben and Ariana.

When I got to the scrum by the Brandenburg Gate, I suddenly looked up.

"Where's Sean?"

"We don't know," Gerry said.

"What do you—?"

Will was staring at his plate. "He means, we don't know. Last time we saw him was Berlin. He was with you until you got to Venice, right?"

"Yes. I…" I swallowed. "I ditched him before I went to the airport."

"Why?"

"I'm…I'm not sure. I thought…I had the impression someone had wiped his mind. Badly, I mean, not like Claudia did it—"

"Like I did what?"

Claudia had emerged from her cabin. Human once more, she'd changed into a swimsuit and cotton knit cover-up and pulled a chair to the table. I would have killed for a body like that, not covering it up under prissy sweaters.

"I was just saying, I think Sean's brain had been…tampered with. He kept trying to get me to stay in Venice, he kept saying Danny would be OK, which was a total turnaround. When I asked him about it, he went kind of blank. When he practically broke my back trying to drag me away from Adam and the figurines—he knew how important it was to me to find them—I began to wonder whether he'd been turned against me. So, just in case, I ditched him."

I swallowed again and reached for the water. "Do you think he was working with Senator Knight? Maybe even those other Fangborn I ran into, back at home? Maybe they wiped him?"

Claudia nodded. "Probably the groups in Boston were working for Knight, in one way or another. But, Zoe, I have bad news."

My stomach clenched. "What? What is it?"

"News from Venice. Professor Schulz is dead, Zoe. And the police are searching for someone with Sean's description."

Chapter 22

"He didn't do it," I said instantly. "There's no way Sean had anything to do with it. He was with me, in Venice…"

I realized Sean and I had been apart since I'd leapt from the vaporetto. But it was still impossible that he would commit murder. He had no reason.

"No way," said Will. "There's been a mistake."

We looked at each other; we still had loyalty to Sean in common.

"I think you're right. I think either the police were given that hint by someone on Knight's team or somehow Knight's people managed to 'suggest' Sean kill him. If that's the case, we're on truly dangerous ground. Knight must absolutely believe killing the professor would be for the good of human and Fangborn kind."

No one said anything; they all seemed to understand the importance of this.

"Uh, why would he do that?" I said. "Seems like an incredibly stupid thing to do."

"It is," Gerry said. "If you believe that it's better we remain hidden. A large minority of the Family doesn't, for various reasons. And…who in their right mind would want to unchain anything that shows up in a prophesy? Never mind Identification; it just doesn't sound safe."

There was a long hesitation. Clearly it was a complicated matter.

"Hey, wait," I said. "If Knight's going to make this announcement—and if he's believed—doesn't that make him evil?"

"No, it just makes him a lousy student of our democracy," Gerry said.

"He thinks he's taking a long-term view in the fight against evil," Claudia said. "We can't confuse political maneuvering with real evil. Fangborn can be willful or wrong about many things. We can disagree, we can do stupid things." Here she looked at her brother, who gave her the finger. "We don't thrive on the unhappiness of others, we don't murder or torture for pleasure, which is how I define evil. It's just that until recently, in the twentieth century, when our numbers started rebounding after the world wars, we've been concerned with survival and protecting humanity. Identification wasn't even a consideration."

"We don't have time for history and philosophy," Ben said. "We need a plan for *now*."

"Agreed," Gerry said. "Bad enough Knight should identify the existence of the Fangborn, but what if he starts chucking magical and mythical objects around, too?"

"We have no evidence of 'magic,' only that which is unexplained," Claudia said.

"OK, so Zoe glowing like a, well, a beacon on Delos isn't magic?" Gerry asked.

Ben and Claudia opened their mouths to disagree.

Will held up a hand. "Let's put it this way: If anyone ever wanted to identify the Fangborn, he's never been in a position to be believed. Not like a senior US senator."

"We need to stop him," Ariana said. "*That's* our plan."

"Clearly he's on this side of the ocean because he's after the Beacon and the keys. He clearly knows about the Orleans Tapestry, so it stands to reason, if there is a connection with an object we can call Pandora's Box, he'll go for that next. It fits with his politics—he wants to expose us to the world." Ben started stacking plates and putting them off to the side.

"I can help with that," Will said. "I'm gonna keep this short, because we need to plan for tomorrow morning. He'll need the fourth figurine if he's going to open the Box. I don't believe he has it, so we need to get to it first. I think that's why he had Professor Schulz killed." He looked at me. "And why he framed Sean."

"We have two advantages, though," I said, trying to ignore the notion I might have led Knight to the kindly Professor Schulz. "The disk and the other figurine—the other key—which is still out there."

Will shook his head. "Wait, Zoe, what are these figurines?"

"OK, the guy in London, Grayling? He claimed they were the keys to Pandora's Box. They are little clay things, like dolls, but they're really ornaments you find on some types of Greek pottery." Score one for me for knowing something Will didn't.

"My specialty is Roman colonies, Zoe. Not Greek pottery. I've never even seen a picture of the type of pottery you're talking about."

"You're the expert, here," Gerry said to me.

It was like he threw a bucket of water on me; I was suddenly breathless. "I'm...nothing of the sort. It took me six years to get my BA. That doesn't make me an archaeologist. It means I've had a thorough grounding in the work and principles, a lot of ancient history, but it makes me—*barely*—qualified to recognize the working end of the shovel."

Ben shrugged. "Well, that is infinitely more training than I've had."

The others nodded. I felt a weight settle down on me. It's not like I picked archaeology because it was easy. I had picked it because...it wasn't about me, not directly. I could wallow in the research. The past didn't bring with it the weight of making rent, dodging my father's family, my growing psychosis.

Now it seemed it did. Maybe it hadn't been a coincidence.

I explained quickly about the figurines I had seen from what I remembered from Jenny. "Thing is, that's just what we archaeologists know. I don't know what they have to do with the document in the Tapestry."

"The figurines you had came from—?"

"I think Delphi, Delos, and Didyma, according to Rupert Grayling." That reminded me, and I pulled out the disk. "I think the last one must be at Claros."

"Why?"

"That's on the map, here." I oriented them and showed them where the site was. "Modern-day Turkey, the western coast. All the marked sites are temples with oracles. Dedicated to Apollo."

"Let's see it."

I was reluctant to let them touch it, but I kept reminding myself: These were people I needed to trust, people who could keep my secrets, because they had so many of their own. They'd helped me save Danny, and that made them family to me, more than any fangs or fur. I watched nervously as they passed it around and explained how old maps of the world were circular, and how I thought this one indicated four of the most important oracles in ancient times, at the height of the classical Greek period.

When it came back to me, the disk was warm. I blushed when I realized it had been heating up in everyone's hands. Maybe it had been my imagination it had pulsed on Delos...

But the others had seen its extravagantly white light, too. Face it, Zoe. You're it.

"Anyway," I said, taking the disk back at long last, "you can see, it looks like a version of the map of Hecataeus, who was from Miletus, on the coast of Turkey, and it's organized the way he described the towns in his work—"

"How do you know that? It seems like very arcane knowledge," Ben asked.

"It took me two and a half extra years to graduate because I was moving around," I said. "Not because I had to repeat courses. And I checked. The places marked are all important oracles sites."

"Our people," Ariana said, nodding.

"What? Greeks?"

"Fangborn. There are oracles as well as vampires and were-wolves. Didn't you know that?"

"Well, kinda." I shook my head. "But I never thought of, you know, Greek oracles as maybe being Fangborn oracles."

"They aren't always, but I think in this case it's a good bet."

I slumped. "I know hardly anything—"

"And that's going to change." Gerry stood up. "People, I'm beat. It's been a long day of outrunning international authorities and hard sailing. I need to sleep. I think, with everyone's consent, we need to head for Claros. You said Knight doesn't have the last figurine?"

"On Delos, Adam Nichols said he only had three," I said. "And…yeah, I sensed only three on the boat when the disk…gave off the beam of light."

"And they don't know where to look next?"

"They sure didn't see this drawing on the disk. Even Ariana and Ben didn't know what was on it."

"Last question: Do they have what we've been calling Pandora's Box?" Claudia looked around. "We know about the keys, so we have to assume there's something they unlock."

I shook my head. "I don't know."

"So we head to Claros and look for the last one," Gerry said. "Then we try to figure out how they work together and figure out how to defang Knight." He pushed his chair in. "It will take a couple of days of motoring, at least, so we can stay under the radar. So I propose to swap off captaining with Ben and Claudia, and I'll get Zoe up to speed on Fangborn culture and try to get her powers under control. They'll be looking for her, not a crowd of yachters, and with any luck, by the time we get there, we'll get this figured out."

No one disagreed, and the idea of a few days of resting, surrounded by people who weren't trying to kill me, was very appealing. There was one thing, however.

"Is there any way we can find out about Sean?" I said. "I don't like the idea of him being alone, and a murder suspect."

Claudia said, "Will?"

Will frowned and looked away. "I'll try. I may be able to reach him, but I think you're right. If someone got to him, I suspect Sean's in Senator Knight's hands now, willingly or no."

We cleared up, and everyone drifted off to chores or their cabins. Will vanished, which was fine. I still wasn't sure I could talk to him about all the personal stuff I probably should have discussed when we were still together, and I wasn't sure he'd forgiven me for ruining his plans to capture Dmitri in Berlin. But I still wanted to follow him.

Chapter 23

It took me a minute to remember where I was when I woke up the next morning. My cabin was well designed, small but not claustrophobic. After an unexpected lurch of the boat rolled my stuff from the top of the cabinet to the floor, I figured out that everything had to be inside a locker or under a net. I'd found the shower last night, so tiny I could barely turn around inside it; but it had hot water and that was good enough for me.

I was shy about going above. After all, I had gone to a lot of trouble throughout my whole life not to draw attention to myself, and last night's revelations about my potential role in Fangborn and world affairs were plain horrifying. Under the sink was a bag of clothespins, so I rinsed out a few things and then brought them up to the main deck with me. A line was stretched out, and I hung them up, making sure they were safely fastened. The wind was picking up a little.

Then breakfast smells hit me. I forgot about shy and beat a path for the table.

Danny was there. He was eating like a horse. He looked tired but so much better, even with the small piece of surgical tape on his nose.

"Hey, you!" I hugged him around the shoulders.

"Hey!"

"I'm so sorry this happened," I whispered to him. "It's all my fault."

"What do you mean?" He stepped back from me, cocking his head. "You're the reason I got away from him."

I was saved from thinking about what I'd eventually do to Dmitri when the others arrived. True to form, there wasn't much talk during the first few minutes. When Fangborn get together, they generally—

I realized I was going to have to tell Danny I was a werewolf. In fact, that out of the seven people on the boat, he and Will were in the single-skinned minority.

Later, I decided hastily. After breakfast, at least. I already had about sixteen things on my "too hard" list, and this one could wait.

A few minutes later, Gerry got up. "OK, orders of the day. Ariana, you've got galley duty today, so you're excused from everything else."

Ben grumbled something about too much oregano.

Gerry—and everyone else—pretended not to hear him. "Ben, you've got the helm today. We'll get underway, and when we're clear of the harbor, Zoe, you and I will start Fangborn school."

I felt my stomach clench. I tried to think of a word that sounded like "Fangborn" I could use to cover Gerry's gaffe.

I turned to Danny, who was scraping off his plate into the garbage. "Uh, what he means is—"

He looked up. "I didn't know you were a werewolf—how come you never told me?"

"Uh, what?"

"Claudia's been explaining." He shook his head. "You never said anything to me."

He was calm, only curious. If Claudia had told him about the Fangborn and me, maybe with a little vampiric push, he was bound to accept the truth. "Um, I didn't know? I thought I was going mental?"

"Oh, Zoe." His brow furrowed. "You poor thing."

I patted his arm, reassuring him so I wouldn't start crying myself. "It's better now. It explains a lot."

"It opens up a lot of other questions, about your family."

I held up a hand. "Yeah, trust me, I'll be looking into that." I didn't tell him of Dmitri's probable connection with my father.

"Do you mind if I sit with you and Gerry? Listen in?"

I shrugged. "Fine with me. You can leave for the naked stuff."

"Fine with me," he said.

"Not fine."

We looked up. Will was shaking his head.

"Can't do it. It would get me in trouble with the TRG, and worse, it would get you into a bad place with the Fangborn. If anyone ever tortured you, you'd spill it all, and we can't risk the breach."

I saw a little flutter in Danny's temple and saw his jaw tighten. "I've *been* tortured. How about you?"

"I have training." Will straightened and crossed his arms. "I have precautions put into place."

"I can get them, too. Forget-me juice in the back tooth or something." He turned to me. "Claudia filled me in on a lot yesterday."

"I'm the only one who's getting paid a government wage and benefits to take the chance," Will said. "I'm the only one with a security clearance and training."

"Fine. Where do I sign up?"

"Danny, you can't do that!" I stared at him. "You have a good job, you have...a normal life. After all we've been through—"

"You think I'll still have a job when I get home? I've been AWOL for days."

"You know they'd take you back in an instant. Call them now, tell them it was a family emergency."

"You think I got the application forms in my pocket?" Will said.

"I think you have a phone with access to websites with the forms. I think you have the authority to hire and fire anyone you like, and at your pay grade, you can—"

"You've been prying into my—classified government documents!"

Danny couldn't conceal a faint smile. "Maybe."

"You could go to prison for this," Will said. He was struggling to stay calm.

"If you can prove I did it, first."

I'd decided this had gone too far. I stepped in front of Danny and growled at Will. Maybe showed a little fang.

"Hold!"

I froze in my tracks. Gerry had barked out the command so forcefully, I had no choice in the matter. Drill sergeants could have taken lessons.

"We don't do that," he said to me. "You don't use your wolfself to intimidate Normals."

"I thought that's what you were trying to get me to do!" I backed off from Will, though.

"In the face of evil, yes. In the face of a spat, no. You can yell, whine, bitch—punch him in the nose, for all I care. Anything a human would do. But you don't show your fangs without real need. Got it?"

I didn't like it, but with everyone watching, I didn't have much choice. Not if I didn't want to look like a serious jerk. "Got it."

"OK." He smiled, and suddenly everything was OK again, my slip forgotten and done with.

He turned to Will. "This is an emergency. I'm not going to tell you who to hire or not, but I think we have to bend the rules a little. He might be able to help Zoe get the Change under control; he's already seen us in action. And he needs to know about the political stuff if he's gonna help us."

Will's fists were clenched; he was struggling to stay calm. "Why not drop him off at the nearest airport and send him home? Why involve him at all?"

"He's already involved. He has information we can use against Dmitri." He nodded at Danny. "You want in?"

"Yes."

Gerry looked around. "Anyone else have strong feelings for or against? Or an option besides Danny being in or out?"

Lots of shaking heads. "We need all the friends we can get," Ben said unexpectedly.

"OK, we're done then," Gerry said. "And if you want to blame someone after, if we're still alive, you can blame me, Will."

"I don't like it," Will said. "But I'm living by your rules out here, just like we agreed. Considering me a kind of ambassador while we're out of the US." He turned to Danny. "If I can't talk you into going home, which would be the smart thing to do, can I get your brief on Dmitri? I know it won't be easy, but it would help."

"Whatever will hurt him," Danny said. "Whenever you want."

"I'll be with you," I said. "When you tell him."

"No." Danny and Gerry spoke at the same time.

"You have class with me now," Gerry added.

"Let me do it with Will first," Danny said. "It'll be easier with…not-family first. I'll tell you after I've sort of gotten used to it, OK?"

I nodded, and tried not to feel hurt. But that was the way Danny did things, hiding away in his own world until he could talk to me about it. I sure wasn't going to make him do anything he didn't want to, not after what he'd been through.

"We got three hours before lunch," Gerry said once we were at the front of the boat. "What do you want first? The cultural stuff or the physical stuff?"

"Cultural, please."

"OK, we'll do that second. That will be the carrot for getting through working on the Change."

I gave him a sour look, which had zero effect. We sat down, and I felt my palms begin to sweat. I really hated wrestling with the Change.

"OK, when your power first started to manifest itself," he said. "You were...what? Twelve, thirteen?"

"Sixteen."

Gerry looked troubled. "Seriously? That's old for us. Was it at the same time as your first period?"

"Oh, jeez, really?" It wasn't my cycle I didn't want to talk about. It was the horrible years of junior high and high school I wanted to avoid.

"It'll help me help you," he said. "I promise it's not for kicks."

"A couple of years after I started. So when did you start... being able to Change?"

He frowned, then nodded. "I was twelve. Puberty and power seems to go hand in hand for most of us, so your case is a little unusual. But with your upbringing, or lack thereof—"

"What was your upbringing?"

"Raised at home until I was ready for school, when we're packed off for special training." He shrugged. "We call it 'Fangborn Academy,' and it's tough—regular school lessons, but lots of extra education on Fangborn history, ethics, that kind of stuff." He looked a little wistful. "Lots of training in 'Scenarios,' how to use our powers. That part was the best."

It sounded nice to me, being surrounded by family, being guided so carefully. But the notion of the Academy reminded me of another institution, the one my mother had escaped from.

"My mother...she had to be Fangborn, too, didn't she?" I said suddenly. I wanted to know and didn't want to know.

"Yes. I mean, we can have kids with Normals, but it's super rare, and you never get a shape-changer offspring. Probably she had some oracular power, if you don't think she was a werewolf or vamp."

If she was an oracle, her hunches—about when we needed to run, trusting Sean to keep her papers, all sorts of things—were starting to make sense. "So why didn't she teach me all this?"

Gerry thought a long while. "I don't know. When we found out about you, we couldn't find any records of your parents. That's odd; we have long, fairly complete genealogies. There are some groups who isolate themselves, some who try to deny what they are. This happened back in the 1930s. I thought almost all of them had been contacted and reintegrated after, but maybe not. Maybe she was brought up like that. There were as many different responses to being Fangborn as there are cultures, but there was the Great Convocation in 1946, and we realized, if we were going to survive, we needed to act with as much unity as we could."

He looked up sharply. "And you are getting me off the point and into the history, which is dessert. All right; you're going to be a tough one, but let me ask you some questions."

He went down a whole list: the first time I felt different, the first time I Changed, what happened after, the times I'd felt the call to fight evil, etcetera. It was a little bit like being head shrunk, which I hated— I'd had my share of guidance counselors and social workers. But privacy wouldn't make me more effective against our enemies. I gritted my teeth and promised myself I would beat them down for all of this.

"No help there," Gerry said after the last question. "OK, exercises. Remember what we tried in Berlin? We're gonna work from there."

I told him about my failed attempt to Change on my own in Venice, on the stairway, with so many people in view.

"That's good. We make every effort not to Change, not to be seen by Normals."

That reminded me of the fight on Delos. After I told him, Gerry shrugged. "We know Dmitri has information about Fangborn, even if he doesn't know everything about us. We got a bigger problem at hand."

I sagged. "Like what?"

"I'm guessing you smoked a lot of dope, drank a lot when you were younger? To keep from Changing?"

When I was younger? Try right up until this trip, bud. "It kept me mellow, most of the time. Which I think helped me keep from Changing every time I got pissed off, which seemed to be always. But the times it didn't work, I always blamed it on the moon. And then it helped me forget, once I slipped up."

"That's a lot of reinforcement to overcome. Let's get to it. Close your eyes."

"Why?" I was tired of him poking, prying, and giving orders.

"Because I said so."

I closed my eyes. I breathed in through my nose and out through my mouth. I searched for my happy place, a quiet place in the universe.

I felt an insistent nudge. Gerry's foot against my side. I opened my eyes. Yawned.

"That's not meditation. That's a nap."

"Sorry."

"You don't seem to be trying very hard."

"You keep telling me to do the opposite. 'Let yourself go,' 'keep control of yourself,' 'just trust me,' 'go with your instincts.' What the hell am I supposed to do?"

"Danny's a Normal, but he's signing up for something incredibly dangerous. You don't even care about him, about our mission, enough to try to bring your powers on deck."

I took a deep breath; he was right, but I didn't like it. "Hey, you're asking me to learn stuff that I should have been taught years ago. I didn't get raised in one of your special schools. I didn't even have a childhood Normals would consider normal—"

"Yeah, I get it, Zoe. But now you have a chance to fix so much of that, and you won't."

"*Can't.* I can't do it. Look, you want me to do something I've struggled my whole life to avoid. I've done everything in my power to resist the Beast, Changing, for the past eight or nine years. It's not going to happen overnight."

"And we need it to." He looked down, trying to think. "Let me think about this. Go help Ariana in the galley for a while. We'll try again after lunch."

The last thing I wanted to do was try again, so helping Ariana was fine.

"That didn't take long," she said, looking up from a grocery list.

"Little break," I said. "Need some help?"

"Not a lot of room in here. How about you take these on deck and peel them?" she said, handing me a bowl full of eggplant. "Ordinarily I'd just cook them skins on, but these are still pretty tough."

Great, I thought as I took the bowl. I'm banished from the galley, too.

I sat there peeling eggplant while the wind whipped my hair. That reminded me: I looked up just in time to see one of my bras go sailing off the line, off into the wild blue—

Will reached up and caught it. He glanced down at it, at me, and smiled.

I just about melted; his smile still did that to me. Then he fastened it back on the line, making sure to loop the bra through its own strap so it couldn't get loose again. He did the same with the other things, finding clever ways to keep them all from sailing away.

Will hanging up my laundry still looked natural to me.

"How's Danny?" I asked.

"Tough morning. We're taking a breather," he said. "This doesn't look like Fangborn Academy."

"It's detention." I shrugged. "I've been fighting my Fangborn nature for a long time, Will." *And I gave up everything to do it*, I added to myself.

He hunkered down and replaced an eggplant peel that had escaped. "There's an awful lot at stake, you know. Beyond our own interests. That's why Gerry's so afraid he'll fail."

"Afraid *I'll* fail, you mean. He's acting like I'm going to get all this in three or four days when it takes a whole culture more than sixteen years to train a real Fangborn."

"You're a real Fangborn, and no, he'll be the one who fails. You're right; you don't have any of the training an adult Fangborn has. You don't have the training an *eight-year-old* has. So when the world has descended into chaos, when the Fangborn are either overwhelmed and exterminated or in a state of civil war, fighting for the right to survive, or the unhappy peacekeepers in a genocidal stalemate, it won't be a twenty-something stray people will blame. It will be the full-grown warrior who failed to get the edge that might have won."

I put down my knife. "As if I couldn't feel any worse…"

"The point's not to make you feel bad. The point is to impress you with what's at stake. It's not just you and Danny anymore, Zoe." He got up, brushed off his hands, and moved aft. He turned back. "It may not even get to that. The last figurine might be missing, and maybe Knight won't be able to get the juice to pull off his plan. But if in the meantime we run into Dmitri again…wouldn't you like to unleash on him? And know you've got control over it?"

He glanced over at the clothesline, a brightly colored row of underwear, merrily dancing on the wind like a row of cancan dancers. He didn't quite turn around before I saw him grin again. He always did enjoy lingerie.

I sighed and went back to my work. If nothing else, I was good at peeling eggplant.

Gerry wasn't at lunch. Things were worse than I thought.

"He's working on something below," Claudia said when I asked.

"Should I bring him a plate or something?" I said. Apologies went better with food.

"No thanks. He ate." She laughed. "Trust me; if he's hungry, he won't stay away long."

He didn't. I saw him on deck while I was helping Ariana clean up after lunch. He was typing quickly on a laptop. "We're gonna try something different," he said without looking up. "I can't do this the way I usually would, in hours instead of years. So I got a plan."

"I think it's risky," Ariana said. She and Claudia had come up on deck.

"It *is* risky," Claudia agreed. "Perhaps impossible."

"You're only saying that because no one's ever done it before," Gerry said. He finished scanning the screen, hit a key, then closed the cover. "What we're going to try to do is suggest you Change."

"I've told you. I *like* the suggestion," I said. "Just not sure how to implement it."

"No, I mean, we're gonna get you to Change, and at the same time, Claudia's gonna give you a little jab with some suggestibility venom behind it. It should incline you, when you think of a certain phrase, to want to Change. To give you a push."

"Yeah, but what's going to make me Change in the first place?"

"I'm going to Change, like we did in Berlin. If we need to, Ariana can, too, but I think she's just here to keep an eye on Claudia."

"What's gonna happen to Claudia?"

"We don't know," she said. "Like Gerry said, no one's ever tried doing this before. There's never, at least not in the records I've seen, been the need."

"We don't know anything's going to happen," Ariana said. "Let's not get excited before something goes wrong."

"Our main concern is you." Claudia caught her hair, whipping about in the wind, and tied it back. "I don't like you having a crutch; if you do ever get the chance to train yourself properly, it might make it much more difficult. And—"

"And we don't know what a dose of vamp juice will do to you while you're in mid-Change," Gerry finished. "Not really."

"What do you mean, not really?"

"Messing with Fangborn blood chemistry is always hazardous, and we know nothing about your blood heritage. Doing something like this, it's so risky it's not sanctioned by the Family. Most of the Families worldwide signed agreements during the Cold War not to attempt this outside a very controlled environment."

I shrugged. "I'm not much use as it is. This might help. Let's give it a shot." I looked around. "Where we gonna do this, and how?"

"Right here. I'll Change, you try to go, and Claudia will bite you."

I remembered what I'd seen her do with Danny. Alarm must have showed on my face.

"Don't worry," Claudia said. "You'll feel nothing. Our fangs are designed to leave no marks, and there'll be plenty of anesthetic."

"No marks unless we want to leave marks," Ariana corrected.

"But first, we need a phrase for you to think on. A mantra, a key," Claudia said, ignoring Ariana. "Something unusual, but not too hard to remember. I don't want you freaking out if you accidentally hear it."

"How about 'trowel bite'?" I said, thinking of Dmitri and my new favorite memory of him, with my trowel stuck in his thigh.

They all thought a moment and couldn't imagine a scenario where it would be commonly used. "Let's just hope Trowel Bite doesn't become the world's next greatest rock band," Gerry said. "Ready everyone?"

We all nodded.

"Here we go."

Chapter 24

Claudia Changed.

I didn't feel it the same way I did when Gerry had Changed; maybe because I wasn't expecting it, maybe because it wasn't the same vibe. Or maybe because it was only halfway: She was now bipedal, dark violet, her hair and lips purple, almost black. Her nose receded, her fangs extended, her claws grew.

I kept telling myself she was a friend. But it was weird, somehow more alien than when I'd seen Gerry as a wolf-man, and I was glad we were at sea. She looked pretty funny, a snakelike monster in shorts and a bikini top, her purple hair in a messy ponytail.

Claudia started talking to me, low, so I almost couldn't hear her words. It didn't matter; I felt the effect immediately. I felt comfortable, relaxed, a little sleepy at the same time. At the same time, I *wanted* to pay attention; I *wanted* to focus on following Gerry into the Change. I was there, on deck, ready to do whatever they wanted.

Honestly, it was the best I'd felt in years. I almost didn't mind it wasn't entirely my will driving.

"You ready, Zoe?" she said.

"Dig in, Claudia," I said. I wanted to be cool about it, but I was too drowsy. A part of me wasn't inclined to watch the process, any more than I could look at a needle going into my arm at the doctor's office.

I felt her take my hand. Warm, dry. A little pressure, the merest *idea* of a bite, somewhere at the back of my thoughts...

Then I couldn't *not* look.

Claudia held my hand, her mouth over my wrist, working in that inhuman way. I wasn't scared, but it was pretty freaky to remember her as I'd met her in Boston. Ariana had Changed, too, and she whispered in Claudia's ear, guiding or anchoring her.

Ariana looked up, her green-and-black-toned scales still alien to me. Her voice was familiar, though her Italian-accented English was now made even more exotic by vampiric hisses.

"Zoe, when you want to Change, remember the words 'trowel bite.' Gerry, go!"

Gerry Changed halfway.

I felt the urge I had in Berlin. This time, I didn't think about it, I just went with it. Let the pull of Gerry's Change bring my own. But this time, it was more like a bicycle drafting behind an M1 Abrams tank.

Claudia let go of my arm, because she got a mouthful of fur and because I suddenly needed all four limbs for balance. I rolled around on the deck awkwardly because my tail was stuck in my shorts.

Gerry had pulled out a knife and said, "Zoe, stay still."

I waited patiently as he opened up the back seam of my shorts, just enough for my tail to stick out. The rest of my clothing hung oddly, but I didn't care. I raced down the stairs to the wheel, woofed at Ben, and turned tail and ran back to the bow. I skidded on the smooth deck boards and would have gone right under the railing and into the drink if Ariana hadn't grabbed the collar of my shirt just in time.

"Take it easy, Zoe," she said. "First you master the Change. Then you master shipboard life as a wolf. Can you go back to skinself? Just think of your phrase and let the suggestion take you."

I tried, and when I thought *trowel bite,* I felt the urge coming on me. I followed it.

With limited success. I was back on two feet, but a wolf-woman.

Before I could get discouraged, Claudia looked up, a little blearily. "Don't sweat it right away. Check it out. Last time you were half-Changed, you didn't even know it. Get the hang of this body, this skin. Can you say something?"

"Of course I can say something," was what I'd meant to say. But my palate and teeth had altered dramatically, and it took a few tries. Thinking about it made it even harder. "Yes."

"Good! Keep working on it. Start with the alphabet, try a couple of tongue-twisters when you get that down. It'll help with your enunciation."

Gerry helped when I got hung up on some of the harder sounds. I watched how he moved his mouth to compensate for the lack of human lip structure, and pretty soon I was very nearly selling seashells by the seashore.

Will came on deck and set down a tray of food. If I'd been capable of blushing, I would have. It took all my self-possession to keep from running away.

He truly knew what I was now.

It didn't matter. We weren't together anymore. So why did I always feel so amped-up crazy when he was near me?

"If you can Change back, you can have a snack," he said, waving a cookie at me.

"It's not obedience training," I said slowly. He was grinning wickedly. "Wait, what's this?" I pretended to fish around in my pocket and pulled out my fist, middle finger extended.

"Good, Zoe! Awesome pronunciation!" Gerry had gone to skinself and made a beeline for the sandwiches. "Thanks, Will."

Claudia and Ariana also crowded Will and his tray. The thought of three hungry Fangborn descending on food I suddenly realized I was craving should have provided the impetus for me to Change instantly.

I got tangled up in my own thoughts.

"If you get stuck, Zoe," Gerry said from around a too-large mouthful of sandwich, "just calm down. Focus, and remember your phrase."

"What's the phrase?" Will asked.

"Trowel bite."

"Trowel bite!" Will said, raising his hands.

"It's a psychological trigger, not a magic spell, you jackass," I said. I even got "trigger" and "jackass" out pretty good, but I still wasn't human. I closed my eyes and tried to center myself, suddenly seeing the point of what Gerry had been trying to teach me this morning.

A sudden shift in perception and swirl in my reality, and I was back in my own skin. One of my own skins, I reminded myself.

No more demonizing the Beast. No more demonizing myself.

There was one sandwich left, and I dove on it, slapping Gerry's hand out of the way. "Nice try, buster. Back off."

"Well, when you finish that, I made you this." He took a folder from Will's tray and handed it to me. Since I couldn't eat it, I hadn't noticed it before.

"What is it?" I opened it and saw a sheaf of papers clipped together. No cover sheet, no index, just a set of lists interspersed with text. "'The Ten Lessons'? 'The Twenty Laws'? I don't get it."

"A Fangborn primer," Gerry said. "Not as good as we keep at home for the kids, but then, we keep very close account of those. This isn't nearly as comprehensive, but it should give you an idea."

"And if the worst happens, and someone does find it," Ariana said, "I can tell them it's part of the prototype for the game I'm designing."

"If the worst happens, it won't be someone finding that," Gerry said. The humor was gone from his face.

"Just because things suck," Claudia said, "doesn't mean we get lax about everything else."

Danny joined us, and that jarred loose memories of *Dungeons & Dragons*, long afternoons with rule books, polyhedral dice, and graph paper. I started laughing so hard I nearly coughed up my sandwich.

"What? What is it?" he said.

I held it up when I could breathe again, tears streaming down my face. "They made me a *Monster Manual*, Danny."

"Good to know there's a manual," he said. "Can I see it?"

I shrugged, handed it to him, and looked around. "You can read the whole thing when I'm done, I guess. Everyone seems to agree you're on the team."

He glanced through it before handing it back. "You know, Ariana, the more original documents I look at, the more I might be able to help. I can get a lot of information from the arcane prophesy sentence structures and word choices that a regular translator might have missed."

Both Ariana and Will looked interested. "We have some copies of the Tapestry text and some others on my machine," he said. "Since you're on the team. The funding at the TRG has been so strapped, we've only been able to deal with the most immediate of problems, so antiquities research has given way mostly to biological research. Anything you could do, we'd appreciate."

"Speaking of what you can do." Gerry turned to me. "Tonight. You. A brief lecture on what we will find at Claros. What we should be looking for and the most likely place we'll find the figurine."

My jaw dropped. "Are you kidding me? I've never been there. I had *one* class on religion and temple sites, maybe heard of Claros just once before...before London."

"But you know the architecture and city layouts, or whatever—you know roughly what to expect," Gerry said. "I said before, Zoe, whatever little you have is way more than what we have. And we all need to be up to speed when we reach the site."

"I can cobble something together, if someone can get me a computer and some Wi-Fi. But honestly? Most of these sites have been excavated for decades, even centuries. There's no guaranteeing the artifact will still be on the site. And even if someone excavated it, there's a good chance it will be in a museum in London or Berlin or Rome or Istanbul or Ankara. If it hasn't been lost, stolen, or sold."

"We have something else on our side, though," Claudia said. "We have Zoe's disk."

"It's a map," I agreed, "but it's very crude. It really only lists those four towns. It's not going to help us on the ground."

"Unless proximity to the other figurines was what caused that column of light."

We stared at Claudia.

"Like, how?" Gerry said. "They were...texting each other?"

"I don't know," she admitted. "When I think about it, I come up with Victorian words like 'resonance' or 'vibrations' or 'refraction.'"

"The more I think about it, the more I think you've been in the sun too long. You're the last person who'd be hinting that these things are magic, Claud. You're the one always yapping about 'science.'"

"Yes. Just because I can't explain something doesn't mean it isn't real. Zoe and her golden disk aren't shining right now, and they weren't before she got to Delos and—more importantly— close to Adam's party. Assuming they had the figurines with them, I think that's what caused that reaction. If that's true, then it stands to reason we may be able to locate the fourth and final figurine by proximity, too."

"And what if the fourth figurine is underground?" Gerry said. "Or smashed into bits? Or...any of a hundred other things?"

"Then we'll be no worse off than we are now. But I think it's a good hypothesis."

Gerry rolled his eyes, but I liked Claudia's notion. "It felt like…it wanted to be somewhere," I said. "It was excited about something. And there was a response, the first time, when I was in my room in Venice. There was a burst of light, and then a kind of… review…of my memories."

Everyone stared at me. I felt incredibly lame. "You had to be there, I guess, but that's what I got."

"I guess that makes it final," Ariana said. "You're the heir to the Beacon."

As tidy as that sounded, I'm not sure I liked my new title and potential status as ender of the known world.

Chapter 25

I practiced several more hours until we found a mooring off a small island to the east by late afternoon. I spent a couple of hours with the reports I had from Professor Schulz and from Jenny Kelner and the images Will got me from the TRG files with the flaky Internet we were able to pick up from the nearby marina. I promised myself that as soon as I had any money, I was going to buy myself an electronic reader so I could download books instantly. It would sure beat trying to re-create notes I dimly recalled from classes years ago.

Ben and Ariana arrived back from the marina with boxes of supplies and something that smelled like fresh-baked bread and cheese—*bourek*. Food was turning out to be a quick gateway into a new language for me. Once the carnage of dinner was cleared away, I got out my notes and, with a nervous glance around, started to talk.

"OK, so, temples are basically the houses of the gods or heroes. Inside, they're made up of a series of concentric spaces that lead you into the holy of holies. Outside, you are led to the edge of the precinct by a sacred way, which is sometimes even paved with marble. This leads to a reception area or propylaea outside the temple area, where people would gather and wait to be greeted by the priests. Closer to the temple, there was an altar, which was outside the temple because sacrifices were to be shared among the populace—only the bones, hides, and smoke belonged to the gods."

I looked around, a little sheepishly. "That, traditionally, was considered to be the doing of Prometheus, for what it's worth. He tricked the gods into accepting the lesser parts, so humans could have the meat.

"Generally speaking, the temple was organized so you moved from profane to sacred. Past the altar, you went up steps to a platform, where columns around the temple on the platform separated it from the outside world. An interior room without windows—the cella—was further divided by a row of columns. Each time you move forward, you're being prepared, in a sense, to encounter your god. The cella also had a porch at the front, the pronaos, and a screened-off sacred space in the back, the adyton, or holy of holies, where the god was housed. Usually that was an important statue, and very valuable. This part of the temple often acted as a vault, housing the treasure from both the temple and town."

I looked around, but no one seemed to have any questions so far. "Most of the temples in Greek sites were located near springs or water sources, also considered sacred. Often there were even earlier temples to other gods here, so there's a kind of pedigree of holiness associated with these sites, going back thousands of years."

"But these are sites in Turkey, not Greece," Ben said. "We have to go through customs tomorrow."

"Right, I mean 'Greek' in the sense that these sites were Greek colonies. And actually, 'Greek' is kind of a misnomer, because we're really dealing with city-states like Sparta or Athens, and not what we think of as the modern state."

I hoped he wouldn't ask any more because I was only about three chapters ahead of my small class. "The towns, too, followed a regular format. They were usually within walls for protection, and the streets were often gridded. They all had acropolises, or high places of religious or secular power, as well as temples, theaters—which were also for religious festivals—and shopping areas or agoras, houses, baths, running water, and gymnasia. Malls, gyms, and plumbing—all you need for a civilized life.

"In this region, the towns usually were on the coast, so they relied on trade; they were often within eyesight of each other. If they failed, it was because their harbors silted up, pirates raided them, or there was an earthquake." I shook myself. "OK, that's enough of generalities. Now for the specifics. This "—I pulled out a map from my pile—" is Claros. It's been excavated by French and Turkish teams, and it's pretty important because so much of the subterranean temple structure is intact. Also, the oracle was supposedly the second most important in Asia after Delphi."

"I thought that was Delos?" Gerry said.

"That's what every oracular site that isn't Delphi claims," Will said. "Big money in temples and oracles, today and in ancient times."

"It's important to us," I said, "because we think that's where the last figurine or key can be found, if it's still undiscovered. I've looked through the reports I have and everything online. I don't see any mention of any pottery with figurines. Usually something unusual like that would be the star artifact, and made much of."

Will looked over at the map. "But most of this temple's been excavated, right? Wouldn't they have found any of the figurines or pottery that might be associated with the temple? I hate to be a buzzkill, but I'm afraid if there was a figurine here, it's long gone."

"Maybe. But we have to check here. The problem is narrowing it down to looking in one or two places—these sites are extensive. So I have to ask you guys: Are there places that you—we—Fangborn—generally leave messages for each other?"

Ariana frowned. "You mean besides our phones?"

"OK, that's why you're in business and not history," I said. "I mean from the old days. Were there traditions of meeting at the nearest church, say, or at the city gates at midnight, or by the local water source?" I thought a minute. "Wait—vampires can cross moving water, right? Go into churches? That's not real, right?"

"Right." Claudia was trying hard to be patient. "I like sunbathing, I like garlic, I don't like silver, but it's not an allergy. I don't feed on humans."

"I do," Ariana said, preening. "But only if they ask nicely first."

"You're a disgrace, Ariana," Claudia said. "So much for getting rid of the notion that all vampires are oversexed."

"I'm not oversexed enough then."

Now it was my turn to strive for patience.

"Grandpa used to talk about meeting at the edge of town, or the city gates or something," Gerry said. "Something about respecting the territories of other Fangborn, I think? Claud?"

"Sounds right."

"OK, so we'll look near the gateways to the temple—propylaea—and for anything that suggests an official entry point. I'll make up a list, narrow it down to probables and possibles." I looked through the satellite images and the maps from the articles. "These are really nice, Will. The definition is very good."

For a moment, the two of us bent over the maps was like the best of the old times. Magic of a familiar sort. Our eyes met. With a raggedy breath, I turned away.

Will cleared his throat and leafed through the maps. "The guys at the TRG can get some time on a satellite for photos, if you give them enough notice. It's even better than a regular aerial shot."

"Why do you need different pictures, Zoe?" Ben asked. "These drawings are much clearer."

"Those are the archaeological surveys," I said. "They are good, but they only show what was excavated—actually discovered—and what was on the ground nearby. The photos are helpful because if you compare it with the drawings—you can see these different colored spots? Those are changes in the ground, and may be some indication of what is beneath the surface. The plants will vary, depending on the soil, and there'll be differential drying out, depending on what's underneath them. You use a little bit of everything that's available."

"Isn't it assuming an awful lot, to go by what we are saying our grandparents said?" he said. "It doesn't seem logical."

"It *is* a long shot, but it is logical. You can get information about what happened within the past hundred years or so if you interview modern inhabitants of old sites—they'll remember what their grandparents told them, as well as their own lives. You can get traditions that might go back much further than that. So I'm going on the premise that we need to blend Fangborn traditions with what I know about archaeology. I think we should also think about how we're going to tackle this. I mean, do we split up and sort of grub around at the most likely places? Do I go around with the disk and—"

"What's that noise?" Ariana stood up.

Instantly, all the Fangborn were on point. Will and Danny hadn't heard anything, but I realized now Ariana was referring to a sound that wasn't quite the lapping of waves against our hull.

Someone was trying to board the boat.

The air was suddenly buzzing, pregnant with the idea of violence. And the urge to Change.

The idea had no sooner entered my head than my resistance to the Change fell away as easily as a prom dress.

My Cousins were also half-Changed, save for Ariana. I was alarmed to see her vanish from her clothing, which, no longer suspended, fell down in a heap. I realized she'd taken her scaleform and, lightning fast, had darted to the side of the boat. She vanished over the side, and I barely heard her hit the water. The only trace of her was a faint ripple, dark on dark, as she moved toward the stern.

I shivered to think of the danger in the water now. Then I shivered to think I was part of the danger on deck. It was a nice shiver; one I wanted to get used to.

My Fangborn cousins might not have been used to fighting as a team, but they knew where the threat was. I wasn't certain what to do until I realized they were all heading for the back of the boat. The problem was I was picking up on other presences.

On impulse, I reached out and got the impression of men—human men—in the back, as well as other intruders around the front.

"Four astern, three at the, uh, front," I yelled. "Don't let them surround us!"

Gerry whipped his head around, nodded, and dashed to the bow. "You and Will get below, watch Danny."

I nodded and grabbed Will. He looked around wildly, unsure of what we were responding to, but aware something was up.

He'd pulled a gigantic-looking pistol out of nowhere. He looked like he knew how to use it.

Never saw *that* trick before, I thought. I tried not to startle him as I led him below decks. I didn't want him blowing my face off. "Go, now!"

He nodded and, looking back at me, jumped a mile. "Holy—!"

I nodded, trying to shove a rush of other thoughts aside. "Still Zoe," I said. "Downstairs."

Somehow, in a tangle, we made it belowdecks.

"Get in there, stay with Danny," I said. It was hard work, enunciating around a mouthful of teeth, but another shove and some pantomime helped get the point across. "Don't come out unless you hear me give the signal."

"Got it."

He went in, shut and locked the door.

I'd never noticed it before, but apparently, along with the propensity to get violent, the Change made me more commanding, more sure of myself. I certainly wasn't the same desperate, pathetic creature bolting across the Tiergarten because my ex thought I was a monster.

I heard muffled noises from on deck and resisted the urge to join them. Whatever else happened, I'd protect Will and Danny.

I wasn't totally confident in my ability to *stay* Changed, however. The door to Ben's room was open. I saw a pile of tools stowed in a cupboard and grabbed a trenching tool.

That felt better. I always felt better with a shovel in my hands, no matter how small. This one had the benefit of having a serrated edge.

Silence, upstairs. I wasn't afraid, just anticipating trouble. I didn't like waiting for what might be coming next. But I did like being part of this response with my Cousins. It didn't feel like mania. It felt like being part of a team.

I tried to "see" who was out there and got only jumbled images in my head. I was probably too unfocused.

I heard screams, a shot, and a boat's motor outside. I licked my lips. It was hot down here. Could I sweat, in this form? Did I have to pant? I had no idea. What was going on up there?

There were footsteps above the hatch. I tensed, readied myself.

"Zoe, get up here!"

It was Gerry, skinself again.

I bolted up the stairs. Ben was bleeding profusely. Claudia was latched onto his arm, trying to stop it.

"He wasn't the one who screamed," I said.

"No, it was one of the men. Right after he shot Ben."

A thrashing in the water, and a shadow slithered up the anchor line, then over the railing.

It was Ariana—I hoped it was Ariana, because it was a very large, very dark snake. All her mass had to go somewhere. Gerry grabbed a towel and spread it out on the deck.

If I thought he was going to dry off the large snake, I was mistaken. He stepped back and the snake slithered under the towel. A shimmer, a frisson of energy, a brief dance of shadows, and suddenly it was Ariana again, shivering and naked as the day she was born.

With a distinctly European lack of body consciousness, Ariana used the towel to dry her hair first. "Is there another towel, Gerry? I'm drenched."

Gerry seemed grateful to have something else to look at. That towel wasn't nearly big enough, and Ariana was luscious.

"I'll let Will know it's all clear," I said to give him another distraction.

He nodded, and I could tell Gerry the fearless werewolf was blushing by moonlight.

I pounded down the stairs and rapped on the door. "It's OK," I said.

The door opened, and there was Will. He was standing at an odd angle, I realized, to conceal his pistol. "All clear."

"Yup."

He stepped out rather than letting me in. "You should probably Change back," he said. "Before Danny sees you. It can be quite a shock."

I raised my hand to my face and realized it wasn't a hand so much as a paw full of claws, which felt a muzzle instead of a nose, several inches more face than I was used to.

"OK," I said, a little embarrassed. I tried to Change.

Nothing.

"Are you kidding me?" I said.

I took a deep breath and tried again.

Will glanced up at the deck apprehensively and back to me. "Zoe, I hear the harbor master out there. The shot must have brought them. You really have to—"

"I know, I know—" I squeezed my eyes shut and tried to block out the panic and excitement of the fight. *Trowel bite.*

"Zoe! You gotta—!"

The irritation I felt at Will seemed to do the trick. I felt the Beast subside, felt my human skin clammy with perspiration and the night chill. "Yeah, thanks, I got it."

He smiled. "Yeah, you do."

Then he leaned over and kissed me.

If I thought Gerry was blushing on deck, it was nothing to what I felt now. A rush of heat from my toes to my forehead loitered pleasantly below my belly. I felt dizzy. At the same time, the close confines of below deck seemed to crowd in around me and spread out in a vertiginous forever.

"What was that?" I said, my head spinning. It was a good question; a kiss was the last thing I expected. I wanted more.

"Positive reinforcement," he said. "I didn't have a sandwich."

"You guys, get up here!"

It was Gerry again, and from the other noises I heard, we were about to be boarded for the second time that evening.

The Greek equivalent of the harbor master was as curious as I about what had happened.

Gerry explained, and Ben translated, that drunk men had boarded the ship and tried to rob us. Ben fought them off, scaring them away. No one was hurt—though I knew that was a lie. I could sense Ben had been hurt, but he'd ditched his shirt, which presumably was covered in blood. They said they'd put out a report and requested Gerry moor in the marina tonight to prevent further attempts.

"How come you didn't know about the men coming at us from the front?" I asked as Gerry maneuvered us to port. Ben was nearly healed, thanks to Claudia, but unhappy about the loss of his favorite aloha shirt.

"Wind was in the wrong direction," he said, then frowned. "How did you know—?"

"I, uh, sensed there were three more."

He looked at me sharply. "What do you mean, sensed?"

What did I mean? "Um, I can...can't you sort of tell when there are people around you?" I waved a hand. "Sort of get a blurry image of someone nearby?"

"Werewolves can't do that," he said. "I mean, we can smell them, hear them coming, sure."

"No, this is more like...a heads-up display, an idea." Then I was confused, too. "I don't actually see them, just...know they're there when I search for them."

"Are you sure?" He was confused and concerned.

"It started in Berlin," I said. "It's been pretty reliable so far."

"OK, that's weird. That's oracle stuff, that kind of...would you call it 'proximity sense'?"

"Sure."

"Well, we'll look into that tomorrow." He adjusted the course a tad. "Why don't you go down and get some rest. Busy day tomorrow."

I went below, but there was no chance of sleep. It was hot, and once we'd moored, the engine was off and there was no AC. There was noise from the clubs along the waterfront, and now there were mosquitoes, too.

Will's kiss didn't help, either. In spite of me taking off on him, did he still love me? Could he love me, knowing I'd occasionally sprout fangs, claws, and an unladylike amount of body hair? Did I want him to love me? Or did he just have a thing for freaky girls?

After an hour of tossing and turning, I went above deck. Maybe if I sat up a while, I'd relax enough to sleep.

I found a place on the side of the ship away from town and the *thump-thump-thump* of the disco. As hot as it was down below, it was starting to cool off here, and a damp was settling down on every surface.

I sat down on the roughened deck, my legs on either side of the bar, my chin resting on top. It was amazing how many noises there were apart from the town. The ship itself was full of creaks and groans, the water sloshed and lapped, and somewhere below, a generator for the refrigerator hummed. Across the harbor, some-one was watching a game show on their satellite TV. No wonder I couldn't sleep.

"Hey."

I was startled. It was Will. Why hadn't I heard—why hadn't I sensed him? Too wrapped up in my own thoughts. "Hey."

"Room for one more?"

I couldn't well scooch aside, so I gestured with a sweeping hand. He had the whole deck to choose from.

He sat down next to me, as close as he could without actually touching. Close enough so I could feel the warmth of him, all the more apparent for the chill in the air.

He'd changed his shirt. I could smell the different detergent, soap and shampoo, and just underneath, faint traces of sweat and motor oil. He'd been helping Ben with the engine, then showered.

The gun was nowhere to be seen, but I'd seen he was kind of a magician with that, so I assumed it could reappear just as quickly another time.

"Quite a day, huh?"

"Yeah."

"If we get through this, we should do some touring. You've never seen Ephesus; it's even better than the books. You'd love it, and it's not too far away."

"That would be nice." I didn't point out we had a lot to get through before we could make recreational plans.

"Nice night."

Will sucked at small talk. He knew *I* sucked at small talk. Why was he bothering?

I shrugged. I was tired and didn't even want to think about what was coming tomorrow.

He nodded and turned to watch the waves. A nice moment, quiet.

Without warning, I was intensely uncomfortable. If I moved in his direction as much as a millimeter, I'd brush up against him. And this wasn't Fangborn instinct; it was human female response.

Why was that a problem? Things were over between us.

The idea of never being able to touch him again was awful. I felt sick at the thought of it. What the hell was wrong with me?

Kiss me, Will, I thought as hard as I could. If I could sense the locations of people around me, maybe I could plant the idea, like vampires could.

His shirt was too big, or he'd borrowed it. The collar sagged back, so I could see his collarbone and the scar where he'd had a nasty accident on site. I remembered the day as if it was yesterday and not two years ago; he'd held my hand so tight in the car on the way to the hospital I'd had marks for days after. The scar was shiny and taut and I knew if I kissed him right at the top of it, at the base of his throat, he'd—

Before I could stop myself, I'd tilted my head and was suiting action to the thought.

He smelled good. He smelled *great*. I nuzzled his neck, his chest.

He startled—he had been looking the other way—but didn't move.

Kiss me, Will.

I was about to pull away, then quickly drown myself, when it struck me. He wasn't shoving me away. He'd had the whole rest of the boat to sit on, yet any closer to me and he'd be in my lap. I didn't hear him screaming indignation.

Maybe this was OK. It was certainly OK with me.

Want me back, Will.

If this was my last chance, I'd better make it good, so I slid my hand lightly across his chest, let it rest on his other shoulder. Then up to his chin, moving it to meet me. I found his mouth at just the right angle.

He kissed me.

Home.

Home was on fire. I was burning up. The more I kissed him, the more he kissed me back, and the hotter it got.

Pretty soon, it was hard to do all that kissing and grabbing around the railing. I tried to edge back without breaking the kiss; no luck.

He stared at me. "This isn't a good idea."

I shook my head. "Probably not." I swallowed. "Do you care?"

"Um, no."

"Me neither."

We scrambled up and tried kissing again, to see if we could find the moment again. It was remarkably easy, for there it was, as if we hadn't broken off at all, not a minute ago, not two years ago. Only now I could feel every part of him against me, and the ache, the need, was unbearable.

I had his shirt off; he was working on mine.

"Wait," I said, pulling away. It was a wrench. "We can't, we don't have a—"

The hurt and confusion on Will's face vanished. He reached into his pocket and pulled out a little packet. He reached for me, but I put a hand on his chest, stopping him.

"Hang on—where did you get that?" He didn't actually carry a condom around, just in case, did he? Call me jealous, but—

He laughed, a glorious sound. "First-aid kit. They're also in the bathrooms, and I bet the galley and engine room, too. Thorben's parties must be wild."

The world tilted—rather, the boat rolled against the wake. We both lost our footing, found it again in each other's arms. We began kissing again, but were confronted with another problem. It was a calculated risk: If we stayed where we were, would we roll overboard? If we moved, the moment might be permanently gone. I'd never been one for open-air adventure, so I grabbed his hand and led him back to my cabin. The door stuck again, opening it; we barged through. Will slid his hands over my shoulders, under my bikini strings, and my vision blurred, giving way to other, finer sensations.

"Door," I croaked. The boat had never seemed so small.

Will stopped what he was doing; I sagged against the wall. He slammed into the door, shoulder first. It banged shut, he locked it, and, in a tangle of clothing and sheets, we were on the bunk.

Roadblock: pressed up against the hull of the ship, just a thin mattress on a wooden platform, my narrow bed was too small for both of us struggling with our clothes. Too many elbows and knees and not enough space. I extricated myself and, standing again, pulled off the bikini and shorts I'd borrowed from Ariana. Will skinned off his shorts, slid as far back as he could, making room for me.

His gaze never quite made it to my face until I slid in next to him.

Perfect fit.

I hadn't let myself remember the simple joy of making out naked with Will. Denied the possibility of it ever happening again, I couldn't bear to recall it. Now the simple friction of our bodies was almost more than I could bear. I ached in all the right places.

He brushed the back of his fingers against my nipples. I threw my head back into the pillow and gasped. We kissed again. I grabbed his butt, urged him into me. He found his way, and we were there.

I wrapped my legs around him and bit his shoulder to keep from howling.

Chapter 26

The next morning, I awoke alone in my cabin. That didn't surprise me until I saw my clothing was not piled neatly on top of the locker, but was flung all over the floor.

I burrowed down into my pillow, testing my feelings.

Well, I felt…*great*. Once I'd gotten the hang of sex, I'd liked it, and with Will, it had always been amazing. Last night had pushed the needle toward "mind-bending."

Even so, I wasn't looking forward to our next meeting. It would have been easier if he'd just stuck around, so we could—

What, Zoe? Talk it over? You were always so very good at that. Maybe another go-round…?

Something like that. My face warmed, and I noticed I was whistling as I got washed up and dressed.

Besides being reunited with Will, something else had changed in me. Fighting alongside my Cousins last night had been a powerful thing. I had a glimpse, the merest idea of what Gerry had been trying to teach me, about being Fangborn. Part of a Family, with a purpose. It had almost entirely obliterated my shameful feelings about Changing. No more fear of the Beast. No more Beast. The Beast was me, and I now understood I was part of an ancient and powerful Family.

I had a lot to think about.

Everyone else had beaten me to breakfast, and their faces were as somber as the day was beautiful. There was no room next to

Will, so I sat at the end. He did wink at me when our eyes met, so I felt pretty good about that.

Not so about the discussion. Even fruit, eggs, and fresh goat cheese couldn't cheer that up.

"We're pretty sure we need to split up, Zoe," Danny said as I ate. "If the men who attacked us last night knew where to find us, it's clear they're looking for the same things we are. They know where we are, and there's just the seven of us against who knows how many of them. If we split into three groups, we can probably dodge them, or at least distract them from our real target."

"The sanctuary at Claros," I said, finally putting my thoughts about Will, and food, aside.

He nodded. "We'll get there this morning. Ben and I will take the ship north. The rest of you will head into town. You'll split up there and, with Claudia and Gerry, find your way straight to Claros. Ariana and Will will head south, then loop around. We'll keep in contact, and if we don't see anyone following us, we'll all meet you at Claros."

"But what about my training?" I said.

"On hold," Gerry said. "Or at least on the fly. That's why we're going together. So eat up, then get ready. Don't take anything more than you need—"

"I don't have anything more than I need," I said, shoveling the last of my breakfast down. I didn't realize I'd been sneaking looks at Will until I saw him smile, faintly, secretly.

Danny sat on my bunk while I packed up my clean clothes. He looked better than he had in days. Actually, he looked better than he had, ever, period, and I told him so.

"This agrees with you," I said. "I wouldn't have guessed it."

"Me neither. I guess gallivanting doesn't bother me as much now that it's on my terms."

"Even getting kidnapped?"

"Even getting the shit kicked out of me."

I must have looked surprised.

Danny's good humor evaporated. "If I ever see Dmitri again, he gets a bullet in the eye."

"Just give me a chance to ask him about my father." I explained how he had a piece of the figurine that matched the fragment my father had somehow acquired. I looked at him. "You've been bullied before, not like this. But even so, this time...you seem different. Better?"

"Zoe, I kept myself *alive*. I'm different because I'm not help-less like a kid is, even if it's just attitude. This time, the only reason it happened was because five huge guys with *guns* were the bullies, and it took all five of them to get me out of that apartment quietly. That could have happened to anyone, but *I* survived. I like know-ing that, and next time..."

"Next time, I'll tear his—no. I'll save him for you."

"Yeah." He looked thoughtful. "Last night, I thought I heard Georgian being spoken. As in Tbilisi, not Atlanta. I think the men who found us were Dmitri's; one of his guys was a Georgian."

It was a good clue; I wouldn't have been able to tell the dif-ference between Russian, Georgian, or anything else. "You should tell the others."

"I already did. Will and Ben and I discussed it this morning. That's why we decided to split up, to keep them and Knight off our trail."

"So..." I wasn't exactly sure how to bring this up. "You know I'm...I'm a werewolf?"

"Yeah." Suddenly he was shy, too. "Can...would you show me?"

I shrugged. "I can try. I need a minute."

I tried *not* to think about wanting to show Danny what I'd always wanted to confide in him. I tried *not* to think about how bad I was at this, how conflicted I was, how worried I was about what the day would bring, my feelings about Will... I shook myself, closed my eyes, and tried to think of nothing. Then I thought, *trowel bite.*

I felt the Change, opened my eyes, saw Danny, agape.

Then, just as quickly, it faded. I was Zoe again.

No, you've always been Zoe. This is just another aspect, I berated myself. *No, don't blame yourself. It will just make it worse.* "Did you see—?"

"I did. It...lasts longer, usually?"

"I didn't say I was a *good* werewolf. But I'm learning."

"You'll get the hang of it. I'm so proud of you." He hugged me.

"You're proud I can turn into a werewolf?"

"Yep. And someday I'm going to find out just how long you suspected before someone told you it was OK."

"Sorry, like I said, I thought I was crazy."

"Well, you're that, too." He handed me my bag. "Time to go."

I shouldered my bag, unspeakably weary all of a sudden. "Don't fall overboard."

"Don't get kidnapped by Russians," he returned. "I can't recommend it."

I said good-bye to Ben and got into the Zodiac. The ride to the marina was noisy only because of the engine. No one was talking. Once we were in the marina and we'd gotten our visa stamps in our passports, Ariana and Claudia went to find a rental car. Gerry disappeared.

Will and I had about thirty seconds to say good-bye.

"So...what's the deal?" I said. "Are we back together, or dating, or having sex or what?"

As soon as the words left my lips, I wanted to call them all back. I just sounded so horrible and defensive and prickly. Same old Zoe.

"Why?" Will crossed his arms, joking, acting tough. Maybe he wondered how much of the old Zoe was there, too. "You got plans lined up, depending on my answer?"

I couldn't pretend to be casual. "I'm sorry, I just...I just want to know what last night was. That's all."

He shrugged, looking just as bewildered—tormented?—as I was. "I don't know. I think we can't make any quick decisions about the future while we wait for Ariana's credit card to clear at the rental desk. I think we need to talk seriously, and we haven't got time."

I nodded, looking away. A thought struck me: What if he really didn't want me? What if my wish had acted like one of Claudia's suggestions, and I'd made him want me?

"If it helps, I'm going to do my best not to get into any romantic entanglements before I see you again," he said, smiling. "And if I don't get to see you again, I'll be very happy we made a bad decision last night."

"Don't talk like that." I wanted to believe last night was the first step to repairing us.

"Don't fool yourself, Zoe. This is dangerous. We all know the risks."

I nodded again. For now, I'd have to be satisfied with the illusion we might be together again someday. "Right." Ariana and Claudia were returning, so I stuck out my hand. "Good seeing you again."

He laughed for real this time and pulled me close.

I tried not to think of it as a good-bye kiss. It was too nice for that. I tried to think of it as a "see you soon, and then we'll see what happens" kiss. For two cents, I would have chucked it all right then and there and dragged him back to my bunk, and I had very nearly decided to do so when he pulled away.

He caught his breath, cleared his throat. He'd been thinking about the bunk, too. "Gotta go."

I couldn't speak; he was right. I just nodded again. *Jesus, Zoe. You may be more articulate as a wolf.*

Ariana hugged the rest of us good-bye, and we set off.

Claudia was driving. I was glaring at the map, because it made it easier to hide my tears. Gerry was fooling with the radio, trying to find something besides Turkish language news, Christian broadcasting, and German disco. Finally we settled for Turkish dance music.

It was a couple of hours driving from Didim to Kusadasi, then to Claros. We had a lot to talk about.

No one was talking, though.

"Gerry, where did you take off to?" I said, finally mastering myself.

"I had to make a call."

A long beat. No explanation. Unlike the usually voluble Gerry.

I finally asked, "Is that a euphemism?"

"No." He shifted in his seat. "I made a few calls to some folks at home, folks I know are on our side. Partly to let them know about Knight's plans so they can keep an eye on his office back home. Part of it was to confirm that it was one of his guys who was leading the group of Fangborn following you in Cambridge."

He stared at the scenery as it rolled by: flat countryside with hills in the distance, all shades of brown on brown. "At first it was some out-of-town Family looking for strays—for you, Zoe. That was bad enough, coming into our neck of the woods, instead of letting us know about you and letting us take care of bringing you in. It's the politics, you see—they wanted one more vote on their side. Then Knight's people stepped in and took over their efforts. He has a lot of sway with the various, more conservative Fangborn factions. He's definitely going to make a move, and he's consolidating power."

"So the Fangborn are…getting ready for war?"

He scowled. "With any luck, we'll stop Knight before he can get that far."

We arrived at the site, a bit of low ground just off the road, surrounded by fields and ringed with hills in the distance. The site was empty at the moment, but we'd passed a van leaving as we pulled up. It was about lunchtime, so we dug into the bag of food we'd brought from the boat. After, Claudia dusted off her hands. "Ready, Professor?"

"Uh, for what?"

"Little tour of the site. Tell us what we're looking at so when we come back tonight we can be ready and acquainted."

I looked around, gathering my thoughts. The air was hot and smelled of oranges from a nearby grove and stale water in ditches around the site. There were huge slabs of marble that contrasted brightly with brown ground, patches of scrubby pale-green bushes, and weedy, prickly plants. There were orchards just beyond the site, leading up to bare, rocky hills. I could see the remains of archaeological field seasons past, as well as some hints of the season in progress: fresh-cut trenches, square and regular; a pump system to drain the groundwater away; a small shelter, hastily constructed with palm fronds and sticks from around the site, was set up over a table. I knew that's where the maps would be drawn, or perhaps the supervisor would oversee progress in the various units from here.

It felt familiar. It made me miss Will all the worse.

Beyond the remains of the temple were the ruins of colossi, of Apollo and Artemis. Pillars tens of feet high gave the idea that once, long, long ago, this place had been splendid.

"OK, I'm going to cover about a thousand years of history and religion and architecture in fifteen minutes." I took a deep breath. "Claros was important for a couple of reasons. For one thing, it wasn't a proper town, but a refuge. It was considered particularly holy, special, even though two towns nearby also had temples. Claros had something else, and I'm starting to wonder whether the something else wasn't Fangborn related. Anyway, Claros was so important that Alexander the Great stopped by here to ask the oracle whether he should build his city at Smyrna."

I pointed over to what looked like the top of a small underground maze. "The temple would have been over there, and beneath that was where the oracle worked. You'd be told to feel your way down those steps and into a gradually narrowing tunnel. Remember, this would all be under the temple, so you'd be in complete darkness. Claustrophobia would be easy to come by, because the walls were closing in around you as you found your way forward. You'd hear echoes of the water, and the space would be filled with weird noises as you moved, literally, deeper and deeper into the world of the sacred and away from worldly life. You'd eventually find a space and a bench, where you were told to sit, and an attendant would take your name to the oracle. Who would...prophesy. Maybe in verse."

I shivered. It had to have been a profoundly weird experience. I led them across the uneven ground, then down the stairs and through the tunnel, to the spring. A grate was over the well, which was filled with green algae and a dyspeptic-looking toad. Not much mystery left here, today anyway.

"There certainly was a theatrical aspect to the oracle's visit," Claudia said. "A theater of prophesy, to get the client into the... spirit of the thing."

Gerry just looked uncomfortable.

I tried to feel the walls, even tried to sense beyond them, but without much success. I couldn't tell if there was a frisson by the well or if that was just a breeze coming down the tunnel. Already the place was playing tricks on me. When the disk stayed cool and dull, when I realized there would be no pyrotechnics, I shrugged. We left the tunnel and wandered past the altar stone, the giant foot from the statue of Artemis, and around the remains of the temple, but still no real luck.

There were a couple of places I thought I felt a...something. A kind of a tingle, a change in temperature to the touch? A flicker before my eyes? Not unexpectedly, these were never at the same time Gerry or Claudia might have sensed something, and for the most part, I was willing to chalk it up to microclimate or plain old hopefulness. Finally we sat on the bench at the propylaea, where pilgrims sat thousands of years ago and scratched their names into the stone while they waited for the priests.

We were starting to draw attention from other tourists and what looked like a few young archaeologists taking their friends for a tour. Their body language and behavior was so familiar, so like mine with Will and Sean, I almost couldn't stand it. When it was clear they weren't leaving any time soon, I gave up.

"We'll come back later," I said. Perhaps the night—and the moon—would bring better results.

We waited until it was completely dark before we dared return to the site. The Turkish authorities took a very dim view of anyone messing with their sites, and I certainly couldn't risk Knight finding us. Praying the moon would give me a boost, I moved to the propylaea, the entrance to the temple, and knelt down. I ran my hands over the inscriptions left by visitors and felt...

...nothing.

I tried hard to remember what I'd felt when the disk had gone crazy on Delos. I reassured myself it was still in my pocket, hunkered down, and tried not to think about what I was doing. I focused on the things outside myself, tried to relax, and thought, *trowel bite.*

A tickle, a tremor—something related to the Change, but nothing I'd experienced before. A surge of adrenaline.

A warning. Was it like the call to Change I'd felt on Mykonos? No. Subtle, too different.

"Gerry, Claudia!" I hissed. "Something...is going to happen!"

"What?"

"I don't know, I need to Change, I tried, and I got…warned, instead. Something's coming!"

"I'll be right over."

Gerry was by my side in an instant. He grabbed my shoulders and said, "Ready? One, two—"

I Changed before he finished. The half-Change snapped into place so quickly, it felt like a slap. Again, nothing like before. "Did you feel *that*?" I was too dizzy to whisper. "What was that?"

He shook his furry head as if he had a bee in his ear. "I don't know, but you're right—that wasn't normal! Something's coming. Claud!"

"I'm on it. You guys, get hid."

"I need to get to the temple ruins," I said. "I need to check out the hot spot in the tunnel."

"Good a place to hide you as any," he said. "Go!"

We zigged and zagged across the site, avoiding fallen ruins and deep excavation pits. I would have laughed with the joy of moving so fast, so silently in tandem with Gerry under that moonlit night sky. But something was coming, and something—the site?—was telling me I didn't have much time.

The oracle's tunnel was darker than the night. It was darker than the shadows around it.

And yet, I flew down the stairs, uneven and slick, as if I was running into my own home, a familiar place I'd never known. The dark closed in around me, but not like this afternoon, when I understood how the suppliants were drawn into an eerie experience by the confinement of the tunnel, the descent into the ground, the sounds echoing from the dark. This was a blanket of black.

Down there—a light, something glowing at the end of the short, narrow tunnel. If I hadn't been absolutely certain we had been the only ones on the site when we arrived, I would have imagined this was some kind of official police light, the strobing bubble on the roof of a cruiser. The closer I got, the brighter it was, until it was so bright, it was nearly white.

Like Delos.

It hurt my eyes, but I kept moving into it. It seemed as though it was coming from the well of the oracle.

Either my eyes adapted or the brightness faded. The stones themselves were no longer granite or marble, but seemed to be made of glass, the light coming from inside them. Behind them? It was like being inside a model of "the visible man," where I could see the entire structure illuminated from inside.

There were no stars over me now. It was as though the temple was now intact. There were walls, fully formed and raised to complete ceilings. No more plain white marble: all of the architecture and statuary was gaudy with painted and gilt color. Chambers that hadn't been here this afternoon were here now, that hadn't been standing for centuries maybe. It should have been impossible to see them—I couldn't see through the walls of light. It was more like the idea of them was now alive in my brain, an instant reconstruction. If I pushed my proximity sense just a little, I had a blurry image of the colossal statues of Apollo and Artemis just beyond.

The well was now complete, just the same, as solid to my touch as any cold stone. It pulsed, as if some giant engine somewhere were rumbling to life.

No mere feeling or hunch now: one of the rocks near where I imagined I'd found a hot spot earlier was glowing aquamarine among the pale blue-white walls. The disk, tucked securely in my shirt pocket, was radiating the same color.

In the discipline of archaeology, we are trained to notice the slightest variations. I giggled, nerves overtaking me: this glowing blue light was, as we called it in the trade, a clue.

I reached down to it, feeling warmth I knew was impossible emanating from stones that couldn't be there. I pulled back before I could touch it, suddenly afraid.

"Hey, guys!" I cleared my throat and tried again. "Anyone else seeing this, or am I about to fall over and drown in this hallucination of the sacred well?"

Nothing. I couldn't even hear wind or crickets, the noise from the far-off road.

I turned back to the one stone, still beckoning to me. Sucking up all my courage, I reached down and pushed at it, thinking to dislodge it.

The warmth confused my sense of touch; the "stone" felt like hard rubber, and I thought it must be a trick of my trembling clawed fingertips. I leaned over even farther, and I understood. My hand had passed through the surface entirely. I was sunk into the glowing stone up to my wrist.

The warmth was all around my hand, and although I couldn't see anything but the blurry shadow of my hand within, *omigod*, the stone. More, I felt something just beyond.

I stretched, almost to the limits of safety. I didn't see the modern protective grate, and the water below me was no longer murky green but a roiling red. I didn't want to find out what would happen if I fell in.

My hand penetrated another centimeter, then—

A sharp pain in my middle finger, as though I'd been bitten. I yelped, and the noise seemed to be drowned out by the thrumming all around me. I pulled back instinctively, but my wrist was seized by the stone, as though I was locked into colonial stocks. Stretched out over that pool of boiling…blood?

"Shit, help! Somebody help me!"

Still nothing from outside, and I could hardly hear my own scream over what was now the roar of a hurricane. The light of the pool was growing, and crazy red shadows played over the glowing white walls. I pulled until I thought my arm would come out of the socket. I threw back my head and howled, long and loud, for all I was worth.

Still stuck.

I was panicking now, wondering if the temple of ice and light was going to collapse into the growing scarlet tempest, my hallucination finally killing me. Desperate, I shoved myself toward the rock, figuring maybe I could force the whole rest of my body through the glowing wall of not-stone.

The red was creeping up the walls now, like blood soaking into cracked glass. Veinlike patterns appeared.

That couldn't be good.

Desperate scrabbling; my claws scraped something. I reached again, a muscle-tearing effort, and this time I grasped something small. Maybe a lever I could manipulate...

The rock opened or the force field relented. I fell backward, hard, my head hitting the stone floor—now ordinary, dark, and *hard*. The stars I saw were all too familiar, friends from my tumble-down and fractious youth. Could werewolves get concussions—?

As the brilliant icy blue and red light faded, I could just make out a figurine, so like the ones I'd had and lost in my hand.

Screams and howls. I could hear the outside world again.

The outside world sounded like a preview of hell.

Every hair on my body stood up. I had the urge to Change fully, but I knew I needed to hang onto the figurine I'd wrested from the wall; it seemed important, a crowned female figure. I shoved the fourth key to Pandora's Box into my bag, tightened the shoulder straps, and ran out to the fray.

Chapter 27

There were men, everywhere. Normals, heavily armed and armored, a blur—

Scratch that.

My proximity sense told me of nearly a dozen Fangborn and Normals. None of them were happy.

I reached out and found Claudia and Gerry fighting other Fangborn. Fighting hard, letting blood. Somewhere else out there I could feel familiar others. I recognized the presence of Dmitri Parshin almost immediately, picked out the scent of his blood. I recognized the other Fangborn because of our common lineage, not because I knew them personally. Not only were the Fangborn and Normals attacking the Steubens, but they were attacking each other. Knight's men and Parshin's, converging, all after the fourth key.

It was horrible, and I knew this was a glimpse of what the world might look like when the Fangborn were revealed, their powers feared and coveted by humankind.

The thought was terrible and I hesitated. I didn't know who these other Fangborn were. Maybe I was supposed to abide by some kind of rules, like Ben had said, some kind of cultural courtesy. Fangborn weren't meant to fight each other, right? Or was it kill other Fangborn? Perhaps if I just hurt them, took them out of the game...

I didn't know who they were, only that they were attacking my Family. That was enough, I decided.

"Zoe, get out of here!" Gerry yelled. His shirt was torn nearly off, and there was an ugly gash on his back. He slammed the head of his human attacker into a marble column.

That was going to leave a stain...

The blood glittering on the marble focused me, drove away my panic. There was blood everywhere, lighting the space almost like the scarlet light in the oracular well.

The battle called and I was filled with energy and eagerness. I looked for where I could do the most good.

There.

A small group of men who were skulking up, trying to get a bead on Claudia. She was slashing out with claws and fangs as she fought a human I'd never seen before and an unfamiliar vampire—blood everywhere, human and Fangborn. In the moonlight, she looked even more inhuman than she had when she was healing Danny. She executed a violent ballet as she fended off the attacking vampire; his reddish scales gave him a devilish look. Venom flew through the air, smoke rising where it hit the ground. He kept her at a distance, distracting her, while the human darted in where he dared.

The men sneaking up on her had oddly shaped guns, almost like toy water blasters. She might have known they were there, but couldn't do anything about them.

I had to stop them before they shot her. Didn't want to find out what was in the Super Soakers by watching them fire on Claudia. I ran and leaped onto the men approaching her.

Two went down with little noise, surprised by the wolf-girl descending as if from the sky. The two left were off balance. I scrabbled up and growled, lunged at the closest, knocking his toy gun aside.

Two hits. Me hitting him in the jaw, him hitting the ground. Out for the count.

I turned to the other, who was shaking his gun. Something must have busted when we all went down. I grabbed it from him and swung it like a bat, connecting upside his head.

This was *fun*. I didn't even have to kill them, I just had to whack them really hard. It was like playing video games with the cheat codes on—

Something bit into my back—and it hurt. I reached for it. My claws knocked something out. Something pointy, attached to a wire, causing incredible, cramping pain—

Taser? Some kind of—?

I turned and threw up all over the ground. When I looked up, I saw that one of the men who'd been knocked down first had recovered. His finger was on the trigger, his other hand fiddling with a dial.

The needle at the end of the wire was pumping out dark liquid. It glistened in the moonlight briefly before it leached into the ground.

My eyes stopped focusing. I staggered back, vomited again. Pain cramped my muscles until I thought I would stop breathing.

I fell. Somewhere beyond me, I heard Dmitri shouting hoarsely in Russian.

No codes in Latin this time, but I still couldn't understand him. He sounded desperate.

As my head hit the ground, blurred shapes of men rushed around me. I couldn't move now and felt my brain slow down, almost as if the blood had stopped in my veins. I was still alive, though, a distant part of me knew. I could hear Claudia screaming.

My sense of smell went berserk, increasing to a level even beyond Fangborn capabilities. There was too much information to process and it overwhelmed me. Even the slightest movement made me retch. Even closing my eyes didn't help as my nose tried to compensate even more. I no longer had any control over my proximity sense; I could see, with crystal clarity, people miles away going about their business. I didn't dare scream at the influx of information and sensation. More noise, coming from inside me, would probably kill me.

The last thing I was aware of was the distant feeling of something—me—being thrown into the back of a jeep. The truck hit an uneven spot, my head hit the floor, and all was glorious silence.

I woke up unhappily, my head pounding and a taste in my mouth like things that had died at the bottom of a swamp a long time ago. I reached out, experimentally, and found to my profound relief that my senses were back in balance. Quiet seemed like true quiet, and the only person I was aware of was me. Smells were of must, dust, and my own unattractive self, but no more. There was nothing left in my stomach to throw up, which was nice, but I missed the illusion of doing something to alleviate the sickness I felt. I settled for trying to sit up.

Mixed results. Being upright helped my head clear, but movement brought on one last spasm of cramping so awful I cried out.

A door opened, letting in light that scalded my eyeballs. I was in a space about the size of a broom closet, just enough room for the cot I'd been on.

A goon in uniform with one of those hateful guns. "The senator will see you now."

Like I'd been cooling my heels in a reception room for the last…I had no idea how much time had passed. No phone, no backpack.

There was no reason to stay here, and I didn't want another blast of whatever toxin was in that weapon—had Claudia and Gerry mentioned black hellebore? I got up, a little wobbly, and followed him down a hallway.

The corridor was like a hotel's, but I suspected it wasn't really. While I thought there might be people and Fangborn nearby, I couldn't tell exactly. Either I was still suffering my cataclysmic hangover or something was blocking me.

A guard outside a door at the end of the hallway stood back to let us in. Behind him was the anteroom I expected, and behind another guarded door was the senator.

I felt the peculiar thrill you get when you see someone in person you've only ever seen on TV. And it was weird, how familiar Senator Knight seemed when I knew him only from the news: tall, thin, receding hair that was gray at the temples. His nose gave his face the hawkish look that had been caricatured in political cartoons for decades.

The only thing that was different in person was his eyes. There was no camera on earth that could capture the depth of them, the intensity, the…age. He was supposedly in his sixties; I knew now he was closer to two hundred years old. Those eyes had seen a lot, and they could see far and deeply.

He eventually looked up from the papers he was reading.

I shivered and turned away after a minute. His gaze was harrowing, with all the intensity of a vampire's understanding, and he made no attempt to conceal it.

"Thank you for coming, Ms. Miller. Tomorrow I'd like you to find Pandora's Box for me."

"Where are my friends? The Steubens. What—"

He frowned; I was off-topic.

"I'm sure they'll be joining us shortly. Now then—"

A rap on the door. Knight frowned again at this second interruption. His eyes unfocused. Then he blinked, refocused, and something like a smile crossed his lips. "Come in, Zimmer."

The door opened. The man I thought of as "Clean-head," the man who'd tortured and killed Rupert Grayling in London and chased me across Paris, entered.

I stood up; a gesture from Knight, and I had the undeniable urge to sit. I couldn't get up, I couldn't talk, but I could growl.

The filth that was Zimmer filled my nostrils; I longed to attack, but couldn't.

Why wasn't Knight reacting to him? Why didn't Knight vault his desk and tear him limb from limb?

Zimmer crossed the room with only a glance of disdain for me. I growled, louder this time.

"Ms. Miller! Behave yourself. Mr. Zimmer is a valued colleague of mine."

Now I couldn't even growl. Didn't stop me hating, though.

Zimmer whispered into Knight's ear, so quietly I couldn't hear. Knight nodded once, and Zimmer made as if to leave.

"Wait."

Zimmer stopped, so abruptly a switch might have been thrown.

"Show Ms. Miller you're not such a bad sort. Sing for her. Something...cheery."

Zimmer turned, opened his mouth, and began to sing.

"A more humane Mikado never/Did in Japan exist /To nobody second /I'm certainly reckoned/A true philanthropist."

I must still be unconscious, I thought dizzily. *That killer is* not *singing* The Mikado *to me. What is going on here?*

"That's fine. Thank you, Zimmer. You may go now."

Zimmer stopped singing instantly and, without so much as a glance at either of us, departed.

"He's been a true asset to me. But where were we?" Knight glanced at a pad—he had a fucking *agenda* for this meeting? "Yes. Pandora's Box."

It took an effort to answer him. "I have no idea where it is."

"I think you do. And you have many reasons to want to find it. You do not want it in the hands of Dmitri Parshin, for example? I cannot imagine you'd allow such an unspeakable power in the hands of a Normal, and a foreign national at that. And there are others like Rupert Grayling out there, collectors who know of our artifacts but perhaps not of us. He certainly was not acting alone in his pursuit. It is imperative we find it first."

"If there is such a thing as Pandora's Box out there," I said, "maybe it's better off lost." The idea of the Box in the hands of someone like Dmitri Parshin was terrifying.

"Oh, my dear. The time for that kind of head-in-the-sand thinking is well past. There is another reason you might want to help me." He picked up piece of paper, glanced at it, set it back. "His name is Sean Flax. He's staying with me. He's a suspect in a murder he didn't commit, and I'm sure you'd prefer he be cleared."

Sean helped me concentrate. "How did you do that? Did you use vampire venom to convince someone Sean had attacked Professor Schulz?"

Senator Knight frowned slightly. "No. I simply had someone paid off. Less obvious, at least in Italy."

I pushed harder, determined to get some answers. "But you were responsible for altering his mind?"

"You never should have detected it, but yes. We tried several times, in Boston, in Berlin, but could only get him to follow you, never to force him to do something against his will." He frowned again, more deeply. "How do *you* change the subject with *me*?"

I felt a strengthening of his concentration. Not a subtle thing, like Claudia's suggestions, but a powerful combination of charisma and vampiric will. It became a rhetorical question.

"Tomorrow you will bring the Box to me," he said. "I have all the keys and the Beacon; my horoscope, cast by the most powerful oracles in the world, says I am the one who will unveil the power of the Box and the power of the Fangborn. And it will happen tomorrow."

I couldn't understand why I felt so...ordinary. Knight was treating this as if it was some kind of routine scheduling issue. I felt none of the anger I knew was appropriate. He was threatening me with Parshin, threatening Sean, behaving as if my abduction was part of a job interview, and essentially telling me he'd throw the world into chaos tomorrow. Business as usual.

Two things occurred to me: Senator Knight believed this *was* business as usual. He was a powerful man and had a reputation for making daring decisions throughout his whole career. He was used to this kind of behavior.

More than that, Senator Knight was a vampire. I realized it fully now. There's no way someone who wasn't Fangborn would have known. But he was pumping out something that made me calm, suggestible, and truthful.

For the first time I understood how scary the combination of Normal power and Fangborn ability might be. How delicate the balance had been, until now. The fight over just the idea of Fangborn power in the shape of the figurines was bad enough; Identification would be a million times worse. It was not as simple as announcing "here we are."

And now he wanted Pandora's Box and its ungodly powers?

"Why me?" was all his compulsion would allow me to say.

"You've been in possession of the elements relating to it for quite some time. You know something of the historical and—I *hate* to use the term—mythological background. And you are an archaeologist. That makes you entirely qualified."

"You can't expect me to find something on command. Archaeology doesn't conform to a deadline. Besides, you're the one with a crew, with the information. With power."

"But we've had no luck finding the thing itself. You will, and you must. Time is running short. In order for me to fulfill the prophesy, I must open the Box tomorrow."

"But…it's not a prophesy. Not the way you think. Oracles are right as often as they are wrong or just plain deranged. You should know better than me."

He gave me a look that mingled pity and disdain. *Of course* he knew these things. He was a corn-fed Fangborn, of an age so great as to make his power almost palpable to humans. "I've had the best minds studying this. My own life has been such that it is clear I'm the heir to this power. And you will bring it to me."

I struggled to speak, the least little resistance. "Or Sean goes to jail. Or worse."

Senator Knight shrugged. "I would prefer he didn't. I don't like to make threats, but I'm willing to follow through on them when I do. One unstable nobody, an accused murderer, in the face of the countless benefits this will bring my people? It's acceptable. Very."

"Yeah, well, I'm your people, you know."

"You are, several times over." He tented his fingers, as if giving due consideration to my point. "You are an American citizen, and I've served my country faithfully my entire, long life. You're a member, albeit distantly, of my Fangborn Family. And I'm doing this for you as much as anyone else. I can bring peace to humanity. I can employ the Fangborn the way they've always been destined to serve. With this one move, I can make the world *better*."

I thought about what Gerry and Claudia predicted would happen. I thought about how I knew humans behaved in the face of change or difference. I didn't think it would be nearly as smooth a transition as he thought, and with all the effort I could muster, I spoke. "We don't even know what is in the Box, if we find it. The Tapestry document says whoever found the Beacon would unchain the Fangborn. That could mean Identifying us to Normals, but it could mean our DNA will unspool or something. It could mean *I* will be the one, because I found the Beacon. You don't know how this will play out."

Senator Knight smiled briefly and stood up. "I believe my intent is what will be channeled. You have tonight to pick the places to search. Neither one of us wants Parshin to win this prize. All of us—not just Sean—would stand to lose a great deal."

He seemed reasonable, even in his threats. Then I thought about what he intended, and knew I couldn't allow it to happen.

I was desperate, eager to throw any impediment at his plan. "You don't understand. I am the world's *unluckiest* person, and as for archaeology, my 'career' hasn't even been in existence long enough for me to have developed a nose. I've never even—"

Knight tsked. "Everything you've done so far has led you to this point. You've gotten as close as anyone ever has to solving the riddle of the figurines and gathering the keys. You stumbled, some-how, upon the Beacon. I would call that very lucky indeed. You're the girl for the job, my little stray."

The pejorative bit hard when he used it. The differences between us couldn't have been more pronounced, and decidedly in his favor. I felt small and weak in every way.

He flipped through to another file, glanced at the top sheet, then at me. He closed it. "I'm not unfair. I will also add a carrot to my sticks. I have information here, about you. About your mother's people and their…situation. I bet you have any number of ques-tions about your past, about why your mother was on the run from such an early age? If you are very quick in finding the Box, I shall reward you with this."

He put his hand gently on the coffee-stained and dog-eared file; I couldn't help but hope he was telling the truth. I desperately wanted that information. I tore my eyes away from the file and tried to defy him, just a little bit.

"You're lying. I'm nobody, you've said so yourself. Why would you have any information on my mother? Gerr—someone told me there were whole communities, scattered and hidden."

He nodded. "That is correct. At the beginning of the last cen-tury, there were groups who removed themselves from the world, some for religious reasons, some because they feared Normals and their narrow-minded ways. Seeing how they treat their own kind, for the slightest of differences, was a powerful inducement to hide. But with the upheaval of the modern wars, on the home front and overseas, and with advances of communication, many of these groups were exposed. While some families were reincorporated into nests and packs, some orphans and strays were made a part of a powerful set of experiments in the attempt to enhance our powers, for the good of humanity and Fangborn alike. There was a war on, after all."

I didn't like the sound of the word "experiment" one bit.

"Your mother was orphaned as a baby and was brought to one of these homes, not knowing who or what she really was. Part of the group she was in was an experiment in 'suggesting' they were no different from humans, a way to blend them back into Normal society with the idea they would use their powers for good, then forget about them." He shook his head. "As you can imagine, it was a dismal failure, but it was a small sacrifice for the greater good."

I couldn't help myself. "You know, a lot of people around that time split up families and tried to reengineer people, 'for the greater good.'"

"Hindsight makes it so very easy, doesn't it, Zoe? You're what, twenty-five? Adrift in the world, wandering through life—how could you have any concept of what we Fangborn have been through?" He got up and paced, showing the first trace of anger. "Your mother was just a child. We were fighting for our lives, for everyone's lives. You have *no* idea."

He took his seat, again composed. "Your mother ran off, never knowing or understanding her oracular powers. We tracked her down, very near the end; the nurse at the hospital where your mother died alerted us and I sent Family for you. But this is all good for you, Zoe."

"Yeah? How?" I didn't like him talking about my mother.

"I can tell you about your mother's Family. I can help you learn about your father's Family, too. The past is so important to Normals. It's more important to the Fangborn, because we are gifted with a purpose. Perhaps that is why your study of the past is so important to you. Poor stray, how *alone* you must have felt."

He meant it; he believed he was being sympathetic. But if I could have killed him then and there, I would have.

"I can make you a part of our Family," he said. "But first I need that one, last artifact."

He straightened the files, put them into a drawer, locked his desk, pocketed the key. "I suggest you get a good night's sleep after you consider where to start tomorrow. You'll have about six hours to do a great service for your people. And you'll learn about your past. If not?" He shrugged. "Sean's fate also depends on your actions."

I knew he meant it.

I was escorted to a small office, bare save for a cot, a table and lamp, and a stack of books and references to the archaeology of the coast. Maps, paper, a ruler, and calculator were there, as well as the figurines and the contents of my backpack. I sank down, staring at the figurines dejectedly.

If the senator hadn't missed the point, I didn't think my luck had improved recently. If it had, I'd be anywhere but here.

I stared at the row of figurines and the gold disk. They weren't glowing now, which surprised me, but after all, they'd found each other. Why go through the effort?

I glanced at the map and compared it to the crude yet elegant version on the Venetian disk. It was remarkably accurate, given the lack of satellites and computational equipment. The ancients certainly knew something about sailing and the stars.

But why was the compass rose located beneath Claros? That didn't make sense, to crowd it so close to the geographical information of the map.

Until I glanced at the modern map, which had been marked in the same place, with a less conspicuous mark.

My hand flew to my mouth. Shocking, how dense I'd been.

It wasn't a compass rose. It was the location of Secundus's treasure, possibly Pandora's Box. In Ephesus. It was a big X, right on the damned map. Big mark equals big importance, right?

Nice going, Zoe. It's only one of the most significant sites in the entire world. And you missed it.

Hey, I wasn't looking for it. It wasn't marked as a city on the map; I thought it was just about the figurines and their home oracles. I was just trying to get an artifact for a crazy Russian and not get killed. And, oh, by the way, coming to grips with the idea of being a werewolf for real, hello? Little bit preoccupied.

As Will had mentioned just a couple of nights ago, I'd never been, but you can't study archaeology and not know about Ephesus. Ephesus is not only important on many historical levels, being nearly three thousand years old, it is huge. It had once been home to 250,000 people, second only to Alexandria in the classical world. Only 15 percent of it had been excavated.

Somewhere on this massive, carefully guarded site was Pandora's Box. All I had to do was find it.

If the senator hadn't been able to find it with his resources, how could I? He was Fangborn, he could wander around with the figurines as easily as I could, and they'd probably just as easily work for him if they were going to. But I had claimed the Beacon, or it had claimed me, and that seemed to be important somehow.

There was no way either of us could cover the entire site before the site opened tomorrow morning. We couldn't cover it in a month just wandering around.

What the hell was I going to do? How could I narrow it down?

I got up and paced. I couldn't even go through all the documentation Knight had left for me. Giant, thick volumes, some in English, some in Turkish, some in French, some in German. I glanced at the clock. No way I could read all this in the next five hours.

I sat back down again, determined not to let the impossible stop me. I put the books in Turkish aside; I couldn't read those at all. My "museum and menu" German wouldn't get me far with the detailed and jargon-filled reports, but maybe I could do something with cognates. Same for the French.

I opened the English reports and employed my best all-nighter-hadn't-read-the-book-yet strategies, skimming tables of contents, chapter introductions, conclusions, and indexes. I spent a lot of time on the pictures. Great thing about pictures, you don't need to speak the language to understand them. Worth more than a thousand words to me now.

No references to the style of pottery like the ones Jenny had shown me. Nothing referring to Secundus or Pandora, or even Vindolanda. In desperation, I looked up "oracle" and "temple," but found too much and nothing that would help me.

Resolutely I picked up the German and Turkish texts and started flipping through the photographs.

My heart almost stopped. It was nothing I should have noticed—in fact, if it had been a better photograph, no one should ever have seen the tiny sequence of numbers and letters. Provenience markings on small, intact objects were usually concealed by the photographer, and sherds were generally marked with their minute numbers and letters in such a way that they would not show when they were mended into larger, reconstructed vessels.

The provenience numbers on one of the vessels looked strangely familiar. They were nearly identical to those I'd seen on the insignificant little sherd of Samian ware from the apartment in Paris.

Chapter 28

I rummaged through my bag until I found the spice jar. It looked like part of my "medical kit" and had been ignored by Knight's guards, who had been focusing on the figurines and the disk. I fumbled with the top, and the plastic bag dropped to the floor. I pulled it out and reexamined it.

The numbers were organized in the same fashion. I maneuvered the lighted magnifying glass around and examined the sherd again. The numbers were clearer now, and I realized what I'd originally thought was a "9" was a European-style "7," with a bar through it.

I tore through the site report, trying to find a description of the way they'd designated the excavated areas, how they correlated the artifacts to the area and level they'd taken it from.

There.

Outside, a distant rumble. I wondered briefly whether this wasn't one of Turkey's famous earthquakes.

No time for geology. I pulled the site map out of the pocket in the back of the report and spread it out across the table.

More rumblings, closer, louder now. That was not an earthquake. But until I knew what was going on, I had to focus.

Flipping back and forth between the book and the map, I managed to find the approximate location of the context in which my sherd had been found. It was well away from the main part of the exposed, touristy part of the site, and also away from more recently excavated areas, on the hilly periphery.

I studied the sherd and pinpointed what I thought was the context: the ruin of a small house on the edge of a recent excavation area, described as "merchants' homes." I tried to narrow it down more, but the door slammed open.

It was Adam Nichols.

He had a gun. He was spattered with a fine tracery of blood, which looked like a jeweled net on the skin of his face and hands.

I licked my lips, swallowed, and looked away. Werewolf or no, I had to get over this obsession with blood. It was creepy. A little vampiric.

"We need to get out of here. Dmitri's men are storming the compound, looking for you and—" He moved toward the table with the figurines on them. "These."

He reached out for the figurines. Before I knew what I was doing, I'd ducked in front of him, sweeping them up together. If anyone was going to hang onto these, it was me. I grabbed the map, the disk, then scattered the books. I didn't want to leave any clues.

He didn't say anything, just handed me my backpack, and I shoved the figurines, map, and disk in.

"Why are you helping me? Knight is gonna know for sure... what are you getting out of this?"

He opened the door a crack, looked up and down the hallway. "Let's get out of here first. Unless you want to be here when Dmitri breaks in? My men almost failed to repel him at Claros, and he's followed them back here. With reinforcements."

I ran. I got too far ahead of Adam, distracted by too many thoughts. When I turned the corner, I practically ran into a knot of five heavily armed men. I thrashed about, trying to Change, but one of them had one of those damn poison-spraying guns and got off a blast. My head was turned away, but the vapor hung on the air and slowed me.

Adam joined us, just in time to punch the guy going for his radio.

One grabbed my backpack while another handcuffed me. I shook my head, slowed by the mist of the hellebore cocktail, and tried to bite the hand closest to me.

Howls and a jerk back. I looked up, just in time to see the fist coming. I was able to move only enough to keep from getting punched square on the jaw.

I caught it on the temple instead, which made the world crazy until I got slammed from the other side, too. There was nothing but wall over there, and I was bouncing off it and onto the floor—

Can't respond if you don't see it coming. Can't anticipate, can't fight back like you have to, and if you're gonna survive…

Goddamned bully. *Bastardnogoodmotherfu*—Focus, Zoe!

Trowel bite!

Grrrrrr. The small noise in my throat was the opening bar to every song on the playlist you use to get moving at the gym. I shook with the deliciousness of it. The growl grew.

For the first time possibly ever, I was pleased with my small stature. A dainty wolf, I slid my paws out of the cuffs with no problem. Ditto my jeans. It wasn't even a hitch in my progression from that one step to the leap that took me toward the neck of Knight's man, who was staring at me with the most idiotic look on his face. He shoved me aside, stumbled back, one step, two, and turned to run.

Adam got him. But there were plenty of armed men left. I was a little woozy from the poison, but I caused enough of a melee that Adam could pick off the biggest problems first.

The five who'd run into us were down, but there was another, just beyond that door, my proximity sense told me. I could smell the evil coming off him in waves.

I lunged at the door, which opened from the other side.

I landed on top of him, heavily. I don't know if it was the actual sight or smell of him, but the same compulsion I'd felt in Mykonos overcame me. Rotting fish, formaldehyde, and pig shit. This guy smelled like hell. I might have whimpered.

There was something else, though. Somewhere beneath all that foulness, I could smell blood, old and drying. I looked over in the corner and saw the corpse of a young woman chained to the wall. Bite wounds and claw marks covered her body.

Horrified, I didn't see it coming when he punched me in the muzzle. My head snapped back; he stumbled. I knew, as if I was reading his mind, that it wasn't just my death he was interested in. The young woman hadn't died quickly.

I launched myself at him without thinking. He was sated, over-full, too slow and too clumsy, and I had just a fleeting glimpse of some truly unorthodox dentistry covered in blood when my jaws closed around his throat.

I felt his neck snap, the sound like a boot crunching through a windblown branch. There was no room for me to chide myself—*who's the bully now, Zoe?*—just a feeling of righteous wrath so complete, it made me stronger, smarter, more focused.

The rush was like nothing I'd ever experienced. The taste of his blood was an encyclopedia. I knew the taste of the woman from his throat. I understood that he was the most evil thing I'd ever encountered. But he didn't taste...human.

He was Fangborn.

But Gerry had said there weren't any evil Fangborn.

I must be getting a better grip on my powers, I thought. *Of course, there's no one brand of evil. It's complex, it's variable.*

Drunk, I threw my head back and howled.

"Time to celebrate later," Adam said, pushing his way into the room. He froze when he saw the two corpses, his face gray at the horror of it. Even a Normal could sense the evil here, and Adam made a living from violence.

He swallowed and handed me my pants as he glanced back down the hall. "We gotta jam."

I got Human in a hurry, dressed, grabbed my bag, and ran.

Not too far ahead of Adam, though. He was good in a fight.

We ran into one more guard running over as a door to the outside closed behind him. He glanced at me, looked to Adam.

"Sir! Parshin's men have breached—"

Adam stepped in and busted his head with the butt of his rifle. We ran outside and I looked around, trying to get a bead on where we were.

Adam jogged toward a jeep and motioned for me to get in.

I stopped. "Wait! Sean! We can't leave him!"

"We can't let Dmitri or Knight have those things. This is our one chance to keep them—and you—out of their hands."

Why did I get the impression Adam was good at making rationalization sound like purest reason?

He shook his head. "I am totally compromised. I *have* to leave. You coming?"

I opened the door but cast a glance back at the compound. "But Sean!"

Adam gave me a venomous look and took a deep breath. "Knight won't do anything with him," he said, trying hard to sound patient. It was almost convincing. "He thinks if he controls Sean, he can control you, so he won't hurt him unless you're there to see it."

He started the engine. "We need to leave. Now."

Another explosion in the compound decided me. I needed to be away from here and take the figurines and my newfound theory with me. I had to keep it out of Knight's hands—and Dmitri's.

I got in. We tore out of there, leaving the rumble of another explosion and the sudden, sharp smell of burning building behind.

"Where are we going?" I said.

"You tell me."

I had to decide whether to trust Adam or not. Again. If he was still working for Knight, it was too elaborate a plot to get from me what I'd willingly give Knight to help Sean and get my file. Adam must really be switching sides.

"Ephesus. There's a spot on the site. If I can find what I think is there..."

He turned away from the road to stare at me. "We can't let Knight get it."

I nodded. "So why the sudden change of heart?"

"Not so sudden. Remember, I was at Delos."

"Yeah, and I remember you were in Venice, too, busting into my room and waving a gun around, taking my stuff. So break it down for me."

Adam tapped on the GPS until he found a route he wanted. "We're going to avoid the main entrance."

I glared at him. "Ya think? Now talk."

He cleared his throat and started to drive. "I've always wanted to serve my country. Knight was a friend of my father's. I learned he was Fangborn—and about the existence of the Fangborn—just a year ago. Only a few of his staff know he's a vampire. I only learned about his other plans more recently."

I waited. "And?"

"And...I couldn't get behind them. We...humans...aren't ready for you guys. You see what we do to each other over the slightest differences in religion or politics? We beat each other up over *baseball* games. We'll kill over the wrong-colored bandanna. What would we do faced with the Fangborn? I was only waiting to see how he was going to reveal himself and out you all, and then figure out how to keep him from executing his plans."

Sounded plausible, even truthful, in parts of it, but there was something about his hesitation and his delivery that didn't quite convince me. He wasn't afraid of violence, theft, lying, or other types of lawbreaking. Still, I was committed to trusting him.

But only for the moment.

It was still dark when we got to Ephesus. Dawn was another hour away. Because we were avoiding the main entrances, we ran out of paved road quickly. Between his GPS and the coordinates I'd taken from the report, I knew we had to look for a small cluster of ruins halfway up one of the rolling brown hills. There was an overgrown path, but rocks and loosened soil made the going treacherous, and there were tangles of thorns and thistles that would deter all but the most determined goats.

I could see pretty well, but Adam was stumbling across the uneven terrain even with a flashlight. We got to within a hundred meters of the right area and I turned to him.

"Keep watch for Knight and Dmitri here. Warn me if they show up." I also wanted a little privacy while I looked for the thing. No sense leaving a trail of breadcrumbs for my enemies.

Plus, I had the sneaking suspicion I'd only find the Box if I was at least half-Changed. I didn't want Adam seeing that again; it would be like letting him catch me getting out of the bath.

It was incredibly hard to navigate the uneven ground quietly, even with my excellent vision. Loose rock and rubble littered every inch, and I slipped a number of times on goat poop. I discovered an unexpected and weatherworn trench when I stumbled into it. It hadn't been on the map. Looters had been here since the end of last year's official excavation. Picking myself up, I found I'd torn my trousers and had a jagged scratch in my leg.

If only I had something to clean it out with. I didn't know how quickly this would heal while I was in human form. There was no sign of my wounds from the fight while I was still a wolf. Interesting. I found myself wondering about my last tetanus shot, and as soon as I thought of water to clean the scratch, I became aware of how thirsty I was. I hadn't come to the site prepared.

With a groan, I realized I didn't even have my trowel. I'd left it in Dmitri's leg.

I got up, took a deep breath, and pushed on for the "merchants' houses."

Secundus had been a merchant.

My heart still pounded, and every noise—rock against rock, the distant crowing of roosters—reminded me that time was short. Only two bare hours until the appointed time. I had to hope I could find the Box before Knight or Dmitri found me.

As the sun rose, I found an elevation marker embedded in concrete and knew I was at the approximate center of the site area. What I prayed was Secundus's house was about ten meters north. I began to count my paces, praying I wasn't on a wild goose chase.

Left, right, left, right. Sinister, dexter, sinister, dexter…

I hope Grayling was genuinely on my side when he directed me to the sherd in Paris, I thought. *I hope he truly wanted to keep this from Dmitri and wasn't just flipping me off as he died.*

Can't second guess yourself now, Zoe. It's all you have. Start with what you know. Work to the unknown from there.

It was hot, even though full daylight was still an hour away. Sweat trickled down my neck and back, and I was so drenched my sleeves made a slapping noise when I moved.

I was there. A series of ruined stone walls indicated the complex I was looking for. Now to find the right house.

Where to start? I had the vague impression of a map I looked at for about ten minutes, a scratch on my leg turning septic by the minute, and a ruined wall.

The wall. Before he was a merchant, Secundus had been a soldier in the Roman legions, seen the world, seen the ruins of cities that had thrived and died long before Rome. He would assume that the walls of the city would be there long after his departure. Ephesus was huge, and although the walls had been largely destroyed, meters and meters of them still stood—

I had to focus on what I had. If I went beyond that, if I tried to figure out all the possibilities, I'd go mad.

Stick with the house. If Grayling screwed you over, you'll move from here.

Three buildings had sections of walls standing. One was outside the excavation area. Two were inside.

The last of my paces brought me right in front of the one still outside the excavation area. The one I believed to be an original part of Secundus's house.

The wall was a fixed location, easy to recognize, comparatively durable, easy to find. It was almost everything an archaeologist looked for when establishing a datum point, the point from which an entire site was mapped and organized. I had to hope this was the last link in my chain of evidence.

I had no trowel, no crew, and no time.

Time to put aside the archaeology and invoke the Change.

I arranged the figurines and disk nearby. I took a deep breath, reached out to touch the wall, and tried to assume my wolf-girl form.

It was always a little disorienting, but now I saw the scratch I'd gotten while in human form fade. The wounds from my fight appeared, but they were already starting to close and heal.

If I thought that I'd experience phenomena like those I had in Claros, however, I was sadly mistaken. Nothing but dead stone and increasingly light skies, and me futilely patting a stubbornly ordinary stone wall.

What if I was in the wrong area? What if it had already been stolen? What if by coming here I had just killed Sean? What if—?

Hold on, Zoe. Nothing's less attractive than a panicking were-wolf.

The figurines had elicited the response in Claros, I told myself. No reason to think, once I had all four together, they'd do anything else.

You're still an archaeologist, even if you've got fangs and claws. Use that.

I took a deep breath and stared at the wall. Nothing unusual about it, what was left of it. Plain plaster, because the painting had long ago been weathered away. There was one patch, smoother and whiter than the rest, though. Almost exactly where I was staring, about four and a half feet above the ground. About as high as a short man could comfortably carve while standing.

Before I could think about it, and maybe stop myself, I reached out and scratched at it with my sharp claws.

It was fragile and fell away in fragments. My distress in having so carelessly destroyed something two thousand years old set my cheeks burning.

Until I saw what was under the plaster.

There was a crude rendering of a phallus scratched into the rock, along with a deeper inscription. The inscription was a series of letters and Roman numerals—or more letters.

...LEG VI VICTRIX.

The victorious Sixth Legion. If you knew some of the standard abbreviations, it was easy enough to fill in the rest. Secundus had marked the wall with his brother's old legionary designation. I didn't know how Tertius had found his way to Vindolanda—his legion would have been stationed in York—but it didn't matter. His brother had left him a clue here.

And the carved image of the phallus? That was just for good luck. The walls and roads of the empire from Scotland to North Africa to Turkey were covered in them. Gerry would have been scandalized.

This particular bit of graffiti was marking something. Had been concealed to smooth the surface under a painted wall, and now it pointed the way to something else.

The sun was rising. I had an hour, maybe, to use whatever I found to barter for Sean and the file. Or would I have to sacrifice them to keep Knight from unleashing the power of Pandora's Box on the world?

I needed to find the object before I could make the decision.

The raking light of the sun made the letters stand out as if they'd been waiting for my approach. I reached out and felt the carving in the stone, which was different from the others in the wall.

I longed for my trowel, but made do with a flat stone and my claws. I chipped away at the mortar, which flaked away at the surfaces but was harder to remove the deeper I went. I worked diligently, my patience rewarded when I realized the stone was moving. It wasn't nearly as thick as the surrounding ones. It was like a veneer, a false wall concealing a space where the original stone had been.

I realized that I was doing the very thing I hated most in the world after bullies: destroying a piece of the past, something meant to be shared with everyone.

Jenny, my friend, forgive me. Sean's future and my past are on the line. Maybe the rest of the world, too. I can't let the others find Pandora's Box first.

It struck me: Secundus had wanted someone to find this object eventually. He wouldn't have left the clues he had, or sent the letter to his brother, otherwise.

It was enough of a rationalization. I didn't need much at this point. Too much was at stake and the only way I could hope to affect any of it was to be the one who found the Box.

All archaeology is destruction, I thought as I worked, trying to ignore the blood welling from the cuts on my clawed fingers. As we dig, we destroy context. But we do it so that we can get the information, more important than the artifacts themselves, no matter how fascinating they might be. I tried to convince myself that's what I was doing now.

The front fell away. There was a space behind it. Too valuable to leave in the ground, too dangerous to be trusted to another man or even to the priests guarding the temple strongbox, Secundus had hidden his treasure within the walls of his own house.

Not caring about scorpions or spiders or snakes, I thrust my hand in and felt a piece of ceramic, heard the familiar clink of pottery on pottery. Very carefully I pulled out the object. It rattled, and I could see what I had: two bowls, one turned over on top of the other, both of the same fine red earthenware as the sherd from Paris. They'd been put together to protect something else. Removing the top bowl, I saw a leather-wrapped parcel in the bottom of the other.

The leather was brittle, and it took me a moment to realize that it was coated with something metallic. Shiny flakes disintegrated as I pulled the bundle free.

I brushed the rest of the metallic substance from the surface. A wax-coated thong tied the top of the leather sack shut, and carefully I worked at the knots.

The leather fell apart quickly. It would, being clawed at, even if it hadn't been two thousand years old.

Inside the leather was a vessel similar to the one in the picture I'd seen in Jenny's office. If everyone who'd been after the figurines was correct, I'd just discovered Pandora's Box.

Chapter 29

A shout from down the hill. "Zoe, we got company! Whatever you're doing, make it fast!"

The sun was up, and I was out of time. I could see two truckloads of men coming from the same direction we had. Knight.

I turned my attention back to my find. The small vessel in the leather wrappings looked like something you'd see in the museum from anywhere in the Mediterranean world: flared mouth, narrow neck, bulbous body, flat base. Although there was an unusual flange around the middle, indented in four places, it was different from the picture Jenny had shown me. More ordinary looking, but odder, too.

It wasn't made of clay. It was metal. It shone dull silver in the creeping morning light.

Just as Secundus had written to his brother. An "unbreakable" vessel, as the text of Hesiod suggested.

The indentations, shaped like footprints, gave me an idea. I had to see if the figurines could be fitted onto the flange around the waist of the vessel. I had to know this was what Knight had sent me after.

There must have been some core of magnetic metal worked into the clay of the first figurine, the one I'd taken from the museum. I had no sooner placed it near the flange then it was pulled into place, upright, standing on the flange. The dull beige of the clay blushed, and, as if it was being suffused with life, the traces of pigments darkened. My female figurine now had dark hair and light blue robes.

A shot whizzed over my head. Knight's men were firing at me. Or maybe at Adam, who was returning fire from behind a pillar somewhere below me. I heard shouts in response; they might want me gone, but they didn't want the Box damaged.

I grabbed the next figurine, the one in the shape of Athena. It bounced back from the lip, like two magnets of equivalent charges resisting each other.

"Zoe Miller!" It was Knight's voice, electronically amplified, echoing through the hills. "You are not, under any circumstances, to handle the Box. It requires controlled, laboratory conditions—"

Knight was hardly "controlled conditions" as far as I was concerned. As if in agreement, the gold disk—the Beacon—began to glow.

"Sean's here with me. He wants to see you."

Even the power of Knight's suggestion, even the offer of talking to Sean couldn't move me. I was enthralled, captivated, enslaved by the vessel and its artifacts.

A bit more fumbling; I was moving too slowly. Suddenly the vessel turned itself around, and the second figurine snapped into its correct place.

Holy shit. Pandora's Box was taking matters into its own hands.

Athena's helm was gold, and the snaky head of Medusa on her shield was black and green, her serpents coiling and darting. I could have sworn I saw gray eyes, too.

More gunfire erupted, this time from above me on the slope.

Dmitri's men had arrived. I was barely paying attention, but it was as though my proximity sense had graduated to high-definition. I could see the men and their movements with crystal clarity, but had no will to do anything but focus on the Box.

The third figurine I snatched up was the one I'd retrieved from Claros. The queenly figure with the elaborate headdress was pulled *out* of my hand into its place. As the paint returned, I could see her golden hair, and there were tiny snakes wound around her arms, reminding me of the statue of the priestess from Crete.

The vessel was whirling faster now, as if it was building itself. Sparks were flying out from it.

Not sparks. Tiny lightning.

The Box was choosing me over Knight, I knew. Just as the Beacon had, back in Venice.

The last figurine was the broken one, the one I'd pieced together from the fragment my mother had taken from my father and the piece I'd torn from Dmitri's neck.

I could smell faint traces of hellebore cocktail. The men downslope were readying their guns. One had Changed into a wolf and was attempting to sneak up the slope far to my left. A familiar snake was slowly slithering into a helicopter that had landed at the top of the hill. Its markings—how could I see its markings in this poor light, from behind a wall?—were green and black.

Ariana. How had she found me?

Knight's voice was eerily omnipresent, disembodied, calling over the scuffles breaking out. "Stop now, Zoe. I'll make you rich if you stop now. You'll end up killing everyone here if you continue—"

A shout and a scuffle below. The shout was familiar: Sean was tearing up the hill. Adam fired over him, just enough to keep anyone from following Sean.

Rock clattering on rock, a miniature landslide. Dmitri was descending the slope above me. Coming for me.

"I think you all want to stop shooting," I shouted. It was my voice, and yet how was it carrying over all the other noises so easily? "I think hitting this thing with bullets would be very, very bad. Remember what supposedly happened last time this thing was opened? I'd back off, if I were you!"

"That's mine!" Knight screamed. "You have no right, stray!"

"No stopping it now. It's going to—"

I fit the last, broken key onto the vessel. It made full contact, and a band of the lightning built up around the figurines. The face of the last one was chipped off, but I now had the impression of a wolf's muzzle and pointed ears; an Egyptian kilt was wrapped around its waist. The area around the missing hand caused the band to be incomplete, and there were weird jumps and flashes of light. Arcs of electricity.

The vessel spun free of my hand, defying gravity. I no longer perceived only shapes of the humans and Fangborn around me; I sensed the connections between them. I could see Dmitri, because I had bitten him, knew his blood, I could understand his orders in Russian—since when do I speak Russian?—to the man next to him, who was a distant relation...

I could see Ariana sinking her fangs into the neck of the helicopter pilot, binding him to her will. I could taste her fears that Ben would not be in the right place at the right time, that her talent for persuasion and control wouldn't be enough...

Somewhere at the edge of perception, I could feel Ben's panic. Claudia and Gerry and Will were closer now, clearer. I could feel the fury boiling off Will and realized his target was Knight himself...

And Sean, somewhere under all that was Sean, scared and massively pissed off.

I couldn't feel my feet anymore. I worried that I was going into shock; the lightning was encircling me and I couldn't extricate myself. I wasn't certain if I wanted to, despite the surfeit of information pouring in, threatening to blow the neurons out of my brain. It was the upload and download of the experience in Venice, but now there was too much information for me to digest.

"Not for you! That is never for you!"

Dmitri, his face a mask of rage and desperation, had skidded down the stony slope. He had a pistol in his hand, and not even the shock of seeing me as a wolf-woman slowed him down. He'd be here in forty-three seconds. I could "see" the engraving on the side of his pistol, could smell the lubricant used on the gun, smell the wound in his leg healing, taste the bitter coffee he'd drunk in haste this morning...

Too much.

I couldn't have done anything if I'd wanted to. I was aware of what was going on around me—both sides readying for a final assault to claim the vessel.

But only distantly: the vessel was still in command.

::but not yet complete::

There was a piece missing. Something prompted me to take the disk from its place on the ledge of the stone wall. It was burning red-gold now, flashing, a beacon...

I knew what to do. I placed the gold disk on top of the vessel. The red-burning gold melted as if it was wax, sliding easily over the surface of the vessel, coating every part of it.

Two more shots rang out. "Clean-head" Zimmer had fired at Dmitri, who was now just twenty meters away from me and approaching fast. Someone from up the slope fired in return. Concern about the safety of Pandora's Box had evaporated in a storm of gunfire.

I had no capacity to respond. I was outside, beyond. I was now...part of the process. I felt structures in my brain tearing and reforming beyond anything human or Fangborn—gods-cursed, gods-possessed, gods-reclaimed—

"Stop it!" Knight screamed. His voice was full of uncharacteristic panic. "Don't hit the vessel!"

Claudia and Gerry fought their way through Knight's men. A hole in the mob, and Will found his way to Knight...

The vessel was open now, and the light I'd seen on Delos now radiated from inside. The others saw it, too.

I reached in. Hesitation was no longer a part of my vocabulary. I was being driven. The vessel wanted me to reach in, and so I did.

Knight screamed, "Sean, stop her!"

Will tackled Knight.

Even though I couldn't see Sean, I knew he was just ten feet away. I could taste the residue of the two inept vampires who'd worked on him, and a third, much more recently. And at Knight's order, I could feel something…switch off…in his brain. Sean was missing. He was a shell, a robot driven by someone else's commands.

No time for Sean.

No time for Dmitri, who was one step away from me, rage contorting his face, greed in his eyes.

No time for petty human wrangling and gunplay; bullets were still whizzing past, profaning the site. The smell of hellebore toxin grew greater.

It didn't matter anymore. The Box had what it wanted.

As my hand passed through the neck of the vessel, the lightning ran up my arm and enveloped me. The lightning consumed and subsumed me. At the bottom of the vessel was…

…nothing. A vast emptiness.

The vast emptiness of space.

I could reach everything in the universe. Numbers filled my awareness, sequences that made no sense to me. Then faces of strangers, places I had never been, followed by texts in languages long dead or inhuman. The vessel was patient as it tried to communicate with me, my monkey brain, even enhanced, still too rigid for easy translation. Finally it settled on pictures.

Fir trees surrounding an ice-cold lake. The water was clear, but the bottom was slick and murky, dense brown with rotting vegetation.

A cave in a desert, empty for thousands of years. A scorpion scuttled across a stone.

The ruin of a wooden temple, the trees around it filled with ghosts.

The cornerstone of a stately home, bricks cracked and mortar disintegrating.

There were four other vessels out there in the world. I needed to find them.

All I had to do was reach out, through the Box, and—

An eternity since his last step, Dmitri was on me.

I had to respond to him, even as the vessel revealed itself to me. The distraction caused me to miss whole segments of information. There was a taste of my own impatience with Dmitri and his ceaseless, selfish violence, in the vessel.

I reached out to him instead of seeking the other vessels.

Billions of souls, past and present, and there was Dmitri Parshin's grubby little being at my fingertips. I reached *into* him and touched...

Dmitri froze, wonder in his eyes.

The lightning around me flickered as the vessel slowed its revolutions and the fragmented figurine whirled past. The break in the figurine caused an imperfect circuit, and there was a sharp crack.

Then, excruciating pain.

Whatever had been dulling some of my senses, and expanding others, was gone.

The neck of the vessel had closed around my wrist. And was squeezing. Like a vise.

I screamed and howled. The Change, always just barely out of my control, now shifted wildly. I felt my molecules morphing uncontrollably among my forms. Fangs, fur, claws, and once, briefly, I swore I saw scales.

Time sped up and the real world—my present—was again at the fore of my consciousness.

Pandora's Box exploded. Its metallic shards hit the ground, scattered like beads of mercury, and melted away.

Sean tackled Dmitri, who raised his pistol.

I fell to my knees, too human now. Shining red all over the wrist that had been bitten by Pandora's Box.

Dmitri's pistol fired into the air.

Another shot from downslope. This one connected.

Clean-head had shot Sean.

Sean screamed. Blood was everydamnwhere.

As the last of the fragments melted away, a voice inside my head whispered,

::what do you need?::

Nearly blinded with pain and unable to concentrate, I gasped. "I...just give me a minute."

Instantly my bitten hand jerked up. I felt a pulse like a shock wave spread out from around me.

Everyone around me—human and Fangborn, friend and foe—fell to the ground.

I stared. I could see something like veins and bone exposed three inches above the bend of my wrist. I was surprised my hand was still attached.

The pain receded, my eyes focused. It wasn't bone I saw on my wrist. There were stones, a bracelet of some kind. Alive, now part of me.

I heard the heartbeats of those around me, and knew they were still alive.

I understood.

Interpreting my blurted request literally, Pandora's Box had given me a minute.

I stumbled to Sean's side. His heart had slowed, but there was too much blood on the ground. When my minute was up, time would snap back into place and he'd bleed to death.

I pulled Dmitri off him, yanked the gun from his hand, and threw it as far away as I could. I tore off Dmitri's shirt, then dragged Sean behind the wall for cover.

I could smell it; the bullet had broken bone and shredded his lungs. Sean was dying.

Desperately I tried to summon the voice that had given me that minute—maybe it could help. "Make me a vampire! Help me save Sean!"

But there was nothing. Less than nothing, because now I was the only one conscious within one hundred meters.

I tried to stanch Sean's flowing blood with Dmitri's shirt, but too much had already been lost. I stared at the blood on my hand, watching it shimmer in the light before the cells died.

A minute isn't a very long time when you're alone and your friend is dying and you can't do anything about it. It is a very long time to anticipate his death.

There was nothing I could do.

At the edge of my consciousness, I felt others start to stir around me.

Sean's fingers grazed my elbow, but then fell away.

"Sean!"

His eyes were open. He was ashen, his torso sodden with bright blood.

"You were...a wolf?" He was Sean again, the vampiric compulsion broken.

"It's OK—" *If only I'd been thinking when I'd been asked what I needed. If only he'd been shot when I could have reached out, repaired him.*

"Zoe. I'm sorry—"

Tears burned my eyes. "Sean, don't! We'll find Claudia or Ariana, they'll fix you—"

He coughed, an awful sound. He reached up to my face, brushed my lips with his bloody fingers.

The blood burned like a brand; my wrist throbbed. I glanced down. The panels of red gemstone shifted, revealing a fractured blue stone.

Sean's grip tightened on my hand. "Zoe, I'm scared."

"I'm right here. I'm right here, Sean." It was so very little, when I'd had such power just a moment before. My tears mingled with his blood. "I'll get you help! Just hang on!"

He was dead.

Too much.

I Changed. I howled. The thorny brown hills echoed with my grief.

A clatter of rocks. Dmitri was there, and he only had eyes for me. Maybe my shiny new bracelet.

Didn't matter. He had set me on this road and as good as killed Sean. If Clean-head hadn't missed Dmitri...

Good, evil, or indifferent, he'd earned whatever I had in me to dole out.

I was on him, seizing his shoulder. We went down.

I struggled to get a better grip, never letting go of the meaty flesh of his upper arm. My jaw ached from hanging on, but there was no way I would let go. He screamed, and I felt the warmth of his familiar blood rushing from his shoulder over me.

He twisted and turned. I held on, but again lost my claw-hold on his torso. Shouts behind me, and a shot; I felt a massive blow as a bullet punched its way through my shoulder. The smell of hellebore toxin was in the air, and I grew dizzy at the smell of it.

I whimpered but held on. I felt my body refuse to move as I wished. Even when I felt...nothing, even when I could not see his unshaved chin, even when I could no longer smell his clothing, detergent, deodorant, blood, I held on.

A roar from overhead, and a hot wind washed over me. That's when I left the whole mess behind.

Chapter 30

I was still a wolf when I woke up. Terrified, I tried to Change back, but could feel nothing but fear. My limbs were like a puddle of warm oatmeal to the extent that I could feel them at all. The thing I'd feared all my life had finally happened: I'd let the Beast out and would never regain my human form. I'd be a wolf forever...

Bright lights and voices, none of which made any sense. I closed my eyes, trying to recall what had happened, where I might be. There was no sense to be had.

So I went back to sleep.

I woke later, the taste of my earlier panic still in my mouth. I still couldn't move, but I worked harder this time at focus and calm. Maybe if I could just chill out, I'd slide back into my human form.

My eyes focused on figures in front of me. A picture. Letters. Too woozy to make sense of the words, written in large block capitals, I studied the photographs.

Will and Danny, Claudia and Gerry, smiling and making exaggerated gestures of happiness. A red cross with a circle around it. An American flag.

Message received, guys. You're OK. I'm in the hospital. Theoretically I'm safe.

I didn't feel much reassured, glad as I was that everyone was alive.

Alive. Maybe not OK.

I dozed again.

When I woke the next time, I sensed company in the room before I opened my eyes. My nose twitched, I whined.

I felt a reassuring hand on my muzzle and pried my eyes open to see who it was.

Gerry.

"Hey, it's OK. You're going to be all right."

Claudia came in, knelt by the bed so she was eye level with me. "Zoe, we've given you something, a drug, to keep you in wolf form, OK? There were complications because of the hellebore and...other things. If you Change back now, you won't heal properly. This will be faster, trust me. You'll be human again soon, I promise."

A weight rolled off me, and I felt I could breathe again. I woofed, a small, gruff noise.

"You were in bad shape skinself, too. This will at least get you better stabilized. When you're stronger, when you've healed, we can work on the human hurts."

My eyes closed halfway. I understood.

"Will's OK, too." She glanced up at her brother, a bemused look on her face. "He's sleeping now, but he's been here until we made him get something to eat."

"Get some sleep now, kiddo." Gerry patted the top of my head gently, about the only part of me that didn't feel like it was bandaged. "Maybe when you wake up, we can get you back to skinself."

Skinself. Wolfself. A little part of me, detached from the principal matters of restoring flesh and bone, noted that Gerry talked about it as just another part of me.

Nice to think that when I woke up, I might be whole, for the first time in my life.

———⏜———

The next time I woke up, I was ravenous. And I was human. There was a tray nearby, full of brown, limp hospital food. This seemed to have a certain tang that went beyond "institutional" and hinted at "military-industrial complex."

I'd never eaten anything so delicious. I licked the plate, craned around for more. I found a buzzer and pushed the button. If it wasn't a buzzer, and it gave me a dose of painkillers instead, I'd be just as happy.

Will came in. With another tray of food.

I looked like seven kinds of hell, I felt like eight kinds of hell, but I would have sung if I could.

Will knew. Will was alive. It was OK now.

It might have been the drugs or the relief, but I was floating.

He set the tray down in front of me, and the smell caught my nose. I ate the second tray, enjoying every bite.

He sat on the edge of the bed, watching me, amused. "I thought I'd lost you. Again."

"Nope," I said around a mouthful of...what? Chocolate pudding? Gravy? I didn't care, but I did put down my spork. Tears sprang to my eyes. "Oh, Will! Sean! I couldn't do anything—!"

Will looked away. "He never should have been there in the first place. Do you have any idea why he came with you?"

I remembered Sean's admission, back in Venice. "Uh, he was under a vampiric compulsion." I tried a weak smile, feeling like a jerk as I lied to Will, but determined to protect Sean. "It was the only time I've ever seen him do anything he was told."

Will nodded but didn't smile. "I'm so mad at him, I can't think straight." He turned away so I couldn't see him while he wiped his eyes. "Sean didn't always do the right thing, but he was my friend and now he's *gone?* How does that happen, Zoe?"

I had no answers; I held his hand. Finally Will grabbed a napkin off my tray and blew his nose. "But I'm even more angry at Knight; whatever Sean's mistakes, there's no way he should have used him like that. It's disgusting, and it's against everything every Fangborn I ever worked with stood for. To take Sean and just... subvert his autonomy like that."

Will shook his head.

"What happened?" I said. "How did you find me?"

"Danny did it. Danny figured out the symbol on the disk marked Ephesus and the location of the Box. He figured Knight would go there, if it meant what we thought."

I couldn't help smiling. Of course Danny had figured it out.

"Once we had the location, we regrouped, and then all we had to do was follow the heavily armed men." Will took the now empty tray and set it aside. "I wasn't sure we were going to get there in time."

"And how did we get out?"

"It was Ariana who hijacked the helicopter Dmitri had—no one knows where he is, by the way, or if he's alive or dead. Ariana sneaked into the helicopter as a snake, then Changed to skinself." He coughed. "I'm sure the pilot was stunned to find a naked Italian hottie wrapped around him, telling him he should take us all out of there."

I smiled, until I remembered my next question. "Knight?"

"The Fangborn shook off...whatever that was you unleashed... a lot faster than the humans. Knight was long gone—his age and strength allowed him to bounce back much quicker than the rest of us. I'm embarrassed to say Gerry had to haul me up the hill in a fireman's carry. Then we dragged you to the copter. But none of us went looking for Knight—our goal was to get you out of there. No one else has seen Knight, either; the news had some little bit about him being treated for exhaustion." He shook his head. "You can imagine the Fangborn families who know about him are going crazy."

I nodded. Not good, but it could have been so much worse. "Where's Danny?"

"Danny is well, he was here, and he'll be back again soon. He's in DC, filling out his forms and getting his clearance. He's as happy as a pig in a puddle with the pile of ancient documents we've given him. He's been working with Claudia and a few of the other Fangborn."

Will hesitated, then said, "You know, we're going to need to spend some time breaking down what happened out there. What happened to you. People saw some seriously spooky—not to mention dangerous—things happening. We need to understand."

I nodded. "Sure. I'll do my best." I held up my right arm. "But you can't tell me there weren't already whole batteries of tests done on this while I was conked out."

There were faint lines in marker on the flesh of my arm, above the bracelet. The sort of thing doctors do to pinpoint a location when using a laser. It looked like I'd been scanned, X-rayed, and a whole bunch of other things while I was unconscious.

Will's mouth tightened. "I worked very hard to make sure you were treated well. That the docs were only making sure this wouldn't harm you."

I snorted. "More likely wouldn't hurt them." I stared at the bracelet. It was made of flat gemstones ranging from deepest violet, ruby, sapphire, and emerald to palest translucence; through the two or three colorless stones, I could almost make out the veins, muscle, and bone of my arm. One dark-blue stone was dull and cracked, its surface blurred. The stones were mounted in thin bands of metallic wire; from a distance it looked like cloisonné or a cheap imitation of some rich, ancient wrist brace, stones mounted in gold and silver.

From a distance. The gold wire really was gold; the silver wire was platinum. Will told me there was an ongoing debate over the nature of the stones, because every time someone had attempted to examine it while I was unconscious, they received an electrical shock.

The bracelet was actually sunk into my skin and bone, a part of me. Nothing short of removing the lower portion of my arm would remove *it*.

"Zoe." Will had that stick-up-his-ass TA look on his face. "You're going to cooperate, right? This is weird, and it's dangerous. I'm worried about you."

"Yessir. I'm going to be good. I'm tired of running. I'm tired of fighting."

"Good." He gave me the most amazing smile, one that knit bone and made me melty all at once. "I'm tired of having to chase you."

Danny came in just then, and I wouldn't have thought he could hug so hard. I didn't care; we laughed, cried a little, and talked over each other. Finally I had to sit back.

"I didn't get him, Danny," I said, a little out of breath. "Will says I didn't kill Dmitri. I'm sorry."

Danny shrugged. "You took a chunk out of him. That's a good start. We'll get him next time."

I loved "we." I loved "next time." Amazing words, the best ever. "You're going to work with Will?" I said.

"Yup. Signed away all my rights, got a TB test, and peed in a cup. I'm now a government employee, and Will can't boss me around anymore."

Will snorted. "We'll compare pay grades and see who the boss is."

"Hey, guys," I said. It was wonderful having them crowd me and bicker. I felt a glimmer of that long-lost summer. "You better take it outside. I'm getting tired."

Danny gave me a kiss on the forehead. "Catch you later, Zo." He was whistling as he shut the door behind him.

As he got up, Will said, "Zoe, you've got a job now, if you want it. TRG-in-training." He cocked his head. "We'll be working together, if you like."

I liked it a lot.

———⌣———

It was great, on paper.

Over the next week, I got my strength back, read up on what I needed to know about the Fangborn, about myself.

Danny and I trained together. I got more lessons in my powers. We mourned Sean.

I made love with Will every night. There is nothing at all sexy about a hospital bed in a military installation, but being with the man I loved, who knew me entirely now—both the good and the, well, strange—made the mind-altering fireworks at Claros seem tame. There were moments where I almost felt the same power I had when I'd been in communion with the vessel. And yet, after, finding myself in a tangle of sweaty sheets, I'd lie in Will's arms, listening to his pounding heart as it slowed to a normal rate, and it was as wonderful and familiar as anything.

And every morning I woke up to him smiling at me. Glorious.

It wasn't a perfect summer, but it was pretty damn wonderful.

Except…

I loved being together with Will, and I was delighted that, after all the trouble I'd caused him, Danny had a direction and a real passion in his new research job, something I'd never seen before. I liked the idea of getting to know my new Fangborn Family. They wanted me to take over researching artifacts and antiquities, and the TRG were willing to send me back to school, all expenses paid.

A real life, with all the trimmings, on a silver platter. A gift from the gods.

But a gift that comes with a price isn't a gift.

The price started showing up in small ways.

The TRG wanted to find out exactly what I was and what my groovy new jewelry could do. I'm allergic to white lab coats and have never liked going to the doctor, so I wasn't keen on hearing "just a few more tests today," with no end in sight. I tried my best to cooperate, and Will and the Steubens had promised they'd look into changing my situation, but I didn't like the way they had specialists asking me questions about my background and my memories, and if I could move the pencil by thinking, and what were the limits of my proximity sense, and were there any other side effects from the bracelet?

I'd started to learn, back on the yacht, that a few things, like my proximity sense, like a limited ability to suggest things, weren't standard on werewolves. I seemed to have a blend of Fangborn abilities. But Gerry and I were the only ones who understood I'd had these abilities before the bracelet. I suspected it was due to the testing Knight had said was performed on my mother, but kept my mouth shut.

Yeah, I admitted, there were side effects, all right. I admitted to headaches and stress, mostly from their tests. I wouldn't tell them the latest side effect I'd noticed, because I realized I was being isolated.

At first I thought something big must be heating up somewhere. My friends had less and less time to visit. And then one day Will didn't visit at all. Or the day after, or the day after that.

At the same time, the Steubens and Danny stopped showing up, too.

This stunk to high heaven. I didn't like it and made the inquiries as carefully as I could.

They were on other business, I was told.

"And didn't say good-bye?" I asked.

I was met with shrugs, a change of topic.

I didn't believe for one second Will would leave me without so much as a word. Danny would have broken any number of rules to say good-bye—and what emergency missions do linguists get sent on, anyway? I wouldn't buy Dr. Claudia, knowing my trust issues, taking off without an e-mail, a text, an explanation. Even Gerry—I somehow knew that, with his Galahad instincts, he wouldn't abandon me, not without a very good reason.

Everyone had left without letting me know? That was just the purest bullshit.

Worse than that. No matter how much I tried to explain, the white coats didn't seem to buy my side of the story. About how I'd activated Pandora's Box and what happened after. I tried to describe the temporary omniscience, the fleeting omnipotence, but they didn't believe me. They didn't even believe I'd discovered Pandora's Box, for the simple reason that there was no proof. No evidence. No one had seen me with it, not even Adam Nichols. Sure, folks could attest to bright lights, loud noises, and odd sensations, but this could all be attributed to the fight, explosions, nerve gas.

"What about this?" I said, holding up my wrist. "I didn't get this at the Duty Free!"

Their response was that it was very interesting, but so far inert as far as their tests went. A funky new brand of surgically implanted self-adornment.

"Are you kidding me?" I shook my head and did an impromptu demonstration: I Changed, assuming each of my forms. Each time the bracelet was there, unchanged each time.

"Wouldn't my Fangborn body spit that out if it was human jewelry? How come it stays put and adapts to the new shape of my arm?"

"We're still looking into it," was all the response I got.

"And what about everyone who was with me, before Ephesus? They didn't notice me taking time off to get implants!"

"You were alone with Senator Knight for nearly a day," they said. "That's what we're trying to investigate. We need proof."

Clearly they weren't telling me everything they knew, trying to sell that weak tea about the bracelet and "proof." They didn't even believe it themselves. They just didn't have a better answer yet, one they could believe.

I understood, sort of. There were too many questions, and I was trying my best to get them answered. But not everyone seemed to agree on what the real questions were.

Before he suddenly vanished, I had been working with Gerry, talking about the different tastes of blood and what it could tell, and I'd become convinced: I'd killed a Fangborn who was evil. "What about the guy in Knight's compound?" I asked. "I mean, I know I'm a noob, but I know evil and I know Fangborn!"

"There is no such thing," Gerry had insisted. "History tells us this. Don't worry, Zoe, we'll work through it. You've got a lot to learn, but you'll get there."

For all his insistence that history never recorded such a thing as an evil Fangborn, I had to wonder. Any history is incomplete; every history focuses on what is most important to its culture. Gerry had been raised drinking the Kool-Aid, I had not. I knew there were evil Fangborn.

"No evidence for that" had been the official response, too.

The bracelet, and my insistence I'd removed an evil Fangborn predator, was my undoing. The investigators began to treat me as unreliable. They kept asking me the same questions in different ways, as if I would change my story. I sneaked a peek at the file one of them had left behind, and it was full of files from my many schools, informing who it may concern that my permanent record was one of noncooperation and truancy, with borderline psychosis or ADHD or dyslexia or lactose intolerance, or whatever the fad diagnosis of the day was.

Well, yeah, I explained. I'm a werewolf who was left on her own to discover what she was. Bound to be a few bumps in the road growing up that way. Really, I'm doing my best now, even without my friends.

And I was trying, until the day one of them slipped and mentioned that the current theory was that there really *was* a Pandora's Box, but I'd given it to Senator Knight.

I lost my shit. I half-Changed and put my fist through the wall. It wasn't that big a deal; it was only sheetrock, but it freaked out the human analyst.

———

I went into a funk for a week. It had only been a couple of months since my mother died. Unoccupied by adventures, I now felt all the grief I hadn't allowed myself to feel. I had the confusion over her past and mine—and concern over what the experiments performed on her had done to my powers.

Alone in a hospital room, grieving, and considerably messed up. It all felt awfully familiar.

I realized I was dying for a joint.

I felt as if I'd lost all the progress I'd made in the past weeks, but eventually I figured out it wasn't lost. *I* hadn't lost Will and Danny or the Steubens; *I* hadn't misplaced my newfound knowledge of myself and what I was. All I'd gained had been *taken* from me, by Dmitri or Knight, and now by my new employers, who were lying to me. Probably lying to my friends, too—or worse. Was it possible Danny and Will had been imprisoned? Perhaps a government vampire "suggested" I'd never existed, or, even easier, that I'd run off again.

That's when I realized that I needed to get out of there. I had to find out what happened to my friends and save myself.

By my logic, there were three possible scenarios: that I was a traitor, having given Fangborn artifacts away to Knight; that I had possession of a vastly powerful artifact, a weapon that was now considered the property of the United States; or that I was a free citizen and could leave any time I wanted.

Guess which I picked.

I started a whole bunch of my own tests. I was no longer allowed outside within the compound, even with an escort. One day, when I got back to my room, I found that the door no longer opened from the inside.

I was only allowed to go out for a run with escorts. They didn't have weapons on them, but I noticed the guys at the guard towers now had hellebore toxin shooters.

I told them over and over that the bracelet hadn't done anything. I didn't tell them about the one new side effect I had noticed.

I was crazy again.

I'd started hearing voices, all the time. Whispering to me. I thought it was tinnitus until I realized I could make out words. The voices were suggesting ways I could break out, which I figured was my own subconscious.

It took a few more days to recognize it was Sean's voice I heard. It sounded just like him, wiseass comments and all. Eventually I realized I was agreeing or disagreeing when he pointed out something I should know. But I didn't realize it might not be insanity, until one night, when I started answering him. And noticed the fractured blue tile in the bracelet glowed with each word I heard.

My mother had heard voices, too. She'd been part of an experimental group of Fangborn, without their knowledge, without their consent, and I wouldn't be party to that. Not even for the good of the nation.

I wasn't good at staying in one place, anyway.

Maybe it was my own paranoia, maybe it was simple bad judgment. Maybe it was the bracelet, or Sean, or guilt, but I had decided for sure.

More than time to go.

I wasn't sure how I'd do it. They were clamping down on me big time, and I'd started to notice I felt dizzy and tired all the time. It wasn't my food; I woke one night to the gentle hiss of a gas coming through my air vents. Hellebore-based, if my nose was to be trusted. It made me drowsy before I could do anything about it, and in the morning I had a headache and couldn't concentrate.

But one day shortly thereafter, I woke up without the headache. I didn't do or say anything unusual, though, and acted as though I was still gassed. I'd wait for a chance.

The chance came late that afternoon. A man in a lab coat appeared in my room. Tall and thin, with dark red hair and freckles that were incongruous on a serious demeanor.

"I know you're not drugged."

I acted woozy. "Huh?"

"I know you're not drugged, because I swapped the canister of hellebore toxin gas for oxygen myself."

"What do you want?" I sat up.

"I want to help you get out of here. We don't have a lot of time. I pulled the security camera offline, but the guy I offered to cover for will be back soon. We need to get going before he finds his station unmanned."

I suspected a trap, possibly a trick to get me to reveal the powers of Pandora's bracelet. "Uh-huh."

The guy wasn't much older than me but was thin and worn. "Look. A number of years ago, I was a college student. I was the night manager for a little art cinema in Massachusetts, and one night after work I was attacked by three guys. I would have been killed that night, except there was a young woman who turned into a wolf and saved me."

My jaw dropped. If he'd announced, "No, Luke, I am your father," I couldn't have been more stunned. "That was you?"

He smiled briefly. "And it was you. Suffice it to say, my interest in werewolves was piqued, and after a long series of adventures, I found myself working for the TRG." He frowned. "But here's the thing. Either the Fangborn are citizens, with all the rights of citizens, or they're not. Until they're going to come out and lock up all the Fangborn, I don't believe they should be holding you. Lying to you."

"Will, the Steubens—they didn't just go away about their own affairs and leave me here."

He shook his head. "I don't know how they got rid of them, what they told them, and that worries me."

"You know, this is a hell of a way for the FBI to treat its employees," I said, remembering Will's description of the TRG in the café in Berlin.

"Things are changing," he said, his face dark. "There's been some reshuffling upstairs. I don't like the direction we're taking now."

"Reshuffling?"

"The director's brought in a new head of the Biological and Historical Intelligence branch. I don't know the new guy personally, but I hear he comes with friends in high places and worked closely with Senator Knight himself."

I felt sick. "You can get me out of here?"

He nodded. "I'm going to trigger an alarm on the far side of the building in a few minutes. Can you get out and over the wall, if it's not guarded, in that time?"

"No problem."

"Is there anything you need to pack up?"

"No." My old backpack had been packed for days. Just in case.

"OK, give me five minutes to get over there and two to get the diversion going."

I grabbed his arm. "Thank you—?"

He squeezed my hand. "Rob Watson. And you're welcome. Thank *you*, Zoe, for what you did all those years ago."

I nodded. It was nice to think my youth hadn't completely poisoned my adult life.

"Seven minutes, OK?"

I picked up my bag and waited by the door, keeping it open a crack after he left.

Seven minutes later, an alarm was dimly audible. I waited until I could no longer sense anyone in the hall near me. I ran out to the main corridor and down to a side office. I threw my bag out, then eased myself out the window.

I thought about Will and the last night we'd spent together. I loved him desperately, perhaps even more than before the first time I left him. And Will loved me, fur, fangs, and all. I knew that. I had to find out what happened, how they managed to convince him to leave me. Or, if it hadn't been convincing but coercion, I had to fix that, too. Same for Danny and the Steubens.

I sneaked down past the main gate and did a wide loop around until I found the outside road. I knew most of the staff were at the other end, so I wouldn't be seen.

I started trotting away from the facility.

I'd find Will and Danny and make sure they were safe, and that they knew I was, too. And then I would have to think of a way to protect them all from the curse-bringer I'd become.

The Fangborn documents, like the Orleans Tapestry, were fragmentary, and they were prophetic; I knew there were as many ways of interpreting prophesies as there were interpreters. Thing was, whichever way you spelled it, I was doom or close enough to it. I was a werewolf, I had a dead man whispering in my ear and a bracelet with powers that defied scientific examination. I'd find a way to undo the oracles' shadowy promises of destruction. I wouldn't let anything, even me, hurt my friends. My Family.

A car, somewhere behind me. I wasn't far enough away yet to start hitching, so I skidded down into the culvert to avoid being seen. A large black sedan pulled ahead of me and stopped. Honked once.

I could tell without looking it was Adam Nichols.

I didn't sense anyone else, or any ill intent from him. It was handy, now understanding that I had more than the usual lycanthropic powers, that I could rely on certain vampiric or oracular talents as well. I was going to have to keep a journal, keep track of just how sharp my powers were getting, or which new ones might appear, as Sean's voice had. Academic habits had been good for me, and they'd come in handy as I tried to correlate the information I had from Gerry's Fangborn rules and lessons.

I climbed up. He reached over and unlocked the door for me.

I leaned into the open window. "You're not bringing me back there."

"No, I'm not. Where you heading?"

"You suddenly find me, when everyone else is being distracted. How does that happen?" I wondered if I'd have to knock him out and whether I dared steal his car.

"I heard an alarm, I thought of you. I went in the opposite direction of everyone else—easy. So I ask again, Where you heading?"

I thought about the letter my mother had left me and the scant details of her youth. "North."

"Oddly enough, so am I."

"Why? You've got a job here. You can probably talk the new boss into whatever you want. The TRG need to find Knight. They have to stop him from starting the Identification." I didn't say anything else about prophesies or my potential role in them.

He tilted his head. "I don't know whether they trust me enough to let me do what I'm good at."

I laughed. "You're not particularly trustworthy. You're not afraid of violence. You weren't exactly Employee of the Year for your last boss, stealing from him, betraying him."

"And yet here you are, talking to me." He reached across to the briefcase that was in the passenger-side well and pulled out a file. Coffee-stained, dog-eared, I recognized it as the one from Knight's office, the one that had my Family's history in it. "Untrustworthiness has its rewards."

I stared at the file. The key to my history, and maybe my crazy powers. I knew I wouldn't like what I found in there, but I had to open it and find out. My own private Pandora's Box.

He looked in the rearview. "I haven't got all day, Zoe."

Sean's voice whispered in my ear. "He's a dick, Zoe. Don't trust him." I looked down at the bracelet and had the impression the fractured dark blue stone had momentarily pulsed with life.

"I know," I said to Sean. Adam assumed I was answering him.

Adam had a car; I had a direction. He'd picked me up twice before, both times saving my bacon and complicating my life. I could take care of myself now, and I wouldn't much mind if he got blown up if I unleashed some new power all of a sudden.

I threw my bag into the backseat, got in, and slammed the door shut. He pulled off down the road.

"Any particular route you want me to take?"

"Just keep going north. I'll tell you when to turn."

"No map? No destination?"

I shrugged. "I'll just know."

He laughed. I fastened my seat belt and stared out the window, watching the woods roll by.

I'd find an answer to all this trouble I'd inadvertently stirred up.

It was time for me to dig into my own past.

END

Acknowledgments

I like "Acknowledgments." I like seeing the connections between people, and I think it's important to take the opportunity to say thank you to everyone who makes the writing process a little less solitary.

First, and most importantly, to my husband and first reader, James Goodwin. You're the reason I could write *Seven Kinds of Hell*, plain and simple. That's why it's dedicated to you. (OK, I *know* that's not enough, and I *still* owe you for those days when you picked up the slack and did extra laundry or the shopping, and went on endless research trips to look at old ruined things, and did the cooking—like I *said*, I'll make it up to you.) But for real, for now, this Fangborn novel and my love. Thank you.

I wouldn't have come up with the Fangborn if it hadn't been for my friends and beta-readers, Charlaine Harris and Toni L. P. Kelner. Writers and editors extraordinaire, they asked me to contribute to their holiday anthology *Wolfsbane and Mistletoe*, which was the first story featuring the Steubens. May everyone reading this find such friends, who both challenge you *and* give you the means to succeed. My FP sisters—y'all rock. Thank you.

Tess Gerritsen and S. J. Rozan read drafts of this book. Tess introduced me to Peter Sommer's wonderful gulet tours of Turkey; the sites we visited inspired much in this book. She also told me I had to write an archaeological thriller; it turned out to be an archaeological thriller *with* Fangborn. S. J. is a sterling writer and one hell of a reader/editor. I was lucky to have her eagle eye and incisive observations. Thank you both.

Many folks gave me advice about factual elements in the book. Mostly I took it; sometimes I fudged minor details to suit the story, taking advantage of the fact that this is a work of fiction. Thanks to Dan Hale, who helped me navigate Paris, and to Konstantin Clemens, Mark MacMahon, Jilles Van Gurp, and Christian Ziech, who came to my aid in Berlin. Joe Basile (Associate Dean of Liberal Arts and Professor of Art History, Theory, and Criticism, Maryland Institute College of Art) helped Zoe with her classical art and archaeology, and helped me with ancient Greek, Latin, and Italian. Thank you all!

To the amazing folks at 47North: David Pomerico (acquisitions editor), Justin Golenbock (PR specialist), Katy Ball (marketing manager), Patrick Magee (author relations manager): Thank you for your support in bringing the Fangborn to novel form! Very special thanks to developmental editor Clarence A. Haynes, who read *SKoH* so thoughtfully.

My brilliant literary agent Josh Getzler is a terrific reader and knows the business; he's also a very nice guy. He and the team at HSG Agency (Carrie Hannigan, Jesseca Salky, and Maddie Raffel) are simply the werewolf's fangs. Thank you all for your knowledge, patience, and enthusiasm!

The wider mystery community has been incredibly encouraging of the werewolves and vampires in my crime fiction. Thank you to the good folks at Malice Domestic and Bouchercon, especially, with a special shout out to Jon and Ruth Jordan. Also, thanks to the folks at the SF/F conventions (especially Boskone) who've welcomed both my hypernatural characters *and* the mysteries in which they were set. Thank you to the booksellers and librarians who keep writers in all genres going.

Every writer has a special community of writers and readers. Our community lost a dear friend and champion when Sally Fellows passed away this year; we will miss you, Sally. Thank you to my friends in the Teabuds, MysteryBabes, BuffyBuds, Mystery Writers of America, Sisters in Crime, and especially to my promotion group, the hugely talented Femmes Fatales. They are: Donna Andrews, Charlaine Harris, Dean James, Toni L. P. Kelner, Catriona McPherson, Kris Neri, Hank Phillippi Ryan, Mary Saums, Marcia Talley, and Elaine Viets. Thank you all so much.

About the Author

 Award-winning author Dana Cameron lives in eastern Massachusetts with her husband and two cats. Cameron, known for her mystery novels and short stories, was short-listed for the Edgar Award in 2010 for "Femme Sole," and earned the Agatha Award in 2011 for "Disarming" and in 2008 for the Fangborn story, "The Night Things Changed." Trained as an archaeologist, Cameron holds a bachelor of arts from Boston University and a doctorate from the University of Pennsylvania. When she's not writing fiction, Cameron enjoys exploring the past and the present through reading, travel, museums, popular culture, and food. More news about Cameron and her writing can be found on her author website and blog, at www.danacameron.com.